BORN AGAIN Sinner

A NEW **M/M** ROMANCE
BY

DARYL BANNER

AUTHOR OF

FOOTBALL SUNDAE
HARD FOR MY BOSS
BROMOSEXUAL
&
GETTING LUCKY

BORN AGAIN SINNER

Cover Model / Photographer
Nathan Hainline

Cover & Interior Design
Daryl Banner

I would like to dedicate this book to

Melissa Mcentyre

a wonderful woman who has left us too soon.

You put a big ol' smile on my face

every time I think of your compassionate, gracious self

and of all the love you put into the world.

I pray I can honor you by following your lead.

XXOO ~ Daryl

BORN AGAIN Sinner

Prologue

CODY

Two months ago, I opened my heavy eyes and found a round, beady-eyed face hovering over mine like an insect.

"Good morning, Cody. Do you know where you are?"

Every appendage was wrapped up like a taco. The last thing I remembered was Pete shouting at me to move. "*MOVE!*" His urgent voice, that one stupid word, echoed ceaselessly up and down the long-ass empty hallways of my ears for weeks on end. The fucker would not shut up.

"Do you know where you are?"

And neither would this nurse. "Fuck off," someone spat back, far, far away from me.

Someone. *I didn't even recognize my own voice.*

I remember trying to move, but everything was so slow. I felt like a bug trapped in a honeyed Petri dish. "Where's Pete?"

"You're at Prairieland Medical. Do you remember—"

"I know where the hell I am. Where the hell is Pete?"

MOVE!

It wasn't until four days later—four fucking days later—that I learned exactly where Pete was, and it wasn't any damned place I'd be returning to anytime soon.

He was back at the base. He suffered scratches. That lucky fucker stood two feet away from me and suffered *scratches.*

And there I was, plugged into machines in a bed with metal in my left leg and arm.

Yeah, maybe I should've moved.

They don't waste any time either, these insects called nurses. They had me rolling left or right on my bed every damned day, sitting up, lying back down, doing pull-ups on the hand grip over the bed—all sorts of circus shit to see what needed attention, to see what was broken. Long story short: fucking everything. I heard the phrase "embedded shrapnel" about a hundred times too many a day. And: "Now try this". And my favorite: "Does it hurt?"

How could anything hurt when all I felt was anger?

MOVE!

Who had time to care about any "embedded" *anything* when I couldn't move my left leg without screaming out in pain?

MOVE!

What kind of stupid shit would I bother to "try" when I knew damned well that the only family I ever had—my brothers in the military—were continuing their missions without me?

"When am I going back?" I asked anyone within earshot. I must have asked just as many times as the nurses asked me to try this, to try that, to move this way and that.

It was on a day two weeks later that I was given an answer: likely never.

What was the point in taking my recovery seriously when the only thing I could look forward to was returning to civilian life in a small town I hated? That was the whole reason I enlisted—to get the fuck out of that town I was about to be condemned to live in once again.

Maybe the insects should have gotten the hint the first time I forced myself out of my bed on my own and almost bled out halfway down the hall because one of my drain balloons fell off, dropping to the hallway floor like a damned Christmas ornament, except the shattering was less pretty.

MOVE!

That's all I kept trying to do, follow Pete's advice that could have saved my life and kept me among my brothers.

Instead, it *only* saved my life.

"You're making it worse," the nurse chirped at me each time she returned me to my bed. "You won't recover if you don't do it properly. You've got to get your head in the game and go through every step of the therapy. No shortcuts. Hey, don't give me that look. Remember what you're doing this for, Cody. Remember."

Remember.

I remember feeling strong my whole life. I remember facing every bully in school with fearlessness. I remember standing up to my dad, who's a lying, alcoholic shit stain. I remember spending years and years working out, strength training, and gaining so much muscle mass that no asshole in their right mind would ever fuck with me again—school bully and father alike.

And now it's all for nothing.

Nothing.

Strength, the one thing I relied on my whole life, fled from my bones as fast as I could count the days slipping by.

"Get your head in the game, Cody."

Yeah, my head was in the game. It was in the game since the day I signed my life away to the Army, and the Army sent me back home a damaged piece of meat. It was always in the game.

And I had already tapped out.

1

TREY

Yes, I know exactly who lives in that house. Everyone does. It's no secret in town who the young man at the end of Willow is.

Every stop sign on the way over tried to ward me away—*stop, stop, stop*—like a bunch of octagonal red flags. I clearly didn't listen to a single one of them.

For being told all my life that I have such a good heart, I also sure as spit have a foolhardy, stubborn one.

And yes, I know what I'm getting myself into.

As I walk down the path between two overgrown patches of grass under the giant shade of an oak tree, I hear the deep breath I took in the car over and over again in my ears. It sounds just like an ocean wave pulling back—or crashing forth, it's hard to tell.

It makes me think of Mom. See, there's this big pink seashell my mom gave me before she died, and I put my ear up to it and listen for the sea every night before I go to bed. It's something of a ritualistic weirdo thing I've done for the past six years since that fateful day. I was only fourteen. Add to that fact me being the gay, motherless son of Reverend Arnold, and you've got a recipe for *living in the spotlight for the most awkward and formative years of your life.* On the surface, all anyone ever saw when they looked my way was a sweet face, a meek and well-meaning smile, and soft eyes that showed none of the demons I'd faced in my life.

I guess a lot like that seashell, you gotta get up real nice and close to hear my secrets.

I bring my knuckles to the door, clench shut my eyes, then give the soft wood two tiny taps.

The door opens before I finish the second. A round face caked with enough makeup to scare away a cat answers the door. "Oh, thank God you're here. Oh, sorry."

Everyone apologizes when they use the Lord's name in vain around me. I guess that's another perk to being the minister's son. I pay her apology no mind because I took no offense; I never do. Now and then, even *I* slip. "Hello there, Miss Davis."

"Call me Bethie, please, everyone does. Come in," she urges, scooting right out of the way.

When I step inside, I feel a chill of repulsion tap-dance up my neck. The house smells of dust, old books, and something *off* that was cooked two days ago. The spring heat is beating at my back, but inside, it's cold as a coffin. The couch is stacked with so many clothes, there's nowhere to sit. A laundry basket with some freshly folded clothes sits neatly on it—perhaps Miss Davis's attempt at quickly cleaning up the place a bit, her effort of which my arrival has interrupted. Next to all of that, there's an old tube TV on top of another TV on top of a giant box labeled "PETE", whoever that is. Apparently if one TV isn't working, you can just hop your eyes two feet lower and watch the other. Through the wide archway ahead, I see evidence of a kitchen with towers of dishes and pots that dare to fall over at any sign of an errant gust. The back door is missing one of its windowpanes, a small square of cardboard stapled at each corner of the opening in its place, hissing and flapping at a loose corner from the outside wind trying to push in.

My eyes clearly betray my inner shock, because Mrs Davis's next words are: "Please don't leave."

I blink and turn her way. "Sorry, ma'am?"

"Call me Bethie, like I said. Look, don't be put off by the—um—all of the—uh—" She waves a hand at, well, everything. "We're in a bit of a transitional period here."

Transitional period. That's cute. I push away all my misgivings—the same ones I was pushing away the entire drive over here—and offer her a polite smile. "Can you ... clarify something for me?"

"Yes. Please. Anything."

"Am I ..." I bite my lip and glance back at the cluttered couch. "Did you hire me as a caregiver ... or a housekeeper?"

Ms Davis frets with her hands for five solid seconds before answering. "A caregiver. And you were ideal because, well, you're a nurse, so if something's wrong, you'd know what to do. But really my son just ... needs someone. He has shrapnel in his leg and arm. He can't walk well. He ... He just needs someone."

He needs someone ...? There is something Ms Davis isn't quite telling me. "Caregiver," I repeat skeptically, standing in a house full of Lord-knows-what. I couldn't even tell you what color the carpet is. *Or if there even is carpet under this filth.*

"Yes. Caregiver." She sounds a touch more assertive. "And you *are* nurse-certified, ain't you? A-Aren't you?"

People also correct themselves a lot around me. That, I can't quite explain, other than they must think I hang out with Jesus Christ himself every weekend and want me to put in a good word.

"I'm a licensed practical nurse," I explain. "I can't do some of the things an RN can do, but ... I can care for your son, look after him, report any serious issues to Dr. Emory, if you like."

She bites her lip, glances at the hallway over my shoulder, then says, "Well, the RNs and doctors couldn't do a dang thing for my son. So maybe you can. Y'know. Without being scared away."

I let out a little chuckle. "I'll try my best, ma'am. Really, I—"

"Bethie."

"Bethie," I say reluctantly. Really, my father wouldn't approve of me calling anyone I don't personally know by their first name. It simply isn't polite. "I just got here a moment ago. I'm not going to be scared away by ... by a little clutter."

I'm probably standing on last week's pizza delivery box and a neighbor's dog that went missing three months ago. *A little clutter.*

Miss Davis smiles warmly. "Really, I think I just need you here two, maybe three days a week. That should make a difference."

To be honest, she wasn't clear about what my precise duties would be when we first spoke on the phone. "Make a difference?"

"Yes. We could all use a little help in our lives now and then, can't we?" she asks vaguely.

I suddenly feel twenty steps behind her.

"Here." She spreads her hands. "Let me show you the—Let me show you around."

Navigating a floor crowded by piles of books, taped up boxes, dirty laundry, and unidentifiable knickknacks, Miss Davis takes me to the kitchen, which looks ten times worse close-up than it did from the foyer. Attached to the kitchen is a small dining room with a table topped by an assortment of dumbbells, loose weights, and metal objects I can't name—maybe parts to a dismantled radio or remote control toy airplane? *Or a rifle*, I realize when I get a bit closer. Our tour loops us around to a small, similarly cluttered den that leads right back to the foyer and living room.

Then we arrive at a short hallway. This is where Miss Davis pauses for a moment to steel herself. "You never know."

She's full of oddly vague expressions like that. "You ... never know what ...?" I prompt her.

"What mood he'll be in," she mutters half to herself. Then she lifts her gaze to me as if coming out of a dream. "You're an angel to come and give this a try. Really, you are. Thank you. I ... had no one left to turn to."

I lift an eyebrow. "No one left ...?"

"Five nurses I've gone through. I didn't even know we *had* five nurses to go through in all of Spruce. It being such a small town, I thought I'd cleaned out my options after the third one up and quit on her second day. Can you imagine what a nightmare it would've been to hire one all the way from Fairview?"

I stare unblinkingly at her. Five nurses, she said? *Five??*

"And after the last one got scared off, and the one before that tried to act like his mama and copped an attitude right back with him, and the one before *that* one acted like I was lookin' for a wife for my son and got *flirty* and tried playin' house with him ... *oh, goodness* ... I got to thinkin', maybe he needs a *male* caregiver." Miss Davis eyes me. "That's logical, isn't it? I mean, my son ought to be comfortable around another *male*. And you're about his age, too, or a lil' younger. So that makes sense, right? Sure does to me."

From all she's said, I'm not sure it matters much the gender *or* age of the caregiver. For a moment, I thought I was ready for this. Now I'm *really* starting to wonder what I've gotten myself into.

But life is full of challenges. My parents never taught me to back down from a single one. "You ... think it'll matter to him that I'm gay? You know I'm gay, right?"

"Oh, of course I do. Year or two ago, the whole town found out like wildfire, wasn't that the way of it? My son was raised in this lovely town, too. And I tell you, he *would've* been there like the rest of the town was to see your father marry off Tanner Strong to that sweet dessert chef ... if he hadn't been overseas. He was taught to respect the gays just as much as anybody here in Spruce, thanks to Reverend Arno—I mean, your *father*—preachin' it right. No, no, he ain't gonna have a lick of a problem with who you like to kiss."

Who I like to kiss. I force a smile on my face, which likely looks as stiff as it feels. "Thank you, ma'am."

"Please don't be afraid of my son." Her face stiffens right up. "He's ... really a sweet, sweet boy deep down."

And then from the depths of the bedroom at the end of the unspeakable hall of horrors comes a deep and hulking voice: "I can hear y'all talkin' shit about me out there."

Ms. Davis takes a deep, patient breath. "Deep, *deep* down."

I stare after the dark hall and the slice of sunlight coming out of the cracked-open door at the end of it. My heart already races in my chest as I stare, unable to make my feet move.

The sweet boy in that room has more to say. "And I don't need no fuckin' caregiver or nanny or exorcist or a new '*friend*'. So you can send whoever it is you're gabbin' with out there right on back to wherever the hell they came from."

Ms. Davis gives me a reassuring smile. "He's just moody is all."

I eye her. "Moody ...?"

"Ever since he's been back," she clarifies. "He's got all of this *stuff* going on in his head, and really, I'm sure that if he'd just let it out and talk to someone, maybe—"

"I CAN STILL FUCKIN' HEAR YOU!"

I purse my lips and stare down the hall. "Doesn't sound much like he wants a caregiver, ma'am," I murmur quietly.

"Boy, I can't shake you out of that 'ma'am' habit, can I?"

"My apologies. It was just how I was brought up."

Ms, Davis takes my hands suddenly and gives them a little shake. "Let me level with you. No filter. *Please* hear me out."

I swallow once, then nod at her to continue.

Her eyes turn hard, and then, still gripping my hands, she pulls me in closer and lowers her voice. "My son ... My son is a mess. He drinks himself dry every day. He goes and shoots off his guns in the backyard. I've gotten complaints. It only makes him worse. He hardly bathes himself, partly due to difficulties with his injury, partly because *I think he just plain doesn't care.* He doesn't feed himself properly like he should. He's turned this house—this beautiful little house his dear grandmamma gave him—into a pig sty. *I can't just sit back and watch him continue to destroy his life.*"

Between her beseeching stare, her bone-crushing hold on my hands, and her words, I can't avoid the weight of responsibility she is dropping on my shoulders.

"You're ... needing more than a caregiver for him," I conclude.

"I don't know what he needs. He just needs *someone*. Someone to rely on. Someone who can care for him. Someone he can really trust. Someone who ... 'gets' him."

"And ... you believe *I'm* that someone."

"Well, I heard a lot of good things about you at the nursing home. And Dr. Emory speaks a lot about you. And, well, you being Reverend Arnold's son and all that. Listen." Her voice is like iron suddenly. "I've only asked for something from God twice in my life. First time was after my husband of twenty years walked out on me. The second time was this morning before you arrived." Her eyes are wet with desperation. "Please. Just one day. Give me one dumb little nothin' day."

There is no way I can say no to that desperate look in Miss Davis's eyes; if I did, the second I got home, I'd be wracked with guilt at turning my back on her—and on that guy down the hall.

That guy who I haven't yet met.

"Well ... I *can* cook ..." I finally concede. "And I *do* know how to fold clothes and wash dishes ..."

"Oh, bless you."

"All of it really goes hand-in-hand with recovery, you know?" I rationalize. "His nutrition and environment are just as important as medication and therapy to heal his body."

"And his soul," she agrees, hope bursting in her eyes.

Lord give me strength. "Let me meet him."

It takes only ten steps for the pair of us to make it from the start of the hall to his cracked-open door.

"Sweetie?" calls out Ms. Davis. "Sweetheart? I'm coming back there. I want you to meet—"

"What'd I just get done sayin'?" he shouts back.

"Damn it, let me help you!"

I put a calming hand on Ms. Davis's shoulder. She looks up at me at once, more angry words on the tip of her tongue, ready to be fired. The look I give her stops them from coming out.

"Let me try," I murmur quietly to her, almost a whisper.

She relents and steps back, allowing me my freedom. I face the cracked-open door and, just as I did at the front door, I lift my knuckles to the wood and give it two tiny taps.

"Fuck off."

I clear my throat. "I'm just here to ... give you a quick medical looksee," I assure him through the door. "Then I'll be gone."

"You can be gone right now."

I've had worse greetings. I did some charity work at a nursing home for a few months while I was getting all my schooling and certification done, and it was one of the most trying times I've ever had. But in that sea of nasty words and foul elderly behavior, there were islands of peace and a soft-spoken thanks or two. *Just do it for the islands of peace*, I coach myself. *Islands of peace ...*

"It'll just be a minute," I assure him once more. "One minute is all I'm askin'. Are you decent? Can I come in?"

Still no response.

I take that as a submission of sorts and gently give the door a push. As it opens, the sunlight coming in from the window pours over me, nearly blinding compared to the rest of the dim, messy house. There isn't much to his room except for an old dresser by the window and a bed opposite it, upon which he's seated.

He looks up at me.

I stare down at him.

Dear Lord in Heaven, I was not prepared.

I already knew he was a handsome guy. That's all anyone ever said about him around town. "Oh, that handsome, darlin' Cody!" "Oh, he's such a stud!" "Cody is the hottest, most charming bachelor in all of Spruce." Of course, those same people turned to their other friends and also said: "Too bad he's messed up in the head." And: "For such a pretty face, he sure has a lotta issues." And my favorite: "Cody is about as dangerous as he is good-looking. Better to keep far away from that boy unless you enjoy tasting a recipe for disaster."

As it turns out, I seem to be exactly the type who likes a taste of disaster, because none of that gossip on the grapevine scared me away. In fact, maybe it's the reason I came at all. When I hear of someone who's fallen wayward, or a person coming on troubled times, or a soul who's in need of help, that's where I go. I go where I'm needed.

Cody Davis clearly needs ... something. But for the first five seconds of being in his room, I can't seem to figure at all what that is because I'm too distracted by *him*. None of the swooning words do him justice. His bright brown eyes are simply dazzling and so deep, the second you look into them it's like you've been reunited with someone long-lost you've known your whole life. He has got the solid, brawny, commanding face of a soldier with the heart-crushing beauty of a runway model. He emanates strength, taking every scrap of your attention and refusing to let go. He has not shaved in a day or five, but it only makes him more striking in that wrecked, tortured-soul kind of way. His rosy cheeks and blunt, commanding chin are bathed in light brown cactus needles.

But enough about his face. Cody's body is a buffet of muscle from one shoulder to the other that continues down to two pert, firm pecs filling every inch of the army-green tank-top he's got on, which tapers down the rest of his long, thick torso in exquisite detail. He's wearing boxers that look like the American flag itself hugs his massive, muscled thighs—red and white stripes up one thigh, and white stars against a blue background down the other.

I can't even produce a proper word at first.

How did I not know someone this devastatingly beautiful was right here in my not-even-on-most-maps Texas hometown all this time? *How have Cody and I never met? Everyone's met in this town.*

And his boxers are not that long. Most of his legs are exposed.

I can't even begin to express how many inappropriate, totally ill-timed, horribly sinful thoughts explode in my brain in this one instant. My knee-jerk reaction is to clench shut my eyes and let out an apology.

Except my eyes don't shut. And the apology never comes out.

Apology? What am I sorry for, exactly?

"The hell you starin' at?"

My eyes flick right up to meet Cody's, which pierce me with the sort of deep, knowing conviction that only a man who has seen death, life, and everything between can have.

I'm not even sure I can tell him what I was just staring at. I don't know if I know myself. He's possessed me. Maybe it's *me* who needs the exorcist. "H-Hi. Hello. Hey there," I sputter, greeting him three times in a row for some reason. "I'm—"

"I know who you are."

His voice is low, deep, and unexpectedly velvety. I didn't hear all of that nuance from his shouting a moment ago. "You do?"

Cody lifts an eyebrow, his forehead wrinkling in the slightest. Just that small, unassuming movement is a sight beautiful enough to crush a full-grown man. He doesn't answer.

"So ... you've been to the church?" I prod him. "On Apricot?"

His silence is torture. His eyes are like weapons. And his voice is so sultry, it somehow matches *and* equally contrasts with his roughened, outer demeanor. Not to mention the way his plush and pillowy lips stay parted between his words, inviting more than just my eyes toward them.

I blink away the dirty thoughts again.

What is wrong with me?

"I ..." My words fill the silence. I need to stay on track. "I'm just here to check on you. Your mother called me at the free clinic where I volunteer. Well, one of them. I volunteer at two. The one off Main Street just past Wicker, and the one right at the ... the ..." I feel foolish suddenly, like maybe I should have heeded all the ample warnings. I sorely, gravely underestimated the effect Cody would have on me in person. "She filled me in on some things."

My eyes drift back down to his exposed legs. I didn't notice all the scars running down them, or the notch near his left ankle, or the unsightly gash on his left calf.

I give a tiny nod toward them. "I hear you have some trouble getting around the house. Does it hurt to walk?"

His eyes burn instantly with the rage of a hellfire.

I still need answers, so I stubbornly persist with my questions. "Does ... Does your left leg hurt more than your right?" Silence. Dead, stubborn silence from the brute on the bed. "I was told your left leg was the one that had gotten—"

"You were told a lot."

His sudden words, fortified with the unyielding, biting glue of bitterness, are like hammers to my ears, shutting me right up.

I promise that I usually have a lot more finesse than this. I'm quick with my words. I'm a confident person, even if I seem meek at times. But there is something about Cody Davis that catches me totally off-guard. I can't seem to hold on to a crumb of courage in front of him before it fumbles right out of my grasp.

"Am I wrong?" I ask, my voice a touch quieter. "Is it your left leg? You injured it? You have trouble getting around the—?"

Before I'm able to finish, Cody pushes himself off the bed in one swift movement, then rises to his feet right in front of me.

He's a whole foot taller than me, which is made all the more apparent with him standing so close. I can feel heat wafting off his muscular body. He exudes such strength that I involuntarily have to take a step away, which slams my back right against his window—as if I'm planning to hop out of it and make my escape.

The presence of Cody Davis so close to me is overwhelming.

To say the very least.

Escaping right out of that window at my back sounds like the smartest idea in this moment. I'd better do it before I get any more involved than I already am. Before I realize I can't peel my eyes off of his chest. Before I do or say something I'll regret.

I mean, *I'm* the one with the minister for a father. *I'm* the one who sits across from him at breakfast every day. *I'm* the one who will have to feel His judgment on my shoulders this Sunday at church, knowing what I did when I entered the home of Cody Davis, knowing the inappropriate thoughts that crossed my mind.

Thoughts like: *What do Cody's lips taste like?*

Thoughts like: *If I touched his chest, would it be as firm and warm and strong as it looks?*

Thoughts like: *Why is my heart racing so fast that I swear it could chase a hare halfway to El Paso?*

"Well?"

I flinch. I literally forgot where I am. "Well, what?"

"I'm standing." His eyes fall on me like two heavy hands from the sky. Did I mention he's taller than me by a foot? "Does it look like there's an issue with my legs?"

Despite all the *crazy* that's going on in my head, I swallow and stand my ground. "I couldn't help but notice your scars. Do you mind if I examine them?"

"Yeah, I mind."

Seeing as he's left barely a foot between his body and the wall at my back, I inch my way around him to give us more space. I kick into a collection of empty beer cans on the way, startling me.

With someone who's as resistant as he is, I can't expect to just be welcomed here. Like I did with many elderly folk at the Caring Candle, I'm going to have to ease into it.

"So how long have you lived out here?" I ask him, sincerely curious. "Your whole life? You said you know me, but ... but I don't know you."

Cody's totally mature response is to cross his arms and tilt his head, staring at me deadpan and saying nothing.

I give him a tightened smile anyway, then lean against the door. That only makes me lose my balance as the door, unsecured, slams itself shut at my back. I clamber for two seconds before finding a new home against the wall, my balance regained. "Y-You look about the same age as me." Here I am, still trying to act cool and collected. "Did we go to school together? Or do you know me from church? Have you attended one of my father's sermons?"

"I don't need no friend or babysitter."

I blink. Clearly my efforts at connecting with him are going so well. "I'm not a babysitter ... and you're not a baby."

"Didn't I tell you to fuck off earlier?"

Why is he making this so difficult? "I'm just here to help you."

"I don't need help."

"Most of us don't think we do. But most of us also don't know what we really need." I speak as gently as I can and keep my eyes locked on his, despite the distracting way in which he's made his biceps bulge just by crossing his arms, all the veins along his thick forearms popping. Tattoos are painted down both his beefy arms. Was I too overwhelmed to notice them earlier? *How are you noticing them now? I thought you were staring at his eyes!* "Cody, you've been through ... a difficult past several months. No one can possibly imagine what you're experiencing unless they've been through it themselves. I wouldn't be so arrogant as to presume to know what all of that's like."

He doesn't respond, continuing to uphold his staring act on me. I don't know if his intention is to intimidate me or just give me the cold, silent treatment, but I can't let it thwart my efforts. He's just a guy who's put up a lot of walls; all it'll take is the right *thing* to get him to let me in. People who need help the most push it away the most. *I'm going to help him one way or another.*

"We don't have to talk about any of that if you don't want," I assure him, hoping that his silence is a good sign. I even permit myself to take a step in his direction. "I can just check up on how you're healing from time to time. A little bit each week, if that's okay. You don't have to see any more of me than that. I'll ... I can even cook you a meal or two." *Provided I don't open the wrong cabinet and send an avalanche of dirty dishes piling over my head.* "I'll keep out of your hair otherwise. How's that sound?"

Again, he doesn't respond. And again, I have to presume that his silence means he's listening to me. Maybe the best I'll get out of him is a wordless approval of my taking care of him. Even if it feels like I'm being hired more as a housekeeper.

"So ... I'll come back tomorrow, then?" He keeps his silence. I smile lightly in return. "Great. It was ... It was a pleasure meeting you, Cody. I'll be back tomorrow."

Then I turn and make for his door, satisfied.

But when my hand is on the doorknob, I stiffen up despite all of my brain telling me to just go. There's something unfinished between us here, isn't there? What if he's just as uncooperative tomorrow? Will I only tidy up his house a bit, cook him a meal he won't touch, then have him refuse another medical examination?

Exactly how far does his stubbornness go?

I turn back to face him, my hand still on the doorknob. "You know, I can't possibly compare my own life to yours. But I know that we ... we're given *tests*. Each of us. We're tested over and over throughout our lives. Sometimes, the tests seem unbearable, like there's no way we can possibly overcome them. I know *I've* had a dark time or two in my life when I just ... I just ..."

I wave a hand in the air to fill the words I can't come up with. Cody just watches me, his eyes fierce and his stance intense, like he's ready for a fight. All his muscles are turned to stone. Cody is a statue of strength carved in granite. Even the scars are beautiful. And the scruff on his face.

And those too-short American flag boxers that hug his big thighs.

I obviously have his attention, so I try to eloquently finish the point I was making. "It's up to us to face those challenges and not balk at them ... or hide. It's the only way we grow stronger. If we don't, then we're just stuck in life. Waiting. Suffering. And by—"

Suddenly, Cody takes a slow, heavy-footed step toward me that seems to make the floor itself tremble. He doesn't stop as he crosses the room.

Before I know it, I've backed myself against the wall—again—and stare up at him as he comes to a stop right in front of me. My heart races at once. For a second, I legitimately feel in danger, like I had just said too much, or gone too far, or persisted too hard.

Then he slaps a hand to the wall right by my head and inclines his body toward mine—almost as if to kiss me—but his face stops inches from my own.

And that's where he stays, his gaze smoldering me. The look in those bright brown eyes of his is as sharp as spears.

I can't breathe as I stare up into them, paralyzed. All of my words are gone in an instant.

Other than his intense face, my entire world becomes his big, massive shoulder, his huge, bulging arm near my head, and his tight, tank-top wrapped muscular chest.

He's not even touching me. Just the presence of him pins me to the wall.

Then, ever leisurely—almost gently—he reaches for the door with his free hand, twists the knob, and lets it creak slowly open. Without once taking his eyes off mine, he grows still again, the door held open and his body staying planted right there in front of me. He doesn't blink. He doesn't even seem to breathe.

After a second to regain my sense, I take the hint. Slowly, my own breath held, I peel my eyes from his gorgeous ones and leave.

Ms. Davis is by the front door, a wounded look on her face as I pass by on my way out. To my backside, she tries to distract me from what just happened, likely having heard every word. "You know, I just ... I just *love* Reverend Arnold's choir. He does such a great job with the whole church. Really. W-Wonderful job."

Outside, I stop at the bottom step of the porch, my back to her, to the house, to it all. It would be rude for me to just leave and not give her a proper thank-you and goodbye.

So why am I not saying goodbye yet?

What's keeping me glued to the bottom step of this porch?

Can I really give up on helping Cody, just like that? *He's just guarded,* I tell myself. *That's normal. Totally normal. Expected, even. Those who need help push it away the most, right?*

My heart still races from the way he put himself right in front of me. I can still feel the heat from his body.

His beautiful, ripped, sculpted body.

Every time I blink, I see his intense stare drilling into me and pinning me against that wall.

It wasn't entirely unpleasant.

Even if a little bit scary.

Maybe I'm worried that if I spend any more time around him, I'm going to give in to all of those *other* thoughts I was having in his presence. Maybe I'm worried that I will want to do a lot more than just help him.

Maybe this is *my* test.

"I ... I understand," Miss Davis says to my wordless back. "You don't have to say it. Really, you don't." She sighs wistfully. "Thank you for trying anyway. It was worth a shot."

I take in a short breath of fresh air, then turn my head toward her. "I'll be back tomorrow, Miss Davis."

2

TREY

I can't stop thinking about him.

Cody Davis, that is.

Oh, and there's a shameless tent in my bed sheets.

My sad butt is wide awake at seven on a Saturday morning instead of peacefully sleeping in—you know, like the rest of the *sane* population of Spruce. I'm lying in bed caught in a stare-off with a proud tent I'm making in the sheets.

No, that tall bump in the bed does *not* happen to be a garlic breadstick left over from last night's Italian.

It seemed impossible to sleep last night. I'm not even certain how I managed to drift off. All throughout dinner, I kept hearing Cody's deep, masculine voice over and over in my ears. As I sat across from my father over plates of pasta and neatly folded cloth napkins, my heart skipped a beat each time I pictured Cody's face hovering inches from mine when he nearly pressed me against the wall of his bedroom.

I seriously could have kissed him right there.

I could have pressed my expectant lips right against his big plump ones, breathed him in like an animal to an intoxicating scent, and raked my fingers down his meaty, muscled flesh.

My cock throbs even harder.

Good Lord, what is wrong with me?

I roll over onto my side with a huff, putting my back to the mild sunlight in the window and commanding myself to go back to sleep. *You are not getting out of this bed until it's at least nine o'clock, do you hear me?*

No, my body doesn't hear me. My body is pumping every drop of blood in my system down to my cock. With every beat of my heart, it grows harder and aches worse.

I roll onto my back once again, and my sheets push upward to make room—you know, for my massive erection. There I am on my back staring down at it once again, my reminder of how totally and endlessly stupid I was for agreeing to be Cody Davis's ...

Whatever I am.

Cody Davis and his cocky smirk. Cody Davis and his big, beefy arms. Cody Davis and that look in his sharp, spine-crumbling eyes that could bring a grown man to his knees.

Me, to my knees.

In front of him.

I shut my eyes and let my hands wander beneath the sheets.

A man like Cody Davis could own me in seconds. He could take me by the hips and lift me right off the ground like plucking a weed from a crack in the pavement. He could throw me over his thick, muscled shoulder and carry me wherever he wanted. I'd be a piece of property to him, nothing else.

He could find me in church before anyone else gets there, and I'd back against a wall next to a stained-glass window, alarmed, and there might be no one there to protect me from him.

That look he gets in his eye—that dark, menacing glint—could pin me in place.

I would be a helpless little treat for Cody Davis to enjoy.

A crispy little wafer.

My hands find a stiff *something* under the bed sheets. I part my lips and let out a sigh of pleasure. My mind continues to enjoy the scenario I've built.

Cody rushes right up to me and slams a hand on the wall next to my head, just like he did in his bedroom not twelve hours ago. *So dominant.* He could easily hook a finger in the waist of my jeans and tug our hips together. I'd feel every inch of his swelling need in his pants, which matches my own. *So powerful.* With just a pull of his strong hand at the collar of my shirt, he could rip it asunder and free my chest from my cottony confines. *So forceful.*

All the eyes in the stained-glass windows would be watching—as well as the tiny portraits of saints over the church organ and the cherubs carved into the backs of all the benches.

All of those eyes watching. All of those eyes judging.

This is so wrong.

This is so, so wrong.

Cody wouldn't care. He couldn't care if he tried. All he wants is me, and he's going to get it no matter the cost—even if it's my soul, my morality, my virginity. He will take it all if he takes any single part of me.

I do realize Cody Davis must eat a lot to maintain that kind of body—and he's looking awful hungry right about now.

I'm just a little morsel to him.

My hand moves quicker, and I moan. I'm stroking my cock under the sheets slowly, yet firmly and calculatedly. The sheets jump with joy at my every stroke, like a fanfare every second. The noise of rustling fabric fills my ears.

I'm certain the whole town of Spruce can hear me right now.

My fist choking my cock under the swishing white sheets.

My jagged, excited breaths I don't deserve to have.

My groans as I live out my fantasy in my mind.

So, so, so wrong.

Cody's mouth is open in front of me as he keeps me in place against the wall of the church. I just know he's going to have his way with me. I'm so desperate for him to touch me. I want him to pull me out of this shell of protection I've lived in my whole life. I know he's the only one who can do it. My father, Reverend Arnold, the beacon of example, of righteousness, of perfection, would be absolutely ashamed at my complete and total lack of restraint.

I am an undisciplined, horny, and *very bad* boy.

The image in my mind of him towering over me is the exact position he put me in yesterday in his bedroom. It's like my mind is trapped with that vision, that experience, that *feeling* he injected right into me. I'm stuck, my brain desperate to purge myself of the obsession that's taken me over.

I want it to happen again. I want Cody in my face. I want lots of stuff in my face.

I'm so bad.

He hasn't even kissed me yet in my dreams, and I'm already so close, I could come right now under my sheets. If I get it out, then maybe I will be free from the spell he's cast on me. If I come, I will get him out of my system once and for all, and when I return to his house, I can just be his caregiver.

I can just be ... his ... caregiver ...

Giving him ... care ...

Lots of "care" ...

All over his hard, sculpted, beautiful body.

I come right there. As I emit an abrupt, choked sound, I do half a crunch as I empty into my underwear. I come so much that I have to be making my sheets wet too, but I don't care. I'm drunken by the moment as I nearly shed tears of joy at how blissful, how perfect, how pleasurable my bodily release is.

And I'm about eighty percent complete with my orgasm when there's a soft knock on my already-cracked-open bedroom door. "Son?"

My eyes go wide as I grip the first thing my free hand finds and slap it over my cock so hard, I might have just broken it. The next instant, my father's head appears at the doorway, warm and oblivious and bright.

"D-Dad," I address him in a croak.

"Thought I heard you awake. I could have sworn I heard you sitting at your computer typing. Perhaps my ears deceived me."

Apparently my repetitive under-the-sheets racket was louder than I realized. "Must've just been … tossing and turning in bed," I mutter, painting a sleepy smile on my out-of-breath face.

His eyes go down to my crotch. "Back to sleeping with Mister Happy, are you?"

I glance down. The "thing" I grabbed is a huge, bright yellow fish-shaped stuffed animal with a big toothy grin on its face.

And that ridiculous fish is the only thing separating my dad's judging eyes from my still-swollen cock and the wet spot I have certainly made in my sheets.

"I sure have," I squeak for an answer.

My father smiles, then shakes his head ruefully. "I remember when you would cuddle with that thing every night. You couldn't sleep without Mister Happy in your arms." He chuckles, and then a glint of hurt enters his eyes. "Those days ..."

He means the days with Mom. "Those were the good times," I agree, my voice still tight. Not that I'm trying to disrespect the little moment he's having here, but I really need him to leave the room, and soon; the wetness under the sheets is growing colder by the second.

"Are you alright, son?"

I lift my gaze to him. "Yes," I answer quickly. "I'm fine."

A dubious look clouds his face as he appraises me. Then, after a moment, he lets out a short sigh. "God bless us for this glorious morning. I'll make us some breakfast." With that, he slips away, leaving my door wide open after his departure.

And I let out a sigh of my own. I feel wet and dirty all over.

I can't believe I let myself do that.

Maybe now, it will be out of my system for good. I can—no, no, I *will*—keep a professional air around Cody Davis. I will respect him as a human being, and I will treat him the same as I do any of my other patients or people I care for.

That's all I will do with Cody Davis. Caring for him.

I peer down at Mister Happy and turn him around to face me. His big, bright, innocently grinning face stares back.

First things first: let's care for this mess I've made in my bed.

* * *

Thoughts of Cody follow me all the way to the church, which is an old but charming L-shaped building at the end of Apricot Street that has stood there for forty-nine years. (It'll be fifty in a couple of weeks.) A forest hugs it on either side, the trees reaching out for its roof with long wooden fingers. The day is still young, yet the sun already beams brightly. There are many folk up and about, strolling down the street enjoying their Saturday. Among them, I see the Shannons, who give me a little wave and two big smiles. The Marvin brothers make their way to the market, Gene griping to Lee about a spoiled crop of cabbage, behind a flock of kids belonging to Margaret Hubert, who are probably headed for the park off Main Street a block down.

When I push through the doors of the church, four guys on the edge of the stage clamber to their feet at once.

Until they see who it is. "Aw, man. You scared the crud outta me," calls out Jeremiah, a gangly fellow with shoulder-length hair the color of straw.

"Yeah," chimes in Robby, another member of the choir who sports a buzzed head and a slender, muscular frame. "I thought you were your father."

I snort as I come down the aisle. "Give me twenty more years, maybe you'll see me at that pulpit." I set the box of pastries on the edge of the stage. "Brought y'all a little breakfast treat."

Robby, Hal, and Burton gasp and dive toward it, crowding around the box like they haven't eaten all week. "Trey, you're the best!" exclaims Robby.

Jeremiah, last to attack the box, swings his legs lazily over the edge of the stage, then helps himself to a pastry. "Made a stop at T&S's, huh?" he asks before taking a hearty chomp.

I lean against the stage, watching them eat. "It was on the way. Billy wasn't there today, but TJ helped me. Figured you guys could use the brain food before bad-mooded Robinson shows up and whips y'all into shape for Sunday's service. Hey, leave some for the others who haven't shown up yet," I chide Hal as he reaches for seconds.

"Our song game's gotta be on," Robby states after swallowing a mouthful of decadence. "Pastor from Fairview is visiting. I hear he and your pops got a rivalry or somethin'?"

I shake my head. "No. We love the Fairview churches. They're friendly people."

"I heard one of them preaches 'love the sinner, hate the sin'." Robby shudders. "I don't get how those people don't realize how condescending and self-righteous that tired rhetoric is."

"I never heard that rumor," I admit, "but it does make me feel lucky my dad is the way he is. I could have a very different life."

"Same with my buddies Billy and Tanner. Shit, they—"

"Mind your dang mouth, Robby, jeez," mumbles Jeremiah at his side as he tucks strands of his hair behind his ear. "You forget you're in church?"

I glance over at a particular spot against the wall between two of the stained-glass windows. It's a spot where a certain "fantasy" I had this morning took place. I can still picture Cody pinning me to that wall and stealing away all of my breath with just one of his deadly looks from those rich, sexy eyes.

He's out of your system, I remind myself. *Cody Davis is totally out of your system. You don't have any more lustful, sinful thoughts of him.*

It feels like I'm coaching myself, yet sounds more like lying.

"It ain't Sunday! It don't count." Robby faces me again. "Billy and Tanner, they might not even be together if it weren't for how Reverend Arnold's opened everyone's minds here in Spruce."

"*Thaaank* the Lord," sings Burton in a silly falsetto, inspiring a muffled chuckle from Hal, his mouth full.

Robby points his pastry at me. "You pro'lly got a sentimental attachment to T&S's Sweet Shoppe, huh? Your pops married them a year ago. First gay married couple in Spruce."

His question distracts me from thinking about my moment against the wall with Cody in my face, and it transports me to a whole other moment entirely. I look out at the seats in the church and remember when they were all filled—each and every one of them and then some—with most everyone in town. The place was so packed, we had to have been breaking every fire code in the book. My dad didn't care; he was bursting with pride that day.

And the very next day, I had come out to him. *"Dad, there's something I gotta tell you. It's eating me up inside."*

"Go ahead, my son. Confess your sins," he said to me in his light, gentle voice, humoring me and thinking I was about to tell a joke.

Instead, I told him: *"I'm gay."*

For the first time since my mother passed away, my father's smile vanished completely. He looked up from the folders stacked on his desk and stared at me hard, all his usual humor gone.

I remember how furiously my heart thumped in my chest. I stood there, terrified, literal nightmares surging through me. I genuinely thought he was about to flip his whole stance on gay marriage and homosexuality. I thought he was going to send me to a gay conversion camp, which is no laughing matter. I thought he was going to yell at me and say I'm wrong and tell me how angry and disappointed my mother would have been. I thought all of these things and worse.

Then he slowly came up to me and wrapped me in his arms. *"I still love you, son,"* he murmured over my head after several—*and I mean several*—minutes slugged by. *"I won't say I'm not surprised. I am.*

I am quite surprised. I didn't see any signs at all. I thought I was going to be marrying you off to Jamie in another year or two. I thought—"

"*She's my best friend,*" I admitted, my voice shaking, the terror still wracking my whole body. "*She was only my girlfriend for a week. She's the first person I came out to, two years ago.*"

"*My, my, my,*" sang my father, and then he let out one tight little chuckle. "*The things in front of you that you never see ...*"

We didn't say much else that first day. The next day, he had had time to think it over, and we sat down over breakfast and had ourselves a very long talk. He confessed, in the spirit of complete disclosure and honesty, that he would need time to reconcile this information with his own expectations of what my life would be like. I then made him realize that my life wasn't going to be much different. I still wanted children. I still wanted to model myself in God's good image. I still wanted to unite in holy matrimony with a good, decent person with whom I'd share my life. The one and only change was that the person may look a little different than what my father originally pictured.

My father was silent for quite a while. Then he told me he would need more time, reminded me that he still loved me with all his heart, and knew my dearly departed mother would be proud of me no matter what.

No matter what ...

Yet since that day, and despite all he said, our relationship has not been the same. He seems *stiffer* now during Sunday service. He gives me a disapproving look when I wear anything too flashy, even if it's just a brighter-colored shirt. I guess he's one-hundred percent supportive and loving to anyone gay, but when it comes to his own son—his own flesh and blood—the game is changed.

I could have it so much worse than I do. I really shouldn't be disheartened by this change between my father and I. *But still ...*

"Yeah," I finally respond back to Robby, returning from my trip down gay-memory lane. "You can say I have a sentimental thing for T&S's. Their bravery inspired my own, I guess."

"I'm surprised there aren't boys lined up around the church for you," teases Jeremiah. "I mean, I'm straight, but dang, you are *good-lookin'*, Trey. Like, better-than-average *good-lookin'*. Ain't he?"

"Yep," agrees Robby. "Even my girlfriend said so."

I have to laugh at them, though my laugh comes out more like a suffocated chuckle. "Vanessa thinks I'm attractive?"

"C'mon, Mister *Formal*. She goes by Nessie. I believe her exact wording was: 'That Trey Arnold is hot to trot.' Her mother adores the shit outta you too, which is pretty damn amazing because her mother adores no one."

"*Robby*," chides Jeremiah yet again for his language.

Robby shrugs. "Just sayin'. Cassie Evans is iron cold."

Vanessa is Cassie Evans's only daughter. The Evanses are the fourth richest family in Spruce next to the Strongs, the Whitmans, and the McPhersons. Since dating Vanessa, Robby started cleaning up his act and denouncing his former ways—which mostly involved dating a new girl every week and entertaining what he used to call his "choir groupies". To say the least, Mrs. Evans is *not* pleased with her daughter's choice of boyfriend, reputation aside.

"Are you gonna stick around to watch our rehearsal?" asks Hal, brushing his hands off on his pants from the pastry sugar.

My mind fills with Cody's striking face hovering inches in front of mine. I swallow hard and shake my head ruefully. "Sorry, guys. I ... have an obligation I have to get to. Right now, in fact. I'll definitely see your performance Sunday. Can't wait to watch you blow the Fairview socks off of Pastor Raymond."

"Obligation?" Nothing misses Robby's attention.

I'm already stressed enough about going. The last thing I need is to spend energy in dodging Robby's nosiness.

I nod as I push myself from the lip of the stage. "A nursing house call," I answer vaguely. "I'll see you boys Sunday."

"House call?" pushes Robby.

Really, he just won't let it up. "Yes, a house call."

"Whose house?" asks Jeremiah, apparently picking up on the vein of suspicion in Robby's voice.

I look between the both of them. "It isn't any of your business, you bunch a' hens, thanks very much," I sass them.

Burton, however, goes and ruins all of my mystery. "I bet it's the Davis house."

He makes the statement knowingly as his eyes narrow with suspicion, slowly chewing on his last bite. If I had to guess, I'd say he either saw me driving over there, or one of Cody's nurses that preceded me made a stink about their experience.

"The Davis house?" Jeremiah whips his head around to look at me hard, his long blond hair swinging. "Cody Davis's house?"

Robby gawps. "You're Cody Davis's nurse?"

Hal doesn't even say anything, averting his eyes to the box, likely wondering if he can get away with snatching another pastry without my noticing.

I can't even answer him before Jeremiah shakes his head. "No. That, my friend, is a very bad idea."

"Bad, bad, bad," agrees Robby. "Shit. I wouldn't even—"

"*Language*," hisses Jeremiah.

"I wouldn't go near him, Trey. You heard he stabbed his pops in the gut with a butter knife?"

I roll my eyes and let out a sigh. "Oh, and then he basked in his father's blood before worshipping Satan," I retort mockingly. "Really, guys, do you believe *everything* you hear?"

"His mama don't come to church no more," mumbles Hal, his eyes still wide and averted.

"Yeah," I agree, annoyed, "and that's because you and the rest of the town can't mind your own. You judge. One family has one major blowout that involves the police, and then no one can stop talkin', the story gets twisted all around, and suddenly the Davis family is a bunch of devil worshippers." My arms are crossed the next instant. "Really, y'all ought to be ashamed."

"Yeah, tell us all of that with a straight face after Cody's tried to poke a butter knife into ya," states Jeremiah flatly.

Robby shakes his head. "He's messed up. There's some serious damage going on in that brain of his. And it ain't just because of the Army. There was something *off* about him back in school, too."

For an instant, I want to defend Cody, even despite how he treated me. The next instant, my own curiosity spills over. "So he went to Spruce High?" I catch myself asking, my voice low.

"Yep, sure did."

"How come I didn't know him?"

Robby shrugs. "He would have been a few years ahead of you. He's about twenty-four, now."

Four years older than me ... "He must've just graduated when I started as a freshman," I deduce out loud, mulling it over.

"There isn't a single person who's close enough to Cody Davis to say they know him properly," Robby goes on. "No one got along with him back then. Like, at all." He shakes his head. "Didn't even have any girlfriends, far as I heard. I think he even cornered Billy Tucker once when he thought Billy messed with his locker. Heard it from Joel who'd heard it from Mindy."

"Ain't the two of them gettin' hitched?" interjects Jeremiah.

"Joel and Mindy? Last I heard, they are. Hey, quit interrupting me!" blurts Robby. "I'm trying to help out my buddy here and you're making me lose my train of thought."

"You can pull the brakes on that train of yours, actually," I tell him. "I think I've had enough gossipin' for a day."

"Aw, c'mon, Trey. You aren't any fun."

"The bottom line is, it really doesn't matter whose house I'm going to," I state as I take a few steps down the aisle, aiming for the door—my eyes deliberately avoiding a certain area of the wall by the stained-glass window, lest certain thoughts reenter my mind during my little spiel. "It's a person in need, no matter. This is what I do. I'm a caregiver and a healer. I give care. I heal. I don't choose who's in need of me. God does."

Jeremiah shakes his head. "You're braver than I am."

"Second that," mumbles Robby.

"It isn't bravery." I eye them importantly. "As it turns out, it's just called being a decent human being."

They stare back at me, dull-eyed and silent.

"I ... didn't mean to imply that you guys *aren't* decent human beings," I add quietly. "I know you're all very good people."

"We know what you meant," Robby assures me, though there is a clear hint of distance in his eyes.

I don't suppose I can amend my words any better than that, so I just nod at them for a goodbye and trust they know I mean well.

"Leave some for the others," I tell them with a halfhearted gesture toward the box. "If Justin shows up and sees that box empty, you know that boy will throw a fit."

"Watch your back, Trey," calls out Burton ominously before I reach the door.

"Yeah," chimes in Robby with a touch more lightness in his tone. "Dodge those butter knives."

Their voices disappear behind the church doors as they shut heavily at my back. I think I have quite enough of a battle in my head as it is without all the choirboys instigating any more—and, as it turns out, quite enough of a "battle" in my pants, too.

3

CODY

"He's supposed to be coming by later," calls my mom from the other room.

I shove a bookmark into the book I was trying to read—*not that I can focus on much of anything lately*—and shout back, "Who?"

"Trey Arnold! He said he'd be back today, sweetheart!"

I shake my head. That woman never gives up, no matter how futile the endeavor. "What're you doin' here anyway?" I retort. "You brought me groceries yesterday."

"If I don't buy them for you, who will?" she fires right back, completely unfazed.

Gently, I push myself off the bed, then slowly, I rise to my feet. Just a little bit of weight sends sharp tingles lancing down my left leg like lightning bolts, which are far more annoying than they are painful. I limp every other step as I make my way to the bathroom across the hall from my room.

"Better get yourself decent before he shows up," my mom is saying from the kitchen right as I shut the bathroom door.

Even just standing here to take a leak is an effort, shifting my balance onto my right leg, which is also sore due to constantly putting all my weight on it. There's something wrong with my left arm and elbow too, so even the small motion of pulling down the waistband of my shorts sends a pinch of pain up to my shoulder, which persists the whole time I'm holding down the waistband to relieve myself.

Can all of this pain just fuck off for a second so I can take a piss in peace?

That brings my mind back to the moment when Trey Arnold was in my room yesterday, and I rose off the bed with such speed, you'd think my ass just caught fire. I did that to prove to him that I was "totally fine", feeling smart and cocky. The truth was, my leg was in so much agony from that sudden, stupid, rash movement of mine, I could've cried right there. The second Trey left, I breathed the deepest sigh of relief and sank right back onto my bed, then stared at the ceiling for hours while my mom droned on and on about how I should give "the sweet church boy" a chance.

When I heard that Trey Arnold, son of the minister of Spruce, had come out to everyone, my first thought was that he'd drown in seven suitors a week knocking at his door. Other than being adored by everyone for being the minister's son, it wasn't lost on anyone—myself included—that Trey was one handsome guy. He might look a bit like a stick-up-his-ass, hair-always-parted, *don't-harm-my-ears-with-your-foul-language* kind of guy, but it never once detracted from how striking he looked. He's classically handsome. He has strawberry-blond hair always parted neatly, buzzed really close and cleanly on the sides and back. His eyes are green and always bright, keen, and curious. His nose is basically a perfect button, and his lips are full and kissable and—

I stop peeing. *What the fuck am I saying?*

I pull my waistband up and slap the handle down, flushing the toilet, then make for the sink and glare at my beat-up-looking face in the mirror. Every scar and scratch on it has a story, and none of them are a story I'll share with Trey-fuckin'-Arnold, no matter how many times he comes over and tries to pry his way under my skin with his words and his "tests". He might have the whole of Spruce charmed and in love with him, but I know better than to fall for that goody-two-shoes act.

It doesn't matter if we have one little thing in common.

That one thing being: we both prefer the company of a man in our bed.

"Sweetheart," calls my mom from the hallway. "You hear any of what I just said? I've been talkin' to myself out here."

Of course, maybe we don't even have *that* in common. Trey is such a Jesus freak, I'd bet he's saving himself for marriage. There won't be a man in his bed until he's been *courting* the poor bastard for two and a half years. Then he'll pop the question over a sweet, candlelit dinner, and they can have their lovely Jesus wedding, congratulate each other on being such perfect, pure, privileged individuals, and skip on their merry little way to Gayville to live out the rest of their perfect days in peace behind a long white picket fence. They'll probably get three cute puppies, too.

He would never choose to be with a damaged person like me. He and I could never, ever happen. Trey Arnold's sweet little idea of paradise is not—*and will never be*—mine.

"Sweetheart?"

I swing open the bathroom door. "What?"

"I'm heading on out." She slings her purse over a shoulder. "If Trey comes by before I'm back, you treat him nice."

"Why are you comin' back at all? Don't you have something better to do with your Saturday other than to hover?" clean house.

Her eyes narrow. "No, in fact, I don't."

"Well, you've done enough. Get on out of here and run your errands and then go back to *your* house. I'm fine as spit over here. I don't need you checkin' up on me all the time."

"If you don't want me checkin' up on you, then *stop scaring away every caretaker I send your way.* You need some help, and if you don't want it from your mama—*Hey!*" she snaps the moment I roll my eyes. "Don't sass me, I swear it, Cody Brian Davis, I *will* throw a fit right here in this hallway."

I pinch the bridge of my nose. "Mom ..."

"That Trey Arnold is a sweet boy." Her voice turns sharp at once. "And he is the last damned one in this town who's willing to come near this house anymore. Do *not* blow it with him."

"You think the minister's kid is the magic button to all our problems? You don't think the magic button might've been—oh, I don't know—*not* marrying my asshole dad in the first place, the man who went and wrecked both our lives, then took off without a lick a' consequence?"

My mother's eyes soften at those words. Then she lets out a long, patient sigh before she gently places a hand on my shoulder. "Sometimes, Cody, I could smack you right across that indignant mouth of yours. And sometimes ..."

"Sometimes?"

She eyes me. "Sometimes ... you just say the truth." She tilts her head, not a strand of hair in her tight hairdo moving. "Your father might've been a poor choice in my life." Then she reaches out and pinches my cheek. "But you weren't. You were *not* a poor choice. You, sweetheart, are my only choice I got right."

Then she pats me on the cheek firmly before turning away to head off. I watch her shadow disappear down the hall, then listen to the front door as it softly opens, creaks on its tired hinges, and shuts resolutely.

Silence falls over the house as I stand there in that dark hall, reflecting on everything.

And ignoring a dull pain throbbing in my leg.

Throb, throb, throb.

It's exactly ten minutes later when I'm stripped to just a loose pair of gym shorts doing bicep curls with my right arm in a chair by the dining room table that I hear a knock at the front door.

I ignore it. That knock can only be one person: Trey Arnold. My mother would've just let herself in like she always does, and there's not another soul I can think of in the whole town who would dare to knock on the door of the Davis house.

He knocks again, a touch harder.

And I ignore it again, a touch harder.

Next, I hear the door swinging right on open. "Hello?" comes his soft voice. "Anybody home?"

I frown and glance over my shoulder, even though the front door is out of view. That's pretty damned ballsy, really, just letting yourself into someone else's house like that.

"Ms. Davis?" he calls out.

I hear him stub his foot into something, then curse under his breath. Even his curse is a whispered, "*Shoot,*" since he's obviously physically incapable of cussing. His clumsy footsteps shuffle closer and closer.

Then he appears right at the doorway of the kitchen area, but he's looking the wrong way, his back completely to me. Today, he is wearing a white polo tucked into a pair of crisply ironed khaki shorts, belted, with low-cut socks and a pair of beige tennis shoes that look like they haven't once kissed a mud puddle. Over his right shoulder hangs a black leather bag.

I deliberately let all thirty pounds of my dumbbell drop from my grip and slam against the floor.

Trey jumps five feet in the air with a shriek and spins around, wide-eyed, both hands raised in terrified surrender. When he sees me sitting here by the dining room table with my weights strewn about me, I watch his eyes drink in every part of me: my sweaty, shirtless, tatted torso, my sweaty gym shorts that stick to my big thighs, and my stern, focused face, with my laser eyes scorching him from across the room.

"Cody," he blurts, then puts a hand on the cluttered counter next to him to keep his balance. He stays right where he is. "You ... You surprised me is all."

I don't say anything. I just stare at him, waiting.

He clears his throat, then lifts something he clutches in his other hand—some message scribbled out on a torn bit of paper. "It told me to come right in," he explains.

I flick my eyes to the paper, then refrain from scowling at it. *My mother's handiwork.* She must've also deliberately left the door unlocked, too, knowing I wouldn't have let Trey in had she locked up behind herself. *She sure thinks of everything.*

Trey shifts uncomfortably as his eyes scope his surroundings, as if all my dishes and cups are infected with syphilis.

As if he didn't interrupt me, I reach down, clasp my dumbbell, and resume my bicep set right where I left off. On my sixth rep, I note that Trey's eyes have zeroed right back onto me. He watches my every bicep curl, eyes glued to the dumbbell and to my bicep as it bulges with each flex and release.

I glower at him. "Enjoying the show?"

Trey lifts his eyes drowsily to meet mine. It's like I just pulled him from a trance. "What?"

I shake my head, then go back to ignoring him as I carelessly switch to my left arm. The moment I start my curls, I feel a sharp jolt of pain, which makes me stop with a hissing wince.

Trey takes a step forward. "You okay?"

I ignore him and give my arm a moment to recuperate. When I think it's good to go, I do another—only to have the same result, stopping once again with a grunt. *Motherfucker.*

"I can take a look at your arm," he insists. "It's no big deal."

I ignore him and just switch back to my good arm.

After a while, he lets out a short sigh, then changes his tone. "Well, you seem to be doing just fine," Trey notes, his voice lofty. "Working out. Getting about." He shrugs, crosses his arms, then reluctantly leans against the counter. It takes him a moment to decide precisely where he ought to lean, with so much stuff for his elbows or arms to accidentally knock over. "Really kinda makes me wonder why your mom thought you needed a caregiver at all."

"Told you yesterday, didn't I?" I grunt between reps. *Fuck, I lost count.* I just presume I'm at five. "Don't need a caregiver." *Six, seven, eight ...*

"Well, your mom thinks you do. And the military hospital you stayed at before you were released also thought so."

I glare at him, my eyes on his as I continue my curls—and ignore the soreness and pain that's building up in my body.

"Your right arm is gonna be *super* jacked," he teases me.

I let the dumbbell drop to the floor again.

Trey jumps. Again.

He lets out a patient sigh. "Your mother filled me in on some things. You refused to do the physical therapy. You also refused the required psychological counseling. Or got out of it. Or blew it off. Your mother wasn't clear about that."

I cross my arms and wait for him to finish.

After another short stare-off, he starts speaking quickly. "I'm really not trying to pry or get in your business. It's just that your mother asked me to help you out, so ... here I am. And while she might've told me all of that stuff ..." He shuffles his feet. "Really, I'd much rather hear it straight from you."

When's this guy gonna get it? I stand up, put all my weight on my right leg, and keep staring at the boy with an intensity I know keeps him pinned to that counter. He doesn't have the balls to come any closer to me—not when I'm staring daggers at him the way I am. No one with a spit of sense would dare come near me.

"Cody, I'm just here for you," he tries one last time. "Just tell me what you want. Anything." His eyes drift to my chest, and then to my arms, like two lost friends wandering in the woods of my body. "Anything," he repeats, a touch out of breath.

I reach down and give my nuts a hearty scratching, utterly disregarding his presence in front of me. His eyes are pulled right to my crotch as I do so. His eyebrows pull together, his forehead wrinkling at my crudeness, yet his eyes don't peel away.

It might've also just come to his attention that I'm free-balling it. No underwear under these thin, meshy gym shorts.

"Any ... Anything," he gets out yet again, a skipping record, as he forces his eyes back up to my face.

I'm still watching him.

This dude seriously needs to get fucked.

Trey sighs and looks away, annoyed. "Well, fine, then. If you want to act like some ... some ..." He waves his hand, searching for the word. "Some untrained *dog* ... licking your privates and picking at fleas in front of your guests ... then fine, be that way. But I'm—"

"You're not a guest."

He looks at me, startled by my voice. "What?"

"You're not a guest," I repeat. "That makes you a trespasser."

Trey scoffs at that like it's the most ridiculous thing. "I have a handwritten note. Which was posted on your front door." He lifts the wrinkled thing in the air and wiggles it. "You literally told me to come right in. Unless—" He sighs, realizing. "Your mother."

I reach behind me—still without pulling my icy stare off of Trey—and grab something off the table. I grab another something, again without looking, and click the parts together. Then I flick open something, pop something else in place, twist another thing, shove two parts together, grab something else off the table, pop it into place, and suddenly I'm holding a shotgun, assembled entirely without looking at it once.

Trey stares down at it, unimpressed. Then his eyes flick back up to meet mine. "Am I supposed to be scared?" he sasses me.

I pump the shotgun—*click, click*—and keep my stare on him.

Precisely ten long, perfectly still seconds pass as the two of us stare each other down, neither of us moving a muscle.

Then Trey lets out one short huff and approaches me.

I wrinkle my face, confused.

He stops in front of me and pulls the shotgun right out of my grip. I let him. Then, before my eyes, Trey pops open the action partway and pulls forward on the barrel. *Click*, the trigger housing pin slides right out. He turns over the shotgun, pulls the cartridge interrupter and cartridge stop out of the receiver, and sets them on the table—*thump, thump*. I watch, stunned. *Click*, and out comes the bolt slide. *Pop*, and off comes the forearm.

He sets the last piece of the shotgun I just assembled back onto the table—all of it in pieces again. Then he looks up at me, his eyes half-lidded. "Where do you think we are?" he asks me flatly. "If there's a fool in Spruce who doesn't know how to properly put together and disassemble a shotgun, I ain't met him."

I stare down at Trey, dumbfounded.

His eyes drift to my chest, and he squints. I can't tell if he's checking me out or lost in thought—or both.

"Alright," he mutters suddenly, deciding something, and then he straightens up. "Keep on with your little silent treatment. I'll go on ignorin' you just the same while I ..." He steps away from me and runs a finger along the cardboard that covers up the missing glass on my back door. "While I tidy up a bit around here."

Then Trey saunters right on out of the kitchen, his tight little tush wiggling invitingly in those fitted khakis as he goes.

My mouth hangs open as I stand in the kitchen catching flies and listening to the soft, scuffling noises of Trey getting to work in the living room.

What the fuck just happened?

TREY

So obviously he starts antagonizing the heck out of me.

What else was I expecting from this big man-child?

"That doesn't go there," Cody grumbles from across the room, then lets out a hefty belch for punctuation, a beer can clutched in his big hand.

I pay his protests no mind. "Really, though, don't you have trashcans in this house?" I work through the living room with a trash bag, picking up the empty beer cans, bags, and pizza boxes. "Maybe you ought to try using them now and then."

"You could also try leaving," he suggests shortly.

That's the extent of our progress, conversationally speaking. Maybe by the next time I'm here, we will graduate to only *politely* insulting one another every five or so minutes, like other dignified adults do.

And if he wasn't so achingly beautiful to look at, maybe I truly *would* have walked out by now, fed up with the ceaseless attitude.

I am so ashamed of myself for being so pathetic.

Half an hour later, I move on to the heaps of clothes on the couch. Cody is on beer number five and has gone back to working out in the dining room, despite the pain he's obviously in. *Why do I get the feeling he wouldn't be doing that so brazenly if I wasn't here?* I have been listening to that obnoxious fool grunting and slamming metal down over and over for the last hour. "Time for laundry!" I announce to no one. "Big grown boy like you can't do your own?"

If he's allowed to press my buttons all day long, I sure as spit can press his right back, can't I?

For a second, I think he's ignoring me. Then his deep, brusque growl reaches my ears: "Don't go puttin' your paws all over my delicates," he shouts from the dining room.

I have a sudden vision of grabbing a pair of his underwear he's worn all day long, thrusting it in my face, and inhaling for hours.

Oh my Lord, what in the world is going on with me??

Despite my fighting away dirty thoughts—amidst sorting dirty laundry—Cody grows bored of working out again and decides to antagonize me some more, charging my dirty thoughts right back up. It's becoming something of a sport to him, apparently. A few minutes into my work, he appears at the side of the couch, still shirtless, but now twice as sweaty.

I could lick that sweat right off of him.

Stop it!

Forcing myself to focus on something else, I also note his limp when he walks. *You're his caregiver, remember?* Yes, I remember; I'm not here to ogle him or his dirty underwear. As I continue sorting bottoms from tops, I sneak glances at the scars down his leg, as if I'm secretly taking inventory of his various wounds and trying to deduce—without being allowed to properly examine him—what some possible treatments might be. Maybe one of the treatments will involve putting my hands on his muscular thighs and—

Nope. Literally every thought that follows *that* one involves something very inappropriate.

Not today, Satan.

"What're you lookin' at?" he grunts at me, having caught me on one of my more elongated sneaked peeks to assess his scars.

Sass is my only defense to the unspeakable thoughts I've been having. So, ignoring his question, I merely nod at the other end of the couch. "You have hands, don't you? You can help instead of just standing there like a soggy tree stump."

"I told you, I don't want your help or your—"

I slap a pair of pants at his bare chest. He catches it by reflex. "Fold those up," I tell him, "and put them on that La-Z-Boy."

He stares at me like I might as well have just slapped his face. I'm ignoring his reaction as best as I can while continuing to grab and sort through the clothes. Yes, this is how I can manage; the tougher I am with him, the less I can focus on how strong his arms look when he crosses them, or how tapered and muscular his backside is, eclipsing the sunlight coming in from the kitchen and back windows behind him.

Suddenly, I find myself worrying that I may be pushing his buttons just a touch too much. After all, I really *don't* know what Cody is capable of. I don't know him much at all, in fact.

And I'm not about to find out on this lovely Saturday morning whether that butter-knife-stabbing story is true firsthand.

I can picture it now, my father reading tomorrow morning's front page headline: *Minister's Son—Death By Butter-Knifing.*

The next moment, Cody drops the pants onto the La-Z-Boy, then trudges out of the room. I look up to catch a glimpse of him before he disappears around the corner. Seconds later, I hear the heavy clinking of metal as he returns to lifting weights.

Is that all he does to fill the hours of his days here? Weights, grunting, and sweat?

If the way he winced and the look of his gashes and scars is any indication, he's not doing himself any favors pretending he doesn't have internal injuries in that big arm of his. Most likely, he's aggravating his injuries and making them worse. He could even be causing himself permanent nerve damage—if he hasn't already, thanks to his stubbornness. Cody is acting like he wasn't wounded at all while overseas.

And that's just on the outside. I'd be remiss to think he isn't suffering the other sorts of wounds, too—the kinds you can't see. He's hurting inside from things he simply won't talk about, not even to his own mother. He lost the camaraderie of his Army buds. Maybe they were his only friends, if I put two-and-two together from what I gathered about his reputation back at Spruce High. Cody is suffering. His emotions are shredded all apart just as badly as I suspect the inside of his left leg and arm are.

Maybe all of that is why I'm so stinking determined to stay here until he's ready to open up to me, or at the very least let me tend to his needs.

Is that really why I'm staying?

It's only an hour later when I've folded up the clean clothes, which are neatly sorted into jeans, shorts, t-shirts, polos, and nicer stuff that I have to find hangers for. I take a basketful of the dirty clothes to the washing machine, which I find in the steaming-hot one-car garage connected to the house by a door I didn't notice in the corner of the dining room. Cody's finished his workout by then, but he's still sitting at the table tinkering with the shotgun parts. Cleaning them, from the looks of it. I pay him no mind on my way to the garage.

Apparently, I really *was* just hired on as a housekeeper.

Thankless work, this is. Just as thankless as my volunteer jobs at the nursing homes.

Just call me Housemaid Arnold.

It's just temporary, I remind myself, keeping focused. *Your real motive here is to get Cody used to you being around. Once he decides to open up, then the real healing work begins. It's just a matter of time.*

I can tell myself that until I've got purple ears; doubt still sits in my chest that a guy as brutish, stubborn, and immature as Cody Davis will ever feel like opening up to a guy like me at all.

And maybe I'm a touch more motivated to stay because the sight of him is so ... pleasant.

I'd be a liar and then some if I didn't admit that much.

While I've got a load going in the washer, I get to the kitchen and start collecting plates, cups, and silverware for a dishwasher load, leaving a stack of not-dishwasher-friendly pots and pans by the sink to be hand washed later. All the while, I keep sneaking glances back at Cody, who still sits like a lump at the table, nearly motionless, as he meticulously cleans his shotgun parts.

Not even a peek my way. Nothing.

After washing and drying as many dishes as I can and starting yet another load of laundry, I return to the living room and begin picking up loose items off the floors and coffee table. He does have carpet, by the way—brown carpet. Lovely discoveries one makes when cleaning a nightmare of a house like this. Since the vast majority of what I see are books, I start making piles to be taken into the den where I noticed two or three long, mostly-empty bookshelves just dying for books to be set on them.

Just when I pick one up, I turn to find Cody standing two feet away from me. How or when he came in is a total mystery to me.

"That stays right there," barks Cody, swiping the book right out of my grip and slapping it back onto the coffee table where about ten-hundred other things are stacked, too.

I'm still reeling a bit from the sudden reappearance of Cody—and that sweaty, gleaming, gorgeous chest of his—that I take a moment too long to form a reply. "Well, it's gotta go someplace."

"I'm in the middle of readin' it."

"So get it from the *bookshelf*," I state tersely, grabbing it right back off the coffee table, "where I am going to *put* it. You know, where *books* belong."

Then he goes and leans against the doorway to the den—right where I was headed. I stop in front of his big muscular form and look up into his eyes.

I think his middle name is Antagonize-Trey. Cody Antagonize-Trey Davis. "You're in my way."

He smirks down at me superiorly—not quite a smile, not quite a scowl—but he's clearly enjoying making my time here miserable.

Why does Cody have to still be totally shirtless, gleaming with sweat from his workout earlier, and wearing nothing at all but a pair of loose gym shorts with *nothing* underneath?

"You need a shower," I tell him, annoyed.

This was all planned, I'm certain of it. This whole day. All of it. *I am in Hell.* "Cody," I state warningly.

He still doesn't move.

So I let out a short sigh, then force myself to slip past him with the half a foot of space he's left me to get by.

This puts my face against his sweaty side for five solid seconds as I squeeze past him.

It also presses my body against his.

Right. Up. Against. His.

His thick, masculine aroma assaults my nostrils, making me drunk on his musk. I could totally stay right here, pressed against his sweaty, firm, perfect body for hours.

Literally, my whole side feels utterly drenched and violated just from squeezing past his firm, slippery muscles.

No, he deliberately doesn't budge an inch.

After getting past him and returning the book to the shelf, I go back for more of the books in the living room. Cody still hasn't moved an inch, blocking more than half of the doorway with his big muscled body.

He's also still facing the same way, which means the view I get now is of his wide, tapered backside, as well as the shape of his two perfect buns in those gym shorts that are glued to them, skintight—two globes of absolute perfection, cleaved right down the middle, a dream and a half of desires I swear away every night on account of keeping sinful thoughts at bay.

Lord help me.

I've thought those words a hundred times an hour, it seems, ever since I first stepped foot in this house yesterday.

Stay strong. Stay focused. Stay smarter than your dirty thoughts.

"Cody," I state to his backside. "Sorting all of these is going to be a lot of work to begin with. If you would kindly stop making it more difficult by deliberately standing in my way—"

"There are *two* ways into that den," he points out in a grunt. "It's not my fault you prefer pressin' your body against mine on your way in when you could've taken your ass around through the dining room." He lifts one muscled arm to point in the direction of the kitchen. "That way."

I glance over at the other side of the den and realize he's right; there's a small archway, and I could've easily gone around.

My face flushes, annoyed. Not caring to argue more with him, I make my way through the dining room instead—but not before taking one last glimpse at his chiseled, beautiful butt before I go.

My heart races at just the sight of him. Just the *proximity* of our bodies in this house is enough to steal my breath away as I continue to clean out his living room, little bit by little bit.

Yes, I'm ashamed of my attraction to Cody.

And no, obviously I can't help myself. Really, can I be blamed? Someone would have to be *dead* to not be instantly drawn to the beefy body, hunky face, and dazzling eyes of Cody Davis.

I am unraveling by the second.

No, I'm not, I state tersely to myself as I carry four more books in my arms—heavy ones, by the way—around through the kitchen, the dining room, and into the den to file them on the shelves. Each time I leave, I sneak another glimpse of Cody's wide backside and bubble butt. It's like a reward for each trip.

No, it's not.

I'm so messed up right now.

I wish he hadn't pointed out the other route to the den. I would totally push past his body a hundred more times just to feel him against me again, just to have him—

No, you don't, I scold myself.

I'm not sure how much more of this emotional tug-of-war I can take before I snap in half.

"I hope you realize that I'm gonna pull all those books right back outta there when I want to read them," he calls over his shoulder, taunting me.

"And you'll put them right back when you're *through*," I retort from the den as I switch around books to maintain an alphabetical order by author, so help me. "Like an *adult*."

"My house. I do whatever I want."

He's so irritatingly childish. I realize I'm holding *A Tale Of Two Cities*. I turn it over, reading the back. "These your grandma's?"

He doesn't answer, but I hear his body shift for the first time since he annoyingly planted himself in that doorway.

After filing the book away in the D's—*Dickens*—I turn around and find Cody facing me, leaning against the wall inside the den instead of at the doorway. He watches with two stony eyes across the dim, cluttered room. I can't help but drown in the sight of him every time I look his way. It's impossible. I can't just *see* him; I have to see every bit of him. Like some unavoidable steamy cloud of hotness, his beauty invades me whether I want it to or not.

Which makes it all the more infuriating when he's acting like a big, muscled brat.

"She has good taste in books," I tell him anyway.

The tiniest of smirks crosses Cody's face.

By the time it's late afternoon, I've cleared off the counter in the kitchen enough to make a pair of tasty sandwiches for us. I suspect Ms Davis is the one who gets the groceries, because I'm surprised to find actual lunch meats and fresh condiments in the refrigerator among some other decent foodstuffs—cheese, milk, a head of lettuce, two cartons of eggs, a few cups of fat free yogurt, and a jar of mild salsa.

Of course, there's also a twelve-pack of beer stuffed in there, as well as several bottles in the door.

Half that twelve-pack is empty, all of it consumed since I arrived.

"Hungry?" I call out to the man-child, who has returned to the table to tinker with his guns. No response. "Me too. What do you like on your sandwich?"

He fumbles with a part. It clatters across the table. He reaches for it with his left arm—winces—then grabs hold of it and sits back in his seat, continuing his busywork.

No, he doesn't respond or acknowledge my existence at all.

I don't let it bother me. "Awesome choice," I announce with mock enthusiasm. "I like that on my sandwich, too."

Not even a scowl breaks on his stoic, statuesque face. Maybe I've maxed him out of reactions and words for a day.

"You oughta play poker," I mutter as I finish up the second sandwich, "with a deadpan expression like that. Don't want you to miss your calling. Lunch is ready."

He doesn't budge an inch other than his fingers as they slowly and meticulously clean each and every part of his gun. I notice it's a different one than the one we both assembled and disassembled before—a rifle with a couple attachments on it.

I come up to the table and set a plate with his sandwich on it right in the middle of his workspace, interrupting him.

He quirks an annoyed eyebrow up at me, squinting.

Paying the insolent look no mind at all, I sit in the creaky chair across from him, whisper a quick prayer before drawing a cross over my chest, then go right on eating my own sandwich without a bother in the world, crunching away at the lettuce. All the housework genuinely worked up an appetite in me, so it isn't some obnoxious show I'm putting on in front of him; I'm starved.

And considering he had a few workouts and hasn't eaten a single thing since I showed up, I know he has to be hungry, too.

Though it becomes apparent after two bites of my sandwich that he hasn't touched his.

I swallow my bite. "It isn't gonna eat itself."

He gently sets down the pieces he was holding, then sits up in his chair and leans forward over his plate. He doesn't look at his sandwich; his eyes are on me, hard and untelling.

Maybe he wants to eat me instead.

Stop thinking things like that!

Then, without any further coaxing, Cody grips his sandwich with both hands, grunts in annoyance, then lets go and only grips it with his good right hand. His pumped biceps, still shiny with his sweat, gleam in the light that hangs over the table revealing every ripple of muscle to my eyes. He lifts the sandwich to his plump, parted lips, then chomps a big, hearty bite. When he pulls it away, chewing, I see a tiny dab of mayo caught on the corner of his lip. It dances as he chews.

His eyes never leave my face. He looks positively deadly.

Satisfied—and trying my best not to continue ogling his arms like some horny teenager who's found his older brother's stash of pornography on his computer—I resume eating my own lunch.

But my eyes betray me, slipping right back to his face.

Cody is still staring at me.

Hard.

I notice the plumpness of his lips as they move with his every crunch. Even the way he chomps off one big bite at a time of that poor, defenseless sandwich is sexy somehow, like he's dominating it slowly, claiming it piece by piece as it goes into his belly.

I really want to be that sandwich.

No, you don't.

Yes, I do.

I notice the sharpness of his eyes, the way he looks like he could seriously devour me right after he finishes that sandwich I made him with my own hands.

Cody is so beautiful. It's impossible not to notice.

Something else apparently notices his beauty, too—*something right below my waist.*

I look away at once, blushing, and cross my legs before going in for another bite. Why do I always feel like I've got the upper hand, then just with a *look* from Cody, I lose all my senses again?

He finishes before I do—considering his bites are twice the size of my own—and then he rises to his feet at once and crosses the kitchen very slowly, limping. I watch him go, my eyes slipping down his smooth, tatted, naked torso, arriving right at his butt again as he yanks open the fridge and bends over.

Can I please pull out my phone right now and snap a shot of Cody Davis's perfect, beautiful, sculpted butt in those shorts?

It's bad enough that his body is made of granite and dreams. *But he's also not wearing any underwear, and that fact is made twenty times more apparent when he bends over like he is right now.*

I'm totally seeing butt cleavage—pure, perfect, pornographic butt cleavage.

I'm dying right now. The sight I'm enjoying doesn't help the problem in my own shorts.

This is so not me.

He straightens up the next instant and slams shut the fridge, a can of beer in his hand now. He braces the can against his chest and cracks it open—*pop, snap, hiss.* The big brute ambles back over to the table and plops right back in his seat to take a long, slurping sip of his beer before setting it down by his empty plate next to two other emptied cans. Then he returns to his work like he was never interrupted, fiddling with a rifle part and a small rag, wiping, wiping, wiping.

Well, at least he ate.

Apparently so did my eyes when he bent over at the fridge.

Mental torture has a middle name. *This is it.*

After taking another bite and chewing on it for a while, I let my insides calm down and reel in all of my focus. My eyes flit over to his rifle, and I search my brain for words. I still have my duties here; let's not get sidetracked with sandwiches and Cody's buns.

"What's that?" I ask with a nod.

Surprisingly, Cody actually looks up. "Huh?"

"That." I nod again at the rifle. "Attached to the rifle scope."

He doesn't even need to look at the thing to answer. "Night vision attachment."

I nod appreciatively. "Never seen one."

"Sure you have."

"Nope."

He scoffs. "You went and took apart my shotgun like you own twelve of your own. Don't play dumb now with my Remington."

I take a bite—a fairly big one—and then respond through my mouthful. "I ain't playin' dumb. I just haven't seen an attach—"

"Don't talk with your mouth full, either," he sasses me right then, cutting me off. "Didn't your mama teach you it was rude to talk with your mouth full at the dinner table?"

I lift my eyebrows in surprise.

Was that an attempt at humor? Is he actually playing with me now? Is this a good sign?

And is he aware that my mother's no longer with us?

"She sure did," I answer anyway—with my mouth still full.

Cody shakes his head and hides half a smirk behind his rifle, which he picks up. "The original scope," he explains, tapping it. "This," he goes on, tapping the extra attachment, "is the night ... the night vision. Attaches to the end of those—*this* here, see?"

I swallow my bite and give him a nod, listening. *He's only just now starting to slur,* I note. *This boy has the tolerance of a yeti.*

He's about to go on, but then something stops him. He squints at me for a moment, and then his whole tone changes. "You're just collectin' a paycheck from my mom, huh?"

I freeze. That was an unexpected shift of topic. "What?"

"All of this." He nods at the kitchen, at his plate, then at me. "Your ass is just here to get a ... a *check*. Runnin' all around my house. Puttin' away all my d-dang books when I didn't want you to. Going through my launder—laundry. Makin' me ... *sandwiches*. Small-talkin' shit about rifles you damned well already know."

"Is it a problem to just ... talk?"

"When you're bullshitting me, yeah, it's a problem."

Cody's face has gone hard as stone, and his eyes would throw a magic spear right through me if they could.

If there's anything I have learned in my time here so far, it's that Cody responds well to strength. Maybe it's a military thing. Maybe it's a Cody thing. Regardless, I know I can't break in front of him. I need to stand my ground just as firmly as he is if I'm so determined to earn his respect. So here I go, putting my elbows up on the table like I'm king of it. I square my jaw and tilt my head. "You must be outta your *gourd* if you think I'd put up with all your crud today for a measly check from your mama."

I might have just weakened my stance with the use of a word like "crud". If I was more ballsy, I might have said the "s" word. *Haven't I had enough bad thoughts today to not add in bad words?*

I get the desired effect, anyway. Cody narrows his eyes, leans back, then drops the subject as he picks up his rifle and resumes right where he left off, tinkering and rubbing and inspecting.

And I sit back and finish my sandwich in peace.

Peace is relative. My mind is a storm of questions and angst and frustratedly unfulfilled curiosities about that young, beautiful man across the table from me. What's his deal? If I listened to any of the stories the choir boys were going on about, Cody's always been this way, even before the Army.

He's always been a loner. He's always been on his own.

I can tell that about him, the way he pushes me away, the way he lives, the way he ... *scowls.*

Somehow, I think it endears him to me, even despite all else.

I'm sort of a loner in a way, too.

None of the confrontation between us just now discourages me. In fact, it only makes me more determined to knock harder on that impossibly thick shell of his. I'm going to crack a fissure right down its middle and let all his gooey insides spill out.

But, you know, in a less visually disgusting way.

It only now occurs to me that I don't know what Cody's smile looks like. I keep finishing my sandwich while I study his face curiously, stewing on that unfortunate, sobering fact. *I would bet a hundred bucks his smile is beautiful.*

5

TREY

My dad's first concern was whether I was being mistreated at all by "the Davis boy".

"No, no. He's totally great. We got along quite well," I assured him after service on Sunday. All of the choirboys sang their hearts out and Pastor Raymond from Fairview pretended to be somewhat underwhelmed—which was a surefire guarantee that his socks were knocked off and he was super jealous of our choir's talent.

My dad was skeptical at best. "I still don't think it's a good idea, you spending too much time with that Davis boy."

Even an hour later when we were headed home, I was still so bothered by my father's attitude about the whole thing. "You said that we ought to help those in need," I argued. "Cody's injured. He needs a helping hand to ... get around, to feed himself, to ... *feel human*. Hell, he even has trouble *bathing* himself."

My dad turned two cold eyes onto me right then. It wasn't until ten solid seconds later that I realized I'd let "Hell" slip right out of my lips. The realization made my face go bright red.

"Bathing," murmured my father, shrinking all of what I just said down to that one word, which now made me feel so weirdly embarrassed and small. I could imagine my father picturing Cody and I sitting side-by-side in a bathtub with a rubber ducky, our heads covered in soap suds.

And then my father went into the house ahead of me, leaving me on the lawn to mull over all of my thoughts. I was so frustrated that I could spit venomous acid on the bright, colorful flowerbed right in front of me. The problem was, I didn't know what I was frustrated about. Was it Cody and how I felt like I made little to no progress with him on Saturday? Was it my father, who gives all his love to the whole sweet town of Spruce and saves his cold, bitter disappointment for me, his gay son?

Or was it myself for letting slip that dumb word on our little walk home from the church?

And that was on a Sunday, too.

"What're you doin'?"

The sound of Cody's voice jerks me abruptly back to present time. It's Tuesday and I'm in Cody's kitchen washing dishes. My hands are buried in the sink with the water running, and I was just staring off at the window, reflecting on Sunday's little drama.

"Lost in thoughts," I answer Cody, who stands by the counter.

Of course, Cody's face isn't exactly bleeding with concern. He looks more annoyed that I'm even here than anything.

I decide to be more specific and share a little of myself. "Well, on Monday, I had to deal with a bunch of stress at the clinic. The one off of Main Street, right past Wicker, that is. The clinic was shorthanded because Marybeth called in—something to do with her daughter—and then the patients were particularly ... *needy*. Of course, that meant that *I* was going to have to—"

"I didn't ask for a whole soliloquy." He turns away and yanks open the fridge.

I narrow my eyes at his back. He wears a loose tank top today. "I'm surprised you even know a big ol' word like *'soliloquy'*."

"I know a whole bunch a' big words." He pulls out his fifth can of beer since I arrived two hours ago, then slaps shut the fridge. "Cunnilingus." He cracks open his beer. "Fellatio." He kicks it back for three hearty gulps, then slams it on the counter as he stares at me, wet-eyed. "Forni-fuckin'-cation."

I set the last clean dish into the dish drainer, then swipe a towel off the counter and dry my hands as I spin to face him, a big smirk pasted on my face. "Boy, you must think you're *really* smart. Entertaining, too."

Cody's dark, half-lidded eyes regard me with no humor when he lets out a deep and resonant belch for a response.

I toss the towel onto the counter and cross my arms. "You're gonna be seeing a lot more of me, Cody. I know you thought you were rid of me when I left Saturday—"

"Can't be that lucky." He takes another sip of his beer.

"But Miss Davis is the one who hired me. So I am here 'til I'm dismissed by my *employer*. Which, for the record, *ain't you*."

"I don't need my mother to dismiss you." Cody sets down his beer with a loud thud, then takes two steps toward me. He tries (and fails) to hide his limp on both steps. "I could get your ass right on out of here if I wanted."

I lift up my chin partly to show strength, but also to keep my eyes on his; standing this close to me, I'd be staring at his chest if I didn't. *Not that that's a bad sight to behold in that loose tank top.*

"Yeah, you heard me." Cody smirks superiorly down at me. "I could pick your scrawny ass up right now and toss you out of my door. I've carried men twice your weight."

"After all I've done for you?" I spread my hands innocently. "Cleaned up your filthy kitchen? Took out your trash? I even put beef stew and chili I made in your freezer so you'd have somethin' other than just sandwiches to eat. That wouldn't be very kind of you to toss me—"

"I'm not a kind person."

"I think you *think* you're not a kind person." I challenge him with my eyes, like a knight throwing down a gauntlet. My words are my sword. My faith is my shield. "But deep down, we're all just doing our best. Inside, we're all doing what we think's right."

"I AIN'T GONNA BE YOUR FUCKIN' FRIEND," he barks out with sudden and surprising strength.

I flinch, my eyes widened at the unexpected burst of anger. In an instant, we're no longer playing with each other; he is truly and legitimately angry, and I withdraw all my sass at once.

He goes on. "I told my pesky mother and I told you—both of you—I don't need any help, *and I fuckin' meant it.*"

"Cody ..."

"What the hell gives you the right to come in here and tell me how to live my life, huh? Put my books over here, put my clothes over there, my dishes, do this, do that. Fuck you, Trey Arnold. I don't give a *shit* whose son you are or what you think of me."

"That's fine," I interject sincerely, keeping my voice calm. I really don't know how much of this is Cody and how much is the beer talking. He has to have a high tolerance, considering his size. Every time I'm here, he's consistently downed at least six cans. "It shouldn't matter at all whose son I am."

"This is *my* life," Cody growls, slapping a hand to his chest like a gorilla laying claim to his corner of the jungle. "*Mine.* I can live my life however I want. I can sit on my roof every night, drunk off my ass, and howl at the moon."

Stay calm. "No one's stoppin' you."

"I can build a fuckin' *fort* in my kitchen out of those books and use my own dirty damned dishes for target practice with my rifle. I wouldn't miss a single one of them."

"Would be a bit wasteful, but be my guest."

"You go on and on about fuckin' ... life *testing* me and shit." He takes another step, towering over me. "You don't know anything about tests. You're as privileged as they come, church boy."

I stand my ground the best I can without matching his anger. The trick is to diffuse; I won't succeed in diffusing anything if I get angry with him, too. Calmness is key.

Of course, that's all a lot easier said than done when you have a guy as big and threatening as Cody Davis nearly pressing his chest against yours.

"Your whole '*we're given tests*' bullshit," he goes on. "Was that a God thing? Is that the gist of all that bullshit you went on about last Friday?"

I blink. Now he's lost me. "Friday ...?"

"In my room. When you first showed up. You actually think God's testing me?" He slaps his bad leg. "With this?" He slaps his left arm. "With this?" Then he jabs a finger at his forehead three times. "In here?"

Recalling it, I actually didn't mention Him at all on Friday when I said my ~~prayer~~ before leaving.

I realize the towel is back in my hand and I'm wringing it, as if neurotically needing to dry my hands a second time.

"It ... doesn't really matter what you believe in, Cody." I am trying not to let my voice shake. "We're all tested in life just the same." Also, I'm stepping away from him, slowly. *What happened to standing your ground, Trey? What happened to showing strength? What happened to not being afraid of him?* "You. Me. Everyone in this town. Everyone in the world."

With one fast swipe of his hand, he knocks the towel right out of my grip. Then he closes any remaining distance between us, his shadow falling over me like a rolling storm cloud. By reflex, I step away. It isn't long before my back smacks against the kitchen wall.

And there we are, just as we were when his mere presence had me pinned to a wall in his bedroom. *And a church wall in my fantasies, all the cherubs and saints and Jesus watching.*

"Well, here's a little news for you, preacher boy," he breathes in my face, his voice a deep, low growl. "There is no God."

A thick, tense silence falls between our bodies. My heart is up in my neck as I stare at his fierce, pained expression.

There's so much in there he doesn't want to say. There's so much pain behind those eyes.

"Cody ..."

"There is no God," he repeats.

It's not the first time I've heard someone say that, by far. But it *is* the first time I've had such words directed right at my face with such intensity and anger.

"This ... This isn't about God," I manage to reply. "This is—"

"God is dead." He practically spits the words in my face like poison off his tongue. "You can take all your God shit somewhere else. Because if I hear one more time about God's plan for me, or how my nearly gettin' blown up and then dismissed from the only family I've ever had is part of His '*test*', or how I should be thankful my deadbeat dad is still alive even if he's a fuckin' lyin' prick and wants nothing to do with my sorry ass ... so help me, Trey, I'll put another hole in that wall." His voice deepens. "*And maybe my next one will be right by your self-important head.*"

Stunned, my eyes drift to the wall next to me. Only then do I see the two big, fist-shaped holes, side by side, right by an empty spice rack on the wall.

Then, just as scathing, he adds one last thing: "Tell me this, preacher boy. Did a bunch of self-important assholes visit *your* house to lecture you on God's '*tests*' after your mother died?"

My instant reaction is to tell myself that he didn't mean it. *He didn't mean it.* If I didn't tell myself that, then his low blow would be enough to literally shove the air out of my lungs.

Despite my efforts, my eyes feel a sting of impending tears—and I am *not* a crier.

I won't cry. Why would I cry? He's just speaking in anger. I went too far. I pushed him too much.

Yet, still ...

He didn't mean it, I tell myself again more assertively. *I'm not going to be hurt by it.* I'm clearly so determined to act invincible. *This is all in anger, what he's saying. He doesn't mean it. This is all ...*

But it's a bit tough to convince myself of that right now.

I lift my chin, part my lips, and prepare to respond.

And the response doesn't come.

My eyes sting even worse, tears threatening to spill out once more despite my efforts to keep them inside.

I am not going to cry.

Stop it.

After another long moment passes, I try to speak yet again. "Cody, I ..."

But words *still* fail me.

Cody's furious stare is too intense to look at, so I just turn my face away, still stunned and hurt, unable to talk. My whole view is nothing but those fist-shaped holes in the wall by my head.

Sorry, I mean: *my self-important head.*

"You ... what?" he spits out. "You'll pray for me? ... Is that it?"

"No." I can't manage to look at his face anymore, no matter how beautiful or striking I found it just moments ago. "I'm just ... thinking about ..."

What am I thinking about?

Then a dry snort comes out of my nose. "I'm thinking about the moment I woke up this morning, got dressed, and decided I'd spend my day helping Cody Davis."

He doesn't respond.

The room is as still as the dead.

I go on. "Y'know, it took me over an hour to plan what nice things I'd try doing for you today. How pathetic is that?"

I let out a tiny chuckle—Or is it a cough? Or a choke of sadness? Or none of those things?

Then I squint at the holes in the wall, aiming all my quiet, calm words to them. "I guess I ... didn't expect to have ... the wound of my mother's death ripped open in return."

A flicker of—something—passes through his eyes, though his face stays flat as a stone. Maybe I don't need him to say anything. He's already said his part, and I suppose now I've said mine.

I slip out from between him and the wall, slowly crossing the kitchen and heading for the foyer.

Before I'm gone, I glance back at Cody one last time. He hasn't moved; he just stands there facing the wall where he had me pinned with just his intimidating presence. I notice his head is slightly bowed now, the only movement of his body coming from his slow, calculated breaths.

Then I gently pull open the front door, step through, and let the creaky old thing shut itself at my back.

I drive home slowly, taking the scenic route. When I reach the first stop sign, ocean waves of my own breath drawing in and rushing out fill the whole car. I can't stop thinking of that seashell I keep by my bed and the day my mother gave it to me.

In, out, in, and out go the waves.

In and out.

It was a lost cause to begin with, I think to myself, grasping for any semblance of reassurance or comfort while staring at that stupid stop sign.

Perhaps I really ought to have heeded all the red octagonal warning signs on the way to his little house at the end of Willow in the first place.

6

CODY

I am such an asshole.

If an asshole had an asshole, I'm that asshole's asshole.

Like father, like son, apparently.

I spend the whole rest of the evening in my backyard as the sun lazily sets. The noise of kids bouncing on a trampoline two houses down reaches my ears, reminding me of the total *lack* of joy and laughter in my own childhood. I always wanted a trampoline. There's something about jumping on an unsteady, bouncy surface that's thrilling as hell to me. You never know where you'll land.

And the more you seek that thrill, the higher you go.

Up, up, up, up, up, up.

My mom texts me when I'm in the backyard staring up at the stars asking if Trey is still here. I scoff at the message, then type out that she'd better not look for a *seventh* nurse or I'll fuck things up with that one, too—then I delete the message before sending it. I can't stomach my mother's disappointment in me. Not tonight. I'm too damned disappointed in myself to fit any other feelings in my loud, chaotic head.

It's easier lying out here in the grass. The noise of the world—crickets, wind, distant talking, creaking patio benches, the wood of fences settling and shifting, a far-away wind chime, the rumble of a car engine—all of that noise comforts me.

It comforts me because ever since coming back home, I don't trust silence anymore.

Silence is stealth and cunning and watching.

Silence is a sniper waiting patiently on the other side of a half broken wall, their good eye trained to your forehead.

Silence is the moment of peace after the pin is pulled from the grenade. Silence is the lull before your best friend shouts, "*Move!*"

Silence is all you hear just before it explodes.

Boom.

Silence is the corpses littering the field of yesterday's battle.

Silence is all the people back home you'll never see the same way again. The sad look in your mother's eyes because she knows she'll never truly be able to protect you anymore from the world, not like she used to when you were a little baby and could be held against her breasts, coddled, and sung to sleep. She'll never truly know you anymore. Her son was ripped away from her the day he went off to join the Army. She doesn't know who you are now.

Silence is counting hours before the sunrise.

Silence is death.

I spend an unhealthy amount of time wandering my backyard at night. Back here, I don't have to hide my weird limping. I have a hundred different places I can sit and read, even at night. My neighbor has this obnoxious porch light that stays on until well after three in the morning, and it casts so much light into my yard that I can actually read for hours.

But there's no reading tonight because thoughts of someone else is crowding my head.

I can't stop thinking about Trey Arnold.

And what I said.

Every time I look back at that house, I think about the look on his face right after I let those angry words slip. His mother? *Really? I had to fucking go there?* There was just something about the way he spoke to me, like he was ready for anything I said, like nothing would surprise or unsettle him, like he felt invincible with an imaginary bible pressed to his chest.

I wanted to see him scared, just like everyone else is scared of me. I wanted him totally unsettled in my presence. I wanted to give myself a real reason to hate him, just like I hate every other judgy-eyed fucker here in Spruce.

I just wanted him as undone as I feel in my head twenty-four hours a day, even if it was just one fleeting second for him.

Well, I went and succeeded in doing just that, didn't I?

Maybe I succeeded too well.

That's my last thought before I drift to sleep that night.

When Wednesday rolls around, there's no Trey knocking on my door. I sit in my house all day and stare at all the different places he cleaned. Then I distract myself by pulling apart another gun, or lying under the sunlight in my backyard, or peeling open a book—which I *do* return to its proper spot on the bookshelf when I'm through with it. I even pull out a container of stew he made me and set it on the counter to defrost for later.

Damn you, Trey.

He doesn't come by on Thursday, either. Friday also flies right on by without one sign of him.

It isn't possible that I miss him, right? That'd be messed up.

And it'd be exactly what I deserve.

It's four in the morning—very late Saturday, early Sunday— when I'm standing in the dark den staring at the bookshelves and all of the carefully sorted books. I stand here and stare at those damned books for a whole hour, seems like. I keep seeing his cute face as he studies the shelf, contemplating where to file the next book, and then going for another bunch of them.

Then it's five in the morning when I'm staring at the dryer—and the load of clothes he left in it that I never put away.

Fuck.

I let out a short sigh, then pop open the dryer and grab a bundle of clothes. It isn't an easy effort to carry them in my whiny arms while limping slowly and tediously with every labored step. I take them to the living room to fold and sort them, just like Trey would have, before bringing them to my room and putting them away into my dresser and closet. Despite dealing with my broken body, the routine of it all takes me right back to the Army and the strict discipline my time there hammered into my head. Up at the crack-hole of dawn. Clothes ironed sharp, ready. Shoes polished. Mealtimes. Workouts. Drills, drills, drills.

Where did all of that discipline go in such a short time?

What the fuck is wrong with me?

When the horizon swells with a bright blue glow through my window, I'm sprawled out like a sorry sack of shit, wide awake on my messy bed. I'm actively ignoring a pain in my left thigh and a worse, emotional one in my chest.

It's right then, staring off at the light swelling in my window, that I realize what I gotta do before I lose my fucking mind.

And apparently I gotta do it on zero hours of sleep.

7

CODY

The hardest effort is getting dressed.

Because suddenly, no thanks to Trey and his chores, I have so many fucking options of what to wear.

I pick the first clean shirt I find—a button-up shirt. One arm goes in at a time, and I wince as my body tries to fight the effort with my left one. I have to redo the stupid-ass buttons three times because I keep ending up one off.

I grab a pair of blue jeans. It feels so foreign, putting on pants for the first time in I-don't-know-how-long.

I slap some water onto my head one-handed, then push all my hair to one side. There isn't much hair to deal with in the first damned place, but I make sure it's all at least *trying* to go in the same direction.

It's the effort that counts, right?

Thirty-two minutes later, I'm standing in front of the church at the end of Apricot Street, drenched in back sweat, armpit sweat, and a sheen of perspiration across my pale forehead. I almost ran over a cat with my truck on Peach Street, and my arm locked up when I crossed the intersection at Main, nearly causing me to veer into a street sign. No, driving with this body wasn't the smartest choice I've made. But after recklessly putting at least two lives in danger on the drive over, here I am.

I'm seriously about to do this. *And I'm fucking petrified.*

When I push open the doors, I find the lobby empty. Service must have already begun because no one is in the short, narrow front room at all. The chapel doors are propped wide open, letting out the echoes of the choir as they sing.

In other words, I'm welcomed into the church by the ringing voices of angels. Hallelujah.

I don't waste any time. I make my way through the doors, my left foot shuffling annoyingly along the ground as it disobeys me.

Three people near the back turn around. Three sets of eyes go wide at the sight of me.

Then come ten more faces turning. Then about twenty. All of them look at me like I'm drenched in goat's blood with an upside-down cross painted on my forehead.

I was hoping for a seat in the back, but every potential space is occupied with a person. Just when I note a spot by the aisle, the lady sitting by it quickly puts her purse in its place, then plays it off like she wasn't just staring at me by innocently turning her old, stiff neck forward.

My heart drums something awful as I stand there like an idiot, sweating twice as much in here as I was outside in the heat. There are still several eyes on me, which I'm not paying much attention to anymore. I don't see Trey anywhere, and he's the only damned reason I stepped foot in this place. I didn't do it for the people of Spruce, or the reverend, or the choirboys—two of which I vividly remember catching behind the bleachers with their pants at their ankles fucking a pair of cheerleaders back in the day. I can taste the hypocrisy of the people in this room who turn their nose up at me, yet swoon at these guys' pretty voices, ignoring all else.

Yeah, things are only pretty if you keep from looking inside them—this church and all its people included.

I should go, I realize as I take a step back, regretting my stupid decision to come here at all. The last thing I need to do is blow up, say something wrong, and prove any of these fuckers right.

It's at this exact point that I finally see him looking my way. Trey Arnold sits in the third row, right by the aisle. His lips are parted in surprise and his eyes are on mine, unblinking.

My feet have planted themselves in place at the sight of him, my escape halted. I can only stare back, a deer caught in the road.

Trey's face softens. His eyebrows lift with hope.

That look is the tether I needed to not take off back to my dim and desolate house. It roots me right in place—Trey and his parted hair, the crisp collar of his polo, his slightly flushed, boyish cheeks and his plump, parted lips and twinkling eyes.

Then the cute bastard scoots over.

Now I kinda have to stay, right?

Against every instinct in my already sore-as-fuck muscles, I push myself down the aisle. Trey's eyes are on me the whole time as I walk, trying my damnedest not to limp. It's a real effort, and I'm objectively unsuccessful, despite how well I think I'm doing.

It takes fucking forever to reach him.

Of course the bastard would sit all the way up in the third row.

When I finally arrive at his row, I realize he didn't really have that much space to lend me in the first place; the whole bench is occupied from this end to the tall glass windows, save the tiny spot he made me at the end that's half a person wide.

Well, I got all the way up here on account of Trey's annoying considerateness. Can't turn back now.

Amidst the glorious and angelic music of cheerleader-fucking choirboys, I take the tiny spot on the bench next to Trey. Half my big ass hangs off of it, but I'm not going to complain. The whole side of my body is pressed up against Trey now. Our thighs touch. Our arms, too. Our shoulders. Hell, even our happy butt cheeks are kissing each other.

All of that makes me too aware of what a great body Trey has.

Even if he's a scrawny, meddlesome little shit.

I eye him out of the side of my face. He's back to paying full attention to the choirboys on the stage, his jaw tightened up and his face flushed slightly from the scandalized attention that his little act of compassion earned him, no doubt.

I'm certain I know exactly what half the room is thinking right now. *"Oh, what a sweet boy, that Trey! He takes pity on the weak and damaged, just like Jesus Christ!"* Yeah, yeah. I bet they're all just creaming in their pants about how selfless Trey is for setting the example here. What a martyr.

He shifts his leg slightly, clears his throat for no reason, and continues listening to the choir. His little movement makes me notice how firm his thigh feels pressed against my own. Nice legs on this guy, really. I wouldn't be surprised if he jogs down Main every morning. Those legs are probably complemented well with that nice tight tush of his—which one of my butt cheeks is getting inappropriately more and more familiar with by the second.

Okay, maybe he's not that scrawny.

When the choirboys finish being holy, no one applauds. The boys step back and take their seats at the side of the stage.

Then a different person fills up the spotlight.

Trey's father, Reverend Arnold.

His eyes are warm and full of love. They scan the crowd and seem to drink in all the sweetness of Spruce from each and every person in the room. He starts speaking, but I'm not really paying attention to a single word; for some reason, I'm just studying his face and his eyes. I'm looking for a false moment. I'm looking for a weakness. I'm looking for the lie between his words.

This is a bad trait of mine, the way I scrutinize people. As soon as I spot the little crack in someone's big mask of a fake smile they wear all day, I decide it's my personal mission to take a figurative hammer to them and shatter them right apart. Really, I feel like I'm doing the person a favor. It's kinda like calling out your friend on their bullshit. The more you give your friend shit, the more it shows you care. It's screwed up, but everyone's like that to some degree. We love peeling people apart. We love *testing* people's resolve. It's like two rough stones wrestling each other as they're dragged down a river's current; by the time they've settled, both of the stones are smoother, stronger, and polished.

Pete and I were like that. Two rough stones caught in a strong current called the Army. Best buds for life, the pair of us.

I clench my eyes shut, pained by even thinking of his name.

Fuck.

When I open them, I find Reverend Arnold staring right at me. His eyes flash, surprised by my presence. It's like he's seeing the dead, the way he pauses whatever he was saying to take this brief, fleeting moment to express his shock.

Then, just like that, the warmth returns to his eyes as he goes on with his words, addressing the room and smiling again.

There it is. His false moment. His weakness. His little lie.

Reverend Arnold can't stand the sight of me.

When I feel Trey's leg flinch, I'm reminded anew the person I am sitting next to. *Maybe the reverend was reacting to your sitting by his son*, I realize belatedly. *Maybe he knows what you said to him. Trey might've run home crying that day, told his father everything, and now his father despises you.*

Guess I don't get any Jesus brownie points today.

The rest of the service drags on until I feel like I can't take any more *repeat-after-me*'s or *and-now-we-read-from*'s. My ass fell asleep an hour ago. I can't feel my shoulder that's pressed against Trey anymore. My leg is bouncing with impatience.

I want to get the fuck out of here before my head blows right off of my neck.

From my mind to God's ear. The service ends and everyone rises. When I get to my feet, pain races down my leg which causes me to hesitate and grimace. It isn't lost on me that every single person who passes by sneaks a glance my way, as if not one of them bastards can believe I'm really here. *Maybe he's come to find God, that poor troubled boy*, they must be thinking. Half the looks I get are skeptical. The other half, pouring with pity.

"You okay?"

I turn at the gentle sound of Trey's voice. *Seriously? He's asking me if I'm okay?* I can't seem to form a response. I just stand there awkwardly and stare at him like he's speaking Romanian.

"Let's get on out of here," he suggests, gesturing toward the doors where everyone is headed. "We're blocking the way."

I scowl at that, annoyed and giving zero shits whose way I'm blocking. But I give in and move along with the crowd anyway, Trey close behind me.

Thank God for fresh air.

The second I'm out of the church, I feel like I can finally take my first breath in over an hour. I'm almost dizzy, like I had been literally suffocating in there.

We stop by a tree right on the curb, the shade of the swaying branches dancing over our heads. Trey has his hands buried in the pockets of his crisp, ironed khakis. His white polo reminds me of the way he looked the first time he came and cleaned up my house. That was over a week ago, yet it feels like yesterday.

"So are you okay?" he asks again.

I wrinkle my face. "Shouldn't it be *my* sorry ass askin' that?"

Trey nods down at my leg. "You made a pained face when you got up from the bench."

Oh, that. "Nah, I'm fine. It just acted up a bit is all."

He steps back and appraises me knowingly. "Always playin' it cool, aren't you?"

I stare him down hard. All of the churchgoers are still leaving, some of them lingering outside the church in groups to chat and make lunch plans. No doubt at least ten of them are sticking around just to see what in the world Trey and I are talking about. I'm sure word's gonna spread from here to the farthest chicken coop at the Strong ranch after today's little event.

"Well?" he prompts me. "Don't you got anything to say?"

I quirk an eyebrow, let my gaze run slowly down his chest, then look back up at his eyes, which hover on me expectantly. "I sure as shit hope you ain't waitin' on me to apologize."

"Apology accepted," he states anyway. "If you haven't totally undone the hard work I did on your house, I'll be back Tuesday."

No, I won't jump up and down in front of him. But I'd be lying if I didn't say I experience a huge weight drop off my back.

"Did you drive here?" he asks me. "It's a far walk from your house. You really need to keep off of your—"

"I drove." I nod toward the small dirt parking lot through the trees. "Nearly hit a cat on Peach."

Trey's eyes widen. "A cat?"

"Nothin'. It's nothin'. I ..." The blunt stares from all the others outside is really starting to get to me. The least they could do is be more subtle about it. Hide under a tree and spy on us behind our backs like a normal human being.

"Yeah?" Trey lifts his eyebrows expectantly, pushing wrinkles up in his forehead.

He looks so damned cute as fuck today.

My eyes catch sight of an old couple near the front steps of the church who are staring at me hard. I return their stare with a mild scowl of my own, which promptly makes them look away.

"I'm gonna head back," I decide with a shrug.

A flicker of disappointment crosses Trey's face. "Already?"

"Yeah. See you Tuesday." I start heading for the parking lot.

"Wait, wait." The sound of his shoes crunching the gravel as he hurries up to my backside makes me stop. I turn to face him. He offers an apologetic smile. "You wanna get out of here?"

"Yeah. That's what I'm doing."

"I meant ... together."

His eyes practically twinkle like emeralds in the sunlight. I am transfixed by them for a moment, like I didn't hear what he said.

His lips go flat. He lowers his voice. "Everyone's staring, huh?"

I smirk. "It's like the fuckers really got nothin' better to do with their day."

Trey winces at my words. *I ought to try saying "fuck" a lot less.*

"Well, let's face it, Cody. You *are* the most interesting thing to have arrived at Spruce Fellowship in half a century, all things considered, so there's that."

"Half a century, huh?"

"Just about. The church turns fifty next Sunday."

I nod appreciatively, glancing back at the building. A score of people turn away, pretending they weren't just staring.

"Fuckin' hell," I mutter under my breath.

Trey nods to the side. "There's a place just down the street. Ken there does these *crazy* good crêpes, if you're still in the mood for some breakfast."

"Country Lovin'. I know it, owned by the Loves."

"Yeah, that one!" Trey smiles broadly.

Fuck, his smile kills me. It keeps giving me pause every time I'm about to say something, like his smile just stuns me and makes me forget what the hell I was about to say.

I don't think I've met anyone before who has had that specific sort of effect on me.

It's unsettling.

"Why's everyone always assume I'm not from here?" I let out, forcing myself to speak to his striking smile. *He's got some pretty great pearly whites, too*, I note randomly. "Shit, I know all the good restaurants in town."

"There's quite a few. Especially since the T&S Shoppe hit that national list and became something of a tourist stop, there's lots of new places poppin' up here and there."

"I even used to hit up the bar on Plum four blocks over every weekend. That is, before the place burned down."

"That was a tough loss. Good thing no one was harmed."

"Good thing," I agree.

He squints as a cloud of dust drifts by from a truck kicking its way out of the parking lot near us. "Country Lovin', then?"

I shrug. "Anywhere but here."

The pair of us turn to cross the road.

The very next second, Trey's hand slaps to my chest and holds me back as a huge truck whizzes right by our faces, nearly taking off my nose with it.

We stay frozen to that curb, our breaths held.

Trey slowly looks over at me. I look over at him, his hand still pressed firmly against my chest.

I could spend an eternity in this moment, watching that look in Trey's beautiful eyes as he holds me away from the danger that just shaved our faces clean. Trey and his look of concern. Trey and the way his very first instinct was to protect me.

That's what a soldier does. You protect your fellow man with your life.

No man left behind.

MOVE! shouts Pete from a deep, dark cavern in my memory.

Trey lets go of my chest at once, withdrawing his hand as his face goes red.

The moment's passed. I'm on the curb again with Trey at my side—Trey and his pretty eyes. I hide a smirk of amusement. "Must be karma for almost hittin' the cat." I hop into the street. "You comin' or not?" I shout over my shoulder as I go, forcing myself to walk properly despite all the pain. The sound once again of Trey's shoes quickly scuffling along the pavement is my answer.

8

TREY

Seems like everyone else from church picked all of the lunch spots in town. Biggie's Bites. Gran's Home Kitchen. That old place farther down Wicker Street. Here at Country Lovin', I only see two other couples and a whole lot of empty tables.

And one gorgeous hunk sitting across from me.

He's drumming the fingers of one hand on the table and one of his legs is bouncing impatiently as we wait for our food to come. He hasn't said much other than giving his order to the server and mumbling something about the heat. The poor guy has sweated straight through his shirt, and he's turned slightly away, staring off at a TV across the whole restaurant.

I can tell his cool-and-collected thing is a front; that much is obvious. I mean, really, when did he last get out of his house? He *must* feel anxious. I still can't believe he had the balls to come to my church. In a weird way, I'm kinda proud of him.

Still, it doesn't change the fact that he's a big stubborn brute. "You know, you really should let me look at that."

He doesn't even look at me when he grunts. "Huh?"

"Saw you limpin' the whole way here."

"Jesus, we're going *there* again?" He scoffs, still looking away.

"Well, I guess you're just a big ol' hunk of *everything's-totally-fine*, aren't you?"

He wrinkles his face and doesn't respond, still looking off.

"That really must've taken a lot for you," I point out with a little nod his way. "Getting out of the house and stepping foot in that place. You must've figured everyone was gonna look your way, yet there you went, walkin' on down that aisle all bravely without a care."

He shrugs it off. "Yeah, and you had to go and sit all the way up in the front."

"Of course. I always do. Being my father's son," I go on to say, "I don't really have a choice unless I want to hear an earful from my dad. *'Why weren't you up in front today? Why weren't you paying attention to my sermon? Why weren't you singing along with the hymns?'* Might seem silly to you, but that's my life. He has this way of ... putting a lot of pressure on me, you can say."

Cody looks at me for the first time since we put in our orders, appraisingly. "Tough old man, huh?"

"Yep. Tough and then some. I mean, sure, he's loving and he's understanding and he's patient. Very, very patient, actually." I let my hand run along the table, feeling the bumps in the wood. The tables here look like they're sliced right off the same big oak tree, bumpy and natural, each of them. "But when you're the son of the minister in town, people look at you a certain way. My dad really drilled that lesson into my head early on. *'People look up to you. They expect things from you.'* Sometimes, I feel like I might say or do the wrong thing around him."

He digests my words with a slow, knowing nod.

After a bit of silence passes, I suddenly feel a pang of shame for my words. "I'm ... I'm not trying to talk my father down, really. He works very hard. He's done amazing things for this town."

"Sure he has."

"He has," I assert with a touch more vigor.

"Wasn't disagreein'."

I study Cody's stoic face. He's so annoyingly difficult to read. There's a tiny scar across the bridge of his blunt, strong nose, and another gash just under his eye. He's so incredibly beautiful—in that tough, beaten-up, will-protect-you-with-his-last-ounce-of-life way. "Thanks," I return reluctantly.

"He's made it good to live here," Cody goes on, his voice just as flat and untelling as before. "Women own businesses and run half the town, makin' just as much as the men do. Boys can be dancers. Girls can be carpenters. People of just about every dang race I can think of live here." He picks at something on the table. "And gays can be gay as all hell, if they want."

It almost seemed for a hot second like he wasn't going to add that last part. "Gays ... can be gay," I agree, keeping my calm eyes steadily on his.

He keeps drumming his fingers on the table. It might be my imagination, but I think his drumming just became a touch more intense than it was a second ago.

I bite the inside of my cheek, figuring out a way to phrase my next question. *Oh, just out with it, Trey.* "So just to be transparent, you know I'm gay, right?"

"Yep."

My pulse picks up like I just took off on a jog. *Yep? That's all I get?* Frustrated, I try to get him to say more. "It didn't bother you havin' a gay guy all over your laundry?"

"Why should it?" He meets my eyes suddenly. "You sniffin' my underwear or somethin' weird?"

I laugh at that, though my laughter sounds strained. Maybe my body was just desperate for a release of the tension I'm feeling between us right now. "I don't think I could pay a *dog* to sniff your rank boxers before I washed them."

Cody snorts at that, the corner of his lip pulling up a pinch.

Wait. He snorted. Did I just make him laugh? *Did I just make the statue that is Cody Davis laugh?*

The moment is interrupted when two steaming hot plates of perfectly-cooked crêpes, eggs, and brown-sugar-sweetened bacon are set in front of us. My stomach literally turns inside-out with excitement as I inhale the decadence.

"Fuck yeah," grunts Cody as he swipes his fork off the table and digs right in.

I, however, clasp my hands together and bow my head. "*Bless us, O Lord, for this food, which we graciously receive from your bounty,*" I murmur quietly under my breath. "*Amen.*" After drawing a quick cross over my chest, I pick up my fork.

That's about when I notice Cody's frozen in place with his big cheeks full of crêpe, his eyes on my chest like he just saw the light.

I lift my eyebrows. "Something wrong?"

"Uh ..." He belatedly points his fork at me. "Was I supposed to pray with you or somethin' before cramming a bite in my mouth? Am I going to Hell now?"

It's my turn to half-laugh, half-snort at him. "If I could count on my hand how many times I've eaten with people who don't pray before their meals—including half the folk from the church— I'd need about a billion hands." I cut a bite off of a crêpe with the edge of my fork. My stomach growls desperately. "My mom always prayed before every meal, even when my dad wasn't home."

Cody nods, then resumes chewing as he watches me eat. The way he chews is slow, yet forceful. I noticed as much when he ate the sandwich I made him at his house. Even the brutish, somewhat methodical way he eats is sexy somehow. *Why do I find such a strange attribute as "methodical chewing" to be attractive?*

Maybe underneath his barbarianism, my brain is still seeking a truth Cody has yet to reveal to me—a softer, gentler truth. I am determined to discover that Cody is actually emotional and sweet under his tough, scar-pocked skin.

"You were close with your mom?"

His question comes almost delicately, like he's afraid that just asking the question might set something off in me. "Yes," I state, my voice firm. "Very. Some people in town used to tease us, sayin' she was my older sister, what with the way we used to interact."

He swallows his mouthful, then studies me for a bit without going for another bite. "You miss her."

"Yes." I take a sip of my orange juice. "I think maybe the one thing I regret is ..." *He didn't ask you.* I volunteer the information anyway. "She passed away the summer between my sophomore and junior year of high school. I didn't get to tell her I was gay."

Cody's eyes drift down to my plate in thought. Then his brows pull together. "Would it have mattered?"

Despite the bluntness of his question, I consider it. "I suppose not." I bite off the end of one of my strips of bacon, chew on it, then add, "I'd be naïve to think she didn't likely suspect it, at least. I mean, she was one smart woman. Like, *really* smart."

"So she already knew."

"Probably."

"So you don't got nothin' to regret, then."

I meet Cody's eyes. They're filled with sincerity, yet strength. He hasn't gone for another bite since we started talking about this. There's something telling about that fact. *Is this his show of respect for me? Is he giving me his full attention?*

Or maybe he still feels bad about this past Tuesday. It was a comment about my mother that sent me out his door, after all.

"Thanks for that," I tell him sincerely.

His eyes pinch slightly. "For what?"

"Maybe I don't have anything to regret after all." I give Cody an appreciative smile. "Maybe life's gone exactly the way it ought to have."

That's right when a pinch of emotion enters Cody's eyes, they detach from mine, and then he picks his fork right back up and goes for another bite.

I had him for a second. Now I wonder if my last comment struck a nerve. *I doubt he thinks getting injured and being ripped from his close-knit Army family with a medical discharge was "exactly the way his life ought to have gone".* I curse myself for saying a few words too many, tainting the moment of connection we just had.

Cody shovels so much scrambled egg into his mouth that his cheeks look like balloons as he chews vigorously.

Okay, maybe he's not as sensitive as I think.

Maybe he was just hungry and waiting for me to shut up so he could eat again.

I lift my chin. "I've decided I have a condition."

Cody glances up from his plate. "Condition?" he mumbles, his mouth still full, his one word muffled through the eggs.

"Yep." I take a languid sip of my orange juice, then set down the glass. "If you really want me to resume visiting your house."

He narrows his eyes suspiciously, waiting.

I finish: "I'm going to start looking at your leg."

"Fine," he barks back, then resumes chewing.

"And your arm."

He stops chewing again, his eyes back on me.

"*And*," I go on, "I expect you to attend physical therapy, just as you were required to."

"Fuck that."

"I'm serious, Cody. You don't know what you're doing to your body. You could be undoing all the hard work you did back at the military hospital, causing permanent nerve damage that therapy *won't* be able to help you with. Then you're gonna need to hire someone to wipe your own butt for you."

He scoffs at that. "I ain't goin' to no hospital. I'm through with hospitals."

"I'll ask Dr. Emory for a recommendation."

"Why don't *you* do it?"

I blink. "You mean ... be your physical therapist? I can't."

"Why not?"

"For one, I'm not licensed to do so. I'm an LPN. I assist nurses. I did *not* go to school for physical therapy, which is a whole other thing in itself."

"You know more than most. You're smart. Can't you just walk me through some exercises I can do at home?"

"Listen, you'll need a *professional* for that. And you'll also—"

"Maybe I don't trust them professionals." He boorishly forks another bite into his mouth, then eyes me. "Maybe I trust you."

I stare at him over my glass of orange juice, which I just lifted to my mouth for another sip. It takes me a second to realize how significant it is that he said those words to me. Cody Davis trusts no one. For him to say what he just said is utterly unprecedented. I wonder if he would even say that about his own mother.

Let alone the minister's son.

Who he's known for barely over a week.

I set down my glass without taking a sip, steel myself, then state my case. "I ... will do regular examinations of your physical well-being, as according to my responsibilities as an *LPN*. Your physical therapy will have to be handled by a *licensed professional*."

Cody doesn't respond, chewing with conviction as he stares at me, annoyed.

"And I am surely no psychologist, either," I go on, "so I can't exactly assess your mental state. That means my other condition is you'll need to start attending counseling sessions. Actual ones. You know, like you were advised to go to."

His eyes go dark.

Yeah, he's clearly not a fan of that idea either.

But I'm not bending. "So do you agree to my conditions or not?"

Cody drops his eyes to my plate. "Your eggs are gettin' cold," he states through his mouthful.

"Do you, or do you not?"

He swallows his bite, takes his time scooping another forkful up from his plate with a loud clatter and a wince-worthy scraping sound that stretches on for a century, then finally states, "Yep."

I return a satisfied nod. "Good."

9

CODY

Trey Arnold can be a bossy little fucker, that's for sure.

"Okay, now try bending it upwards," he coaches me, doing it himself as an example, "like this. Then stop at the precise moment you feel any pain whatsoever."

We've been doing this for a while. He's jotting down notes in a tiny spiral pad of his, "measuring" how far (or not far) I can bend or extend my appendages. As of now, the whole process seems a lot more annoying than it does healing or helpful.

"Yeah. Good, good," he murmurs, observing me. "Now try it like this, the other way."

I was so fucking close to coming out to him at that restaurant on Sunday. *So fucking close.* But I held back. I couldn't get the words from my brain to my lips. Then suddenly we were talking about his dead mother, and how the hell am I supposed to compete with that? You don't just change the subject when you're talking about someone's parent who's passed away, even if it was years ago.

"The problem is," Trey starts explaining to me a couple hours later when we're sitting at my dining room table, "the shrapnel that's still in your leg and bicep might be sharp. If your body has already encysted the shrapnel—"

"Say what?" I cut him off, face scrunched up.

Trey smirks at me. "Mister *Knows-Big-Words.*"

"Just talk in human words."

"Encyst. You get something stuck in you—like shrapnel—and your body sends ... things that spit out cytokines and proteins to cause an inflammation response. Your body tries to eat anything it can. Well, not really, but ... you wanted 'human words' ..."

"You callin' me dumb?"

Trey ignores that. "Anyway, if it can't eat it, then all that ... *mess* ... starts to form a thick ol' tissue around your shrapnel to isolate it. Like, in a cyst. Encyst. A cocoon of scar tissue, basically. It's to encapsulate that foreign object—the shrapnel—and protect your body from being harmed by it."

Trey sounds sexy saying all those big words. Even if it bothers me to only understand two of them. "Alright," I grunt, pretending to follow his gist.

"Problem is, if that shrapnel is sharp," Trey goes on, "then doing physically exertive things—like working out—can cause it to rip through all that protective 'cyst' tissue your body just got done building, resulting in internal bleeding. And if there's anything toxic in that shrapnel, it can ... well, poison you. So no more lifting," he orders me, giving one of my dumbbells on the floor a gentle kick, "until further notice. The doctors couldn't remove all the shrapnel, from what I understand. Am I right?"

I'll admit, I'm a bit too distracted by watching the movement of his lips as he talks to fully pay attention to his questions. Really, all I want to do is shut him the fuck up by slamming him against that wall and devouring his face.

I still remember the way his body felt pressed against mine in the church. I enjoyed the whole side of his firm, sexy body for over an hour. The memory of his butt cheek against mine is vivid.

"Well?" he prompts me.

I shrug. "One doctor said to remove it. Another said to leave it in. Some other one said I should consider a tendon transfer. Pretty much none of them know what they're fuckin' doing."

Trey bites his lip and frowns in response.

I shrug. "Whatever's still in there, one of the medics said my body might push it out in time. Some weird shit like that."

"That's a possibility, too." He glances down at his spiral pad, rereading some of his own notes. "So ... can you tell me what meds they have you on?"

The questions go on and on. Some I know the answer to. Some of them, I just answer with a blank stare or a shrug.

The truth is, I'm fucking attracted to Trey Arnold. Badly. And it's getting to the point where I don't know if I can handle myself a second longer around him. He's going on and on about treatments and health and cysts and bullshit, and all I can think about is how my dick would feel surrounded by his tight, firm butt cheeks.

"Let me see that spot in your arm one more time."

I put my arm on the table, my eyes squarely on his.

He squints as he runs a searching finger down the length of my bicep. He gently taps here and there—ever gently, like he's afraid I'm gonna break. He squints as he slowly inspects me, doing whatever the hell it is he's doing.

Just the feel of his fingers playing along my skin sends bumps racing down my arms. Blood starts pumping somewhere.

Somewhere inconvenient.

"Alright ... alright ..." he mumbles to himself as he pinches my elbow gently. He flicks his eyes up to meet mine. "This hurt?"

"Nope."

"Not at all?"

I shrug. "I just feel a bit of pressure is all."

He goes back to moving his fingers along my arm, presented to him like a leg of lamb as he pinches gently, poking at spots. And I go right back to feeling electricity prickle all over my body at his soft, caring touch.

It's been so fucking long since I let myself be touched.

I'm so hypnotized by the sensation of him touching my arm that I barely notice another situation developing.

A situation in my shorts.

"This is where some of the shrapnel is?" he asks softly as he carefully sets his fingers on a spot.

I nod and mumble an unintelligible syllable.

I'm getting harder.

"Hmm, I see." He keeps inspecting me.

And I keep getting harder.

What the fuck is he doing all of that touching for? Hasn't he taken enough measurements? Hasn't he driven me crazy enough?

His inspections have made me so fucking hard right now.

"Alright. Let's try something with your thigh," Trey decides suddenly, letting go of my arm and standing up. "Get up."

Uh, shit. "W-What?" I sputter, my dick throbbing in my shorts as I look up at him. Did I miss something?

"It'll just be a quick thing," he insists, completely unaware of the situation between my legs.

Sticking my dick up your ass would be a quick thing, too; I'd come right on the spot, I'm so pent up. "Let's do it later. I'm kinda—"

"No more procrastinating. C'mon, get up." Trey claps eagerly. "To your feet, Cody. Let's do it."

What is he now? My personal trainer? "Just give me a sec, man."

"No better time than the present."

Yeah, I got a big, hard present for you—and it's in my fucking shorts. Not to mention I can still feel his fingers all over my arm as if he never stopped touching me.

Alright, those thoughts aren't helping my "situation".

Then he goes and grabs my hand, presumably to help me to my feet. Reflexively, I yank my hand back, refusing to stand.

The result, however, is Trey fumbling forward.

And falling straight into my lap.

While he's fallen against me, he struggles to regain his footing for all of two seconds—*all while being completely oblivious to my hard-on*—before I'm forced to rise from my chair to get him back on his feet and balanced.

And then we're two dudes standing in front of each other, my hands on his arms, holding him in place.

With a giant sideways tent between us.

This is an example of a time when wearing loose gym shorts with no underwear around the house is not a smart fuckin' idea.

He glances down. His eyes stay glued to it for one, two, three, four, five, six, seven solid seconds. Then he looks up at me with two wide, unblinking green eyes, adorably speechless.

My face is a stone-cold blank expression of "*So?*"

Trey turns his back on me at once and steps away, putting distance between us. Nothing is said.

Well, I know my dick is big, but he's just flattering me now if he thinks it needs *that* much distance between us.

"Don't go actin' all scared of it," I tell him flatly. "You're the one who was in such a hurry to *try somethin' out*."

"I'm givin' you a minute," Trey throws over his shoulder.

"A minute?"

"Yes. A minute. To go and ..." He waves his hand. "To handle yourself."

I squint at the back of his head. "What? You think this shit is on purpose? I told you I needed a second, and there you go pullin' me to my feet anyway."

"Well, here's your second. Take sixty of 'em." Trey crosses his arms, keeping his back turned.

I just stand there, letting my eyes drift down his back. When they land on his plump little ass in those tight khaki shorts he chose to wear today, I feel a second, powerful wave of blood rush south, inspiring my dick to flex and throb in response.

Yeah, my mighty meat sure ain't calming down anytime soon.

"What exactly are ya expectin' me to do back here?" I ask, my words like sledgehammers. "Wank off to get rid of it?"

Trey makes a sound somewhere between a scoff and a squeak.

I wrinkle my face. "Shit. Being a gay guy, I kinda figured you would be used to seeing this sort of thing all the time. Why are you actin' like such a prude?"

"Cody ..." he throws over his shoulder warningly.

"Seriously. It's just a dick."

After a short sigh, Trey finally turns back around to face me. His eyes, notably, are *glued* to mine. He absolutely, clearly, utterly refuses to give my enormous stiffy any more attention.

Which is too bad, because it could really use some right now.

"I was just surprised by it is all," he explains, his voice as even as a scolding schoolteacher's. "And for the record, I am *not* seein' that sort of ... *thing* all the time."

"You have an internet connection. I'm gonna call bullshit."

He folds his arms tight across his chest. "Are we really going back to playin' games with each other now?"

"This," I declare, pointing down at it, "is *not* a game."

"I can't do anything while you're …" He huffs, gestures at me, then throws his eyes upward. "… *like that*," he finishes, flustered.

His uptightness is so adorable. "Just give me a bit."

Trey starts tapping a foot impatiently. Then he looks off at the kitchen as if some imaginary pet jumping on the counter caught his attention.

"At least my *dick's* still working right," I point out.

"Stop it."

"Just lookin' at the bright side, here."

"We were just talking about shrapnel. Where in there did I ever mention … big boobs? Or hot, sexy women in lingerie and …?" He shrugs. "Whatever the hell you're into." Then he curses under his breath. "Shoot, you made me say '*hell*'."

I lean against the back door, watching his little fit. "It's just a word. I think the great bearded bro in the sky forgives you."

"I think you're the last person to speak on His authority."

"I think you're a little too freaked out about a boner. Clearly you've never been in the company of a bunch of dudes before."

"Clearly."

"Didn't you go to college, college boy?"

"Two years, in fact," he answers, his words clipped.

I smirk at him, shaking my head. "Can you venture a guess as to how many of my fellow soldiers I woke up next to who had morning wood? Like, all of 'em."

"I commuted. I didn't stay in a … in a …"

"In a dick-packed dormitory?" I offer helpfully.

Trey turns his sour face to me with a glare.

"Seriously." I change my tone with him and take a few steps across the kitchen. "Just relax, Trey. Shit. Actin' like you don't got one of your own swingin' between your legs. We can still do your little thigh thing you wanted to try."

"I think that doggie's dead, thanks very much."

"Don't talk about dead doggies in my house," I deadpan with mock sacrament. "It makes me sad."

"The *donkey's* dead, then. I don't care."

"Really, it's so disrespectful." *I couldn't care less.*

"Maybe we're done for the day, actually." Trey grabs his bag off the chair and slings it over his shoulder. "I'm going to head off. We can continue next time."

"Thursday? C'mon. You've only been here a few hours."

"I've already done my part. Just remember, no ... working out or anything until we get more information on what's happening inside of you." Trey stops by the door to the kitchen, then shoots over his shoulder, "Other than spontaneous, untimely erections."

"Oh, listen to you and your newfound sense of humor."

"It wasn't a sense of humor," he sasses. "You will know when I'm being *funny*." Then he continues for the front door.

For some reason, I can't let him get away so fast. "Hey, Trey."

He stops with his hand on the doorknob, turns his face back, and lifts an eyebrow expectantly.

I lean against the doorframe leading into the kitchen. "I really liked your beef stew. Ate every bit of it."

Trey bites his lip for a second, then gives me a nod. "I'll bring you more next time. It's easy to make."

"Why don't you come by tomorrow?" I offer.

"I have a shift at the clinic."

His voice is a touch softer than before. That much, I notice. *And that much, I pick right up on, like a thrown rope.* "So come on by after. Ain't like I got somewhere to be." Trey's eyes shift a bit. He's considering it. "You can do your little thigh thing tomorrow, since you're still pissin' your pants about seeing another dude's wang."

Trey rolls his eyes. "I'll think about it. For now, I'm leaving." Then, his confidence returning, he pulls open the door and adds, "Maybe you can use the privacy I'm giving you. Y'know. To go and take care of a little *business* on your own."

"Shit. Sounds like I'm already puttin' the Devil right into you," I fire back at him. "Sense of humor. Telling me to rub one out."

"I'm going." He steps through the door.

"Is that your official doctor's orders?" I call out at him with a smirk on my face. "To rub one out?"

The last thing I see of Trey is him trying not to smile as he shuts that door, sealing me in the silent, still house.

I go right up to the living room window and push apart some of the blinds to get a final view of his tush as he walks down the path toward his car parked on the curb.

I'll give you one guess where my hand goes next.

Right there in my living room, fingers poked at the blinds, I let my shorts drop right on down to my ankles, spit down at my hand, then jerk. I jerk while I watch Trey stop by his car and pull out his phone to check something. I jerk, thankful as all hell for the view. I jerk until my arm is sore and I'm breathing heavily, eyes unblinking. *No working out, my ass.*

10

TREY

It's such a slow day at the clinic that I find myself picking at a loose thread on my scrubs at the front desk while the two women I work with today are gabbing by the window sipping mugs of coffee. They're never short on juicy gossip to share, and being "the gay", I'm basically obligated to hear every syllable of it.

"Oh ... muh ... gosh," moans the thirty-something Marybeth, curled up on the bench by the window, slits of bright afternoon sunlight painting her giant curls of blonde hair through the blinds. "*Tell me* you heard about Jimmy Strong."

Carla, a slender twenty-something with a braid of rich, silky dark hair running down her neck, gasps from the nearby spinning office chair. "Jimmy? Tanner's little brother? Which part??"

"Uh, like, *all* the parts! Oh, is that Henry?" Marybeth squints through the window. "Nope. False alarm."

"Dang it. Don't hold out on me. What is this about Jimmy??"

"Hey, darlin', you'll wanna hear this!" Marybeth shouts at me.

I can already hear every word whether I want to or not. I poke my head up from the front counter. "I'm busy sorting patient files."

"No, you ain't. Get over here!" Marybeth scoots over and slaps the bench next to her with her free hand, a mug hovering by her face with the other. Her giant moon-shaped earrings dance when she talks. "It's super big. Like, super, super big."

"If it was all that super, I'd ought to have heard it by now," I reason, but give in anyway, coming around the counter and taking a seat by the window with the two of them. "Y'know, if Dr. Emory comes in and we're all sittin' over here by the window ..."

"Henry always takes long lunches on Wednesdays. Cool your tits. I can't *believe* you haven't heard this bit about lil' Jimmy."

It's kinda weird that Marybeth calls Dr. Emory by his first name all the time. "He ain't so *lil'* anymore," I mumble, to which Carla lets out a guffaw into her mug that she cuddles close to her mouth. "He's a senior now, right?"

"Yes, darlin', he is! Now listen up. Jimmy wanted to take this girl in his dance class—Jazzy—to prom," Marybeth explains, her hand and long fuchsia-painted nails dancing in the air as she tells the story. "They made all these big, big plans. Heck, Jimmy's mom went all out, got them a limo, the whole ten yards."

"It's nine yards," mumbles Carla.

"Don't interrupt! Anyway, you know how ol' Nadine Strong is. She's always gotta be the biggest deal in Spruce. But listen to what happens next: Jazzy goes and *dumps* Jimmy for none other than Anthony Myers ... a *week* before the dance."

"What a ho!" hisses Carla, wide-eyed.

"Oh, no, no, no ... it gets *even better.*" Marybeth eyes me. "This is where you gotta keep your ears open, darlin', y'hear?"

"I never closed them," I assure her, eyebrows lifted patiently.

"So Jimmy is, like, basically best friends with Bobby Parker. You know Bobby Parker," she says, narrowing her eyes. "Patricia's boy. The sweet one on the soccer team. He's gay. He came out after Tanner and Billy's wedding. Hey, kinda like you," she throws my way with a toothy smile.

I return her smile tightly. "Like me," I agree.

"It was such a beautiful wedding," sings Carla wistfully.

"Anyway, Jimmy decided he wasn't gonna let some little fickle girl like Jazzy mess him up. I mean, Jimmy is a *Strong*. He's got the Spruce Juice Tanner for an older brother, right? So yesterday, he does the one dang thing you ain't ever gonna think of to make *him* the new hero of Spruce High."

Carla is on the edge of her seat, gripping her mug now tightly with both hands. "What'd he do?? Did he put a bunch a' tarantulas into Anthony's locker? Did he spread rumors that Jazzy has the clap? Did he—"

"Goodness, no! Jimmy has *class*, sweetheart. And you will *not* guess what he did, no matter how many guesses I give you."

"So out with it already!" squeaks Carla, annoyed. "What'd he do?? I'm about to have a coronary. Was it in the paper?"

"He went and asked *Bobby Parker* to the dance."

"NO!" gasps Carla, slapping a hand over her mouth. "No way!"

"Yep! Straight boy Jimmy, lady's man, dancer, struttin' the halls of Spruce High. He goes and asks his gay best friend to prom, just two ol' friends makin' the best of it. He does it in front of the whole dang soccer team, too. Like, the school must have *exploded* after that. *Can you imagine??* Bobby didn't have a date. Jimmy just got dumped by his girlfriend. It was just the most *beautiful* thing."

"You're talkin' about it all like you were there or somethin'," Carla sasses her, smirking with half-lidded eyes.

"Oh, my daughter told me everythin'. I mean, she's just a freshman, but still, she saw the whole thing." Marybeth turns my way and swats my arm with the back of her hand. "See? See why I wanted you to hear all that? Ain't it just *darlin'* ...?"

I nod vaguely, a smile still pasted on my face. Judging from her searching eyes, she must be expecting me to respond in some way. "It's … It's really a sweet thing," I agree. Her searching eyes want more. So I say more. "A really sweet thing Jimmy did for his gay best friend. Wish I had a straight buddy like that with as much confidence in himself when I was in school. Of course, I wouldn't expect much less from the little brother of *the* Tanner Strong."

"Yeah, but a town like this wouldn't even *exist* if it wasn't for your father," Marybeth sings with a gesture of her hand my way, the red bangles on her wrist rattling together. "We'd pro'lly all be boring, judgmental sticks-in-the-mud shooin' away the gays like they do in Fairview if it weren't for him."

"Praise Jesus," murmurs Carla with a brief lift of her mug.

I smile at that thought, despite my private pang of misgivings about my father. He's a complicated man. It's difficult to judge him too harshly, even being his son.

Especially since we both share a demon: the tragic and sudden and *senseless* loss of my mother.

"What's wrong?"

The question comes from Carla and is aimed at me. I suppose my face went strange when thoughts of my parents took over. I put my smile right back on and part my lips to speak.

"No freakin' way," exclaims Marybeth, cutting me off before I even start talking. She's looking out the blinds. "What's he doin'?"

Carla's on her feet in an instant panic, literally searching for a place to hide her mug for no good reason at all. "Dr. Emory's back already? It's early! It's early! Oh, crap, did anyone call back Miss Herring? Did you call in her prescription yet, Marybeth??"

"No, no. It's not Henry. It's *him*."

"Who??"

"The crazy-hot soldier at the end of Willow."

My stomach turns into a bouncy castle. "W-What?" I sputter as I hop to my feet as well.

Marybeth turns two wide eyes our way. "He's comin' up to our door. What in Sam Hill is he doing here?" She looks over at me, her earrings jangling. "Should I lock the door?"

Carla nods vigorously. "Yeah, lock it. *Lock it!*"

"I should lock the door and tell him that we're closed," agrees Marybeth. She still hasn't blinked once. "He'll just have to—"

"You ain't gonna do any of that," I spit out, offended.

Marybeth and Carla look my way, startled by my outburst.

To their frightened faces, I add: "You *do* realize I'm lookin' out for him, right? Like, as his sort-of hired caregiver?"

Carla's voice is quivery. "S-So ... so it's true."

Marybeth looks like she's seen a ghost. "I thought you were just bein' nice on Sunday. Lettin' him have a seat and all. I didn't know you—"

"Well, I don't know why you two are acting like he's an armed gunman," I scold them. "I've had many interactions with him and find he's just ... totally an okay guy."

"*He is an armed gunman,*" whispers Marybeth. "*Professionally trained by the governme'int!*"

She just turned "government" into four syllables.

I'm officially ready to clock out for the day.

The very next moment, the doors to the clinic push open, and Cody Davis eclipses the sunlight coming in. He's wearing a pair of tight jeans—*Lord help me*—that wrap around his densely muscled thighs so exquisitely, I can't help but let my heart race away from me at the mere sight. He's got on a plaid short-sleeve button shirt opened to reveal a white tank underneath, the material of which pulls across his pecs in a very inviting way. Just his body below his neck is ripe with sexuality, strength, and unabashed confidence.

Then there's the issue of his handsome face. And it *is* an issue. It's an issue what that strong, flexed jaw of his does to me, the way Cody always looks like he's literally *chewing* on his every tense, tortured thought. His blunt, strong eyebrows are pulled together, giving him that sort of permanent scowl he always wears, and his short hair is messed up all over, whether from the wind or his lack of fixing it, I don't know, but it reminds me too much of the way he might look after waking up in the morning—or after sex.

Sex?

Why did my mind go there?

"Trey," he states for a greeting, one abrupt word, my name, a mallet of sound smacking against the cold silence of the room.

"Cody," I force myself to say back.

He glances to the side, taking note of Marybeth and Carla, both of whom have moved to the front counter where they stay, frozen in place, watching us like scared-off kittens.

I experience a pinch of concern. "Is something wrong?"

Cody turns his head back to me. "Nah. I just thought ..." Then he goes silent, his eyes drifting down to my chest.

I lift an eyebrow, waiting.

After another ten seconds go by, I decide he's either clueless, insane, or just doesn't want to talk with two women staring at us from the other side of the lobby. It isn't a very big lobby, so really, it feels a bit like we're all three waiting for him to say something.

I speak instead. "Did you walk all the way here?"

"Nah. I drove."

"Again?" I admonish him. "I thought we decided after your little *stint* on Sunday that you wouldn't be driving anymore."

Cody's face wrinkles up. "How the hell else am I supposed to get around town, then?"

"By ..." Well, walking is just as bad. I'm not sure I had a proper rebuttal prepared. "I don't know. You shouldn't be using your bad leg is all."

His voice softens. "I ... I just thought I would come and pick you up from the clinic."

Those words surprise me for two reasons. First, he thought of me. Second, the way he said them sounded almost ... *sweet.*

Sweet.

Cody Davis. *Sweet.*

And then, naturally, my reply is a nasty: "Why the heck would you pick me up from the clinic? My house is just a five-minute walk down the road. I don't even take my car here."

"Forget it." Cody turns abruptly and slips right out the door.

Shit. "Wait," I call out, pushing through the doors behind him.

He stops on the curb and turns to face me, a scowl over his hot and bothered face. *Wait, is he hot and bothered, or am I?* "I said just forget it," he barks at me.

I lift a hand to shield the sun from my face. "Didn't you want me to come over after my shift? Wasn't that what we decided?"

He puts his hands in his pockets, then stares down at me with a deadpan expression. "Yeah."

"I didn't mean to ... confront you in there. Marybeth and Carla are a bit nosy. And judgy." I throw a look at the window—where both Marybeth and Carla's eyes are poking through the blinds. My hard glance makes both of their faces vanish. I turn to Cody again. "I didn't even bring a change of clothes with me. I was just curious why you drove up here. I'm on the clock for three more hours."

Cody surveys my scrubs with a smirk. "They've got your ass workin' eight-hour days?"

"Yeah. I mean, it's my job, really. Dr. Emory's my boss."

"I thought you just volunteered."

"I do. At a different clinic, sometimes the nursing home near Fairview, depending on where I'm needed." I kick at the pavement and sigh. "It's a slow day, if I'm being perfectly honest."

"I was thinkin' we could ..." His voice trails off as he looks away toward the parking lot, squinting into the distance.

I look up at him. "We could what?"

"Do something. Go to the park. I dunno. See a fuckin' movie." He says all the words while looking away, then shrugs, apparently completely incapable of talking to my face.

I wonder if he feels embarrassed about yesterday suddenly. I know I overreacted a bit to his whole spontaneous boner thing. He was just being such a cocky jerk about it, and the more he pushed my buttons, the more I wanted to push back.

And the whole thing was so strangely erotic. I mean, what did I do or say that inspired such a reaction from him? Was he not even paying attention to what I was saying? Was he daydreaming about some porno he was looking at that morning before I showed up? The last thing I expected was to become intimate with the size and breadth of Cody Davis's erection.

The size and breadth of which, by the way, are immeasurable.

I obviously have no means whatsoever of comparison, but I know largeness when I see it. And Cody Davis was *large*.

But none of that matters. My priority is and has always been Cody Davis's health. One of the first things I told his mother was that his mental wellbeing is just as important as his physical one. If I'm to put my money where my mouth is, then taking him to the park or to a movie is a means of taking care of him, right? I'm still doing my job if I oblige his emotional needs.

Even if it toys with my own.

"Maybe I can take off a little early," I finally answer him. "Just so happens, we haven't had a patient in two hours. And I think the women are more than capable of holding down the fort if the doctor lets me go."

Cody and I both glance back at the clinic and find the women peeking through the blinds yet again—and again, their tiny faces vanish the moment we catch them staring.

"Should I go in there and scare 'em?" mumbles Cody partly to himself, still staring back at the windows.

"That doesn't sound to me like an ideal way to make friends," I point out, also staring.

He turns back to me and eyes the side of my face. "Who said I'm tryin' to make friends?"

All my attention is pulled right back to him. Just from those words in Cody's masculine voice, my pulse picks right up. "Friends aren't a bad thing," I reply vaguely.

"Didn't I scare the shit outta *you* when we first met?"

Cody's face looks so handsome and beautiful in the daylight. He really ought to be out in it more often. "If we're being honest here, I find I was rather ... disappointed the first time I met you."

He squints at me dubiously. "Disappointed?"

"Yeah, disappointed."

"And why's that?"

I cross my arms. "Well, everyone in town made this whole big deal about you. I was expecting my life to be in danger when I stepped into your house. I thought I'd be battling demons daily, fending for my life, and dowsing out Satan's flames ... considering all the hullaballoo about you."

Cody keeps staring at me, trying to figure out whether to be offended or not by my words.

Then I add: "But instead, I get just ... *you*."

He grunts. "Me?"

"Yeah. You." I give him a quick scan of my eyes. "As a matter of fact, I don't find you much scary at all."

Then our eyes meet. There's an unspoken, unintended sort of "challenge" in my words. While our eyes connect so potently after my cocky little declaration of confidence to him, I feel the drum of frantic heartbeats in my chest.

Cody finally breaks the silence between us. "Maybe you're puttin' in a judgment too soon, Trey Arnold. You ain't seen my worst yet."

My response is instant. "Oh, I doubt your worst can scare me either, Cody Davis."

It's the last thing I say to him before heading back inside. *I pray I meant those words I just said to him, because I sure can't take them back now.*

11

CODY

He's let off early, just like he wanted.

Trey Arnold always seems to get what he wants.

Guess that's one of the perks of being the town minister's son, I have to reckon.

"Keys," he orders me, the bossy little bitch he is.

I frown. "The hell? You ain't drivin' my truck."

"Yes, I am."

"No, you're *not*."

"For the sake of all the dear sweet little kitty-cats wandering the streets of Spruce, *yes*," Trey retorts tersely, "I *am*."

I glare at him for all of five seconds before surrendering my keys to him. He then saunters triumphantly to the driver's side and pulls himself up into the cab.

I could throw that damned boy over my knee and spank that attitude right out of him.

"Where to?" he asks after I'm sitting in the passenger seat.

"Movie. Park. Like I said. Something."

I'm so fucking helpful.

Trey lets out a short sigh. "Well, both of those are literally within walking distance. Park is just a block over. Movie theater is down the other way and around the corner." He quirks a patient eyebrow at me. "I don't know what movies are playing."

"I dunno. We could just drive anywhere then. We can go right on and get the fuck outta this place."

He studies the side of my face. Since I'm just staring through the windshield, I don't know if he's annoyed by my ambivalence, or if he's thinking it over.

Turns out, he was thinking it over. "Y'know what? I have the perfect place in mind," he announces, then gently twists the key in the ignition.

Off we go.

With the windows down, I hang my elbow out and let the air slap my face silly as we breeze down Main. Trey goes the whole length without hitting a light—*even the lights give him what he wants, the lucky bastard*—and then he continues on even after the road splits off and the buildings of Spruce are at our backs.

"We headed to Fairview or some shit?" I ask him.

"Not quite." He reaches for the radio and flicks it on. "What do you listen to?"

"Anything with a beat."

"Country music, in other words?" he asks.

I shrug. "I'll listen to anything with a beat. Like I said. Shit, Trey, do you really need me to repeat everything I—?"

Heavy metal blasts my ears the next second.

Trey winces apologetically, turning the volume down. "Sorry. I was just sick of hearin' your voice."

I fight an involuntary chuckle and look off out the window at the grasslands and farmlands as they go by, smirking and sucking my tongue.

It's about ten minutes later that I squint into the distance. "Damn. We headed to the Strong ranch?"

"Nope. That's the other way."

Then he turns off the main road and starts down a narrow dirt one that outlines a long thicket of trees, cutting a path carelessly into the middle of nowhere.

"This shit oughta look scary as fuck at night," I mumble.

"Beautiful, actually. I've seen it." Trey shrugs. "I mean, unless you're afraid of the dark. Or nature. Or anything that's beautiful or remotely pleasant. Which I suspect you might be."

"Fuck you, Trey," I throw at him with half a smile.

"I'm gettin' used to your terms of endearment," Trey notes. "Vulgar as they may be."

After another minute of driving my truck near the woods, he slows down, cuts off the engine, then pops open his door.

I do the same, stepping out of the truck. Twigs and dirt crunch beneath my feet when I follow him into the trees, which grow more dense at first, and then more sparse the farther we go, eventually revealing what I believe to be his intended destination.

"Bell Lake?" I call out to his back, since he's several paces ahead of me. I didn't fall behind deliberately, but I'd be lying if I said I wasn't enjoying the view of his ass. "This what you come to show me? Bell fuckin' Lake?"

"And the least you could do is not spit out your curses now that we're here," he throws over his shoulder. "You'll scare away the fish and all the beauty about it this time of day."

When the trees are at our back, nothing but the wide bank of the lake stretches out ahead of us: broken twigs, tiny stones, and a lot of wet, dark chocolate dirt. The surface of the water is rippling from the wind and shimmering with the near-blinding glow of the sun, which is halfway on its descent in the west.

Trey sits on a log right by the water and proceeds to peel off his shoes and socks, stuffing his socks in his shoes. "I always come here when I need a breather. Floods real bad when it storms, but otherwise, it's the perfect spot for a getaway." He looks up at me. "Well? C'mon. Get them shoes and socks off. That plaid shirt, too. Keep the tank on if you want."

I frown. "Shit, if I knew we were gettin' in the water ..."

"This wasn't exactly a planned thing, Mr. Spontaneous. You're the one who showed up at my work unannounced." He pulls off his light blue scrubs top, revealing his fitted white undershirt.

I'm trying not to stare, but Trey Arnold is literally getting undressed in front of me. The fuck else am I supposed to do?

"Shirt. Shoes. Socks." His words come out like a drill sergeant barking orders—badly. He doesn't even look my way when he says them. "We only have so much sun before it turns 'scary' out here."

That last comment was a taunting stab at me, but I only smirk, refraining from responding as my fingers go for my shirt buttons.

And then he goes and peels off the bottoms of his scrubs, revealing a pair of black boxer briefs.

Fuck me standing. I thought I knew the epitome of sexiness when I saw his butt in those tight khakis of his. I had no idea what was waiting for me underneath them. Already, I feel blood rushing below my waist, my whole body desperate to stiffen up my dick so I can stick it into him. Every fiber in my body feels a magnetic pull toward Trey just at the sight of that plump, pert ass.

If I wasn't so uncertain whether he was cock-teasing me on purpose, I'd take him right here in the dirt. I'd take him so hard.

I flick my eyes away. *He doesn't even know you're gay. Why the hell would he be trying to entice you? He thinks you're into big boobs and women in lingerie, remember?* All of my sexual hunger turns into red hot annoyance as I peel off my shirt, kick off my shoes, rip off my socks, and then slip right out of my jeans, leaving me in just a pair of boxers. All my clothes end up in a pile next to his on the log.

When I look up, I discover Trey already up to his knees in the water, and he's looking back at me with a strange, faraway look on his pretty face. *Was he watching me undress?* His lips are parted slightly, like some professional hypnotist just swung a big watch in front of his stupefied eyes.

Then he shakes out of it like a statue coming to life. "So you getting in or not?"

"What the hell are we doin' anyway?" I call out, standing on the bank like a stone.

"What do you think?" His hands go into the water, waving them around a bit as he steps deeper and deeper in.

I smirk. "Swimming? We're going for a swim?"

"Get in here."

Trey is up to his nipples in the water now, even though he's still wearing his undershirt. *Is he shy or something?* A part of me is disappointed; I was kinda looking forward to seeing what he looks like with his shirt off.

Fuck it. I peel off my tank top too, fling it at my pile of clothes, then make my way toward the water. If Trey was hypnotized a second ago, he's turned into a full-on puppet now. Instantly, that boy is under my damned control. I could walk in twenty circles around him and his eyes would follow, twisting him up twenty times like a playground tetherball around a pole.

The water is cold to the touch, but the sun beats over my skin with unapologetic heat as I go deeper in. The bed beneath my feet is bumpy and uneven, full of little rocks and things, but nothing too sharp. My feet are pretty much made of shoe leather anyway, for as many rough-ass terrains as I've put them through.

The water is up to my chest by the time I come to a stop next to him. "Now what?"

Trey is shaken from his trance by my words. "E-Exercises," he sputters for an answer. "Exercises. To work your legs properly."

"You serious? We came all the way out here for *exercises?*"

He sounds nearly affronted when he answers, "Yes. We did."

"I thought you said you weren't licensed to do any—"

"You don't like my idea?" He spreads his hands like the lake is his own to present.

"And you want to do fuckin' *water aerobics?* What am I, eighty-eight years old?"

Trey huffs at me. "It's easier on your legs. Stop being a baby."

"I ain't doin' water exercises. That's for pussies. I'll race you to the dock over there." I nod at it. "You a good swimmer?"

"We're not swimming. Listen." He jabs a finger at his chest. "I have a job, remember? My purpose is to take care of you. And you said today we can try my 'little thigh thing', remember? Well here we are, about to try something better. And we're doing it in a lake because I'm not a reckless person, and ... while I'm not a certified physical therapist, I ... I *care* about you. And also I'm considerate."

Considerate. He cares about me.

I could pop him in the face with my knuckles if he wasn't so damned cute. Already, my eyes are pulled to his lips, which are wet slightly from him dipping slightly down into the water. His eyes seem to shimmer from all of the reflections coming off the lake, which the sun has set aflame.

"Couldn't we have gone to a swimming pool?" I ask.

"Sure, we could've," reasons Trey, "if you also wanted half of Spruce watching you do your *water aerobics*."

He has a point, even if he's being a little shit in making it. I give him a curt nod anyway, conceding. "Fine."

"Fine?"

"Alright. Fine."

"Hey." His voice goes softer suddenly. "Just think it all over. Seriously, Cody. Don't you want to eventually get around without limping everywhere?"

"I ain't limpin'."

"Yes, you are. And don't you want to work out without aching all the time or feeling that pain in your arm? Don't you want to get back to one-hundred percent?" He doesn't wait for me to answer. "Then you gotta take baby steps. Little bit at a time. The water's your friend. I'm here with you, and we'll do it together. Alright?"

I just stare at him, not caring to hide my dubiousness.

"To be honest," he goes on, "I'm wingin' it from what little bit I *do* know. Plus a little common sense. And the help of Google."

"Google."

"And then afterwards," he goes on, ignoring my skepticism, "we can do whatever you want. Go catch a movie. Get a bite. Order a pepperoni pizza with pineapple on top. Whatever you want."

I'm looking him right in his bright green eyes the whole time he speaks. I don't know what it is about him that reminds me so much of ... *someone I knew.* Despite how much I'm fighting it, I feel so disarmingly comfortable around Trey.

He doesn't put up with my shit. He doesn't give up on me easily. He's loyal to a fault.

He snuck right under my skin like a puppy into my bed sheets when I wasn't looking, and now I can't get him out.

There's a sincerity in his eyes that I know is a rare fucking treasure in this world. I believe him because he makes me feel like I should. I trust him as much as I trust a bed when I drop into it, or a chair when I put my weight on it, or a crutch, or a trampoline.

Or a trampoline ...

Shit, maybe I'm the one who's getting hypnotized here.

"I hate pineapple," I grunt.

He smirks. "Just pepperoni, then."

"Alright, therapist." I take a breath. "So let's get to it already. What do I do?"

"Easy," he says at once. "Just don't be a big stubborn jerk, and follow my lead. We'll start with your right leg, then move on to your less-abled left. Now hold on to my arms. We don't have one of them bars at the side of the pool, so ..." He shrugs. "We're gonna improvise a little."

I stare at him. *Improvise?*

"Arms," he snaps impatiently, then lifts his arms level to the water. "Up, grab 'em. C'mon."

I let out a sigh, then oblige, gripping his extended forearms. I'm surprised at how firm and secure they feel. *Maybe not quite as scrawny as I initially thought at all.*

"Now try your right leg. Lift it up, like this. Knee up."

I look down. I can't see jack shit through the water. "How the hell am I supposed to know what—?"

"You need me to show you? Here, hold my shoulders instead," he commands me, then moves his hands under the water without waiting for my reply.

For one split second, I open my mouth to stop him and jerk my leg away. The next second, my balance is thrown by his sudden missing arm-rails as I fumble to grab hold of his shoulders. Then I'm frozen in place as his hands slip around the back of my thigh under the water, cradling it.

My heart rate picks up. Just the touch of his hands on the back of my right leg sends all my juices pumping south. I suddenly can't concentrate on anything else in the world.

I want his hands somewhere else—somewhere very close to where he's got them, but not quite. *And I want them there right now.*

"Up," he guides me as he pulls on my thigh, causing my leg to lift up, bent slightly at the knee. "To about a ninety-degree angle, if you can. Stop, of course, if you feel any pain."

No pain, not when I'm in your hold—not when anything of mine is in your hold. I completely surrender my leg to him as it slowly lifts under the water.

Yeah, something else is lifting under the water, too. *Something that's rock hard and throbbing with every hungry beat of my heart.*

"Any pain?"

"Nope," I grunt out, barely audible.

"Hmm." His hand never moves or slips, supporting my thigh with firm, reliable strength. "Feel anything at all?"

You can say I'm feeling quite a lot, actually. "Nah."

"Just the sun on your neck, huh?" Trey teases, then suddenly shakes his head, as if embarrassed by his own joke. "That heat isn't going to be pleasant after a bit, actually. I should've thought to bring some sunscreen. You got any in your truck?"

I give him a look. "Shit, Trey, where do you think we live? If you're in Spruce and don't have permanent burns all down the back of your neck, you're not in Spruce. Sunscreen is for little bitches who stand in the middle of a lake askin' for sunscreen."

He gives me a scolding look. "It isn't healthy. And there's all this sun around us reflecting off the water, too."

"You worry too damned much. Just focus on whatever it is you're doing with my leg."

"You ought to be doing this instead of me," he points out. "It's an exercise, after all. You should be holding both my arms, not just one. At least, from what I read—"

"I like you doing it."

The words come out without my even meaning to say them. He stares at me, the words I just let slip swelling between us like an ill-timed fart at dinner. His hands remain firmly glued to the underside of my thigh.

My boner bobs under the water between us, pointing at him accusatorily.

"You know," I go on, feeling the blush creep up my face as I try to cover up my weird exclamation, "because then my lazy ass don't even have to move a muscle."

Trey recovers just as quickly, grasping somewhat reluctantly onto my joke. "Yeah, sure, alright. I bet you're so lazy, you'll want me to 'show you how to do the exercise' with your other leg, too."

"Yeah, be my guest," I challenge him.

"Don't dare me. I will."

"Maybe I *am* daring you."

Or maybe I'm literally begging you to touch my other leg, too.

And then holy fucking shit, the sexy, evil little bastard obliges. Next thing I know, he releases my right leg and slips his soft, cruel hands under my other thigh and gently lifts it. Somehow, the tiny pull and shift in my center of gravity causes me to hop once under the water, bringing me that much closer to Trey's body.

Too close.

My rock hard cock pokes him right at the waist.

He looks up at my eyes at once, his hold on my leg slackening as he tries to assess what exactly he just felt.

My insides squirm with a special blend of fear and excitement.

"What?" I blurt out defiantly, as if daring him.

Then, completely without my damned permission, my dick flexes under the water, poking at him again.

This time, it's unmistakable. Trey, completely thrown by what just poked him, fumbles clumsily with my leg, unsure where to go or what to do, then lets it go entirely and takes a step back.

Except I won't let him get away. Before my hands slip off his shoulders, I pull him to me and reach around his waist, anchoring him against me so hard, the water splashes between our bodies.

Trey's eyes go wide. He becomes a mouth breather at once, practically panting as he searches my face, confused.

So I unconfuse him by grabbing his hand, yanking it under the water, and shoving it down my boxers.

"It's my dick," I announce, answering a question he sure isn't asking out loud.

"I *know* what it is." His voice is jagged and his words are curt as he stares down at the water, seeing nothing, knowing nothing. He looks back up at me, lost. "What are you doing?"

"Tryin' to tell you something."

For once, I have completely knocked Trey off his self-assigned pedestal of certainty. He is completely, utterly derailed. He looks so damned clueless, I almost feel sorry for the poor bastard.

Also, he still hasn't let go of my dick since I thrust his hand down my boxers and put his fingers around it. Clearly he likes the gift I gave him.

"Well?"

"I ... I'm ..."

Trey can't even make any proper words. Shit. My big dick has literally rendered the poor guy speechless.

I try again. "Well? Do I gotta spell it out for you?"

"This ... This isn't r-right."

"The hell do you mean it isn't right? Don't go throwin' some bible verse at me."

A flicker of anger rushes over his face like a forest fire before he snaps his eyes shut, his face flushing red. "I shouldn't be doing this. I shouldn't do this. I shouldn't—" Then he flaps open his eyes and glares at me pleadingly. "Why are you doing this, anyway? Is this some sort of game to you?"

The tone of his voice makes me hesitate. "Game?"

"Messing with a lonely gay guy? Torturing his mind like this? Knowing exactly how b-badly he wants you, dangling a carrot, and then pulling away and laughing all the way home?"

My face goes blank. *Whoa, wait a minute.*

There's practically tears in his eyes when he speaks. "Are you just determined to make me so crazy, I actually give up on you for good, because you can't take *anything* I do for you seriously? Your only means of thanking me is to h-h-humiliate me?"

He whips his hand right out of my boxers, then shoves away from me and turns to wade his way back to shore.

Until I grab hold of his arm and spin him around. "Wait a sec."

"I ain't waitin' another *damned* sec," he shouts back.

"You got the wrong idea, Trey."

"I had the wrong idea since the day I agreed to help you. I'm leaving. I'll *walk* back home. I don't even care if—"

I grip him by the shoulders and spin him around to face me. "Trey, I wasn't toying with you. I meant it when I said I was tryin' to *tell you something*."

The intense look on my face must sober him at once, because he grows very still in my grasp and meets my eyes importantly, waiting for me to say more.

I've only told one other person what I'm about to say out loud, and that one other person lives in the hallways of my ears late at night, still shouting, *"MOVE!"* over and over.

"Trey, it was ... your hands all over me that did it."

He doesn't blink. He stays there and listens, waiting for more.

"Back at my house, yesterday, when you ran off like a scared little bitch." For some reason, I can't just tell him I'm gay. It's far easier to tell him the roundabout way, tossing him the pieces and letting him put the big picture together. "Your hands all on me ... is what did it. Just like now. You touchin' me."

Trey's eyes detach and drift down to my chest in thought.

I huff, annoyed suddenly. "Damn it, don't make me say it."

"Are you tellin' me ...?"

"Trey," I spit out warningly.

He gives himself another minute to process what I'm saying. I let him have all the minutes he needs. Then, slowly, he starts to nod. "Okay," he murmurs quietly. "Um ..."

I'm still gripping his shoulders. Now it's *me* who's so desperate for him to say more. "Um what?" I prod him, impatient.

"Maybe this whole water thing was ... a dumb idea."

I blink. "Uh, shit no. It was a perfect idea."

"Maybe we should get you back to your house."

"Trey. Get the fuck over it."

The expletive makes Trey Arnold's eyes go so wide, they just might fall right out of his self-important head if he doesn't blink soon. The indignant Trey I know so well makes a very abrupt and necessary return.

"Yeah, you heard me," I say right to his face. "Get over it. My dick gets hard when you touch me sometimes. I can't control it. It's human nature. I'm still your fucking patient."

His eyes flash. "C-Cody ..."

"So what if I'm ... *attracted* to you?" I go on, the words feeling so alien in my mouth. "I haven't had anyone fuckin' touch me like you are in ... in ... I don't even know how long. I can't help how my body reacts any more than you can tell yours to stop breathin', or stop pumpin' your heart, or stop pushin' blood through your veins. It just works that way, don't it?"

Trey presses his lips together, studying me pensively.

"Are you gonna get over it or not?" I demand of him, my voice stern as a stone.

"We ..." Trey takes a deep breath, then lets it all out at once, the water in front of his mouth rippling in response. "We will do the exercises. Then I'll take you back home."

I feel like I just messed everything up. How fucked up is that? I messed it all up just by letting my body do what it wants to do. What a hypocrite, the way Trey is judging me right now. *If that's what he's doing in that complicated mind of his.*

"Left leg up," he instructs. And up goes my left leg.

This time, sadly, without his hand's underwater assistance.

12

TREY

The drive back to his house is long, silent, and confusing.

Long.

Silent.

And so, so confusing.

I have no idea what to make of what happened at the lake. It completely blindsided me. There was nothing at all that could've prepared me for that moment.

It's too darned silent. I flick on the radio. Cody doesn't flinch a muscle with the sudden addition of some country singer's twangy voice filling the whole cab.

To be fair, I had already dealt with an *erect* sort of situation with him before. I thought that first time was a total fluke. Maybe even a prank on his part.

Now that I know the real reason ...

That he's genuinely responding to *me* ...

That the big and scary Cody Brian Davis is attracted to men ...

I can't even fathom it. I literally can't process the thought. In some dark library within the labyrinth of my brain, I actually *still* believe Cody is pranking me somehow. I can't believe he's gay or turned on by me. Instant denial is my knee-jerk reaction.

Twice I look over at Cody. Both times, he's glowering out of his passenger side window. His intense, beautiful eyes are half-lidded as he glares at the world outside the way a resentful cat does when its ears fold back. His elbow is propped up on the door, his head resting against his hand. That gesture makes his bicep in his right arm bulge distractingly.

The wind pushes through the vehicle and sweeps over my skin, gently drying my clothes and hair. Everything smells like the lake—and like him, somehow.

We were so close to each other in the water. It felt intimate. I can't remember the last time I'd been that close to another man. Other than two clumsy kisses in high school and a month-long stint with a guy in college two years back, I have not had anyone in my life I can remotely call a boyfriend.

And then Cody goes and sticks my hand down his boxers in the middle of a lake while we were all alone, not a soul to find us but the sun over our heads and the tiny fishes in the water.

And the trees swaying all around us along the shore like tall, silent observers.

And the wind sighing over our wet shoulders.

Why am I reacting so viscerally to all of this? Don't I want him so badly I could cry? Didn't I literally admit that fact to him, humiliatingly, when I thought he was pranking me on purpose?

Haven't I been secretly dreaming for this to happen?

I haven't even completely processed my thoughts by the time the familiar buildings of Spruce surround us. I'm turning down streets driving Cody's truck without even paying attention to the signs, and suddenly there we are in front of his house.

"Trey?"

I flinch at the sound of my name. When I turn to look at him, he almost appears calm, all signs of anger and resentment having fled his face. His eyes practically glisten in the lemon sunlight that cuts in through the rear window of the truck.

"Do you ..." He clears his throat. "Do you wanna at least come in for a bit?"

"No," I answer immediately. Then I shut my eyes with a slight grimace. "Sorry. I mean ..." I sigh. "I mean I probably—"

"We didn't eat," he points out. "Your ass hasn't eaten since ... well, when? Since your lunch break at work some odd hours ago?"

I haven't given much attention to what's in my stomach. I've been much too consumed with what was in my hand barely an hour ago. "Well ..."

"Just say yes. Come in and we'll order a pizza."

Cody Davis, although a totally stubborn, argumentative, and sometimes downright rude individual, is beautiful. He even has these unexpected moments of tenderness and concern that come out of nowhere. And in these moments, I can almost be convinced that he really can be attracted to a guy like me.

I kill the engine, pull out the keys, then dangle them his way. Cody gives them one short, annoyed glance, then snatches them out of my hand. "So?" he grunts. "You comin' in for a pizza?"

"Yep." The answer comes out before I'm ready to say it. Then I look up into his eyes. "With pineapple on it."

He tries not to smile, masking his amusement with a scowl my way. "You fucker."

To his brash term of endearment, I catch myself smiling back.

I wouldn't have believed it if God himself broke through the heavens to deliver me a vision of the future, that I would be sitting in the living room of Cody Davis sharing a liter of Pepsi and a large pizza—half pepperoni, half pineapple—while watching cop shows on TV. But there I am in the dim light coming in from the evening sun sharing a couch with Cody Davis, and I'm making the dumbest small talk about criminals, policemen, and everything in between.

I can't remember the last time I've kicked back like this with anyone. Even during our lazier days at the clinic when Marybeth and Carla are feeling "gossipy" and nothing important at all is going on, I don't feel this relaxed.

But all of that comfort and fun can't shake away the nagging worry still sitting on my lap—not to be confused with my empty paper plate that once held a slice of pizza, also on my lap.

My nagging worry being the thing that Cody tried to "tell me" at Bell Lake. With his cock poking me under the water.

His hard cock.

That would be the second time we've been acquainted in some way.

He hasn't brought it up at all. I wonder if I should do the same, continuing to avoid talking about anything important. After all, I'm not here to get fresh with Cody; I'm here to help him, to look after him, and to tend to his health as best as I can.

Still, it's impossible to ignore the amount of magnetism I feel just sitting next to Cody on this tiny couch. My body literally feels *pulled* into him, as if just one shift of my weight might cause me to fall against him like a pillow. And now that I know he's attracted to men ... *Now that I know he's attracted to me ...*

"You ever had a boyfriend before?"

Cody's question reaches right into my chest, grips something, and squeezes it right up. My grip on my empty paper plate—which I've already been holding unnecessarily for nearly an hour—goes and tightens even more just at the sound of his question. All of my insides are stirred around like a soup.

"Not ... Not really," I finally admit.

"Seriously? Not a single guy at all?"

My heart is racing and all he's doing is asking me innocent questions. *Calm down. Be cool.* "There was a guy I kissed back in high school ... in a janitor's closet. It was ... a confusing thing, and then the guy freaked out. That's not a boyfriend, though."

"No, it ain't. What about college?"

"It didn't last long. He was a stuffy guy, but couldn't handle my needs. He got impatient when I wouldn't put out, then broke up with me. I saw him with a new guy the very next day."

"Ouch."

"Yeah, ouch." I chuckle, then tilt my head. "To be honest, it didn't actually bother me. I was too focused on nursing school, anyway. I wonder if I just wasn't ... emotionally invested in him."

"You were just with him to not be alone?"

"Maybe. I don't know. He was nice at first." I pick at the edge of my paper plate, then sigh and fling it like a Frisbee toward the empty pizza box sitting on the coffee table in front of us. "I found with him that sometimes ... being with someone when your heart's not in it ... can make you feel even more lonely than being alone."

I feel Cody's body shift next to me as he blows air out his nostrils and grunts, "I hear you there."

I halfway turn my head to him. "Do you get lonely?"

After the question slips out, I wish I could take it right back. The TV blathers and murmurs on with its noise and police sirens, but the tension on the couch just tripled from my innocent, little, meaningless question.

To my surprise, Cody answers. "Well, yeah. Sure I do. Who the fuck doesn't?"

I nod vaguely, relieved by his answer. "True."

"I should cuss less, huh."

His self-commentary makes me laugh. "Be free to be yourself around me, Cody. Speak however makes your heart comfy."

"Do you get lonely?"

My eyes drop to his leg, which is so close to mine. Just a little nudge of mine his way and they'd be touching. "I ... have a lot of people in my life."

"That don't answer the question."

"Yes." My second answer is much firmer. "Yes, Cody, I do."

Why is he asking me that?

My heart is drumming so strongly in my chest, I feel sick.

Maybe I shouldn't have eaten so much pizza.

His leg is so close to mine. *Has it gotten closer? Did he move it?*

Why do I suddenly have a new thought every five seconds?

"I didn't mean to ..." Cody sighs quietly, grunts with clear and assertive irritation, then tries again. "I didn't mean to ... freak you out back at the lake."

"I'm not freaked out," I answer so fast, I barely let him finish his sentence.

"We're just two simple guys, Trey. We get lonely like anyone else, don't we? Shit, I'd be a damned idiot and a coward if I didn't tell you how fuckin' ... how attractive I think you are."

There my pulse goes. If my heart beats any more frantically, it's gonna end up in my neck, and I'll suffocate to death. That is not how I prefer my Wednesday evening to end. *Or my life.*

Then Cody Brian Davis sets his hand on my thigh.

I let out a jagged breath, terrified, then flinch away from him. "Cody. I'm just here to—"

His hand is off my thigh the next instant. "Look, I ain't gonna force nothin', Trey. I'm not into that."

I sit up. "I didn't mean to imply—"

Suddenly he sits up too, his eyes hard as two stones. "If there is somethin' that's gonna happen between me and you, then it's gonna be because *you want it*. Not because I ... fuckin' seduced you or manipulated you or got pushy. I ain't gonna force it."

"You're not forcing anything," I blurt right away.

He turns his face to me. Cody's bright brown eyes shine with urgency when they smolder me. I'm paralyzed just by the sight of them. *How does he do that?*

Then he goes and asks: "Are you even attracted to me?"

I stare at him, stunned and speechless.

When my cell phone goes off on the coffee table, I literally let out a shriek, surprised by it. For half a second, I think the fire alarm has gone off until my eyes focus on the lit-up face of my phone as it shakes like a rattler's tail, ringing loudly.

I swipe it off the table. My heart sinks when I read the name of who's calling.

"Sorry," I murmur to Cody, who just sits there with his jaw set tightly as I rise off the couch and move quickly into the dark den to answer my phone. "Dad."

My dad's voice is light and curious when he speaks. "Where are you, son? You being kept late at the clinic?"

I close my eyes and grip my temple with my free hand. This phone call does nothing to lessen my anxiety. "I'm ... um ... no." I can't lie to him, yet can't stomach telling him the truth, either.

"Where are you? You usually come right home. I was trying to figure out what we might do for dinner tonight."

Dinner? I glance over at the window, then pull the phone away from my ear to take a look at the time. *When did it become evening so quickly?* I slap the phone back to my ear. "I'm sorry, Dad. I was ... I was just ... w-well, see, after work, I ..."

Can I not even form a lie with my mouth?

Am I physically incapable of telling my father a lie?

"Yes?" my father prompts me.

I clench shut my eyes. I can't believe I'm about to say this. "I went out for a bite with some of the girls from the clinic. We had a long day at the clinic and ... and just wanted to commiserate a bit."

The lie came so easily off my tongue, it's worrisome. I didn't even stutter but once, and the words came right to my mouth like I'm actually telling the truth.

Like I actually believe my own lie.

"You and the girls, huh?" My dad lets out a little light chuckle. "Well, of course. I wouldn't dare keep you from them, then. Have fun. I'll fix myself something on my own, then. Of course, I'll say a prayer for you. I always do. Will you be home soon, you think?"

My father's question hovers before my eyes and dances a very evil dance with Cody's question, which I still haven't answered. *Do you find me attractive?* The sensation of his fingers on my thigh are still so fresh, I can swear he's right here still touching it. Emotions are flooding me from my brain and from my cock. I'm all twisted up like a wrung, drenched towel dripping in abundance.

What do I do? What do I say?

The words come out as fast as the lie did. "I will likely be a bit late. We may hang out even longer after this. A lot to chat about."

What am I doing??

"Hmm. Alright, then. I'll leave the porch light on."

He didn't even hesitate. He trusts me completely. I am such a horrible son. "Goodnight, Father," I state almost primly, then hang up the phone and stuff it in my pocket, red-faced.

The redness of my face isn't helped when I return to the living room to find Cody standing there with an unimpressed smirk on his face. "Hangin' with the girls, are you?"

I open my mouth to say something. Nothing comes.

Cody lets out one bark of laughter, then shakes his head. "Boy, you are scared shitless of upsettin' your daddy, huh?"

I'm indignant at once. "No, I'm not."

"Shoot, if he knew you were over here ..." Cody lets out yet another heartless laugh.

I sigh. "I'm sorry, Cody. I didn't mean ... I didn't mean to act like I'm ashamed of being here or ... or ..."

Well, to be honest, I'm not even sure why I didn't just tell my father the truth. That I am spending time with Cody Davis. That there is a slim possibility that we are actually bonding. That we may be becoming friends. Or something.

"Listen," he tells me, "I still smell like lake water. I don't know about you, but my ass needs a shower. I'm gonna go take care of that and ... you can do whatever you want. Watch some more cops on the TV. Dust a counter off. Hang with your girls. Stay. Leave. It's up to you."

After studying him for a moment, I stiffen up my back and decide to inject some more confidence into my words. "You smell. It's about time you finally do something about it."

He chuckles at that, then turns to go, tossing the remote he was holding carelessly at the couch. He limps as he moves down the short hall toward the bathroom.

"You better be careful with that leg of yours," I shout at him.

"If I need your help," he calls back over his shoulder, "you'll hear the bang of my body hittin' the floor of the shower."

With that, the bathroom door shuts behind him.

I don't allow myself a moment to process my confused tangle of emotions; I start cleaning up our little mess on the coffee table right away, which includes an emptied liter bottle, pizza box, and plates. I note that he didn't drink any beer tonight. *Interesting.* When I'm done and have washed my hands, I return to the couch, pull out my wallet and phone, and toss them onto the coffee table. Then I stare at the screen of my phone, wondering how long I dare stay here tonight. Just the thought of spending more time with Cody keeps my heart at a steady jogging pace, refusing to let up.

Then I hear a loud, jarring *bang.*

I turn my head at once, perked up like a deer in the woods. I wait and listen. All I hear is the running water of the shower, which sounds like static noise now, not shifting and dynamic like it was a moment ago—evidence of a body moving under the water.

"Cody?" I call out, concerned.

Nothing.

I rise from the couch, move down the hall, and stand in front of the closed bathroom door. I knock on it. "Cody? You alright?"

Still nothing.

I make a quick decision and push open the door.

Cody stands there in the shower, completely naked and wet, the side of his fist pressed deliberately to the wall, and he's staring right at me. A grin spreads across his face.

13

CODY

Oops.

I guess there's worse ways to get a boy's attention.

Trey stands at the door to the bathroom with eyes stretched as big as his face. They're glued to my dick, too, which salutes him like an obedient, ready soldier to his sergeant.

"Hey there, preacher boy."

Trey's eyes flick up to meet mine, and a glint of resentment bursts in them. "What in the heck is this? More games? I thought you fell and hurt yourself!"

"Nope. Just beat a fist against the shower wall. But ..." I point at my back. "I do need help with a few ... *hard-to-reach* spots."

His eyes narrow. "Cody ..."

"This is what you do, isn't it? As my caretaker? Come here."

"You're naked."

"Of course, I am. I'm in the damned shower. Do *you* shower in your underwear or somethin'?"

Trey sighs and shakes his head. "Look, if you need help, and I'm talkin' *actual* help, then call me. Otherwise—"

"I do need your help."

Despite all of his protests, his eyes keep going to my dick, and my abs, and my chest. He tries to pull his eyes away from me over and over, yet they never seem to take in their fill.

I like being a never-ending tall glass of water to him. I like his thirst never being quenched. And for some sick reason, it turns me on that the one whose attention I've so completely captured is none other than Reverend Arnold's kid—*the preacher's boy.* A pure and completely virginal hottie.

A guy who literally trembles in my presence.

Though, I guess being buck-ass naked in front of him is to blame for that particular reaction.

And hard as a motherfucker.

I cock my head and stare him down. "Trey Arnold, do I gotta ask again, or am I gonna be forced to step out of this nice, warm shower, walk over there, and drag your ass over here?"

He lifts two dark eyes to mine. *Yes, they drifted back down to my junk.* "Don't you mean *limp* over here to drag my ass over there?"

Oh. He's got attitude. Anyone else's sass would piss me off.

Trey's turns me on to no end.

"Boy, I'm gonna give you to the count of three—"

"Three," he states haughtily.

Yep. He's asking for it.

I'm out of the shower the next instant. All of Trey's coolness is zapped out at once as he gapes at me, slack-jawed. He can't seem to believe what he's seeing as I cross the bathroom, water dripping from my hair onto my body and all over the bathroom tile. The cool air rushes over my skin, but everything is on fire when I reach that boy and his stunned, adorable face. I grab his arm, then drag him across the bathroom to the shower.

If his uncontrollable sputtering and unblinking eyes are any indication, Trey isn't entirely upset by the prospect of what I'm about to do to his sorry ass.

And if he had any doubt whether I would actually do it, he is now made a believer as I pull him right under the hot stream of the shower with me.

"Cody!" he shouts in protest as the water pours over his head and back, drenching his light blue scrubs.

"Yeah," I agree. "That's exactly what I want you shoutin' out."

He meets my eyes in shock. "Wh-What?"

"My name. Loud and clear."

And then I grab him firmly by the shoulders and take what I've been wanting for too long: his lips.

I am a ravenous beast and his mouth is my favorite treat. He tastes so fucking sweet. Maybe it's how he always tastes. Maybe it's something in the sugary soda he drank earlier. Maybe it's his lip balm. I can't kiss him hard enough. I can't push my lips any harder against his than I already have.

But I try anyway.

I could fucking eat him alive.

At first, he is like stone in my palms. He doesn't pull away, but he doesn't know what to do either. The water has saturated every inch of him by now, and my firm hold of his shoulders tells him there's no escaping from me or my lips.

Then slowly, I feel his body melt against me. His lips open to mine, giving in. I invite my tongue right in, not wasting a moment. I slide my hands down his frozen-stiff arms, then reach around his wet, slender backside and pull his waist against mine. My bone-hard dick presses against his soaked scrubs, reminding me too well that he's still dressed.

Should I dare to strip this boy of his clothes after already just stripping him of his right to avoid my advances any longer?

Who am I kidding? He's wanted this as badly as I have.

Every moment his gaze lingers too long on mine.

Every effort he makes at connecting with me, listening to me, and watching me with those keen, rich, knowing eyes.

He and I were destined to crash into each other.

I tuck a finger into the front of his bottoms, then invite my hand into them. He doesn't stop me. His breaths start coming out in crashing ocean waves over my cheek while our lips remain glued to each other's. Slowly, I let the weight of my hand and arm drag down the bottoms of his scrubs, slowly revealing his soaking wet black boxer briefs underneath. Drenched as they are, they reveal to my exploring hands every single contour of Trey's slender hips, tight thighs, plump and perfect butt cheeks, and his very hard dick and tightly confined balls, which I cup greedily.

I should concern myself with the fact that I'm pushing him beyond any comfort zone he's ever defined. I should be sensitive to the fact that he may be a total virgin and is saving himself for a committed relationship. I should exercise discipline and stop right now. But I can't. I can't fucking hold back for another damned second what's happening any more than Trey can, clearly. Our mouths have a mind of their own. Our tongues, too. My hand won't stop kneading and squeezing and rubbing his perfectly inviting—and thoroughly wet—crotch.

And his confined dick won't stop throbbing and flexing in response to my every knead, squeeze, and rub.

Stop denying yourself. He wants it, too.

Fed up with just exploring his crotch, I let go and thrust my hand under his waistband, inviting my hand inside and right onto his swollen, pulsing dick.

Trey's mouth opens in response, our kissing ended, as he lets out a breathy grunt of surprise at my touch.

He still doesn't stop me.

So I keep going.

With my hand around his dick, I start pumping it, stroking him gently at first, then quickly picking up pace. Trey squirms in my clutch, a hand still planted on the small of his back to keep him held firmly against me. *Not that he's getting away.* His mouth is still against mine, yet we aren't kissing, simply breathing and letting our lips go slack as all our focus stays glued to what's happening in Trey's boxer briefs.

I thought I had him lost to the moment. Then his voice pulls me right out of our frenzy. "Cody, I don't know if I can do this."

I don't stop moving my hand, but I look into his eyes. A mere inch separates our face.

I've kissed guys before. Three, in fact, all in the Army. I've even had sex with one of them, but I've never *felt* close to any of them—not in the way I feel with Trey right now.

This is a whole new level of intimacy I've never breached.

"You need my help?" I ask.

Trey is confused by the question. "Help? What?"

"You're freaked out." Despite our jagged breathing and what's going on in his underwear right now, I speak calmly and evenly to him. Strange as it may seem, I'm the one with the experience here. "You've never done anything like this before, have you?"

"No," he answers at once, out of breath. "I haven't."

I put a gentle kiss on his cheek. "But you want it pretty badly though, don't you?"

"I ..."

Another kiss goes on his other cheek. He lets out a deep, deep exhale full of aching and want. "Tell me, Trey," I urge him. "Your body is begging for me not to stop. Am I right?"

"Cody ..." His objections sound more like pleading.

Pleading for me to keep going.

Pleading for me to ignore his second-guessing.

Pleading for me to give him exactly what he craves.

"I meant what I said on that couch." I kiss the left side of his mouth. "I ain't forcin' nothing to happen here." I kiss the right side of his mouth. "If you want me to stop ..."

Trey lets out a whimper.

I put another kiss right on his lips, full and plush and parted. "Just say the word, Trey. I'll toss your ass right out of this shower. I'll order another pizza and you can pray to Jesus to bless every damned pepperoni, to forgive you for your lusty sins, to—"

"There's nothing to forgive."

I pull away from his face. Trey's eyes are closed. He's lost in a land of ecstasy. "What's that?" I ask.

He hesitates. I can hear it in his breath, the way it stops, then resumes, then stops again. And then Trey says: "Keep going."

I smirk. "Keep going?"

"Please," he whimpers. "Please, please. Don't stop."

Who am I to deny him?

I go right into his face and bite down on his lip. Trey groans in response, then bucks as his dick flexes within my fist. Despite my waiting for his answer, my hand never stopped moving.

Trey must be close already. Not a surprise, considering how pent up and horny he must be.

So of course I decide to make this worse for him.

I pull my hand off his dick, then grip his boxer briefs by the waistband with both of my hands and tug it right on down. Wet as they are, they fight me for a second by sticking to his thighs, but I muscle them down anyway, and down they come.

His dick pops out, nothing left to restrain it. Trey Arnold has a beautiful one. It might be totally hard right now, but it is perfectly proportional to his balls, which are pulled up nice and tight and expectantly, smooth and plump. The length of his dick is just right to fit in my hand with some to spare.

It's also the perfect size to invite right into my wet, warm, hungry mouth.

I have never wanted to suck someone off so badly.

I want to know what he tastes like. I want to know how crazy I can make him if I wrap my mouth around his dick and bathe its every inch with my soft, wet tongue. I can imagine how sensitive it must be, considering all of my playing with it, and how horny he must be after our little stint in Bell Lake. Just one touch of my tongue to his dick, and he might lose all control.

Am I really willing to be responsible for undoing this church boy? Do I really want this on my conscience?

Without answering my own questions, I exert a bit of effort to lower myself to my knees, which throws Trey off balance since his mouth was still hovering in front of mine, waiting indefinitely for our manic making out to resume. My effort causes a spear to shoot up my leg, and I let out an involuntary groan of anguish. Unable to get to both my knees, I end up in a sort of down-on-one-knee pose, like I'm about to propose to the motherfucker's dick.

He glances down at me, bewildered. "Cody? Are you—?"

"I'm fine," I murmur up to him, shifting my weight.

There's no fucking way I'm gonna get comfortable down here. My left leg throbs, demanding me to stand back up. My right one aches, taking all of the weight my left one refuses to.

Am I really gonna let all of this stupid broken-body shit wreck the mood with Trey?

"Fine?" he mutters dubiously. "You don't look—"

"I'm fine," I state one more time through my grimace, then part my expectant lips. I have a high tolerance for pain, and Trey's dick is the perfect reward for it. "Fucking fantastic, actually."

"Cody ..." he moans, realizing what I'm about to do.

"That's right," I say up to him through the steam and the mist of shower water swirling all around us—and the pain I'm actively ignoring in my awkwardly half-bent legs. I'm sick of my body. I'm determined to be strong and unbroken, even if just for a damned moment. "Keep sayin' my name. Say it fuckin' loud."

Then I wrap my lips around his dick and take it all in.

All of it. Every inch. From his pink, perfect cockhead down the whole length of his shaft. You would think I've sucked a hundred of them with the way I so expertly invite him all in without once gagging, but when you want something this badly, you go for it.

"Cody!" he howls above me, his whole body tensing. "Oh my God, oh my God, oh my God ..."

Three times I just made the horny fucker use the Lord's name in vain. Three.

Should I keep score?

I'm hard as fuck in an instant. Something about having all of Trey in my mouth makes me so fucking crazy, I could burst right now without even having a hand on my own dick. My whole head just became a part of Trey, a tool for his pleasure, a fucking toy.

I love every second of it.

And every inch of him.

The bottom of his soaking wet scrubs shirt, which he still has on, plays on my hair and forehead as I start to bob up and down on Trey's dick, sliding it right on out to the tip, then diving right back on. Every inch of his dick goes in, then every inch but one comes out, over and over. I grip his thighs and push and pull with my every go, jerking the motherfucker off with my mouth. I do it with so much force, you'd think I was angry about something.

I guess I'm just so damned horny, it makes me aggressive.

His hands go to my head instinctively—maybe to hold on for dear life, maybe to balance himself, maybe to stop me, maybe to encourage me, I don't know. All I know is that the simple act of his fingers tangling in my hair turns me on to no fucking end.

Also, he isn't pulling away, and he isn't begging me to stop.

"Cody!" he shouts again, his voice bouncing around the echo chamber of my steamy shower.

Yeah, he's definitely not begging me to stop.

While continuing to suck him off, I let my hands slide around to grip his tight little butt cheeks. Just grabbing them makes my dick jump with desperation. He's so tensed up that even his ass cheeks are like two firm rocks, totally flexed, as I run my fingers over his smooth, slippery skin. I can't help but let my fingers explore wherever the hell they feel like going, and that includes right down his crack. The second I let my fingers tease there, he moans over my head and his fingers clamp down, clutching hold of my hair like he's trying to win at a game of tug-of-war.

Fuck, I love it when he grabs my hair like that. I love seeing Trey's strength and being the reason for him exercising it. He comes off so soft and fragile all the time, but I know better; Trey is one tough nut.

Let's test that strength. I let an experimental finger slide between his cheeks, tracing the whole length of his crack until it grazes along his sensitive hole and settles there determinedly.

I wouldn't dare finger him, right? Surely he's done it before when he jerks. This can't be *totally* unfamiliar territory for him.

Without letting up at all on sucking his dick, I push a finger at his hole. Call it dipping a toe in the water. Call it giving a light little knock-knock on his door. Call it whatever; I want inside.

And as slippery as our bodies already are, I wonder if I can get my finger to slide right in.

I'll tell you one thing: Trey Arnold is one tight motherfucker.

I feel more weight on my head, which can only mean that Trey is literally buckling over at the sensations I'm forcing him to enjoy. With my mouth working his knob off and my finger teasing at his back door, he has to think he's dreaming right now.

And what am I thinking? I feel like I've been dropped right in the middle of a dessert buffet of my own dreams. I have every inch of Trey Arnold at my pleasure. His perfect, tight little ass is in one of my palms. His hole is being played at with a finger. His dick is filling my greedy mouth from one end to the other. My own bobs between my kneeling legs with so much blood pumping to it, I can count my heartbeats with every one of its desperate nods.

"We have to stop," he announces to the shower walls.

I let his dick fall out of my mouth—still hard as stone—and glance up at him. No, my finger doesn't move away from his hole or my other hand from cupping his ass; he's made enough false protests since this whole sexual landslide began for me to let go.

Trey looks down to meet my eyes. He still grips my hair.

He also isn't saying anything else. "Stop ...?"

Trey parts his lips, but nothing comes out.

I smirk knowingly. "Sure," I mumble back up to him. "I get it. 'Stop' because ... you don't wanna pop your load in my mouth."

Trey's face wrinkles right up as if the thought actually *hadn't* occurred to him until just now. "I ... I wasn't ..."

"You're a virgin, aren't you?"

Now in addition to scoffing with a sad attempt at indignance, his whole face goes red. "I'm ... I've ... I've been ..."

"Is having my face this close to your swollen dick making it difficult to form a complete sentence?" I ask him with mock sincerity, then give the tip of his meat a long drag of my tongue.

Trey quivers with pleasure and sucks in air.

"Or is it my finger," I go on, "which is *so ... fucking ... close ...* to slipping right inside of you?"

"Yes, I'm a virgin," he states shortly, ignoring my taunts as his eyes close up tightly.

I give him another long lick. "I'm not." I give the tip a kiss. "I know what I want, and I know damned well that you want it, too."

His eyes flap open. He stares at me, speechless.

"So if you want to stop ..." I eye him. "And I mean *really* want to stop ... then you better say so now. There ain't no turnin' back after I wrap my lips around your dick again."

I squeeze his butt cheek for punctuation.

Trey Arnold does nothing but stand there and stare down at me, tiny glass beads dripping from his hair.

I don't want to draw out any corny metaphors here, but if he isn't some angel floating above me with a halo of righteousness glowing over his head and I'm not some devil from the darkness below trying to pull him under my evil, sexual spell, I have no idea what's going on between us in this steam-filled shower.

"That silence," I state, coming closer to his still-achingly-erect dick, "sounds a lot like an answer."

Trey's lips part. He still says nothing.

And that tells me everything.

I close my eyes and descend on his dick once more, but this time I have no plan to stop. While my mouth engulfs every inch of him, my finger keeps teasing at his tight hole, daring to slip inside at the first sign of him relaxing. Trey turns into stone again, his fingers curling in my hair, and I bring him to the edge in seconds.

My heart races with hunger the more I suck him off. Each big inhale and exhale he lets out above my head encourages me. After weeks of drowning out all feeling with alcohol, books, and letting my guns fire in the yard, this moment is waking up every cell in my body and filling me with a joy I didn't know I was capable of.

It isn't exactly a selfish joy, either. Something tells me what I'm doing is perfect for Trey, too. He's a hard-shelled little fucker, and despite all his piety and strict moral code, I think he's been waiting for someone to crack him wide open.

I'm determined to be that someone.

And if all of this is filling me with so many grand thoughts and feelings, Trey has to be going downright crazy by now. This has never happened to him. He's been given permission, maybe for the first time in his whole life, to feel anything he dares to feel and to enjoy a whole world of sexual pleasure and freedom that he might have been denying himself all these years.

Maybe I'm corrupting him.

Maybe I'm freeing him.

Maybe in most contexts, there's not a difference between the two.

Suddenly, I can't ignore my own needs any longer. I let one of my hands go from his butt cheek and wrap it around my dick. I jerk so hard, I can hear every slap of fist against skin. With his dick filling my mouth, the finger of my other hand teasing his hole, and my own dick getting jerked with feverish determination, I'm too soon drunk with lust.

When Trey starts moaning, I realize he's close again—maybe too close. My finger feebly pushes at his hole, desperate to get in, but from the flexed, pulsing of his cock I can feel in my mouth, it's obvious something else is ready to come out first.

"Oh my *God!*" he shouts out as his hips thrust forward, almost gagging me. "Oh my *God!*"

Four times in vain. Five times.

And then he empties into my mouth.

I couldn't possibly predict how it would be like, to have a guy come in my mouth. I've never let anyone before. The moment he does, I hear it before I feel it shoot all over my tongue. Vicariously, I feel deep relief from the way his body almost folds over mine while jet after jet of his jizz fills my mouth. The taste is unexpectedly clean and doesn't make me gag or recoil, despite how damned deeply he apparently insisted on jamming his dick down my throat. It's a good thing he isn't hung like an elephant; I'd be lucky to still *have* a throat after a mouth-fucking like that.

With my mouth filled with nothing but Trey, I let loose my own torrent between my legs, gushing into the rushing water circling the drain. A moan erupts from the depths of my chest as I release all of my pent-up frustration, wave after merciful wave.

The constant rain of shower water takes away my last, ebbing moans as they die off. My finger, once teasing his hole, has come to rest somewhere at the back of his thigh, and before long, I'm holding myself steady with Trey's body as my center of balance.

He didn't pull out when he finished; he stays right in place, breathing heavily. I wonder if he's afraid to move. Maybe he's looking down at me right now, aware that I've gone from sucking him dry to practically hugging his knees for dear life.

And the shower water keeps pouring over us endlessly, the rhythmic noise almost therapeutic.

His dick stays hard the whole time as it rests on my tongue. It all happened so fast, I'm not even sure if I swallowed any of his jizz yet, or if it's still in my mouth. Somehow, I don't care either way; I'm so fucking happy right now that I could cry.

It's not lost on me how intimate we just became in the space of a second. I feel oddly vulnerable. I feel more naked than I am, like a different kind of clothing just fell right off my body, a piece of clothing you can't see with your eyes.

Slowly, I pull off of his dick, swallow, then bring a hand to my mouth for one lazy wipe of my lips. My eyes drag up his body and meet his face.

He *was* looking down at me the whole time.

The pair of us stare at one another for so long, I can't tell if he is feeling pleasure, pain, or something between. I'm still holding on to him like he's my raft and a hungry river is trying to yank me downstream. With the sound of the shower, it wouldn't be hard to believe that very scenario if I just close my eyes.

My right knee has gone completely numb. My left leg tingles, aching right at the thigh in particular. Maybe I overestimated my own physical strength. Something smarts deep in my left leg that's gone ignored for way too long while I kept all of my focus on Trey. *Motherfucker.*

"Hey, Trey," I mumble up at him.

He lifts his eyebrows expectantly. "Yes?"

"Do you wanna ... be my nurse for a second and help me the fuck up?"

Without hesitation, he bends down and grips me under my arms. With a little tug, he gets me to my feet—which feel like they are made out of numb, stiff Ken-doll plastic, for fuck's sake—and then the two of us are right where we began: two boys in the shower staring one another in the eye.

After a minute, Trey murmurs, "What did we just do?"

I don't answer his question. I grip the bottom of his shirt and slowly draw it over his head, then fling it out of the shower. It lands on my bathroom floor with a wet, slapping sound. Then I go for the soap and start up a lather on his chest, washing in slow, thoughtful circles. He doesn't move, but he's looking into my eyes. I bring the soap down below and circle all the places I've been. I'm trying not to think that I'm cleaning up any evidence of my being down there—any evidence of what just happened between us.

"I hope you don't think less of me," he croaks.

I scoff at him. "The hell would you think that for?"

"I don't know what came over me. I was ..." His eyes search my chest for the words. "I was possessed, it felt like. For days, even. I couldn't stop thinking about—" He shuts himself right up and shakes his head, frustrated.

"About what?"

"Nothing."

I bring the soap behind him and drag it down his ass where the bar slips right between his cheeks.

Trey's bright green eyes go right to mine indignantly.

"Calm down. I'm just cleaning you up," I insist in a tone that paints a bright, shiny halo over my head. "For spending all this time in the shower, we didn't actually *shower* much, did we?"

"I'm still wearin' socks," he points out.

I scoff at him. "What weirdo wears clothes in the shower?"

He throws me a look.

I love fucking with him. "Let's take that shit off."

Without waiting for him to respond, I set the soap aside and grab behind his thigh, lifting his leg right up from under him to reach his foot—because I don't think I can afford to kneel down again. Trey loses his balance for a split second before grabbing hold of me, stabilizing himself. When his fingers dig into my skin, his eyes meet mine, and the whole clumsy situation turns into something sexier. With his eyes still on me, I slip off his socks one at a time, gently, letting him shift his weight to lift his other foot after I'm done with the first.

"There," I say, flinging both wet socks out of the shower as carelessly as I did his shirt. "We all better now, you big crybaby?"

"Who are you?"

I'm thrown off for a second by his question, then thrown off for another second by his striking eyes and the rich, bottomless well of wisdom in them. I'd give anything to know what's going on inside his mind. Did I go too far? Should I have exercised some restraint when I devoured him a second ago?

"Sometimes I don't know," I answer him truthfully. "But right now, I can tell you I'm just a man who ... had needs."

He squints skeptically at me. "Needs ..."

"And you just fulfilled them."

"I did?" He nearly scoffs at that. "Felt more like I was just ... standing here doing nothin' at all. You were the one who was all busy down there doing ... doing ..." He gestures down at his dick, which only now is starting to deflate.

"I had fun *doing*," I taunt him.

"Oh, and your leg!" Trey exclaims, his tone changing. "Cody, you really shouldn't have knelt down like that for so long. I told you several times ..."

"It's fine," I return dismissively.

"Cody, I saw you wince. I saw you in pain."

"I'd do it again," I answer honestly. "Boy, I'd suck you off for hours and hours and hours."

He bites his lip.

If I'm not careful, my words might get him hard again.

"And you know," I go on, "if I don't scare you off like a little bitch again, I plan to fulfill your needs just as much as my own, over and over again, as many times as I want, as many times as you can handle ... whether I'm on my knees or otherwise. Seems a fair trade to me for your being my 'caregiver' and all, don't it?"

Trey's eyes detach, and that's when I see a strange sort of spark ignite in them. Is it excitement? Is it anticipation?

Is it lust?

Doesn't make one lick of difference, I suppose; Trey Arnold is still standing in front of me, and even after going all animal on him in this shower, the fucker still hasn't run away. *Yet again, his speechlessness says it all.*

14

TREY

I'm not sure what I'm doing here in Cody Davis's house.

I'm not sure what I'm doing at all.

"Pass me the ranch, will you?"

I glance at Cody on the couch next to me. He's in nothing but a loose pair of silver-gray basketball shorts—sans underwear, as usual. A box of chicken wings we ordered along with another pizza (because apparently our exercise in the shower worked up Cody's monster appetite again) is balanced precariously on his abs, each of which is defined with distracting detail. It's difficult not to notice those things when you're in the same room with a shirtless Cody Davis. I mean, even his big *calves* have definition, propped up lazily on the coffee table as they are.

"What do I look like?" I sass him back. "Your butler?"

"Well, you *were* my maid this past week, so ..."

I smack his shoulder for that—hard. Not that the firm meat of his shoulder does anything in retaliation except punish the side of my hand by making it ache. *It's like punching a brick wall.*

"So pass me the ranch."

I smirk as I swipe the cup of ranch off the coffee table and hand it to Cody, who takes it to use as a dip for his wings. I wrinkle my face as he takes the first bite. "The barbecue sauce isn't tasty enough? Gotta go and douse it in ranch dressing, too?"

Cody shrugs. "I want it, so I get it," he retorts through all the smacking of his mouth. "What's the big deal?"

I wince. "The big deal is you talkin' with your mouth full." He chuckles at that and goes for another bite. I watch him curiously. "You always ... heed your wants so openly?"

He quirks an eyebrow at me, chewing. "What do you mean?"

"You want sauce, so you go for it. You want to fire off a gun in the backyard, you blast away. You want a big ol' pizza with a side of barbecue wings, you're on the phone in a hot second."

"I'm not hearing a problem yet," he says while obnoxiously smacking on his food.

I squint at him. There's a big elephant in the room, and it has everything to do with why my clothes are tumbling in a dryer right now and he's half-naked. "Are we gonna pretend we weren't just in the shower together? And ... did things?"

"Who's pretending we're not?"

"I'm ..." I sigh, unable to articulate what's going through my head. "Listen, I'm trying to say I—"

"You need to chill the hell out, man. Kick back with me. Look at the TV. Take off that stupid shirt."

"It's the closest thing in your closet I could find in my size," I point out.

"I haven't worn that ratty thing since high school."

"Well, I *would* be wearing my own scrubs right now, but they happen to be tumbling around in the dryer at the moment thanks to a certain *someone* gettin' them all soaking wet."

"I warned your ass with a three-count before pulling you in, if you recall correctly, Mr. Three."

The quip leaves me red-faced and biting my lip.

Yeah, he isn't exactly wrong there. When Cody challenged me in that bathroom, I felt a surge of sexual anticipation that began and ended with the tall, glorious sight of Cody's muscular body. I wanted him so badly.

And then he pulled me into that shower.

And everything else happened so fast.

"You havin' regrets?"

His question throws me. I clear my throat and bristle a bit on the couch. "No."

"Bullshit. You're scared you're goin' to Hell now."

"I never said—"

"Prickly Peter's gonna turn your lusty ass away at the gates, you big sinner."

I roll my eyes. "I don't think making light of my beliefs is the ideal tack to win me over."

"Who said I'm tryin' to win you over?"

I sit up and turn to give him a look. He freezes with a wing halfway to his opened mouth, staring at me quizzically.

I change my tone, opting for something less jokey. "Cody, I don't regret anything that happened in the shower. I don't."

"Good," he returns flippantly. "Neither the fuck do I."

"Everything we did, I ... I wanted to do."

He points his chicken wing at me accusingly. "You hesitated."

"This is new territory, Cody. I reserve my right to ... hesitate." I glance back at the TV to gather my thoughts, which does little except fill my eyes with two cops slamming some angry guy to the ground and shouting unintelligibly at him. "This is all very new to me. My heart wanted every second of that to happen, but ..."

"But your brain is shouting, 'Oh, shit. What did we do? Fuck!'"

I let out a dry chuckle. "Something like that, perhaps."

"Why don't you quit tryin' to make so much dang sense out of everything? You're stressin' me out."

I turn back to face him with a smirk.

"For real," he presses. "Just relax. Let it be."

Does everything go right over his head? Does he even realize what sort of walls, rules, boundaries, and morals I took a sexual sledgehammer to in the space of seconds in that shower? I don't even know if I can look my dad in the eye for a month now, let alone go to church on Sunday and not feel wracked with guilt for all the places my mind has gone. I'd need a full seven days just to get all my confessions off my chest.

"Or you could just go." Cody tosses a bone he just cleaned off at the pizza box. "Y'know, if it's so damned uncomfortable to be around me and my irresistible self."

I don't know if he's teasing me or being serious. Is all of my anxiety bothering him? Does he really want me to go, now that he's had a taste of me?

A sudden knot twists up in my chest. Was I that bad? Is he angry I didn't reciprocate in the shower?

Was all of this a game to him?

I push myself off the couch. "I suppose I've been here long enough, anyway," I announce, collecting whatever little scraps of dignity I have left. "We've spent the whole day together. I'll ... I'll just see myself out, then."

He doesn't say anything. I don't look back at him, not wanting to see indifference or apathy or ambivalence on his face; I feel like that would kill me right now. I make for his front door.

"Your scrubs are still in the dryer."

I stop with my hand on the knob, my shoulders tightening up. *I'd forgotten.* "Indeed, they are."

"Probably dry by now."

"Indeed, they may be."

"Also, you'll have to figure out a way home, considering you drove my truck here."

I clench shut my eyes. *I'd forgotten that, too.* "Well, I ... guess I'll have to ..." I huff. "I'll have to walk home, then. In the dark."

"That's a near hour-long walk across town."

I let out a sigh of exasperation all over the door that I'm still facing, then spin to shoot him a look. "Well what do you propose I do, Cody? I'm not having you drive me home."

"Stay."

My eyes flash. "Stay?"

"Yeah. Just stay. You were gonna come over in the morning anyway, weren't you? It's Thursday tomorrow, your usual day to come over and annoy the hell outta me."

I press my lips together tightly. Even after all of what we just did, the thought of staying the night here with him is ludicrous. I can't even consider it as an option. My father would wonder why I never came home. Someone might have watched me arrive at this house—like Burton or nosy-and-observant Robby—and then by morning the whole town will think I was kept prisoner in Cody's secret military bunker dungeon.

"Stop thinkin' about it," Cody barks out, annoyed. "I see all of that anxiety in your face. You're worryin' over it too much."

"But I have to—"

"You don't ha'fta *anything.* People know you're my caregiver. Your car ain't in the driveway. Just stay the damned night. We can watch cop shows 'til we pass out. Like two buddies. Then you can make us breakfast in the morning like a good caregiver."

I narrow my eyes. "You know damned well it isn't that easy."

"Actually, it is."

I glance at the front window that overlooks his living room. Through the blinds, only a faint trace of blue light swells in the distant sky, pulling the day away with it like a warm blanket over the bed of the world. *I already lied to my father about staying with the girls*, I reason. *Maybe he'll think I've stayed the night at one of their places. That isn't too farfetched a notion. Maybe it is that easy.*

Cody rises from the couch, which brings my attention back to him. All of his weight is on his right leg, I note. He limps over to me, not caring to hide it at all, then twists the blinds closed tight, shutting out our view of the street and the waning light.

Then he just stands there next to me looking down into my eyes with heavy, warm emotion burning in his own. He is silent and strong as he towers over me. The effect his presence has is the same as it was the first day I saw him. My heart races. My mouth goes dry. My fingers twitch with anticipation—though I can't say with any certainty what, exactly, I'm anticipating.

"Just stay," he murmurs softly.

He wants me to stay. And judging from the uncharacteristically gentle tone of his voice, he wants me to stay pretty badly.

I don't know how much longer I can continue denying myself. Before long, I'm going to be throwing all of my discipline aside and giving in to every single impulse I have around Cody.

"I won't do anything you don't want," he says to me, his voice still achingly gentle.

I close my eyes. I feel the heat coming off his bare chest.

"Just two guys," he murmurs.

"Two guys ..." I return quietly.

His hand touches my cheek. My breathing quickens as I turn stiff as a tree, my face inclining ever slightly toward his palm like a weak branch bending at the faintest wind.

Cody's face grows closer to mine. "Just two ... lonely-ass guys."

Then his lips touch mine.

I melt against him, my mouth opening right up.

My hand slips off the doorknob and goes straight to his body, clinging, as our feet drag us across the room, stumbling, limping, shuffling. Cody collapses back onto the couch, our lips still locked, then pulls me onto his lap. Instinctively, I straddle his thighs and continue to kiss him, unable to resist his mouth for a second.

Am I even in control of my own body right now? Is it even physically possible to resist the chemical deluge that my nervous system is experiencing?

Just two guys ...

Just stay ...

Do I even have a choice?

His hands slide down my backside, slip under my shirt, and come to rest on my butt. The temporary pair of shorts I put on from his dresser—*also his*—are so loose that his hands slide right inside, cupping my bare cheeks greedily.

The way his hands keep gravitating between my cheeks, it is starting to drive me crazy. In the shower, I squirmed from his evil finger that kept working my hole, but never quite slipping inside. Cody was so persistent, it's like his finger had a mind of its own.

His exploring hands are giving me a hunger for something—a hunger I have never, *ever* had.

And then: "Do it again," I blurt out between our kisses.

My heart flaps like a baby bird's wings.

I flush bright red at what I just asked.

Cody pulls away from our kiss, eyebrows lifted. "Do what?"

I open my lips, then find I can't quite say what I want him to do. I'm too ashamed. I'm so outside of my usual comfort zone, it's like this is some sort of alternate reality when I can let loose and do or say whatever the heck I want without any fear of retribution or fatherly disapproval.

Has this hunger been living inside me all along?

Have I just been ignoring it?

Then Cody moves his hands inward slightly, his rough fingers teasing at my crack. "You mean this?"

I shut my eyes, bite my lip, and try not to squirm. Straddled as I am over his lap, thighs spread, my butt cheeks are pulled apart and exposed to whatever his fingers dare to do to me.

"This?" he murmurs, much quieter, as the fingers of one of his hands tickle between my cheeks.

Now, I can't help but squirm despite myself.

I even let out a tiny whimper.

My hole is so excruciatingly sensitive. Every bit of my focus is pulled straight to what he's doing down there. I feel every little flinch of his finger, every little brushing of his fingertips along my crack, every tiny rhythmic movement.

"This?" He brings one finger to my hole, circling it tauntingly.

"Stop saying 'this'," I breathe out, almost trembling under his cruel, slow, teasing touch.

"Well, I'm glad you want it," he tells me, throaty and soft, "but I sure as hell ain't getting a finger up there dry."

"Don't go in, then." I'm out of breath. Every word is an effort, desperately attentive to what he's doing. "Just keep doing what you're doing. Don't stop."

Cody smirks. "You like it, huh?"

"Don't stop."

"You like it a whole lot."

"Yes."

"Fuck, you're hard."

My eyes flap open. I peer down to find my cock swollen hard and pushing against the front of my shorts. It's practically aimed right at Cody's face.

"Aww, look at that," he taunts me. "Your dick already misses the warm, wet feel of my mouth."

"Yeah. It does."

Who am I? What has happened to Trey Arnold? Who is this horny, uninhibited, crazy person who's controlling my body right now?

"And why's your ass trembling?" he asks, clearly insisting on toying with me as much as he possibly can while he's literally got me in his hands. "Is it begging me to put my finger in it?"

Oh my God. "Yes, please."

"'Yes, please'? Am I servin' you seconds at the dinner table? What the hell is this polite shit?"

"Put your finger in it."

"What was that?"

"Put your finger up m-my ass, Cody," I beg, my face going red as I say the words I can't believe I'm actually, physically saying. "Do it. Please. Please do it."

He appraises me like a piece of meat, his eyes running up and down my form. Then he grunts. "Well, like I said ... your ass is no good to me dry. Looks like we'll have to improvise." His grip on me tightens. "You ready for this?"

I blink. "R-Ready for what?"

In one swift movement, Cody thrusts me off of his lap and flips me over. I barely have time to gasp before he's got me bent over the coffee table, my shorts—*his shorts*—still halfway down my thighs. I am completely confused about his intentions until I feel his palms cupping my cheeks again and pulling them apart—and then the cool, wet touch of his tongue.

I pucker up at once, eyes wide. "Oh my *God* ..." I breathe out.

"Six times ..." he murmurs, the breath of his words like a soft breeze on my exposed hole.

"Six what?" I throw over my shoulder, exasperated.

He lets out a tiny chuckle. "Nothin'."

And then I feel his tongue drag up my crack.

Considering how sensitive everything has become down there in the past hour, it is impossible not to squirm. Cody has me in his hands and controls every ounce of pleasure I experience. With each flick of his tongue, I fall apart more. With each time it grazes over my hole, I quiver and let out the slightest moan.

There are several things that go through my head. For one, I have never once desired another man's tongue around, on, or *in* my hole. Now that it's happening, I don't want his tongue to leave, and I'm experiencing more pleasure than all of my best and most satisfying masturbatory sessions combined.

Secondly, while I've never partaken of any recreational drugs in my life, I am convinced without a doubt that what I'm feeling now trumps the effect of any and all drugs in the world.

Thirdly, and worst of all, I already want to come again.

I've not even so much as jerked off twice in one day. Heck, I usually don't even do it but once every three or four days. To go from that to wanting an orgasm twice in the period of an hour or two is literally unfathomable to me.

All of these thoughts are crammed in my head, shoving each other in their competition for my full attention.

None of them win when Cody does what he does next.

"You ready?" he grunts over my ass when he stops.

"For what?" I ask, terrified, excited, nervous, exhilarated.

His tongue is replaced by the unmistakable tip of his finger. I tighten up right away, anxiety flooding me quicker than the thrill of sexual release did.

"Relax, Trey. Relax ..."

"Is it gonna hurt?" I throw over my shoulder. I feel like I'm coming undone at my carefully stitched and tightened seams. "Am I going to feel any pain?"

"It's just a fingertip. I'll stop if it hurts. You know my stance on forcin' anything, Trey, don't go dumb on me now."

"I ain't dumb," I spit back, my attitude returning.

The attitude is gone the next second when I feel his fingertip slip inside me.

"Oh my *GOD!*" I belt out, then slap a hand to my own mouth. It nearly knocks into the pizza box on the coffee table next to me on its way to my parted lips. "Cody, Cody, is it in? Is it all the way in?"

"Just to the first knuckle. Barely any of it at all."

"That's just the first knuckle??"

"You really need to relax. You're clamped down on my finger so damned tight ..."

"Sorry."

"Your ass is like a Chinese finger trap."

"How the heck am I supposed to relax when you're trying to get a finger inside me? You're putting something *in* my *out* hole. It's not how the body's built!"

"You sound like every homophobic prick whose ass I beat up back in school," Cody grunts at me. "You don't think we've been stickin' all sorts of things up our bored butts for millennia to feel sexual pleasure, gay and straight men alike? It's called a prostate."

I glance over my shoulder. "Thanks for informing me—a licensed practical nurse—what a prostate is."

His finger slips in more.

My whole body bucks without my permission, and I slap both my hands to the coffee table and cling. "H-How much is in now?!"

"Barely to the next knuckle. Why do you think I'm sayin' all this stuff to you?" he asks with a hint of amusement in his voice. "I'm distracting you so your stubborn ass relaxes."

He's playing me like a fiddle, that's what.

"And maybe if we're lucky," Cody goes on, "I can get a second finger invited to the party before you call it quits like a lil' bitch."

I narrow my eyes. Staring ahead, my whole view is filled with his living room window (through which I pray that the blinds are adequately concealing all of this activity) as well as a bunch of cops and flashing police lights on the top TV.

The bottom TV reflects my face back at me like a mirror. I see myself—albeit warped by the convex bend of the TV screen— sprawled over the coffee table like I'm anticipating a spanking, and Cody's muscled form sitting on the couch with a hand at my ass—a hand with a finger that is halfway inserted into me.

Every little movement of his finger, I feel with precision.

Every tiny effort he makes to slip in deeper, I know.

I am teetering on the brink of feeling like this is all too much, or not enough. I want him to pull out, or I want him to plunge all the way in and make my eyes rock back.

I want him to give me a hands-on lesson in what good the prostate is for—a lesson no med school would've taught me.

Maybe my confusion is because I *am* too tight.

Maybe I really do need to relax.

"Easier said than done," I moan.

"What's that?"

"Relaxing."

"Well, better relax in a hurry, 'cause all we're going on for lube is my saliva, and that's sure to dry up quickly."

I squirm a bit. "Maybe it already has."

"Easy to fix."

The next instant, his finger—however much of it he actually managed to get inside—slips right out. His tongue goes in its place.

I'm plunged right back into a state of ecstasy as he licks me without relent. Unlike his finger, his wet tongue teases with so much fervor, I am practically doing breaststrokes on the pool of this squatty table as I squirm. A moan as pornographic as they come wriggles out of me, filling the room.

I can't believe I'm capable of such sounds.

I can't believe I'm capable of feeling such heights in pleasure.

All of this is Cody's doing.

He must gather that I'm enjoying his tongue twenty times more than his finger, because he doesn't stop for one second. The sensation is endless as he licks, tongues, laps, and glides over my hole. He might literally be driving me insane down there.

Without stopping, his fingers hook into my shorts and slowly pull them down. My legs come together enough for him to get the shorts right off of me, and then they're flung to the floor under my body. While police sirens flash in the top TV screen, I watch through the reflection in the bottom one as Cody reaches down and takes hold of my freed cock. He keeps his face buried in my ass while gently stroking me.

It is literally seconds later when I feel too close to hold back.

"Cody," I let out for a warning. "C-Cody ..."

I feel as melted apart as a cone full of ice cream in the sun at noon, all the tiny fingers of sticky cream trickling down my hand, down my arm, down to the pavement. I'm just melted goo all over Cody's coffee table, a puddle of pleasure and sweat and nothing.

In the screen of the TV, I watch Cody lift his face from my ass, suck a finger, and then bring it right to my hole. I have no idea how it's any different from what he just tried a minute ago, but his finger slips right in.

Everything in me hardens like cement.

Bolts of pleasure chase down my legs and up my torso.

My cock is so hard, it could literally explode.

"Oh my GOD!" I cry out.

His finger keeps moving. His other hand keeps jerking me. I'm a ragdoll for Cody's uninhibited pleasure as he drills his finger into me. Deeper and deeper he seems to go. Faster and faster he jerks me. My heart is racing so fast, I could pass out.

And then I come without warning, unable to hold back the dam he's built up so quickly inside me.

The release is unprecedented. I thought I came in the shower. I didn't—not like this. This is my real orgasm.

It feels like pulling a world apart by all its stones and oceans.

It's ripping a forest to pieces by its roots, its vines, and its countless families of rustling leaves and wildlife.

It's thrusting the massive fist of a giant into the bowels of the deepest ocean, then watching as monumental tsunamis the size of mountains race across the world.

I don't even notice when Cody slips his finger out. I feel a presence of his hands at my sides, and then my torso is lifted off of the coffee table and I'm falling back into the couch next to a thick, warm body. Cody's body. His arm comes around my neck and he hugs me against his side, and then all I hear is the pair of us as we slowly breathe.

I count our breaths as they fill the room. I don't even hear the police sirens anymore, or the drone of their interrogative voices, or the crunching of gravel as they pursue runaway criminals.

All I hear is Cody. All I feel is Cody. All I know is Cody.

"Am I still a virgin?" I ask suddenly. My voice sounds so alien, disturbing the peace of the room and our breathing that sounded like the pushing and pulling of ocean waves.

Cody lets out one chuckle, his chest bouncing. "Yeah. I don't think my finger counts."

His words make a loose, yet brave implication—that there is something else that might one day find its way into my ass.

Something that *would* take away my virginity.

Something between Cody's legs.

I close my eyes, sinking against his body, seeking comfort in the one thing that's terrifying me: Cody Davis, the person who has, in a matter of hours, unwrapped me like a gift I didn't realize I was giving. An expensive gift. A one-of-a-kind gift.

A gift that can cost me everything.

Cody rises from the couch suddenly, causing me to fall over from having been leaning on him. He limps into the kitchen where I hear the sink run. Left in his wake is a vacuum that both breaks my heart and fills it up at once. In an instant, I'm put in a state of not wanting to be anywhere but right next to him, comforted by his strength and his experience.

The very next instant, I want to run home and hide under my bed sheets where I've been safe all twenty years of my life.

It's easy to say that I should relax and drink it all in, but it is impossible to relax when I'm stuck here juggling knives—a knife of guilt, a knife of satisfaction, and a knife of freedom—and any of those three airborne blades can land wrong and cut me deep.

And then I'm nothing but the punch line to a joke: a handless or armless juggler, depending on where the knives land.

I wonder if Cody feels anything I'm feeling, or if he really is just the big block of sex and attitude he pretends to be, washing himself up in the kitchen sink.

This night is unreal to me. I can't stop questioning all of my emotions, as if I can't believe they're even there. Maybe I didn't just come twice. Maybe I haven't lost all control and crossed lines I can never uncross with Cody Davis. Maybe I didn't really just lie to my dad on the phone earlier about where I am.

Or maybe I did all of those things.

Maybe I'm a different Trey Arnold tonight—a whole new person.

"You alright?"

I lift my gaze up to Cody who stands at the doorway to the kitchen with his dark eyes hovering on mine, waiting.

"Yeah," I answer finally.

"You came on my shorts."

I lift an eyebrow, confused. "Say what?"

He limps over to me, slowly bends down with a small grunt of discomfort, and retrieves the pair of shorts I was wearing off of the floor.

I peer at it.

Oh. That's what he said.

"I'll throw it in the wash," he decides with a dry snort. "Can't believe you went and made a mess all over my shorts. Damn. Talk about a rude-ass way to repay my hospitality."

I'm a completely different person tonight. I'm the new Trey Arnold, a guy who stays out at night, who lies to his dear and loving father, and who definitely messes around with the bad boy in town everyone warned me about.

"Guess I'm just markin' my territory," I throw back, propping an arm on the back of the couch as I twist to face him.

He snorts. "You're a funny guy, Trey."

"And you surprise me."

Cody stills at my words, then squints dubiously. "How's that?"

I shrug. "You just do, Cody."

He doesn't seem satisfied with that answer. "The fuck does that mean? I 'surprise you'?" He wrinkles up his face and takes two limping steps toward the couch. "You tryin' to say somethin'? How the hell do I surprise you? Say it."

"I'm just saying I ..." My eyes trickle thoughtfully down his chest. "That ... I had one idea of you earlier today ... and now I have this whole other idea of you."

He studies me for a bit. "What idea did you have of me?"

"At first? That you were a stubborn jerk."

He crosses his arms. The shorts hang loosely from his grip.

I wince. "You gonna put those in the wash? I'm sort of staring at them and—"

"So I'm a stubborn jerk, huh?"

I give him a look. "As if *that* comes as any surprise." I tilt my head—new Trey, new confident Trey, new bad-boy-seeking Trey—and ask, "You wanna hear what idea I have of you now?"

Cody smirks as he stares at me skeptically, not answering.

So I tell him anyway. "I think you're soft and emotional and sweet underneath the hardness you exude all the time. I think you want someone in your life who can look at you and really *see* you."

He still doesn't reply. His face remains completely unchanged after my words, as if I might as well have said nothing at all.

I lift an eyebrow. "Well? Am I wrong?"

He doesn't respond. Then, after another moment of nothing but a cop muttering to the camera on TV, he turns away and limps off to the laundry room. I hear the click of the washing machine lid as it creaks open, then the slam of it shutting.

I shake my head, my eyes wandering back to the TV, but I'm not really watching it. I'm teetering back and forth between liking the nonresponse I got from Cody, which might as well have been his way of indicating that I was spot-on with my thoughts of him, or being annoyed that he's not man enough to admit I'm right.

Assuming I'm right.

I could have this all wrong, I realize. *I could just be the score he was trying to make. A quickie. A sleazy lay.*

I don't like how that notion makes me feel at all.

"Get up."

I turn at the sudden sound of his voice. "Huh? What for?"

He's next to the couch. "Get up," he repeats, then limps over toward the hallway.

Figuring I don't have any reason not to, I oblige, rising off the couch and following Cody down the hallway. He heads into his room and stops at the side of his bed where he just stands there, that permanent scowl sitting on his handsome face and causing his eyes to sparkle with intensity.

I join his side, my gaze on him. "What's wrong, Cody? Are you showing me something?"

"Yeah. I'm showin' you how soft and sweet I am."

Before I can say anything, Cody wraps an arm around my neck and takes me down to the mattress in a headlock. I let out a bark of surprise—*or laughter, I can't tell.* I fight him for exactly three seconds before he wraps both of his big arms—*and* his good leg—around my body, wrestling me into submission. I struggle to break free as he nuzzles his chin into my neck, holding me close.

"I give!" I choke through his tight grip.

He still doesn't let go. Only after I stop resisting completely and let my body go slack, he lets off a little, and then we're just lying there on his bed, me trapped in his arms.

I realize belatedly that the two of us are cuddling. Honest-to-God cuddling. Me and Cody, on his bed, with his big arms wrapped tightly around me like he never wants to let me go.

His breaths drift over the back of my neck, slow and steady.

I find a knowing smirk creeping onto my face. *Soft and sweet,* I tell myself, victorious, as I stare into the darkness of his room, just one shard of bluish color coming in from the TV in the living room casting its light down the hall.

"We're cuddling," I taunt him in the darkness.

"Don't make me sleeper you like a bitch," Cody warns me.

I smile, then take a sharp turn in attitude. "I like being in your arms, Cody."

As per usual, he doesn't respond to that sappy sentiment.

Really, I wasn't expecting him to. Maybe it's too early to let out any emotions with him. Maybe I'm still riding the high of all our sexual exploration tonight. Maybe new Trey has locked up the old one and stuck him in a treasure chest deep in my heart.

Maybe I'm just an idiot and all of this means nothing to him.

Maybe this feels so good that I don't care either way.

I could live here in Cody's arms forever. I've never felt so safe before.

"Maybe I'll just stay a little longer," I decide aloud. "But just a little longer. Then I'll enjoy a peaceful nighttime walk home."

To the sound of his gentle breaths—and lack of reply—I slowly let my eyes close while enjoying the warmth of his body against mine. I don't know what to make of this night—or this whole day, really. All I know is, despite all of the joy swimming around in me, much like our legs wiggling under the water of Bell Lake, I will eventually have to return to my life and face reality. My dream—this dream with Cody—is the best I've ever had. But I know I will need to wake up from it.

Just not yet.

15

CODY

There's a vast, sandy wasteland. It's high noon. Everything's so fucking bright, yet I can't seem to find the sun. I can't tell if all the light is coming from the cloudless sky, or from the dirt and the bright, smooth, windblown rocks on the ground.

There's nothing for miles. No trees. No grass. No cactuses. No mountains on the horizon. No cities. No ruins. No hills.

No people.

No sound—not even wind.

It doesn't make sense. Even when I walk forward, I don't hear the crunch of sand beneath my boots. I walk for a mile and it's like I haven't moved at all. Everything looks the same no matter how far I go. Everything is silent.

And I hate silence.

But despite the lack of sound and the vast nothingness around me, there is one fact I'm fucking certain of.

I'm not alone.

I turn around. No one's there. I turn again. Still no one. It's endless wasteland for miles and miles in all directions. My vision is perfect. There's not even dust in the wind to mask my view. My eyes clearly tell me there's nothing around me in all directions.

Yet still, I know I'm not alone. I can feel it. Someone is there.

Someone is watching.

My heart picks up speed.

I can't accept what my eyes tell me.

I can't trust what my eyes tell me.

I'm not armed. I have nothing to defend myself with. Even if I do find the threat, I'm at the whim of my skillful hands and feet and all my combat training.

But even with all of that training, I'm fucking scared to death.

I spin around, wide-eyed, searching.

Still, nothing.

No one.

Then I feel a prickle on the back of my neck. A tingle. An itch. A tickle. The feeling of a tiny spider as it descends from the ceiling and makes a safe landing on the back of your neck. The suspicion that a tiny fly has landed there. It's just soft enough of a touch for you to doubt it—and yet there you are, waiting to feel another tiny flick of movement, waiting for the spider or the fly's stealth to run out and reveal its presence.

I hold my breath. I listen.

Then one word explodes in my ears at head-splitting volume, shattering the thick and perfect silence: "*MOVE!*"

I jump and let out a shout.

I blink. The wasteland is gone. The light I see comes from the window ahead of me—my bedroom window. It's morning sunlight.

I blink several times as my brain slowly pieces together the details of my room. The dresser in the corner. A pillow on the floor. The half-open closet door. The hum of a TV left on in the living room from last night.

I glance down. Trey is in my arms, his head turned toward me, eyes open, drowsy and confused.

"Cody?" he croaks sleepily.

I grunt, "Nothin'," and lay my head back down with a huff, but somehow I can't close my eyes. The wasteland and the silence and Pete's distant cry of "*Move!*" is still too fresh to trust the darkness behind my eyelids.

Trey shifts a bit in my arms to get a better look at me. His face is an inch from mine when he turns, his head resting on my arm. "You alright, Cody?"

"Fine," I mumble.

"Was it a dream?"

"Said I'm fine."

A look of frustration crosses his face, but it's short-lived. He takes a breath and turns his head to look at the window. Then, as if it's just now dawning on him, he sits up slightly, propped up at his elbows. "It's morning already?"

"Your ass fell asleep."

He turns back to me, alarmed. "We fell asleep?"

"Yep."

"We fell asleep together? Here? I slept over?" His wide eyes blink a hundred times. He jabs a fist into them, wiping. "I didn't ... I didn't mean to—"

"What's the big deal?" I cut him off.

"I didn't mean to fall asleep." He hops out of the bed and slips out of the room.

I watch him go with a frown. "You're overreacting."

"Oh, no," he groans from the living room. "Four missed calls."

Either he's overreacting or his daddy is a control freak. "So shoot your pops a text and tell him you're all good," I call out at him. "Problem solved."

He doesn't respond, but I hear the tapping of his thumbs on his phone over the drone of an infomercial—or whatever it is that's on the TV we left on overnight.

I swing my legs over the edge of the bed. Ignoring a throb in my left one, I push myself to my feet and limp down the hall. Trey stands by the front window with his phone out, yet his thumbs have grown still. He's biting the inside of his cheek as he stares off, aloof and silent.

"Trey?"

"I gotta go," he states suddenly. He seems to reconsider for a second, then shakes his head. "No, I definitely gotta go."

He spins on his heel and darts through the kitchen. I hear the click of the dryer door popping open a moment later, then the ruffling of clothes.

I limp slowly to the doorway and watch him as he pulls off the shirt of mine he was wearing, then slips his underwear and blue scrubs back on in a hurry.

The longer I watch him, the more annoyed I get. Not that I was expecting the two of us to wake up to a gay, glorious sunrise and share chocolate chip pancakes or anything, but I didn't see our morning starting out with him rushing the hell home because he's afraid daddy is gonna put him in time-out.

"You're panicking for no reason."

Trey huffs at me while he folds my shirt. "You can tell me that *after* I go home and perform a tap-dance for my dad." He sets my shirt down on the table, then stares at it thoughtfully. "I ... never thought I'd need to do something like this."

"Like what? A high school teenager sneaking around behind his parents' back?"

His eyes become two spikes of flint aimed my way. "I could really go without the extra mockery, thank you. You have *no* idea what my father can be like."

"He *knows* you take care of me. The whole town does."

"Tuesdays, Thursdays, and Saturdays. *Not* Wednesdays."

"It's Thursday," I point out facetiously.

"Yesterday it wasn't. The day I was here. The day we went to the lake together. The day that ... *everything* happened." Trey slaps a hand to his forehead so hard, it surprises me. "I even lied to him. About where I was. I never lie to my father."

"Yeah, we know this. But it's not like you're at a drug house, or a strip joint, or out robbing a bank with your *hoodlum friends you don't have.*" I shuffle over to him by the table. My foot knocks into one of the chairs, which I ignore, my eyes on Trey. "Call him, tell him you're here, tell him you're fine, and tell him you'll see him tonight when ..." My eyes trail down his form, then flick back up to his face. "... when I'm through with you."

The words do the trick. Trey's gaze moves to my chest where a squeeze of sexual anguish tightens his body. He parts his lips, likely letting a thought or two race past his mind.

"Haven't we done enough?" he chokes.

Despite the pang of protest in my leg, I force myself a few steps farther, bringing myself to his side. I grip his hand by the wrist, pull it off the shirt he folded up so nicely, then shove it down my shorts.

"Does it *feel* like we've done enough?" I return to him.

I'm not hard, but I doubt I need to be to get the point across. If his hand stays down there any longer, though, I can't guarantee it won't come to life in a haste.

Trey meets my eyes. There's an unexpected pinch of sadness in them. "Is that all we ... 'do' ...? Touch each other? Give in to our desires whenever we want? Practice no restraint?"

I frown. "Why do you gotta go and make everything so serious all the time? Why can't you give yourself permission to just ... *let go* a little? Stay out at night? Make a mistake? Do somethin' a little bad now and then?"

"Are you the Devil?" he asks. "Yes, I'm genuinely asking," he adds after throwing his free hand on his hip.

No, he still hasn't yanked his other one out of my shorts.

Yes, I'm getting hard.

I smirk. "It wouldn't be the worst thing in the world if you had your hand down Lucifer's pants."

His eyes go dark.

Of course, I can't stop myself. "Maybe there's a reason Lucifer was God's favorite angel."

The next instant, Trey's hand is free, and he's halfway across the kitchen in pursuit of his shoes in the living room, which he plops down on the couch with attitude to put on.

Is this a bad time to mention how turned on I get when I piss him off?

"Maybe we should up you to five days a week," I call out to him as I lean against the table and cross my arms. "I'm feelin' like I need a lot more *caring* from my *caregiver*."

"I'm going home," he calls back, his voice strained as he pulls on his shoelaces, tightening them.

"So who's gonna feed me?" I taunt him. "What if I gotta scrub my back? Or jerk off? You know my arm's actin' up. How can you leave your patient here all helpless?"

He rises from the couch, then throws a look over his shoulder as he goes for the door. "I doubt you're helpless at all, Cody Davis."

"You still don't got your car, y'know," I remind him. "At least let me drive your scared ass home."

Trey's heavy footsteps stop, and then he abruptly returns to the kitchen, bringing his face an inch before mine. "I'm *not* scared. I'm being *responsible* here."

"Oh, is that what you call all that fear in your eyes?" I could kiss the motherfucker and end his resolve. Somehow, I recognize that would be unfair—a dick move—so I practice restraint. If a kiss happens, it'll be Trey who initiates it. "Tell me, preacher boy. What, exactly, is your responsibility? To please your daddy? To *look* a certain way to everyone else in town?"

"My responsibility sure isn't your dick," he sasses back.

"And it sure ain't all the watchful fools in Spruce, either. Fuck Spruce." I betray myself and reach around his back, cupping his tight, supple ass with my whole palm. His body stiffens under my touch. "Don't you want something real for once, Trey? Something you actually want for yourself ... instead of what everyone else wants for you?"

Trey swallows hard. He's considering my lips. He wants to kiss me; I know it.

"Just give yourself permission," I urge him. "You're the only one whose permission you need to *live your damned life*."

"Says the person who hides in his house for months refusing physical therapy and counseling," he fires back in my face.

I lick my lips. Just that tiny act threatens to glue our mouths together from sheer want. "I won't lie, Trey. I would probably take more offense to that if I wasn't so bone-hard right now."

"How did you even get out of all the physical therapy?" Trey goes on, tilting his head. "I'd figure the Army wouldn't have given up on you so easily. They'd push you through the therapy. They'd make you whole again. I'm almost certain they have put men in conditions five times worse than yours back into the field."

"Guess I'm too broken for them to fix." I squeeze his ass. *God, I fucking want to be inside him so badly right now.* "That's why I got you here to fix me."

"I have to go."

"You're mine now, Trey."

Finally, he swats my hand off his ass and steps away from me, then heads for the door. This time, I feel a pinch of victory when he leaves. The morning sunlight pours in and dresses the whole house as I watch him stroll down the walkway to the street before the door's own weight pulls it shut.

16

TREY

I am a sweaty mess of terror by the time I make it to my side of town.

Every person I pass on the street seems to stare me down like I've done something awful. I might as well have robbed the Wells Fargo on Wicker. Or been the one who burned down that one bar. I'm like the town pariah, shamefully trudging home with my tail tucked and my ears folded.

Even Spruce Fellowship stares me down as I walk past its cold, sightless face. *Stop judging me, church*, I think as I go. *You're about to have a second over-the-hill birthday, you old, creaky thing!*

That exclamation, even if only mental, just makes me feel more ashamed.

Then I'm standing in front of my house. The clean shrubbery in the yard. The pruned fig trees on the left. The cross that sticks out from the middle of our colorful flowerbed. The wind chimes hanging on our front porch, tingling and singing a taunting *told-you-so* tune as the morning breeze dances by.

I take a deep breath.

Cody's right, I suddenly hear myself think. *It's just your dad. You don't need to fear him all the time. You have a right to live your life.*

A right to go home with the bad boy.

A right to let him suck me off in the shower.

A right to squirm and moan like a porn star when he slides his slick, wetted finger up my ass.

I clench shut my eyes. *Maybe if I get kicked out of my house today,* I reason, *the Tucker-Strong residence might have a spare bedroom.*

That's all I'd need, to be Tanner and Billy's scraggly stray gay cat they're bringing in off the street. Oh, what lovely bittersweet icing to top my cake of shame with.

I push myself down the walkway I've walked a thousand times and bring myself to the door. After one more deep breath taken through a constricted throat that's trying to choke me, I put a sweaty hand to the door handle and give it a shove.

It swings open. No, my father never locks the door. *"What sort of villain would dare to rob the town minister?"* That's what he asked me before. Many folk around here have followed suit regardless. I guess it's a small town thing to have a crime rate the local police chief describes as "virtually nonexistent, save the chance high school brat or two just lookin' for a way to pass on by their Saturday with a laugh or a prank".

Right now, *I* feel like the big ol' laugh in town.

I've been pranked by thinking I could do what I did and get away with it.

I step inside and gently close the door at my back. I look up at the banister of the second floor that overlooks the foyer, but see no one there. To my left, the empty dining room stares back at me, all the white and beige colors of tablecloth and sunlight filling my eyes. To my right, a silent seating area greets me, its sole chair carrying no father of mine.

I walk under the curving staircase into the living room, which is just as unoccupied as the front of the house. The TV is off. The kitchen, which overlooks the living room, is silent and still. I hear no noise coming from the hallway where the master suite—and my father—primarily reside. I wonder if he's even home.

Then I notice movement through the tall back glass windows. Seated on the back covered patio area is my father next to a mug with a book opened in his lap. He's facing the backyard with his legs crossed and propped up on the chair next to him. As I watch him, he slowly reaches toward his mug at his side—eyes still glued to the book in his lap—fumbles for the handle, then slowly brings it to his lips where he takes a long, unhurried sip from it before gently setting it back down.

I'm not sure why I expected to come home to him holding a wooden cross and pressing a bible to his chest, reciting scripture to ward away the demons that have come home with me. As far as I know, he doesn't know where I was.

Or what I did.

I shake my head and sigh. *Just get this over with.*

The sliding glass door pulls to the side, and then I yank it shut at my back. My father, unworried and calm as ever, lifts his chin from his book and acknowledges me with two light, curious eyes. He studies me for exactly four seconds before a word comes out of his mouth. "Morning."

I instantly clasp my hands in front of me like a boy about to ask his grade school teacher for forgiveness. Then my hands go back to my sides, then awkwardly get shoved into the pockets of my scrubs. "Father."

He studies me for a moment, then turns back to the book in his lap and murmurs, "I can't remember the last time you spent the night with any of the girls from work."

Crashing at one of the girls' place. That's the lie I fed him via text before leaving Cody's house.

Lie number two. Or is it three? I've lost count.

Lord help me, that is not a number I want to lose count of.

"Me neither," I return through my tightened throat. *I have ass sweat. I'm so nervous, I can actually feel sweat trickling down my ass.* "So, Dad, how was your—?"

"Must've been back in high school, if I had to reckon."

I lift an eyebrow. "S-Sorry?"

"Since the last time you stayed over at one of the girls'." He turns a page in his book. "High school, or so."

I nod stiffly. "Perhaps."

"Something the matter?" he asks, his eyes still on his book. "You're glued to that door like you've got somewhere else to be."

I realize I haven't moved a foot away from the sliding glass door. There's a healthy ten feet between my father and I, as if a great chasm of hellfire separates the pair of us.

"I'm ..." I clear my throat and step away from the door. "No, I am just feeling a little tired is all. I may go take a nap, actually."

"Didn't sleep too well last night?"

I close my eyes, as if literally keeping all of the dirty images and memories and thoughts from spilling out into the open. Just at a mere *mention* of last night, my heart speeds up like Cody himself is behind me gripping and kneading my ass, his face nuzzled in my neck, and his deep voice growling, "*You're mine,*" tickling the tiny microscopic hairs in my ear.

A shiver chases its way down my back. "You can say that," I reply anxiously.

Maybe I should've stayed at Cody's, after all.

"Better get you some shuteye then before ... well." My father shifts in his seat, lets out a short sigh, then finishes. "Before your obligation this afternoon."

It takes me a full ten seconds of staring at the back of his head before I realize what he means. "There's really no set time that I have to be ... that I have to go to Cody's." I swallow hard, annoyed with my stubbornly overactive nervous system. "It's ... whenever."

He doesn't respond, simply reading his book and paying my answer no mind.

I despise stuffing down my anxieties. Can't we just say what we really feel to our loved ones and not fear constant reprimand? Can't I just ask my father why he's changed ever since I came out to him years ago? *Can't I just ask my father why his love for the gays seems to be reserved for everyone in the world except his own son?*

I shove myself the rest of the way toward him in pursuit of topic-shifting conversation. "What're you reading?" I ask lightly.

His demeanor is just as abruptly softened as mine. "Oh, just an old book I found." He hesitates, then a smile lightens his face as he decides to elaborate. "An adventure about a princess stolen away by a marble dragon. The prince has hired a wizard's apprentice to rescue her, but the apprentice—our hero—is quite bad at magic, and he finds himself twisted up in this quest to end the tyranny of a jealous sorcerer who turns creatures and people into stone, into glass, and—you guessed it—into marble. I suspect the sorcerer will be responsible for having turned the dragon into marble, and maybe the dragon will turn out good in the end and—" My father lets out a big sigh and shakes his head. "Oh, listen to me. Sorry, I get too enthusiastic about these books. Turns me into a clueless teenager each time I crack open the pages."

I catch myself smiling. "It's great, Dad. Sounds really great."

He rolls his eyes. "Right, yes. And I'm sure you're wondering why I'm reading *this* instead of the good book. Just so happens, I have read the good book a hundred times, and I find pieces of its knowledge in all other books I read. Even this one. The apprentice is much like Job, in fact. His faith in magic—and everything he believes in—is tested when he loses everything despite all of his hard work, including his wizard mentor, his unborn son, and even his dear wife—" He draws silent after that last word, staring off into the yard, lost.

I bite my lip. *Mother.* After too many seconds pass, I put a hand on my father's shoulder. It almost startles him, jerking him out of the rabbit hole of darkness he just slid down.

I offer him a smile when he looks up at me. "You don't have to justify why you read so much fantasy. I get it. We all need escapes. And I'm proud to have a dad like you who ... isn't so pious that he thinks books like this are beneath him, or sinful, or evil."

My dad returns my smile with a tightened one of his own. "Do you know that Pastor Raymond admonishes anyone who reads Harry Potter, as he likens it with practicing witchcraft?" He shakes his head. "It really rather disappoints me, what he's done with the Fairview church. I used to consider him a close friend."

I chase an impulse and hug my dad from behind, which is a slightly awkward effort since he's sitting down and I'm not. He brings a hand to my arm and gives it a little appreciative rub.

"You know, I told your nurse friend Marybeth last night—when I spoke to her on the phone—that I have something for her daughter," my dad then tells me. "I think she'll like it."

My insides freeze. My eyes flap open. "What?"

"Marybeth. Oh." He chuckles. "I called her last night. Didn't she tell you?"

"W-Why?" I'm still hugging him. I haven't let go. I can't let him see my face.

"In my worrying about where you were last night, I called your friend from the clinic. Since she was one of the two who were working yesterday, I figured she was one of the ones you were hanging with after work. 'Course, you were in the bathroom and weren't answering your phone."

I swallow hard. "Yes," I state flatly. "Right."

Somehow, affirming the lie with my voice in person—instead of via text or on the phone—is twenty times harder to do, even when I'm not looking my dad in the eyes.

"Marybeth told me this morning that you had crashed at her place. I thought it a little odd, what with her having a daughter and just living a quick ten minutes from here. I'm guessing you two were having a lot of fun."

"Loads of fun," I agree, my head spinning—and still clinging to him from behind. I had only _one_ missed call from Marybeth last night, which I had suspected was some silly "Henry"-related work thing, but apparently was rather her giving me a heads-up or an interrogation about my dad.

She covered for me, I realize belatedly.

She also saw me leaving the clinic with Cody Davis.

My heart stops. _She knows._

"Have you had breakfast yet?" asks my father lightly, utterly oblivious to the panic painted over my face behind him. "I was just daydreaming of a big ol' plate of crispy brown sugar bacon and Belgian waffles for some reason. How's that sound?"

My stomach growls in response. "It sounds like I didn't realize how hungry I was."

He pushes up from his chair and turns to face me. For a brief moment, I think he's about to give me a proper hug. Instead, he sets down his book, nods stiffly at me, then heads into the house with a strangely plastic smile pasted over his face.

My father's trying. That's the important thing here, right? He's making an effort.

In the form of brown sugar bacon and Belgian waffles.

And I'm repaying him in lies and cover-ups for my super scandalous affair with Cody.

But when I'm inside a while later seated across the counter from my father with plates of bacon and waffles beneath our hungry mouths, I watch the inspired glow in his eyes as he talks to me about his ideas for Spruce Fellowship's special fifty-year anniversary service this Sunday. I note how spritely he's acting, how happy he looks, how pleasant the words between us are.

I also note the lack of consequence for my actions.

I realize how easily he believed all the lies. It was *easy* to do what I did last night and get away with it, free from judgment.

The thought—plus the tasty mouthfuls of brown sugar bacon that my dad hasn't made in months—fills me with an unexpected sense of confidence. Should I call this bravery, what I'm doing? Utter foolishness? Acting with total abandon?

Being a really, really bad boy?

And I can do it again if I wanted. Who's going to stop me but myself? I can go right back over to Cody's house today and spend the whole rest of my afternoon doing ... whatever it is I want.

The mere thought tickles my insides.

I can do whatever I want.

"These taste *sooo* good," I suddenly hear myself sing, mouth full of maple-syrup-dripping waffles, sweet and perfectly cooked.

My dad lets out a short laugh, pleased, then forks two more slices of bacon onto my plate. "You need to put some more meat on those bones of yours, son! Have seconds. There's plenty."

There's always been plenty on my plate ever since I was a kid. Plenty of space in my house. Plenty of space in my bedroom—and my bed. Plenty of food on the table. Plenty, plenty, plenty.

Plenty everywhere—except for my heart.

Until now.

Now, it's filled to near-bursting with the fiery, addictive lust that I have watched fill endless others' hearts. A lust I have never understood. A lust I have always looked down upon.

Now I get it.

"Thanks, Dad." I stab a slice of bacon and bring it to my mouth, feeding my inner glutton.

And now, I only want more.

17

CODY

The knock on my door comes sooner than I expect.

The second knock comes because I'm a broken piece of shit and can't move fast enough across my house to answer the first.

"Damn it, hold the hell up," I call out as I make my slow-ass way from the laundry room.

I pull open the front door with a grunt.

Trey Arnold stands there in a small red t-shirt and shorts, his eyes on me with a look of urgency in them, tension in his face.

I frown, concerned. "The hell is wrong with you?"

"Nothing," he states at once, his voice light and sweet, in total contrast with his expression. "Are you alone?"

"Yeah, 'course I am. My mom don't drop by no more without calling first." My eyes slide down, then back up his body. *Damn, he looks good.* "Not now that you're comin' by and still got the job."

"Good," he says simply.

And his lips are on mine the next second.

I stumble backwards into the house as his arms fling around my neck—whether to strangle me or hold on for dear life, I can't tell just yet. A foot kicks the front door shut. An unlucky heel hits a leg of the coffee table, causing a loud protest of glass and wood and a grunt from my throat. We fall back onto the couch, our hungry hands fumbling with each other's bodies, shirts, belts, and anything else they can reach. Our breaths crash over each other's faces with so much damned force, it's like we're both angry about something, filling the room with the noise of our frenzied passion.

Well shit, this is certainly one way to spend my afternoon.

* * *

As it turns out, lip-locked is exactly the way that Trey intends to spend the evening, too.

"What the hell came over you?" I ask him as we're sprawled out on a blanket in my backyard staring up at the clouds and the orange inferno of the sunset. He keeps kissing me between my sentences, his hands on my body—which I haven't managed to keep a shirt on in over two hours, thanks to this greedy, horny hottie I've got attached to me like a monkey. "One second, you're panicking like a bitch 'cause you slept over. Now, you're—"

"Watch your mouth, Cody Brian Davis." He bites his lip, then adds, "There's nothin' wrong with ... appeasing one's needs."

I snort at that. *This boy is so damned ridiculous sometimes.* "That is surely one fuckin' polite-ass way to describe the ravenous way you've been actin' since you came through that door."

"And besides, we aren't hurting anyone, now are we?"

"Unless you count my dick and whether or not we're goin' in for round three anytime soon."

He pounces me and thrusts a hungry kiss on my lips before smirking in my face. "So how about you just let it happen?"

"Let it happen?" I thumb the house behind us. "You mean like the fevered mutual-jerk-off session and then the follow-up *try-the-finger-up-my-butt-thing-again* bit you initiated on my couch before we planted our lazy asses out here under the sun to bake? Just 'let it happen' ...?"

Trey's fingers rake up my abdomen and arrive at my chest, where he then gives my left nipple a sudden and very stimulating pinch. I grunt and shut my eyes. "And please," he murmurs, his voice deep, "quit questioning my sexual mood swings."

Sexual mood swings. I open my eyes on his face, gritting my teeth as his fingers continue to knead my nipple. "Were you this much of a cock tease back in school?" I ask him. "Did you drive all the other boys crazy?"

He lets go, then replaces his fingers with his lips. I suck in air as he drags his tongue across my nipple playfully, teasingly, and yet with enough aggression to make me question whether he wants me to feel pleasure or pain.

"I take your answer as 'drive the boys fuckin' insane'," I grunt while he works my nipple.

He lifts his face up, bringing it right over mine, half-eclipsing the sky. "High school was a very cruddy time for me."

Cruddy. I smirk. "Makes two of us."

Trey starts to draw shapes on my chest as his eyes detach. I can see the memories of the not-so-good ol' days running past them as his finger drags along my skin. "Tell me what it was like."

I quirk an eyebrow. "What *what* was like?"

"Being *you* at a school like Spruce High."

I consider it for a moment. "I think the grownups assume that just because it's all fine and dandy for *them* in this town, it must be the same for all their precious, well-meaning kids in school. But fools like you and I know that ain't the case."

Trey grows still, his finger stopped. His nonresponse is noted.

"What?" I prompt him, eyebrows pulling together. "School was great for you? You didn't experience nothin' negative at all at Spruce High? Is that what you're trying to tell me?"

"I'm not tryin' to tell you anything," he throws back to me, his voice as innocent as a butterfly. "I'm just listening is all."

I grip his hand and pull it off my chest, then bring his finger to my mouth. Trey watches as I kiss it once, then twice, lightly. "I can figure it all out without you saying a damned word," I say to his finger. "You were the preacher's son, for Pete's sake. People kinda *had* to respect your ass, I'd reckon. If they didn't, it was like committing a mortal sin or somethin'."

Trey is watching me hold his hand, a glint of curiosity in his eyes. "I wouldn't go that far."

"People *wanted* to be good with you, 'cause then they were good with God. And the whole rest of the town. And their parents. And their teachers. Shit, you probably had it made in school."

He lifts two half-lidded eyes to meet mine. "I think you sorely underestimate how *isolating* that is for a guy like me who's spent half his life craving nothing but normalcy."

"What do you mean?"

"Every person who tried to get close to me just ... felt fake. Like they only wanted something from me. It was hard to trust when someone was being nice to me, they weren't just doing it for the exact reasons you so brashly listed."

"So I'm right?" I ask, pulling his hand to my mouth for a kiss.

Trey shoots me a look, which softens as he watches my lips. "That doesn't mean I was happy. So many 'friends' around me ... I still felt invisible. Like no one saw the real me. And add to all of that the fact that I was gay and no one knew. Well, no one except my best friend Jamie. We were boyfriend and girlfriend for a week. Then she tried to kiss me, and I shoved a cheeseburger between our mouths and told her I was gay." He winces. "She didn't take it well for about five seconds. On the sixth second, she realized we were destined to be best friends."

I frown. "So where is this 'best friend' of yours now?"

"In California on a full-ride scholarship. What're you doin' to my hand?"

"Getting your fingers all wet and slippery so I can stick a few of them up my butt," I tell him, straight-faced.

Trey lifts an eyebrow, then glances off with a sigh. "Anyway, we talk now and then. On the phone. Sometimes Skype."

"You Skype with my butt?"

He shoots me a look. "I'm talking about Jamie."

"So why haven't I heard of her 'til just now?" I ask, bringing his hand to rest on my chest. "When's the last time y'all Skyped?"

After a second of discomfort, Trey retracts his hand and then relents. "A year ago."

"That don't sound like a best friend to me."

"She's busy," he insists, defending her at once. "Her school is really ... really mega difficult, considering what she told me. Such a high workload they put on her. And she has all these tests and ... and schoolwork, and ..." His voice trails off.

I nod slowly and knowingly. "You don't gotta say it."

"Say what?"

"It isn't like I'm hearin' from my military buddies every night or anything. Fuckers haven't even tried to contact my sorry ass since I left Prairieland Medical. Not even—"

Move!

I shut my eyes and give my head a shake, as if to try and shake loose the damned memory and Pete's booming voice. I wonder if I'm even accurately remembering it or if it's been so distorted in my memory that it's not his voice anymore.

"I don't suspect it's easy," murmurs Trey thoughtfully. "To keep in touch with family and friends back home. When you're ... over there. Or even just on base."

I don't answer him. Instead, I shift right back to our first topic at hand. "School might have been full of fake fuckers for you, but at least you *had* friends. People were too damned scared of me to even bother sitting with me at lunch."

"Aww." Trey frowns with pity. Then his voice turns playful. "*I* would've sat with you at lunch."

I roll my eyes. "Like hell you would've."

"Why were people so scared of you?"

"How would I know? I wasn't the big, flashy Tanner Strong, the Spruice Juice everyone loved. I wasn't acting in no school play. I wasn't on the yearbook crew, or in band, or ... fuckin' anything, really. My old man never let me forget that, either. That bastard made me feel as small and worthless as a pimple on his ass."

"You were lost," murmurs Trey, watching my eyes in wonder.

"I didn't become anyone until I enlisted. The Army gave me a purpose. And a family I could rely on. It created me."

His hand moves to my arm suddenly. I stop talking, my focus pulled completely to the touch of his fingers on my skin. Trey's eyes say it all; he understands without my having to spell it out. *The Army made me who I am. The Army also took it away.*

Trey scoots over a bit on the blanket, bringing his body right next to mine. My eyes drop to his, the hunger returning to me.

"You will find a new family," he tells me, his voice lowering. "You have a life here. You will survive no matter what happens, because you are a human being, and human beings adapt."

It's hard to argue with Trey when his face is inches from mine and all I can think about is kissing the fucker until his eyes rock back and our bodies grow hard with need. "Human being."

"And regardless of how *stubborn* you insist on being, you are going to go to physical therapy and counseling," he goes on, his voice a touch firmer. "I'll even take you."

"Is that so, caregiver?"

He nods. "Yes. That's so."

Unable to resist any longer, I lean in and plant a firm, wet one right on Trey Arnold's lips. He shuts his eyes tenderly, drinking in the sensation as we kiss.

When our mouths separate, a smile is stretched over his. "I'm off the rest of the week from the clinic," he points out, nearly giggling. "Don't go back 'til Monday."

I lift an eyebrow. "Yeah? The hell you gonna do with all your time off? Bum around?"

"Bum around. Oh, yeah. I'm gonna be *bummin'* around a lot, you might say."

With that, he reaches over and gives my ass a light swat, which makes my heart flutter excitedly. *Is he already edging toward round three?* Then he retreats his hand, his face blushing, and he laughs at himself, as if astonished at what he just did.

I shake my head. "I don't fuckin' know who you are."

After biting his lip, his voice turns pensive. "You ever spend so much of your life dreaming about a certain something, and then out of the blue, you get a taste of it, and then—"

"Fair warning," I cut him off, "my dick's hard, and I'm good to go whenever you are."

He narrows his eyes at me. "Excuse me, but I was trying to have a *deep moment* here."

I lean back and put my hands behind my head, lacing all my fingers together. "Go on, then. Have your moment."

Trey snorts and shakes his head. "Never mind."

After a moment of watching the side of his pretty face, I purse my lips and nod thoughtfully. "I know all about gettin' a taste of it, then obsessin' over how damned good it feels ... and how long you've been missing that certain something that, 'til then, didn't even have a name."

Trey studies my face, then flips over onto his stomach, his face hovering near mine. "Tell me about your first."

I shake my head. "Nah, we're not doing that googly-eyed shit. My first time wasn't love, or a flame of passion, or whatever dumb thing you wanna call it."

He shrugs. "So what would *you* call it?"

"It was a blowjob in a supply closet. That's what I'd call it."

Trey scoffs at that. "You did more than just that, Cody."

"Of course, I did. I fucked him in that supply closet a week later, too. Twice on the same weekend. Then we fucked a handful more times over the course of—"

"I can't believe all of that happened." Trey lets out a muffled giggle suppressed by the hand he just slapped to his mouth. "It's so scandalous and ... and *bad*. I mean, weren't you worried you'd get caught?"

"Nah. You get to know the ins and outs of everything. And it was just sex, nothing more. We didn't even talk most of the time."

"Wow." Trey's eyes wander down my chest. He seems to be eyeing my nipples again, which makes my dick swell expectantly. *Just a look from him gets me so fucking excited.* "Is that ... Is that all *this* is to you?"

My jaw tightens. "What do you mean?"

"This. Is this just sex, too? Ugh, never mind." Trey sits up and shakes his head. "I'm being dumb. What do I expect? Of *course* this is just sex. I mean, we barely know each other."

I don't respond. I just watch him work it all out on his face and with his rambling, waiting.

"And sex is a human need," Trey goes on, rationalizing every little thing in his life until it's become a tiny box he can place on a shelf in his brain, nice and tidy. "You and I are two young men with blood in our veins—"

"And dicks."

"And ... yeah, there, too. And we need sexual gratification. If that's all this is, then ... I'm fine with it. I'm fine with it because we are both benefiting from this ..." He waves his hand in the air, gesturing toward my body for some reason. "This arrangement."

"Does the arrangement have to do with my dick?"

He pays my comment no mind. "And really, why does this sort of thing have to be looked down upon? Casual sex. Sex at all. Why is it a ... a *dirty* thing? I think it's rather beautiful, in a way. You are in need of it. I'm in need of it. I'm here to care for you. And we're both caring for our sexual needs."

"I got a sexual need." I point at my dick, which is now poking straight up inside my shorts. "And it needs taking care of."

"And it's not like we're emotionless, cold, or evil," the grand philosopher Trey Arnold goes on. "We also care about one another on an emotional level. I mean, *you* might never admit it out loud to any living being. But I'm totally able to say that I care about you, Cody. I don't just *want* you. I also ... want you to be happy."

"My dick wants to be happy, too. Your lips would make it very happy, actually."

Trey thrusts a hand under my shorts and takes hold of my dick so fast and so forcefully, I nearly jump, alarmed.

And then Trey resumes philosophizing in his same casual, ponderous demeanor. "So if we both care for one another, and we respect one another, then there's nothing wrong at all about what we're doing. It's a good thing, really. A beautiful thing. I might even be so bold as to say that this is God's work."

His hand slowly moves up and down my dick.

My eyes rock back. After two rounds in just a matter of hours, how the hell am I still this damned horny without my dick aching in protest?

"Somethin' wrong?" he asks me.

"Nope," I blurt out, eyes closed as I enjoy the feel of his hand stroking my swollen hard dick. "Go on. Keep doin' God's work."

Then I feel his hand replaced by something warm and wet. My eyes open and I do half a crunch to pay witness to Trey Arnold as he descends on my dick for his first-ever blowjob.

Not that you'd notice.

The guy has the mouth of a fucking tornado.

Instinctually, I reach down and touch his hair, then weave my fingers into it as he bobs up and down—halfway down my dick, then back up, over and over. Trey twists his whole mouth around my knob so expertly, I can't believe this is his first time.

He comes off of my dick suddenly. "Am I doing okay?"

I stare down at him incredulously. "You fuckin' kidding me?"

He grins, then plants kisses all over my dick from the base to the tip. After that, he starts licking it like a damned popsicle, the whole length, sensuously, thoroughly, every inch, over and over.

My face contorts in the sort of overwhelming pleasure that's almost like anguish. It isn't enough stimulation to push me over the edge, but it's enough to drive me there and make me crazy.

Meanwhile, one of his hands slowly starts creeping up my torso, the fingers bumping along my abs, then tracing up the side of my body.

I could fall apart from the way his fingertips feel along my smooth, sensitive skin. He knows what he's doing to me.

God's work, remember?

Then just as his lips wrap around my dick again, his fingers find my left nipple and pinch with conviction.

"Fuckin' hell, Trey!" I groan out, then any other words I try to say melt into unintelligible vowels as I rock back, lips parted and muscles tightening up.

Now he's got me right where he wants me: a toy in the palm of his righteous little hands.

His fingers won't stop working my nipple, already sensitive from him playing with it earlier. With my dick in his mouth, we've got ourselves a serious situation here.

"Close," I warn him, shocked that my bitch-ass is already saying that word.

He comes up off my dick and replaces his mouth with his hand, jerking me the rest of the way off. The slickness from his saliva has me bounding over the edge in seconds, and when I let it all out, I'm grunting with enough volume that I'm certain every neighbor from here to three streets over can hear my shameless ass coming like a bitch.

While I'm busy swimming in the euphoric chemical cocktail inside my head, Trey snuggles up by my side. I guess, just like after our fun on the couch, we're just going to kind of ignore the mess he just made with his mouth and hand.

"Was it good for you?" he asks playfully, his voice humming on my chest.

I let out one dry bark of laughter. "Well, well. Look who's got a big ol' head now."

"I've never done that before."

"Now you have."

"I want to do it every day."

"I wouldn't stop ya."

"Well, except for Sunday." He turns his head slightly to look at me. "It's the fiftieth anniversary of Spruce Fellowship. There'll be a big important service. I have to attend and help my dad prep for it. A lot of planning has gone into it. It's a big deal. I'll probably spend Saturday helping him out, too, come to think of it."

I nod thoughtfully. "Alright. I'll be there."

"You crazy? You hated how everyone stared at you the last time you waltzed into that church," he blurts, stiffening up. "No need to put yourself through all of that again. Not to mention—"

"You don't want me there?" I cut him off.

He turns to face me and frowns. "I didn't say that. I mean, it'll be long and boring, Cody. And how're you gonna get there? I don't want you driving on that bad leg and hittin' any innocent cats."

Sounds an awful lot like a bunch of excuses to me. "Innocent cats, huh. *That's* what you're concerned about."

"And everyone staring at you. Don't forget that."

"I think *you're* afraid of everyone starin' at *us*."

Trey doesn't much like that argument. "When did I say that?"

"You don't have to. The fear's written all over those scared lil' eyes of yours."

Now he looks downright indignant. "I'm not afraid."

"Great. Then I'm gonna get my ass to that old church one way or another, and I'll sit on that bench 'til my cheeks go numb and listen to your dad talk for an hour."

"Two hours," he states tersely. "And I wasn't afraid."

"Sure, you weren't." We're right back to my normal routine of antagonizing the poor bastard. "I'll be there."

"Well, then you might as well plan to torture yourself with the after-service reception at the Strong's." He eyes me. "They're hosting a big ol' party at their ranch. Of course I'll have to make an appearance, since it's in my father's honor—or the church's, if there's a difference between the two."

"I'll come to that, too, then."

He sighs with exasperation. "On what legs? Cody, don't be stupid. You can't drive all that way."

"I sure as hell can. And I do got legs. You were just between them a second ago suckin' me off."

Trey's eyes narrow. "An *injured* leg."

I grab hold of his shirt and pull that fucker right into my lips. Trey shuts right up as our mouths lock. Seconds later, two tongues wrestle between us, two combatting ocean waves of breaths push forward and pull back, and two bodies grow steadily stiffer, hotter, and squirmier.

I pull away and get a good look at him. "You gotta face him."

Trey, out of breath from my spontaneous assault on his lips, wrinkles his face in confusion. "Face who?"

"Your *daddy*." I'm still holding a fistful of his shirt. "You can't hide what's goin' on here forever. Your doors have to burst open soon enough."

A look of frustration crosses his face, and he shuts his eyes. I am a second away from saying something when he blurts, "I'm not afraid of you being there. Or ... my *dad*. I *want* you there, Cody. It's just that—"

"Good. Then if you ain't gonna let me drive, you're comin' and pickin' my ass up." I slap his shoulder, then settle back on the ground with my hands behind my head. "Now that all *that* shit's settled, let's talk about where the hell you learned to give head, 'cause I am *not* convinced that shit came naturally."

Trey shakes his head as he stares at me. "Oh, Cody Davis. The heck am I gonna do with you?"

I always get my way.

18

TREY

When Sunday morning arrives, I'm awake at exactly 5:58 AM. That's two whole minutes before my alarm clock goes off.

"You ready?" calls out my dad an hour later after I've taken a scalding-hot shower, dressed up in my finest shirt and tie, and got all our things together to take to the church.

I changed my tie six times. And now I'm changing it a seventh. "Gimme one more minute," I call back to him.

The first rays of sunlight make my bathroom window swell with its deep blue hue to go along with the birdsong and rushing morning wind outside. *I've never been a morning person.*

Yes, I do realize my neuroticism this morning has less to do with the actual church service and more with a certain someone who absolutely *insists* on attending.

"Well, hurry up, son," comes his voice from somewhere in the kitchen.

After undoing the tie yet again, I catch my own gaze in the mirror, freezing in place. *Scared eyes,* I note. I try not to hear Cody and his taunting words a few days ago when we were side by side in his backyard watching the sun setting.

"I ain't scared of nothin'," I mutter at the mirror.

My dad's face appears at the door. "Did you say something?"

I nearly jump out of my pants. "You can't sneak up on me!"

"Of course I can. I'm your dad. It's my job." He smiles cheerily. "What's the issue?"

"There's no issue." I glance down at the counter where my graveyard of ties resides, wondering if I should try the purple one again or the cerulean.

My dad taps a heavy finger on the green tie. "That one."

I quirk an eyebrow. "You are *not* giving me fashion advice."

"Your mother bought you that one, remember?"

His words pull my gaze right up to meet his. He doesn't look saddened by the words. He said them as casually as if all five-foot-nothing of her was standing right there by his side, smiling.

I feel a pang of emotion swell inside me. "Green one, it is."

"Looks more like teal to me. Or sea foam." He shrugs lightly. "But what do I know? Brings out your eyes."

I'm trying to have a moment with my dad, and all I can think of is what the look on his face will be when he sees Cody show up at the church. Will he be bothered? Will he actually be pleased?

I swallow hard. *Cody was right. I'm such a wuss.*

"Wear it," he tells me. "Then we will all be there together to celebrate Spruce Fellowship's anniversary. She would like that."

I meet his eyes. I don't quite know what to say.

My dad disappears before I figure out what to say anyway. His soft footsteps carry him back to the kitchen where I hear the crinkle of plastic bags, then the door leading out to the garage opening and closing.

I sling the green one around my neck, tie a quick and tidy Windsor, then appraise myself in the mirror one last time. I push a stubborn hair to the side. I flatten a tiny cowlick. Then I narrow my eyes. "Stop lookin' so dang spooked," I scold myself.

After a very short drive in my car to the church and an hour of setting up, we're ready for service to begin at nine. Already, there's a buzz of early birds outside chatting in groups and couples by the trees, on the grass, and in the parking lot. Half the choir has shown up and they're singing scales at the piano with Robinson, who is in an uncharacteristically good mood for once.

Figuring it's about time to pick up a certain someone from his house, I pull away from the church and head over to my car that's parked by the curb.

I make it halfway before a voice stops me. "Where you off to?"

It's Robby. He looks particularly snazzy today in a crisp white shirt and black tie. "Just running a quick errand," I blurt before realizing I could have (and perhaps should have) simply told him the truth. "The rest of the choir is warming up inside."

"I heard you've been heeding our advice about as much as Hal heeds street signs. Don't ever take him up on an offer to drive you home from a bar, by the way. That iron-footed fool is a dangerous driver, and that's stone sober."

I'm in front of my car door fumbling with my keys. "Heeding your advice? What're you talking about, exactly?"

"A certain Mr. Davis," Robby answers, his posture stiffening. "You've gone over there a heck of a lot of times, so I hear."

Blush creeps up my neck. "So? I told you all I would."

"True." He shakes his head. "I guess I should be thankful that you're still standing, and here, and emotionally sound."

"And without butter knife stab wounds," I point out as I at last manage to unlock my car with the stubborn key fob.

"Not that I *wanted* to be the one to say told you so ..."

"I'll be back in twenty minutes." I reach for the car door.

"Errand's on the other side of town?" Robby leans against my hood and crosses his arms. "Obviously you aren't pickin' up sweets from T&S's Shoppe, since that's just a five minute walk *that* way," he conjectures, nodding his head toward the street at my back.

I sigh. "You're an observant one, Detective."

"Observant enough to notice a change in your attitude, too."

"Attitude?"

"You're bouncing around all the time. Coming and leaving the church in a hurry. You haven't dropped in on a single one of our choir rehearsals this week."

"And you know dang well why," I tell him as I open my door and get one foot in. "I'm taking care of Cody. It's my job, now. That plus the clinic, and you're not left with too much time to spend in a church listening to Burton struggling to hit a high A-sharp." I pat the roof of my car. "I gotta go. I'll be back in twenty."

"I've got an eye on you," Robby says with a tap of his finger on his nose. "Just lookin' out for my buddy."

"Better look out for Burton's A-sharp instead." I slip into my car, pull the door shut, and thrust the key into the ignition.

I'm not sure how much more anxiety my body can take in one early Sunday morning.

As it turns out, it can take quite a bit more. I nearly miss a stop sign on the way to Cody's, my mind everywhere else but on the road. Gripping the wheel so tightly that my knuckles look like eight fat teeth, I drive through morning fog to the other side of town where I pray to every angel in the sky that Cody Brian Davis is dressed, ready, and waiting for me.

He's that and a whole bunch more. Cody picked out a fitted blue dress shirt that glues to every curve, ridge, and taper of his muscular body. His arms look totally sick in that shirt, bulging the sleeves near to ripping them, and the material pulls across his pecs exquisitely, cleaved down the middle by a sharp black tie. His pants are slate-colored and so distractingly formfitting that all I can do is dream of what his ass looks like in them.

"How do I look?" he asks at the door, then gives me the turn-around.

His ass looks like a dream. That's what his ass looks like. I bite my lip so hard, I might be drawing blood.

"That good, huh?" he asks with a short, dry chuckle. "Shit. I ought to dress up more often. You look so horny right now, I could suck you off right here on my front doorstep and—"

"Please, it's Sunday," I cut him off, ignoring the desperate racing of my heart at his totally crude and sexy words.

"I know what day it is." His lips purse, a glint of hunger in his eyes. "You look sexy as hell, by the way. As nice as those clothes might be, though, I'm sorta itchin' to rip them the fuck off of you."

I wince, despite how hot he's making me. "Cody! Lord help you, I'm gonna make you eat a whole dang bar of soap on the way to the church."

"Is that a euphemism for giving road head?"

I shut my eyes. *Lord, please don't make me regret this foolish act of so-called bravery.* "C'mon, Cody. We're gonna be late."

"Wait. I forgot somethin'."

"Dang it, Cody!"

Just when I think he's going to go get something, he presses me to the back of the door in an instant with his powerful hands pinning my shoulders in place and his warm, ferocious mouth on mine. He tastes minty fresh. His skin smells of soap and spice.

I can't explain it, but his tongue has clearly gained a few skills in the past few days since I last saw him.

And if the stiffening in my pants is any indication, my brain is already wondering where else his dexterous tongue might go if I spend another second here.

"*Cody*," I manage to hiss between our fevered kisses. "*We gotta go. We ... We have to ...*"

"That church ain't goin' anywhere," he tells me, unsmiling, his eyes feral and his nostrils flared from his passion.

And then the door shuts at my back, a green tie gets ripped off of my neck, and two heated bodies drop onto the couch like a pair of dogs wrestling for dominance with our deep, rasping breaths, snapping jaws, and uncontrollable paws.

19

TREY

By the time we make it back to the church, I'm in a panic over how late we are.

Twenty minutes late, that's how much.

"There's still people in the lobby. The service hasn't started," I realize with a spike of relief—which is swiftly followed by a spike of fear. "Oh, no ... My dad's held off the service for me. That has to be why it hasn't started. Oh, gosh."

"Calm down, it's alright," grunts Cody at my side as we slowly make it to the doors.

When we enter the lobby, I find only a few groups of people who haven't gone in to take their seats yet. They are dressed up more than usual, one woman even going so far as to wear a gown you might see at some fancy ball complete with a decorative hat.

Through the crowd, I see my father by the door. His face turns and finds mine, and then he hurries across the room to me.

Gulp.

"Hey there, Dad—" I start to say.

"I was a second away from calling you," he murmurs, a glint of frustration in his eyes. "What took you so long, son? I figured you'd forgotten something at the house, or—"

Then his eyes lift to meet Cody's. Cody, not helping in the least to diffuse any tension, stands there like a dang bodyguard, hands clasped in front of him, eyes untelling, face stoic as a stone.

My father, too polite to show any disapproval on his face in front of anyone but me, pastes on a plastic smile. "Cody Davis," he murmurs for a greeting, his voice falling as flat as his smile. "I'm ... pleased to see you could come."

"Happy to be here," is all Cody returns, his voice just as flat.

My father's eyes flick back to me. "You'll be needing the car, I presume, to take Cody home after service. I guess I'll ... get a ride with Robinson to the Strong ranch. Then, we—" His gaze lowers to my shirt suddenly. His eyebrows pull together. "Your tie."

"What about it?" I ask, bringing a hand to my chest—where I make the unfortunate discovery that I left my tie at Cody's.

You know. After he ripped the thing off of me in our wild making out.

"You took it off?" The sound in my father's voice might seem calm and polite to anyone else in the world. To me—to someone who knows him better—I hear an unmistakable pinch of hurt.

"I ... I was trying to fix the knot," I exclaim at once, the lie slipping off my tongue as easily as silk sheets off a dirty, filthy, *naughty* bed. "I'd made it too loose, actually. And then I lost track of time and ... and I forgot to put the tie back on. It's on Cody's bathroom counter. *Shoot*," I add with due frustration—and for the added effect of supporting this tale I'm spinning.

No matter the lie, it doesn't betray the *actual* hurt I feel inside.

The subtle wounded look on my father's face he's trying not to show makes it worse. I might as well have just resurrected my mother by some Heavenly miracle, slapped her in the face, then sent her right back to the grave.

Suddenly out of any words to utter to the despicable likeness of me, my father simply gives a stiff nod toward us, then turns to coax the rest of the stragglers into the chapel with soft words and bubbly enthusiasm—enthusiasm I know he's forcing on account of my having already ruined this momentous day.

"C'mon," grunts Cody with a slap to my shoulder. "It's just a stupid tie. You can borrow mine if it's that big a deal."

I really can't fault Cody for not knowing the significance of that particular green tie—which is lying abandoned somewhere on the floor of Cody's living room right now like a discarded tissue, like some dirty sock.

"Here." Cody turns me to face him. I watch him pull off his own tie. "You need it more than I do."

"No, you don't understand. It isn't *just a tie*. It's—"

"Stop whinin'. You'll look sharp in this one."

I thought he was going to just hand it to me. Instead, he flips up the collar of my shirt and wraps the black tie around my neck. I freeze, my eyes meeting his, as he gently starts to tie the knot. His hands are forceful yet caring, his eyes zeroing in on his slowly-moving fingers, calculating each step in the knot he's tying. He lets out a small grunt when he pulls it tight, smooths it out with a brush of his hand down my chest, then flips down my collar neatly over the tie. When the job's done, the corner of Cody's lip curls up in satisfaction, and he gives his work a quick nod of approval.

I smile mutedly at him. "Thanks."

"*You look sharp as a motherfucker,*" he whispers to me.

"*Sunday,*" I hiss back at him.

With us being the last in the lobby to go, Cody gives me an unexpected swat on my ass as I move on ahead of him toward the chapel. I fight off a blush and privately pray that my dear mother understands the mishap with the green tie.

Regardless of whether *she* understands, I somehow doubt my father ever will.

The chapel is packed from one end to the other. My father reserved a space up at the front for me, I belatedly recall, as we walk the aisle in search of a seat. Front row. As Cody labors with every step on the way, I feel the noise of the room gently ebb away as more and more eyes land on us, watching as we slowly trudge to our seats. In finally arriving at the front row, I realize there's—once again—only enough room for one person. Miss Martha, the lady by my spot, is kind enough to scoot over when she takes note of my extra guest. Her annoyed son and sleepy-eyed husband oblige us as well, and then Cody and I take our seats.

To my surprise, Cody glances over at her and grunts, "Thanks very much, ma'am."

She seems about as surprised as I am by his words, unable to even respond. Poor Miss Martha just stares at him with a tight, stony smile and beady, glassy eyes that make her look as if she's about to either faint, cry, or pass a kidney stone.

When my father takes the pulpit, the room stills to perfect silence. My father's eyes scan the room for a moment during that long stretch of quiet, as if to drink in each and every face that took the time to be here today.

"Thank you," my father states to the congregation. Even as calm and gentle as his words are, they reach every corner of the room. "Thank you for being here. Thank you for celebrating fifty long, enriching years with Spruce Fellowship. Thank you for your compassionate faces. I stand here, humbled by you."

No one makes a sound. This is perfectly normal, by the way. There is such reverence given to my father's words each Sunday, no one ever makes a peep until the very end.

In a strangely casual gesture, he comes around the pulpit and stands in front of it, arms crossed. "You know," he goes on, "I'm standing here, and I'm appreciating the silence of this room—the peaceful, trusting, beautiful silence—and it makes me realize that we live in a very *noisy* time, don't we? There is so much *noise* in the world today. Friends yelling at friends with their opinions and politics ... Right? Don't you hear it? Family shouting at family over trivial things ... Married couples fighting ... Noise, noise, noise.

"And then I stand here in this church, in Spruce Fellowship, here with all of you lovely people ... and I find I rather appreciate the silence. I do. I appreciate the *love* in that silence. The *trust* in that silence ... the *peace* we have within these walls.

"With so much noise in the world, it's a difficult time to be a follower of God. A confusing time. What do we believe is the right thing to do? Do we listen to those who campaign to restrict the rights of our women? Do we listen to those who demand that the good book be the law in this great country? Do we listen to those who fight so vehemently to deny human rights ... to our LGBT friends and family?"

Those last words make me freeze in my seat, astonished. It's been a while since he's said anything specific about gay people in church. His words of compassion are usually a sort of generalized blanket of "love everyone, no matter" he throws over us with his all-inclusive sermons. Hearing my father say those letters—LGBT—makes me feel a timely stroke of pride in him.

In the same thought, I still feel so terrible about leaving that green tie at Cody's. That was so irresponsible of me. So unlike me.

Not to mention my lying to him, over and over again, about

where I've been and what I've been doing.

These are the thoughts that loiter around in the "silent" and "super peaceful" mind of a guilty man, I taunt myself, frustrated.

"How can our love for God be heard in a world with so much noise?" my father asks the room. He begins walking down the aisle as he speaks. "I ... sadly know how some God-loving people are seen in this noisy, noisy time." He stops halfway down the aisle and addresses the left side of the room. "A gay couple hears that a God believer moved in next door to them, and that gay couple worries they'll be judged and looked down upon. Is that how we wish to be seen?" He faces the right side of the room. "We are all seen as riding on high-horseback. We are all living with our noses in the air. That's what all of that *noise* would have you believe."

My father returns to the pulpit. Everyone's eyes follow.

"I dream of a day ... hopefully soon ... when we start listening to one another again. Truly listening. Maybe that's what I hope that Spruce Fellowship could do for this noisy world of ours. We must humble ourselves at times to not defend our egos or 'win' an argument. When all of us are shouting into the noise, each of us trying to win ... we *all* lose."

My father faces us at the front, and I see a familiar twinkle of hope in his eyes, a twinkle I haven't seen in ages. For a moment, for *this* moment, I'm not sitting next to Cody. I'm sitting next to my mother, and the pair of us are watching with joy in our faces as my father does what he loves to do.

"I dream of a day when a God-believer moves in next door to the gay couple ... and the gay couple *sighs with relief.* 'Ah, yes, thank God,' they might say. 'Thank God we have good people next to us who will love us, break bread with us, and open their doors to us when we are in need.' I dream of a day when the portrayal of us on the news isn't to show what latest company we're protesting, or whose funeral we're picketing. Instead, we will be the ones supporting the less privileged. 'Oh, thank God *they're* here to feed the poor, support the grieving, and share their wealth.' What a dream it would be to spread the good word with the intent of making this world a better place instead of lining the pockets of mega-church celebrities and false prophets who live in mansions while their fellow man starves." He smiles. "That, my dear friends, is—and has always been—the vision of Spruce Fellowship. For fifty long years, it has never changed. Let us pray for fifty more."

Some brave soul in the back of the room applauds at that, shattering the silence.

For a moment, no one knows what to do. Even my dad seems surprised by it. But then, in a very short amount of time, the rest of the room follows suit. I'm not sure if my father's done yet, but he smiles into the rage of passionate applause that sweeps over the whole chapel—choirboys and Robinson included.

I feel the muscular movement of Cody's arms at my side as he applauds too, which pulls me out of my strange daze. I start to clap as well, though it is slow and distracted, my mind too deep in the muds of my oftentimes confusing relationship with my father. Do I sit here and be proud of his accomplishments and contribution— no matter how tiny—to making this big, loud world a better place? Or do I sit here and resent how he changes when we are alone?

Or am I just being a big baby, and his occasional aloofness isn't really all that bad compared to how he could be?

When the applause dies down, my father resumes his sermon. After the rest of it, followed by two beautiful performances from the choir (in which Robby was given a solo, to my half-surprise; after all, the boy has got a seriously beautiful, infectious voice) and a curious history lesson about the origin of Spruce Fellowship and my great-grandparents, the chapel is adjourned to enjoy their Sunday, to be kind and compassionate to one another, and—most importantly—to head on over to the big, extravagant Strong ranch where the celebration and festivities will continue all day long and into the evening.

Feeling somewhat obligated to do so, I stay in the lobby to greet and thank people as they leave, several of whom are heading to the Strongs'. I smile so many times at so many different people, my cheeks hurt and I'm nurturing a headache.

Cody stands awkwardly on the other side of the lobby against the wall. He bites the inside of his cheek, his face half-collapsed into something of a handsome, pensive scowl as he stares out the window, all the morning sunlight pouring over his face and, likely unbeknownst to him, making his eyes sparkle beautifully.

He looks like an angel.

And it gives me such a private firework of joy in my soul that I get to put my lips on that hunky, smoldering angel.

As well as do other things to him.

I shut my eyes. *Save them naughty thoughts for another day, boy.*

My father appears at the doorway. I've prepared a whole list of things I want to say to him, but he shuts all of that up when he puts his arms around me and pulls me in for an unexpected, tight hug. "Love you, son," he murmurs over my head. "It's a great day. It's a really great day. I wish your mother was here to see it."

The hug was unexpected as is. The tightness of it, I'm not sure I can trust. Is this a performance for the people still left in the lobby who are undoubtedly watching? Is this genuine and my dad feels bad for the words we had before the sermon? Is he just riding a high of giddiness after his service went so well? *Am I a crappy son for thinking these things?*

"She is," I mumble lamely into his chest as he hugs me, feeling like my sentiment is utterly insufficient, and having no idea in the world how to feel.

He lets go of me and pats my shoulders stiffly. "I'll see you at the Strongs'. Drive Cody home safely."

"He's coming with me," I blurt out.

My father takes precisely three long seconds to process that information—*one, two, three*—and then he simply says, "Very well. I'll see you at the Strongs'," he repeats, offers me a flat-lipped smile, then is buried the next instant in the crowds of people leaving, utterly lost to my eyes.

I sigh. I suppose in the end, my dad will come around. Really, he doesn't have a choice. Like Cody, he will just have to drop his stubborn, emotionless act and get used to the idea of Cody being more in my life, whether it's just at church events, or knowing that I am spending time alone with Cody in his house.

The thought suddenly leads me down a far less comfortable emotional road. Is it really Cody that my father is reacting to? Or does he suspect something's going on between us? *Is he okay with my being gay as long as I'm not actually ... being gay?*

I fight the scowl on my face, wrestle it into submission, and form a smile. *These are just thoughts and paranoia*, I convince myself. *Until you and your dad actually have it out, you don't know how he feels.*

Straightening up, I glance over the room at Cody. The little moment I had with my father must have pulled his focus from the window because he's looking right at me.

Despite the stone in my belly, I offer Cody a reassuring smile. Cody offers me a civil, microscopic nod in return.

Before I can cut through the room to join him, a sudden, unwelcome presence at my side stops me. "So you wanna tell me what Wednesday was about?"

I turn to the sight of Marybeth's face, which isn't unlike that of a disapproving mother's, her spaghetti eyebrows lifted so high they're lost in the forest of her bangs, and her lips pursed into a bright pink heart.

I wince. "Sorry 'bout that."

"I mean, what the heck, Trey? Your daddy reverend called me, I did a quick reckonin' in my head, and then I done lied to a man of *God* for you."

"Really, I'm sorry. I don't even know why I—"

"Why you scurried away from work with that Cody Davis and then lied to your daddy reverend about where you were?"

If she says "daddy reverend" one more time ... "Marybeth, listen. I need to say *thank you*, firstly, for covering for me. And secondly, I'm sorry that you even had to."

She takes a short breath, eyes Cody across the room, then turns back to me. Her voice lowers so much, I barely hear her next words. "So dish. I'm gonna find out one way or another."

I lift an eyebrow. "Dish?"

"Out with it. You know my main fuel is not food, or chocolate, or even hot guys at the supermarket. Ever since Jack up and left me and my daughter last year to pursue a career on the road—may his dear, groupie-lovin' memory rest in *piss*—I rely solely on one beautiful thing for my happiness: *gossip*. Pure, juicy, and totally delicious *gossip*. And I have a suspicion that *this* gossip will trump even that of the Jimmy Strong story I shared last week at the clinic." She swats me on the arm. Yes, it stings. "So *dish*."

I scowl at her resentfully. "There's nothing to ... *dish!* Cody and I have just ... bonded over this whole caretaking thing. He's actually a very ... cool guy. He's thoughtful. And he's funny. And we have quite a bit in common, hard as it may be to believe."

Marybeth squints at me so dang hard, it's like the woman's threading a needle. "I *know* there's more to it than that."

"There isn't. Sorry to disappoint."

"But you *slept* there, too. You know as well as *I* do that that is *not* proper protocol for a *patient*. We do not *sleep* at their houses unless *somethin'* is going on. And I *know* that *somethin'* is goin' on, *Trey Arnold*."

She's punching way too many words for my taste. I have the distinct feeling that if I don't give her more than just a crumb to nibble on, she isn't going to give up until I'm whittled down to the dang bone. "If you say anything—"

"Cross my heart and swear to Prada, won't tell a soul."

Yeah. Says the town gossip.

I glance back over at Cody. He's crossed his arms—*damn, they look so big and muscular and do something inviting to his chest*—and turned his attention back to the window, staring at the crowds as they dissipate into their cars or continue chatting on the grass.

I know I shouldn't say what I'm about to say. I know it with every fiber of my being that it's wrong. I've always been an honest and honorable person my whole life.

What's happened to me?

"Cody and I ..." I let out a sigh, then bring my voice down. All of Marybeth's attitude vanishes the instant she realizes I'm about to spill. Her face lightens and she leans forward, cocking an eager ear my way. "Cody and I ... Cody and I are sorta seein' each other. Sort of. I think."

Her eyelids flap open so wide, I'm shocked her eyeballs don't fall straight out.

"*Don't freak out*," I hiss beseechingly at her right away. "*It is very new. It is very sudden. And I am* trying *to keep my cool here.*"

Through her look of astonishment, Marybeth murmurs, "I just can't tell if you're toyin' with me, or ... or if you seriously ... truly ... *actually* just unveiled to me Spruce's second biggest secret since Tanner and Billy."

"Marybeth ..." I groan warningly.

"I'm still gatherin' myself here. You gotta give me a minute to process. I mean ..." Her eyes search the air in wonder. "You ... and Cody *freakin'* Davis ...?"

"*Marybeth!*" I hiss.

"Oh my *gosh*. You two ..." She lowers her voice and cocks her head. "*You two are doin' it??*"

"Stop."

"*And you're doin' it behind your daddy's back? And you're usin' me as an alibi??*" She shakes her head, her big hoop earrings dancing and bobbing against her neck. "I mean, goodness gracious, is it my *birthday* today? This is the best!"

"You can't tell anyone. Please."

"Cross my heart and *oh my gosh, I still can't believe it.*"

"Marybeth!"

She takes a deep breath, sneaks one more glance over at Cody, then lifts a hand with one-inch pink nails to fan herself. "*Lordy ...*"

"Are you headin' to the Strongs'?" I ask her at once, desperate for a change in subject, or to distract her from all her very visible reactions. "We're just gonna make a quick appearance, then—"

"Oh my gosh, you two are a 'we'. 'WE'! I can't stinkin' believe it. Your daddy's gonna marry the two of you, I hope you realize."

I let out a frustrated huff, then give up entirely. "I'm leaving. I'll see you at the Strongs' ... or not, I don't care."

"You better not play hooky from the clinic," she warns me as I head off. "I can't be your alibi for Henry, too! Hey, I *will* see you tomorrow, bright and early, Trey, you hear me??"

When I reach Cody, his eyes come down on mine. The tiniest hint of a smirk plays on his lips as he studies me. Just that slightly faraway, cocky look in his eye undresses me, stripping me of more than just my clothes; my worries fly right on out of the stained-glass windows in Cody's presence, too. I feel invincible.

"You ready?" asks Cody. "Because my ass is *starved.*"

I bite my lip, my eyes wandering down his body. I fight a very untimely urge to tug on his shirt and pull his face to my lips. "Mine, too," I confess, though I know it's far more than just my stomach growling in desperation for him.

20

CODY

I'm not looking forward to being in a house full of people I don't give two shits about.

I'm not looking forward to eating food across from eyes that won't stop staring at me, terrified of me for no good reason.

Or maybe for perfectly valid reasons.

I can be one scary motherfucker, given the right context.

"Thanks for doin' this," Trey suddenly volunteers.

I turn my head to him. "For what?"

"I know the only dang reason you agreed to get out of your house today and do any of this was on account of me." He shrugs. "It's nice to see that you care. So ... I just wanted to ... say thanks."

I'm not sure what to say to that, so I just slowly nod as I return my gaze to the front, watching the fields of corn whiz on by. It's true that I came out here for him. It's true that I would've kept my ass home otherwise. I wouldn't disagree with any of that.

But hearing him thank me for it makes me freeze up like a jagged cube of ice. What the hell do I say to that, anyway? *You're welcome? Thank you?* I'd be lying if I said this was easy for me. All I want to do is turn this car around, yank Trey's cute, tight tush into my house, flip him over, tear off his clothes, and make a man out of him bent over the edge of my bed. Literally, that's the only thing I want to do right now.

Instead, I'm swallowing anxieties, ignoring the swelling dread in my stomach, and putting on a face for Trey.

This shit does not come naturally for me.

The sprawling Strong ranch, despite being located way out in the middle of farmland-bum-fuck-nowhere—barely within the Spruce city limits—is the biggest, most extravagant piece of land I've ever stepped foot on. Having lived all of my life in this town, with the exception of the few years I was away, it's apparently unheard of that someone has never been out to the Strong ranch. Namely: me.

Well, here I go, ready to pop my Strong ranch cherry, thanks to the one and only Trey Arnold.

I gotta say, it doesn't disappoint. I'm staring at the expansive property out Trey's car window, and we haven't even turned onto their mile-long driveway yet. The main house is two stories, but those are two very big, very tall stories. I can't imagine how damned high their ceilings are. They could probably damn near fit a roller coaster inside.

The size of the house is damned intimidating. All I can think about is how many motherfuckers that place can hold. The church was one thing. This place is another entirely.

"You alright?"

I don't look at him. I just swallow hard, stiffly nod, and grunt a simple, "Yeah."

"You just tell me if you aren't," he murmurs. "Give me a sign or somethin', or just say it outright. We don't gotta stay long."

"Sure," I mutter back.

We park behind someone's beige minivan quite a ways down the driveway, since there's nowhere closer to the house to park, all the spots taken. That forces us to walk a good distance, which Trey sighs and bitches about. I insist it's no big deal and am first to hop out of the car.

It isn't quite noon yet, but the sun's cooking the air enough to wring a decent amount of sweat out of my skin by the time we're anywhere near the house.

"We're almost there."

"I'm fine," I grunt back to Trey, half-annoyed.

"Not too much farther, now."

Trey's trying to be encouraging, I know, but it just comes off as belittling, like I'm his little child who can't keep up.

Instead of being a whiny, annoyed little bitch on this big day, I nod toward the house looming ahead. "So you been here before?"

"Several times," he admits. "This isn't the first time that the Strongs have hosted a post-service gathering. This just happens to be the *biggest* one. Tanner and Billy will be there, obviously. I'll have to introduce you to them."

"Yeah? They your butt buddies?" I tease him. "Best fuckin' friends forever?"

He sighs and shakes his head. "I thought you were working on cuttin' *down* your cursing. Not increasing it like a foulmouthed—"

"I see." I nod knowingly. "So I'm right, then. I mean, it makes sense, y'all bein' butt buddies. There are only so many gay dudes that can fit in one small town."

He stops and faces me, a whole arsenal of sass on his face. We are just mere feet from the front steps of the wraparound porch. "For the record, Billy is a very busy man, and visiting his pastry shop is not something I do every day, as is evidenced by my small and *supple* figure."

I love provoking Trey like this. He gets so cute and spouts the damnedest things, like calling his own build "small and supple".

"So regardless of what you might think, Billy and I don't know each other all that well at all. Same goes for Tanner." He eyes me. "Now are we gonna play this jealousy game every time there's the possibility of another gay man in my presence? Or can we maybe have a little relaxed *fun* here at the ranch?"

Now it's my turn to stiffen up. "Jealousy game? When'd I say I was jealous? I ain't jealous."

Trey smirks victoriously. "Actually, I kinda like you jealous."

"I ain't jealous."

"Mmm-hmm." With that, Trey hops up the steps of the porch, then swings open the door to the house and looks back at me. "You comin'?"

Noise pours out of the door from the countless people who've already arrived from the church in droves. *Fuck me.* I begrudgingly follow behind, grunting as I force myself up the steps of the porch. Passing through the threshold is like entering a bubble of crazy. Unlike the atmosphere of the church where everyone is reserved and polite, here they let loose, laugh louder and freer, and don't hold back. There's a few faces here and there I *do* recognize, like the brother barbers Cale and Edison near the TV who used to cut my hair when I was a kid. Also there's Quincy sitting on the couch, who I went to school with, squeezed next to his uptight girlfriend (*shit, those fools are still together?*) whose name I can't recall. The rest of the room is a sea of unfamiliar faces, and a number of them are starting to take notice of us.

Is it in bad form if I tell them to fuck right off with their staring?

"You alright?"

"Quit askin' that," I retort. *This living room alone is one and a half times the size of my whole damned house.* "Said I'm fine."

"If you want to just chill here at the table," he suggests with a tiny nod at the barely-less-occupied-than-everywhere-else dining room, "I'll make my rounds, play my little part in this, and then be back to get you."

My instinct is to beg him not to ditch me here. The very next second, I'm resenting my own instinct, straightening my posture and lifting my chin to him in the face of all this anxiety flooding my system. I blame the lack of alcohol in my system these past few days for my jumpiness. I think that's what's making me a bit of a dick right now, too. *I should work on that.* "Nah. You go on and ... do what you gotta do," I tell him, keeping my tone firm. "I'll be fine."

"You sure? I mean, the other option is to drag you around this big ol' house with me and—"

"I'll be fine."

Trey gives me a short nod, a whispered thanks (which sounds more like an apology), and then the only damned reason I'm in this house disappears into the thicket of people beyond.

Somehow, his departure invites a shit ton of curious eyes my way. I ignore all of them and turn toward the dining room.

You don't have much more of this to endure. Just tough it out.

I stop by the big dining room windows, which show the rest of the porch as it wraps around to the side of the house. There are steps that lead to a (crowded) cobblestone area, which overlooks a wide, rectangular, crystal blue pool I'm sure could house a damned whale. A giant tent is erected there under which tables of food are set up with people gathered in clusters of laughing faces, gobbling mouths, and fluttering hands (all those sorry fuckers out there are fanning themselves). Beyond the pool, a path hugged by a white picket fence cuts across the field to some distant guest house or something, after which the path goes on to the woods and who-the-fuck-knows-where.

I wander to the other end of the dining area near the side door and kitchen, which is full of people fussing around, talking, and laughing loudly. A potbellied man chats with a tall woman by the counter. Three elderly women I recognize from the church drink together and cackle in the corner. A little girl by them curiously pokes at a cupcake in her hand, then licks the blue icing off her chubby finger like it's a strange and rewarding discovery every time.

A pinch in my leg makes me wince, stopping my meandering, so I finally take a seat at the long, fancy dining room table to wait out the rest of my sentence here. With my ass comfy in this chair and my weight off my stupid leg, I put my elbows on the table and bring my hands together, lace my fingers, and wait.

Maybe I can talk Trey into doing some of those "exercises" of his with me at Bell Lake after this to work out this kink in my leg. *Maybe our horny selves can come up with a few new exercises.*

"This seat taken?"

I look up. A bright-faced and handsome guy my age stands by the table, his watery hazel eyes on me. His plaid shirt—rolled up at the sleeves—is wet in spots, whether from sweat or from various liquids and ingredients spilling on him, I can't tell. I know who he is right away, but suspect from his demeanor that he hasn't yet recognized who *I* am. The poor guy offers me a lip-pressed, tired smile that suggests his day is already far too long.

I give him a short shake of my head no.

He yanks the chair out and plops himself right in it, all his due politeness gone. "I've about had it with dough. I don't wanna look at another blob of it that refuses to rise properly, or tastes too dry, or isn't flakin' the way I'm bakin' it. By the way, have you ever looked out for a table full of food in this damned heat?" he goes on, exasperated. "It's a shit show, I'm tellin' you. And then I get here and the food isn't plated right for the guests—*It's all about the presentation*—so I'm thinkin' I ought to have done it all myself. Call me a control freak, but that's how I roll. And of course I don't wanna let down Mama Dini, because that woman can be one very ... *very* particular individual. I mean, don't get me wrong," he adds quickly. "I adore my mother-in-law. Adore her down to her four-inch heels and up to her hair extensions. But boy, she has a *way* she wants things, and if she don't get it, then—"

He stops suddenly, then gives me an apologetic look.

"I'm sorry." He slaps a hand to his cheek and lets out a long, tired sigh. "I don't even know you, and here I am, dumpin' all my crap on your lap. Don't take this the wrong way, but you just look like a guy who ain't puttin' up with all this pomp and prestige any more than I can, and I happen to find that rather comforting." He extends a sweaty hand. "I'm Billy. I don't think we've met."

Despite wishing I was home and away from all these people, my back straightens in the slightest and I meet his hand with my own in a firm, solid shake. "Cody," I return, "and we *have* met."

He doesn't let go, but the handshake freezes as his eyes shrink and narrow on me, dubious. Then a bomb of recognition explodes over his face. "Holy crap. Cody Davis?"

I grunt for a yes, then let go of his hand and fold my arms on the table.

He lifts his eyebrows and lets his eyes wander, taking me in. "Wow. You ... You've ..." He shakes his head. "You've changed a lot since high school, Cody. I know it's been quite some time, but ... I mean, it looks like you've gained a person worth of muscle. You're big. You're jacked. Oh! Where are my manners?" he blurts suddenly, his eyes lighting up. "Thank you for your service, Cody. I know you were discharged and ... well, *everyone* does. I just haven't run into you around town since you've been back."

Billy's kind words about my service roll off my back like wind, forgotten the second they're uttered. "I ain't been back that long," I point out. I slap my arm suddenly thinking a mosquito had found it. There's nothing there. "Is there any beer around here?"

"Not here at the house. Only soda, juice, and punch, sadly. I could really go for one right about now, too. Well, y'know." Billy leans in. "*If I wasn't on the job, that is.* Would a soda be alright?"

No. "Sure," I make myself answer.

He gets up right away to fetch one. I watch as he goes. For a second, I was gonna ask him where they are and get up to grab it myself. The still-throbbing ache in my leg, however, made me think twice. *Sometimes, I just want to cut the fucker off.*

Then I think about some of my fellow soldiers who didn't have the luxury of a choice.

I close my eyes, annoyed with myself.

The sound of Billy dropping back into his chair jerks my eyes back open, and then he slides a cracked-open can in front of me with a smile. "Bottoms up."

I grunt a thanks, then kick it back, not caring what it is. *It's Dr. Pepper, by the way.*

"So where's your ma?" he asks. "Didn't see her at the service."

"I didn't see *you* at the service," I throw back.

"Admittedly, church has never been my thing, but I *was* there for the first half. I snuck out to make sure things were settin' up nicely here. We were expecting a stampede." He gestures toward the house around us. "We *got* a stampede."

After swallowing my sip, I set my can down heavily and shake my head. "My mom stopped goin'. Guess she didn't feel welcome anymore, being freshly divorced and the talk-of-the-town and all. I guess she was tired of the special brand of judgment you can only find in a small town church."

"Oh." Billy smirks in frustration. "Sorry. Didn't mean to rub up against a salty cut there."

"Not salty at all." I throw my can back again. I really fucking wish this was a beer; it sure ain't doing shit for my nerves. *Where the hell are you, Trey?*

"Strange that your mom felt judged. I mean, Reverend Arnold was just preachin' about how he means Spruce Fellowship to be the exact opposite of that. A safe place. Peaceful silence."

"Y'know what?" I spit back. "I fuckin' hate silence."

Billy doesn't say anything after that, perhaps uncertain how to respond without inviting any more of my anger. To be honest, I'm not sure why I'm acting so bitter. Billy's given me nothing to be annoyed about. If anything, he's downright pleasant.

Maybe that's what I'm having such a hard time getting used to. My buddies back at the base, we gave each other a hard time. We heckled each other ceaselessly. We pranked each other a lot. We'd spit insults at each other and cuss thirty times a sentence.

I don't do polite.

I don't do small talk and feelings and "saltiness".

And I don't do silence, no matter how long Reverend Arnold preaches about loving it so damned much.

"I didn't go to the service with my mom," I state, steering the subject back on track. "I went with Trey."

Billy lifts his brows in surprise. "Trey Arnold, really?"

"Don't pretend like you and the whole town didn't know he was comin' to my house to ... do his *nursin'* thing on me."

Among some other things.

Billy narrows his pretty hazel eyes at me. "You'd be surprised at the amount of gossip that *doesn't* make it past my ears. I try to keep out of it. Heck, between my business and Tanner's students, I've got too much noise in my ears to pay attention to much else."

I nod, then clutch my can with both hands and lean forward, hunching over it. "So where is the big man?"

"Tanner? Oh, he's around here somewhere." Billy looks over his left shoulder, then over his right. He appears to spot someone. "Hey, Mindy! You seen Tanner around here?"

A young woman I recognize from school turns away from the sink where she was rinsing something out. "What do I look like? His babysitter?"

Billy scowls. "Mindy, dang it."

She snorts. "I'm teasing. Jeez. I think he's helping at the tent." Her eyes meet mine, and her whole expression changes. She wipes her hands absently on her thighs and comes over. "Hey there."

That greeting was for me. "Hi," I return as dryly.

She tilts her head curiously, her dark locks of hair sweeping to one side. "You don't leave your house much."

"Don't got much of a reason to."

Billy gestures at me. "What got you out today, then? Trey?"

Both their gazes are on me expectantly. I shrug. "Well, yeah."

"He's our friend, so that makes you ours as well," Billy reasons with a nod. "You remember Mindy from school, too, I take it?"

"He sure does," Mindy answers on my behalf, eyeballing me. She shakes her head in wonder. "It's good to see you again."

I have no idea why she'd say that. Like Billy, we never knew each other. "Alright," I mumble back, unsure what to say.

"There you are!" hollers out a voice from the front door a second before it slams shut. It's Tanner Strong in the flesh. The man lives up to the reputation I remember him for: strapping, muscular, hot as fuck, but it's clear that the years of coaching the high school football team has softened his body a bit. Even though he and Billy don't have any little ones of their own, I can see a bit of "dad bod" in his abdomen area. In a t-shirt and jeans with a pair of shades over his eyes, he comes up behind Billy and grabs him muscularly by the shoulders with a deep growl. "Have you been hidin' from me or what?"

Billy throws him a teasing eye roll, then nods in my direction. "Hey, babe, you remember Cody Davis?"

Tanner flips his sunglasses up to get a look at me. "Well, look what the cat dragged out of the tree."

"That ain't the expression," mutters Billy with a smirk.

Tanner extends a hand toward me. "How's it goin', man?"

I take his hand and shake it firmly. For a second, it's like we're in an impromptu arm wrestling competition. Then I let go and nod at him. "Fine. Just fine."

"You're lookin' good. Hey, I'm awful sorry to hear about the circumstances of why you're back home, but thank you for—"

"Don't be sorry or thank me for nothin'," I cut him off.

Tanner presses his lips together, frozen for a second, and then he shrugs it off. "Alright."

"Take a seat," Billy tells his man, yanking out the chair next to him. "We're keepin' Cody company."

Tanner sits down and wrinkles his face. "What's goin' on?"

"He doesn't know anyone here other than Trey, who he came with. So we're—"

"That shit ain't true. He knows us," Tanner argues, then goes and gestures at the whole room. "He might know half the people here from high school or around town. He grew up here. Hell, I—"

"*Tanner*," chides Billy, kicking him under the table.

Tanner clears his throat, grunts, then folds his hands in front of him and faces me. "So tell me somethin', Cody. Why didn't you ever try out for the Spruce High football team? I always thought you had the drive and the body for it. You could've made it, easy."

Mindy and Billy lean in, curious about my answer. My eyes flit between the three of them. I'm not really used to having all this attention on me, especially after being in my house for months and interacting with exactly no one other than my meddlesome mother and, recently, Trey.

"I don't know," I answer honestly. "Guess you can say I ain't much of a team player."

"Bet the Army changed that in you," Tanner says back.

I consider it. Pete's face comes to mind. He's laughing, then slaps me on the arm and says something crude, which makes me laugh in return. It's the first memory I've had in a long time that wasn't him screaming, "*MOVE!*" at me. The thought puts me at ease, despite the stone of hurt still sitting heavily inside me.

"Yeah." I nod slowly. "It sure did."

"Some of the boys and I sometimes hit the fields out here," he tells me. "You should join us next time. Play some ball."

"*Tanner. His injuries,*" Billy whispers at him—loud enough for us to hear perfectly.

Tanner amends his statement. "Y'know. When you get better. You're doin' the whole physical therapy thing, I take it?"

Something between a pinch of annoyance and a stab of shame hits me. "Fuck that. Those quacks don't know what they're doin'."

Tanner lifts an eyebrow. "The hell you talkin' about? 'Course they know what they're doin'. They know a hell of a lot more than me or you would, that's for sure. You don't think I suffered my own fair share of injuries out there on the field? Shit, if I skipped physical therapy and my coach found out, I'd get my ass whooped right off. And that ain't no sexy euphemism."

Billy snorts at that and rolls his eyes.

It's right then that I spot Trey coming down the stairs. At his side walks the tall, bird-legged, curly-haired, giant-eyed, thin-as-a-pole-with-melon-boobs figure of Nadine Strong, Tanner's mom. Ever since Billy and Tanner came out, Nadine blossomed into a sort of Spruce gay mascot. I can't imagine what sort of spells she worked over on Trey the second he came out. She must have been ecstatic and invited him over for gay tea the very next weekend.

As I watch Trey and Nadine descend and vanish into the living room from those stairs, I turn my face back to Tanner with half a glower. "Tell me why the hell everyone in this damned town is so determined to get into my business like they got none of their own? Like they gotta get to the bottom of everythin' they hear?"

"The only thing *you* need to worry about gettin' to the bottom of is that can," Billy retorts with a nod at my soda. "And the trick to the Spruce hens—*if you need a trick*—is to not give one single flyin' fruitcake about anything in this town except for yourself."

"Unless it has to do with *actual* fruitcake," cuts in the slightly nasally voice of Nadine Strong, who appears like a ghost from a graveyard—a very tanned, thickly-make-upped ghost. She gives Tanner's shoulder a squeeze, leans down to kiss him on the cheek, then eyes me from across the table. "How are you doin', Mr. Davis? I didn't expect you to turn up. You're lookin' awful snazzy."

I straighten my posture, my face flat and unsmiling. "Thank you, Mrs. Strong," I reply simply enough, palming my Dr. Pepper but refraining from taking a sip in front of her—something about manners and being a decent guest.

"You're welcome. 'Course, you always were. I don't know why you don't come out more often. You got the dang face of a Grecian God or somethin'."

Trey is by her side. Likely from the long, tireless conversation and neuroticism of Mrs. Strong, the poor boy wears a somewhat stressed expression, yet otherwise looks calm as a breadstick.

Tanner leans forward suddenly. "Look, I wasn't tryin' to get all into your business," he says, returning to the subject Nadine's arrival interrupted. "I'm just sayin', one dude to another, you can't ignore the long-ass recovery process. It sucks, but you ain't really livin' your life if you spend every day being stubborn and in pain."

I stare at Tanner, expressionless and silent.

"About time someone *else* told him," mumbles Trey as he jabs his hands into his pockets.

I eye Trey just as coolly, still silent.

"Oh, y'know what? I was just talkin' to Trey here about you," Nadine practically sings, cutting off Tanner who looked like he was about to say something else. Her hands dangle in front of her to show off her polished, talon green fingernails that match her flashy green getup as she talks. "You are a *brave* young man, Mr. Davis. Served three years in the Army, now did you? That is just simply honorable. Hey, Billy," she says suddenly, speaking a mile a minute while she snaps her fingers. "Outside needs your attention. I don't think your sweet well-meaning employees know what in tarnation they're doin' with your teriyaki skewer thing-a-dings."

A look of dread passes over Billy's already overtired face. "Oh, mother-lovin' crap." He's out of his chair and through the side doors the next instant, calling out someone's name in frustration.

Nadine slaps the table at once, yanking my attention right back to her. "You went to school with my boys, didn't you?"

I let go of my soda and cross my arms. "Sure did."

"Why the heck didn't you join the football team? You look—"

"Already been through that, mama," Tanner throws over his shoulder with a pinch of annoyance, then he nods my way. "Was just givin' him a hard time about not doing his physical therapy."

"Oh, I know a *great* therapist," Nadine sings. "He's a doll. He does this amazing thing with his hands ..."

Tanner lets out a loud sigh. "Mama, that's a *masseuse*. Cody here does not need a damned *masseuse*."

She smacks her son over the back of his head. "Everyone needs a masseuse!"

Mindy, as if coming to life, comes around the back of Tanner and puts a gentle hand on Nadine's arm. "Mrs. Strong, weren't you gonna show me a brochure for that nice place with the water wall Joel and I can have our wedding at?" She eyes us importantly. I suspect she thinks she's doing us a favor by pulling her away.

Nadine, oblivious as ever, perks up with excitement. "Oh, oh! Yes, yes! It's up in my room. Come, sweetheart. I'm about to *blow your dang mind.*" Off the pair of them go.

Trey scoots into the chair Billy was sitting at, then leans in close to me. "We can go already if you want," he murmurs quietly. "I've pretty much made my rounds. I mean, there's a few people I could talk to, but I don't have to, really. I know you've been ready to go since the moment we walked through that door, so ..."

My eyes survey the room as I consider his question. Nadine and Mindy are halfway up the stairs, arms linked as Nadine talks the poor girl's ear off. Through the window at my back, I see Billy bossing around the others at the tent while he repositions and corrects the ample plates of food set out along the tables. The scene almost makes me chuckle. Why the hell weren't the pair of us friends back in the day? Billy's a pretty decent guy, even if he's got a bit of a stick up his butt all the time.

If I'm being honest with myself here, I can't remember the last time I actually felt this relaxed outside of my house.

And I'm not even drinking.

"Cody?" he murmurs, concerned.

I face Trey and give him a shrug. "Y'know, I'm ... thinkin' we could maybe hang around a bit longer."

The look of surprise on Trey's adorably rosy face is enough to make me smile.

21

TREY

Six hours later, we're still at the Strong ranch.

News update: Cody found the beer.

Well, more accurately, Billy went and snagged a case from their house, which is down the path lined by a white picket fence that leads into the woods where a small lake is. Their house rests by that lake with a long pretty dock and a ton of fish. I went with him while Cody and Tanner sat by the pool, kicked back, with plates of Billy's food left over from the party. By the time we returned, Cody had finished two helpings of just about everything. I was equally impressed and unsurprised.

After most of the guests had made their departure, only the four of us remained plus Mindy and a couple others who were in the house with Mrs. Strong hanging out. They basically banished us out here while they chatted, likely due to them wanting to gossip in secret about stuff—*cough, Cody Davis, cough*. So with our legs kicked up in our poolside chairs, we've been enjoying the evening breeze as the sun sets fire to the tips of distant trees.

I don't know if it's the beer or if Cody's really getting along with Spruce's famous gay couple, but we seem to be cracking each other up with all of the stories, Army anecdotes, and ridiculous overshares between us. Maybe this is what Cody's needed all this time: a kick-back with a trio of gay guys where he can be himself.

Except Cody's not really being himself. *If he was being himself, he'd have his hands all over me right about now.*

Considering he's sitting in the chair right across from me and keeps scorching me with his eyes, it's a surprise he hasn't simply leapt from his chair to pounce on me, regardless of our present company. I'm afraid that every time I look at him, I'm provoking him worse, and if I'm not careful, he very well *may* pounce on me.

Our stare-off is interrupted with another college anecdote from Tanner, who apparently had experimented in a fraternity for exactly one and a half months before realizing what a horrible mistake it was. Cody makes some crude comment I don't hear, and the two lovebirds burst into laughter.

"Shit, you're a lot more fun now than you were back in high school," Billy exclaims after emptying another can of beer and tossing it behind him at a pile they started hours ago.

"The hell you mean?" Cody snorts at that. "I was the funnest motherfucker in our graduating class."

Tanner shakes his head. "Nah, I think that reward goes to the sassiest bitch Spruce has ever known: Lance."

"More like *bitchiest* bitch," Billy retorts with a huff.

"He was hilarious!" exclaims Tanner. "That guy wouldn't take crap from no one. I know *you* don't like him, but—"

"Yeah, well, last I heard, that queen took off halfway across the country for fashion school. I couldn't get him to talk to me if the life of Timmy Tackler depended on it."

"Tackler? Your mama's cat?" Tanner laughs. "The hell would Lance care about your cat for?"

"Never mind, I'm drunk. My analogies are poor. Why are we like that, by the way?" Billy wonders aloud suddenly. "Why do gay guys, in the presence of other gay guys, sometimes act all aloof and uninterested in even a simple hello or acknowledgement of each other's existence? As if being complete dicks to each other is the way to attract one another."

I can't help but let out one dry chortle. "Sounds familiar," I mutter to myself with a sneering look at Cody.

Tanner and Billy look my way.

Shoot. I didn't mean for that to be so easily heard. "Nothin'," I say right away, shooing them off. "I just meant—"

"Is there someone in your life," Billy asks, his voice carrying the tiniest hint of innocence, "who's givin' you shit?"

I look anywhere but at Cody. "Nope."

Billy squints at me, dubious.

"No *Lance* in your life?" asks Tanner teasingly.

Sparing me the opportunity to answer, Billy huffs and spins to face his husband. "All that Lance bitch ever did was ignore me in high school—a time when we *all* need friends—and prance around like a peacock. I *pray* there isn't a Lance in Trey's life."

Tanner snorts. "He probably wanted your nuts."

"I wasn't even attracted to him! I definitely wasn't a threat to him, either. Hell, we could've been friends. Ugh, I will *never* get it."

I decide to shift the subject a tad. "Tanner, I heard what your brother did for prom. Marybeth at the clinic told me."

"Oh, you mean Jimmy's little attention-stealin' stunt?" Tanner laughs and shakes his head. "Askin' Bobby to the dance. I swear, that kid will do anything if he knows it'll get all the girls swoonin' over him."

Billy snorts. "Askin' a boy to the dance is gonna make the girls swoon? That doesn't seem like sound logic to me."

"Of course it is. They know Jimmy's straight. The fact that he would go and do somethin' so *sensitive* and *thoughtful* and shit for his gay buddy Bobby? That's a sure recipe for pussy-melting if I ever heard it."

Billy gags and slaps a hand to his cheek. "My husband did *not* just say 'pussy-melting'."

"Every guy needs a buddy like that," Tanner goes on, ignoring his husband's dry heaving. "A loyal buddy who'll go to the ends of the planet for him. Fuckin' beautiful, really."

I find myself nodding, a faint smile on my lips. "Yeah. It's a beautiful thing, for sure."

My tiny comment draws too much attention my way, which I promptly notice. Billy, picking right up on the awkward silence, eyes me with importance. "Trey, if you don't want to tell us who you're seein', you don't have to."

I scratch a spot on my neck. *Time to play the evasion game again.* "Who said I'm seein' anyone?"

"You haven't been to the Shoppe but once in the past few weeks," Billy points out. "Mindy says you have that look about you, and she's basically a relationship psychic. A couple days ago, Marybeth said you've been acting odd. So I figured it's either drugs or a guy. And it sure as spit ain't drugs."

I feel my stomach trying to climb right out of my mouth. Billy has always been a bit persistent. "Are you kidding me?" I throw back at him, playing it off. "Relationship psychic? Acting odd? I ain't actin' any differently than I usually do, and that's a fact. Besides, I don't think you know me quite well enough, Billy, to know whether I'm actin' funny at all."

"He *is* acting funny."

The new comment comes from Cody himself. I turn my eyes to him, wide and unblinking, clearly and utterly unable to contain my astonishment.

"Yeah! Isn't he?" Billy shakes his head. "My instinct is never wrong. Look, just tell us and put *yourself* out of your misery."

"Yeah, tell us," pushes Tanner as he kicks back his beer.

Cody leans forward in his chair, his elbows propped on his knees. A superior sort of smirk rests on his face as he stares at me. "Yeah," he prods me just as ceaselessly as they do. "Go right on ahead, Trey. Tell us who's got you wrapped around his finger."

I stare Cody down so hard, I swear it ought to be peeling his face right off. Seeing as I don't have that superhuman power, I guess it just looks like I'm trying to leap into his mind and figure out what game he's playing right now. Does he *want* me to tell them? Or is he testing me to *not* tell them?

I scoot forward in my chair, bringing my butt right to the edge of it. Billy and Tanner, like two lazy fools in the back of a movie theater, remain leaning back in their chairs, but their undivided attention is on me, waiting for the spill.

"Okay," I finally relent. I tilt my head, feeling smart. "I can tell you one thing. The guy is, at times, a total *prick*."

Wow. Listen to me. Using words like "prick". On a *Sunday*.

I'm such a big boy now.

Cody, however, looks entirely unaffected by my statement. In fact, I might say that a pinch of pride just crossed his otherwise affectless expression.

"He's definitely moody," I go on, staring right at Cody as I do so. "Totally insufferable. Sometimes, I'd even say he's arrogant. I mean, this guy thinks he knows everything."

"Ugh, those ... are the *worst*," Billy moans—his tone suggesting that he's far more turned on by the description than put off.

The look of amusement still lives and thrives on Cody's face. He is getting a major kick out of this.

"So?" prods Billy, waiting. "Is he hot?"

I smirk. "*He* sure thinks he is."

"Yeah, yeah, but do *you* think he is?" asks Tanner impatiently.

With my eyes never having left Cody's, I bring my voice down. "Yes. He is. I'd be lying if I didn't say ... how affected I am around him. He takes my breath away. And he ..." I struggle for the words. A breeze plays at my hair as they come to me. "He challenges me."

The smug look on Cody's face is now gone. It's collapsed into something far more sincere. I don't know if I'm going too far to say my words are inspiring emotion in him, or moving him in any way he wouldn't be caught dead admitting out loud.

Or maybe he privately thinks I'm full of crap.

"How does he challenge you?" asks Billy.

Just in time, the click-clacking of high heels meets our ears as Mrs. Strong slips out of the house and saunters over to us. "*Bo-o-o-o-oys.*" She stretches that one word out like sticky toffee, making three and a half syllables out of it. "I'm bringin' y'all some yummy munchies from the kitchen. Couldn't fit them in the fridge." On the table between our chairs, she sets down a platter full of odds and ends. "Mindy's about to head out, Billy, and ... you might want to talk to her. She's havin' *thoughts* about Joel."

Billy sighs. "Thoughts? Jesus, can't the two just get freakin' married already?" He pushes out of his chair and trudges toward the house, but not before throwing over his shoulder, "I'm gonna get more out of you, Trey, when I'm back!"

Mrs. Strong watches him go for a second, then spins onto us, eyes wide and bewildered. "What did he mean by that?"

"Nothin' at all," I bellow out too quickly.

As if able to literally *sniff out* the gossip on the tip of a person's tongue, she cocks her hip and gives me a look. "You and I, hon, are overdue for grabbin' a brunch after one of your daddy's services or something. We have a *lot* to talk about."

"*Mama* ..." complains Tanner, apparently knowing where this is going already.

"Hush, you. Now, Trey, listen up." She props a hand up on her hip and tilts her head, all her curls and highlights bouncing. "There is this fine ... *fine, fine, fine* young man from Fairview I want to introduce you to. I am *certain* that the two of you—"

"I'm not really, uh ..." I straighten my back. "What I mean to say is, I'm not really lookin' for anyone. With all due respect."

Mrs. Strong looks like she was just fed a sock. "Excuse me, young man? 'With all due respect'? Do you *know* who I am?" she bleats rhetorically, a scandalized hand to her chest. "I mean, did you hear me properly? This boy from Fairview is a *catch*. He is stinkin' *adorable*. He's *smart*. And, well, maybe he's got the sense of humor of a tortoise, God bless him, but he is *schooled*. Just like you! Five years in a really prestigious law school. And y'know what *that* means." She wiggles her eyebrows suggestively and pinches her fingers together—*money, money, money.* "I'm not gonna hear any more about this. I'm settin' up the date for next week, whenever you're available. Are you off from the clinic Monday? Yes or no?"

"Really, Mrs. Strong," I persist. "Please. Don't schedule a date. I'm not looking for anyone."

"And why not?"

"Because Trey's already found himself a man!" blurts Tanner to the sky, to the yard, to the pool, to the house, to the heavens. *That boy has a voice that carries.* "So leave the poor guy alone about it, will ya? We were *just* tryin' to get him to spill before you came!"

She about craps her pants. "Holy Lord. Are you yankin' my noodle right now?"

Tanner slaps a hand to his face. "*That ain't the expression.*"

"Dear Diary, who?" she sings as she takes a seat on the chair Billy vacated and crosses her legs, her eyebrows lifting as high as her pitch just did.

My throat's tightening. I think I'm allergic to something Mrs. Strong is wearing. Or saying. Or doing.

"Just a guy," I answer with due vagueness. "I'd really rather not talk about it just yet. Not today, not right now. It's ..." I shut my eyes, likely visibly frustrated by my lack of being able to come up with a lie quickly enough. "It's something I'd like to keep private for now. I don't even—" Blood rushes up my cheeks like a fire. My eyes flap open and search for Cody's across the way. He is still staring at me with that same blank, unreadable look. "I don't even know if it *is* a ... thing."

"Hon, you know that anything you tell me stays between us."

I find my balls and eye her. "Yeah, yeah, you and your whole *Saturday romance book club.*"

Mrs. Strong finds that twenty times more hilarious than she does offensive, throwing her huge head of curls back and cackling. "Oh, Trey, you are just *darling!* See? This is why we need to do regular brunchin'. We just have so much dang fun together! Anyway, has your father already left? He said he was going to take home the rest of the carrot cake and didn't."

I grab hold of her shift in topic as desperately as a boy lost at sea clings to a life raft. "I'll be happy to take it home to him."

"Good boy, very good boy." She pats me on the cheek strong enough to almost be a slap, then grabs hold of my chin and faces it to her. "You need to come to one of our Strong family dinners. I'm tellin' you. They're huge. And you'd better bring this mystery boy of yours, too." She lets go of my face, rises, then heads back to the house. On her way, she throws over her shoulder, "I *will* find out who it is, Trey. I've got my ways."

After she's gone, a calm silence falls between the three of us who remain. The only sounds that fill that silence is the steady breeze, the tiny trickles and giggles of the pool water lapping on the stone, and Cody's strangely deep, resonant breaths.

My eyes lift to meet his. The look of amusement has returned to them.

"It's you two, ain't it?"

Cody and I both look over at Tanner, who's frozen with his beer halfway to his lips, his knowing eyes on the pair of us like he's been waiting for an hour to say those very words. I don't say a word in response as I stare at the football star of Spruce, paralyzed by his bluntness toward us.

Then Cody answers: "You're damned fuckin' right it is."

22

TREY

It is a very surreal, unexpected emotion I'm feeling as I drive away from the Strong ranch. It's pitch black by now with nothing but the darkness in all directions, making the narrow farm roads nerve-wracking to navigate. Add to that the extra jolt of terror that suddenly revealing ourselves to Tanner planted in me, and you get underarm sweating, nerves, and a tight grip on the wheel.

"You look freaked the fuck out," notes Cody helpfully from the passenger seat.

I keep my eyes on the ridiculously skinny road. I'm probably driving ten miles per hour, if that. "Can you make sure the carrot cake isn't tipped over or wonky in the back seat?" I ask, my voice strained with tension.

"It's fine," Cody says without actually looking. He props an elbow up on his door. I feel his eyes burning the side of my face. "What's the issue, then? You mad at me?"

"No." I swerve for a moment, thinking I just saw a rabbit dart onto the road. False alarm.

"Well, you're mad about somethin'."

"I'm just trying not to get us *killed* out here on this dark road."

"We probably could've stayed at the ranch," Cody points out. "I mean, it ain't like they don't have the space."

"Didn't want to impose more than we already had."

"Impose? You kidding? Billy and Tanner, the way they were lookin' at us like a pair of hot fudge sundaes with cherries on top, hell, they might've even been interested in a four-way if we drank a little more."

I feel sick, like tiny electric fish are swimming around inside me. "I wasn't drinkin' at all, if you didn't notice." I squint, unsure if the main road is coming up yet or not. *I better not have missed it. If I missed it and we're lost out here circling farm roads for hours ...*

"Oh, I noticed." Cody snorts, then turns serious. "Pull over."

"Why?"

"I'm horny. Pull over."

"No. You crazy? I'm tryin' to get us home. It's so dark that my headlights are blinding. And I—"

He cuts me off by reaching into my lap like an ape going for a banana—*my* banana—and he undoes the button of my pants.

My hands grip the wheel tighter as my eyes flash wide open. "Cody, damn it!" I shout out, then feel a stab of shame for letting myself curse. "Stop!"

He succeeds in freeing my cock—which went hard the second it realized what he was doing—but then he lets go when I protest, lifting his half-lidded eyes to me. "The hell is your problem?"

"You!" I shout out, my face flushing red. Whether it's with anger or lust, I can't tell just yet; my emotions are very confusing right now as I awkwardly tuck away my cock one-handed. "You're talking about *four-ways* and ... trying to get me out of my clothes *in the car* ... while I'm trying not to *drive us into a cow* or somethin'."

"There ain't no dang cows out here."

"Telling everyone about us was just as much my decision as it was yours, and you ripped that choice away from me!"

The slight shift back in topic gives him pause. "Huh? Ripped the choice away from you? Shit, you're such a drama queen, Trey. Everyone already knows about you. You didn't reveal anything tonight. It was *me* who came out."

"But you came out as ... my ... *person-I-was-involved-with.* That's something I wasn't quite ready for yet. And I ... I'm ..."

Suddenly, the moment in the church earlier today when I confessed the whole thing to Marybeth rushes forth. *I did the same thing, and Cody wasn't even at my side to react or share in it.* Shame floods my system, shutting me up. It mixes in with my anger to create a nervous cocktail of confusion inside me.

How can I be so indignant to Cody when I become the world's biggest hypocrite in doing so?

"I see," he mutters, settling back into his seat. "I guess it all makes sense when you look at it that way."

I flinch, still angry, still confused. "What way?"

"You only have a problem with it 'cause it's *me*. I'm the bad boy you don't want nothin' to do with. Not in public, at least."

"That ... That isn't true." I think I see something on the road, jerk the wheel, then let out a frustrated sigh all over my hands. That's twice now I swerved for something that wasn't even there.

"Yeah, it is."

"No, it isn't. I brought you to the church this morning, didn't I? I brought you to the Strongs'. I'm not ashamed to be seen with you in public. Not at all."

"Yeah, well, as long as it's in the context where you come out lookin' like the white fuckin' knight." He chuckles darkly at that. "As long as you're still the righteous, pure, perfect Trey Arnold who's comin' to the rescue for troubled, wayward Cody Davis."

I shake my head. "That's not it and you know it."

"Sure sounds like it to me. Makes a shit load of sense, too."

"Do you even know what it's like to be me?" I ask him. "To not even know what it's like to give your body to someone else? Just a *kiss* outside of wedlock feels like I'm betraying God's great plan for me. And it isn't even the gay thing. Man, woman, it doesn't matter. My body is sacred. And until I met you—"

"Yeah, yeah. I went and ruined that image you're trying to uphold. The whole town watches your every move. Your *daddy* judges you. I get it."

No, he doesn't. It's not that at all. But I'm too heated and too confused to make an intelligent argument, so I simply shake my head and lower my voice. "Never mind."

He sits there for a while, staring at the side of my face. "Is it the four-way thing? Did that piss you off? I mean, they're not my type. I was half-kidding."

I snort. "*Half*-kidding."

A hint of concern touches his voice. "What? I was."

"They're not your type?" I get out, unable to help myself. *I said I was going to shut up, and here I go, acting on yet another impulse.* "Tanner Strong? Bulking muscle, gorgeous face, and attitude for days? Billy Tucker? His cute smile and sexy bod? They don't do it for you? You really want me to believe that?"

"Sounds like you're a lot more attracted to them than I am."

"Do you even know what that sounds like to a person like me? A person who's been ... repressed and disciplined and praying for God's good grace my whole life? I'm not one of your Army buddies. You can't talk about ... about *dick* and *pussy* and ..." I shudder, feeling the blood in my face. "I just don't see sex the way you do."

"Sure, you do," he argues back. "You get horny, don't you? You want things. I oughta know. I'm the one you're wantin' those things with. Difference is, I'm able to say it out loud."

I don't respond, choosing to focus on the road completely. Of course, that's an utter lie; my focus is thoroughly divided. I'm thinking about Cody's words, which sting me to the core of who I am as a person. I'm thinking about Tanner's reaction to me and Cody being a "thing", whatever we are. Tanner will tell Billy. Billy will tell Mindy. Mindy will tell Joel. Any of those four loudmouths will tell Mrs. Strong—a louder mouth. She'll brag to her friends. Her friends will whisper to *their* friends. Come next Sunday, the whole church will be abuzz with the news. Every single person.

Including my father.

Why does that scare me the worst of all?

"Listen to us," mumbles Cody, his tone calmer. "We're already an old married couple, bickering on the way home from a party." Cody chuckles at that, shaking his head and slapping a hand to his face. I don't make a single sound. "Fuck, I am drunk and sleepy and horny all at once. Wouldn't recommend this combination."

He's trying to smooth things over, I tell myself. *Take the bone he's throwing you. Don't be a little moody snot.*

But I don't take the bone.

I stubbornly still don't say a thing.

"There it is," he murmurs, pointing. "The road you're lookin' for, I think. The way out."

The way out, he says.

There's no way out of this.

I turn onto the road, and then it opens up to a far more decent size and carries us toward the welcoming lights of Spruce. It isn't a very bright town at this time of night, but after the pure and silent darkness of the farmlands—which don't even have streetlights, by the way—Spruce shines like the damned sun at noon.

"Can you at least talk?" he murmurs. "Say *somethin'*, Trey? I hate the silence. I really ... *really* fuckin' hate the silence."

I still don't say anything, not even to relieve this wordlessness between us he's so bothered by. *Let him be bothered by it.*

As I drive the more familiar streets, mercifully and brightly lit by the occasional streetlight or lit-up storefront sign, I keep my lips closed and pay attention to every stop sign. They so remind me of the way I felt that first day driving to Cody's house, how the stop signs all looked like octagonal red flags, warning me over and over to stay away.

I'm not used to arguing. I hardly ever do it. It's a skillset I am not particularly experienced in. I don't know how to negotiate. At times, I don't listen very well. I get angry first, frustrated second, then give up and retreat into my shell to listen to the ocean waves pull in, rush out, pull in, rush out. I know I have growing up to do.

It would be a lot easier to do with my mother still here.

See, whenever I hide in this shell of mine, I think of her. Her laughter. Her soothing words. The touch of her holding me in one of her tight, understanding embraces. I think of that seashell by my bedside, the one sitting right next to Mister Happy, the one my mother gave me. I listen for the ocean every night before I sleep.

Except that night I stayed at Cody's.

Is that when everything went wrong? I let go of a lot of things that night. My personal inhibitions. My discipline toward myself. My honesty with my father. My innocence of others.

Others like Cody. Does he even know what he took from me?

Does he know what I gave to him?

I come to a stop in front of Cody's house, pulling the car into park, then the pair of us sit there in silence. Cody doesn't move. I don't push him out of the vehicle. We sit and do nothing but listen to one another breathe.

"I don't do apologies."

I blink. *Really? That's what he's gonna start with?*

"Do you know why I don't do apologies?"

I press my lips together, wordless, and simply shrug.

"Because everything I say and do," he tells me, "is somethin' I *meant* to say or do. Even if it's wrong. Even if it's somethin' I'll be ashamed of later. When I kissed you at Bell Lake, I wanted to. And I had good intentions. I wasn't tryin' to hurt you when I took off all your clothes here at my house, either. I wasn't tryin' to hurt you when I dragged you into that shower with me. I'm not gonna go and apologize for turnin' your life upside-down, Trey Arnold, and I hope to fuck you don't expect that of me, because I *ain't* sorry."

I face him, my eyes like two watery stones as I hear him out. His jaw is tightened up with so much tension, I see a dimple buried in his whiskers I never noticed before. *It's a really cute dimple.*

"I told Tanner 'bout us 'cause I ain't ashamed. I don't care who the hell knows. Maybe you ought to grow some balls and not care either."

"I wish it was that easy," I state, my voice dry from not having said a word in the past twenty minutes. "But do you have any respect—any at all—in your heart for a union of holy matrimony? M+F only Doesn't that level of commitment mean anything to you?"

Cody's eyebrows pull together. "Of course it does."

"I ... want that someday. I want what Billy and Tanner have."

He tries to get ahead of me. "You're sayin' I'm not worth it."

"No, that's not what I'm saying."

"You want a husband. You want a man who's gonna be there for life, stand by you like a rock, and never abandon you."

"Yes, all of that. But I'm not saying that you're not—"

"And you think because I tease about foursomes that I'm not wantin' the same things," he says, getting to the point. "You think I'm disrespectin' their marriage by joking—whether serious or not—about us havin' dirty, naughty, impure sex with them."

"Cody ..." I sigh. "It's getting late. I need ... I need to get home. You need—"

"The point I was tryin' to make wasn't to piss you off," he goes on. "It was to make you see that you're an alive and sexual person just like anyone else, regardless of what you believe in. It was to make you see *how very fuckin' alike we actually are.*"

I stare at him, my lips parted, any words I might have uttered staying frozen to my tongue like chips of ice.

"The damned truth is ..." Cody undoes his seatbelt to turn his body completely my way. "I don't want anything with anyone else. In a way, I never have. Not like this. The soldiers I messed around with before? They might as well have been your sloppy kisses from high school, or that so-called boyfriend from college who lost patience with you. Shit, do you see what you've done to me already? Do I look like the same man I was when you first walked down my hallway and I went and shouted at you to fuck off? That was before I got a look at your face." His eyes drift down to my lips. "That was before I got a look into what makes you ... *you.*"

I bite my lip, too aware of the subtle change in his tone. His words have become softer, yet deeper, full of that rich and wanton need I know I'm feeling in my own body—ever since his hands went for my pants.

Have I had as much of an effect on Cody as he's had on me?

"Come inside," Cody urges me. I don't want to say it sounds like begging, but he's exhibited more emotion in the past few minutes than he has the whole time I've known him.

I swallow once, my eyes on his, and then I look away at the steering wheel, frustrated. "Cody, you know I can't. Not tonight."

"Yes, you can. Just get right on out of the car and walk me to my door."

"It's late. Already hours later than I was supposed to be home. I need to be home. My father—"

"You need to come inside. And I'll tell you why."

"I can't."

"You need to come inside because somewhere deep inside you and that complex mind of yours," he tells me, "you're wonderin' if I'm right."

I close my eyes, my head heavy and reeling.

"You're wonderin' if maybe ... *maybe* ... you're just as much a sinner as the rest of us."

Still, the silence swells. I can't respond. If I say a single word, I'll be tempted to walk into that house with him. If I look at him, I will want nothing more than to be invited into those big arms of his. I'll dream of nothing but where to put my lips. Despite all my efforts to resist him, I'll know nothing but his taste, his touch, and my own ravenous hunger as I devour him from head to toe.

The click of his door opening startles me, but I keep my eyes closed. I hear him shuffle out of the car. Just before he shuts the door, he leans in and says one last thing.

"I ain't gonna give up on you, Trey Arnold."

When I lift my eyes at long last and turn them his way, he's made it up to his door already. I watch as he slips into his house, then gently shuts the door behind him.

I stare at that door for a solid minute.

Damn.

I lick my dry lips, take in a deep breath, then put the car back into drive and take off.

Every stop sign I pass suddenly has a different message than before—and a different effect on my already conflicted emotions.

Red flag: Don't go home.

Red flag: What are you doing, leaving Cody behind?

Red flag: *You're going the wrong way.*

I was able to practice discipline my whole life. I've known the "right thing to do" as certainly as I know the sky's blue or what the letters in the alphabet are. Of course I knew I would be faced with certain trials and challenges the older I got, but I never quite anticipated such a trial—or a challenge—as difficult or morally complex as this one.

As difficult or morally complex as Cody Davis.

I could always resist temptation with anyone in Spruce. I was proud of how strong I was. Casual sex was never something that called to me. Having crude fantasies or imagining myself in bed with a hot guy were never really things I did, so I never missed them. After all, how do you miss something you've never had?

I could resist the boy in high school. I could say no to the guy in nursing school. I could turn down twenty different suitors Mrs. Strong lined up for me from here until next Christmas.

But then Cody Davis went and crashed into my life.

Now, I've been burst open like Pandora's box. Everything is spilling out into the open, and I'm a fool to even try stopping it.

Maybe some cruel, selfish part of me even thought that before Cody went and revealed us to Tanner, I could have still denied what was happening between us if questioned. I could have still covered it all up so that no one would know—like it's our secret. I could have shrugged off this beautiful, pleasurable, sexual part of my life like a jacket to don my good-boy suit whenever needed. And if things went awry between us, maybe I could've even talked myself into believing that all of this never happened. It'd be like I never left my pious, righteous, clean, virginal, naïve little life.

That's no longer an option. I am permanently tainted.

Ignorance has been stolen from me.

In many ways, maybe I'm not the man Cody first met, either. Maybe I don't want to be. Maybe if I've come this far, why not go farther?

What's stopping me now?

The next time I park my car, I'm in front of a house. I thrust myself out of the car, slam shut the door, then race up to the front steps. I don't knock; I *beat* that door with the side of a fist, over and over and over.

When it swings open, Cody's face is there, his eyes wide with surprise.

"You're right," I declare, out of breath.

Our lips connect the next instant. I shove my way into his house, our hungry hands fumbling for each other's clothes as the door slams shut at my back.

23

CODY

It's the kind of kissing where you lose your breath.

You literally can't breathe.

And the best part is, you don't fucking care—*because this is surely the most beautiful way to suffocate.*

When we finally pull our mouths apart to get a look at one another, all of our clothes are on the floor around us. The energy of the room shifts from a frenzy to absolute stillness.

I'm afraid to say anything. I don't want to wreck or test the courage Trey clearly built up to come back to my house. I still don't know what he wants, if he wants to stay, or if he just came back to get naked and make my lips sore.

Trey, still not speaking, puts a hand on my bare chest. I watch him, silent. He appears curious, his eyes alight, as his hand slowly runs down the ridges of my muscles. His sexy fingertips are gentle, causing goosebumps to pop up along my skin.

His hand arrives at my dick.

He finds it hard as stone.

Then he turns around slowly. When he faces away, he brings his back to my front, pressing up against me. My hard dick flattens against his ass, throbbing worse from the pressure.

Trey reaches around behind me, grips my ass cheeks, and pulls me even harder against him.

My eyes roll back. *Fucking hell, he's a professional tease.*

His butt starts to wiggle invitingly, pressed against my dick as it is. His fingers claw my cheeks as they hold me firmly against him. It's killing me not knowing what's going on in his mind, but it is clear as day what's going on in his head—his *lower* head, that is.

It strikes a fire in me, knowing how badly he wants it.

But is he ready?

Is he really ready?

"*Trey ...*" I whisper.

"Put your arms around me."

I slip my hands under either of his arms like a seatbelt, then slide my fingers up his body slowly. Trey bucks in the slightest under my touch, melting against me as my hands come to rest on his warm chest that rises and falls with his every eager breath.

I can't press my dick against him any more firmly than I already am. *I want inside of him so badly.*

"You feel that?" he murmurs into the silence of the room.

As my hands rub and massage his front, I nuzzle my face into his neck from behind. Leaving a trail of kisses, I move my lips from the soft nape of his neck up to his ear.

"Do you feel that in your heart?" he asks. "That warm *thing* inside you that tells you you're alright?—*that tells you you're safe?*"

"*Yes,*" I whisper, kissing his ear.

"I want to remember this feeling." He takes a breath as I bite the lobe of his ear gently. He issues a moan. "I don't ever want it to become comfortable. I don't ever want it to become casual. I don't want this feeling to lose its specialness. I want to remember this excitement, always ... this ... this *fear* ..."

"Fear?"

"It's almost like fear. I'm afraid of being let go, I think. Don't you feel that, too?"

My nostrils drag over his hair. My eyes are shut as I breathe him in, thinking of what I could have lost, of what I could still lose.

Move!

My heart races. "Yes," I admit with another kiss to his neck. "I feel it, too ..." *Maybe more than you'll ever know.*

"It's scary ... but I don't want to forget it. I want it to feel this way every time we ..." He draws quiet.

I kiss his other ear, kiss the other side of his neck, then open my eyes to the side of his face. My hands gently slide up and down his front, feeling every inch of his skin. "Every time we ... what?"

"I ... I want you to ..." His body tightens up.

I know what he wants.

I know what he craves so badly.

"*Say it,*" I whisper into his ear, close enough for him to *feel* my words.

"I want ..."

"*I want to hear you say the words.*"

He takes a breath. Just that little breath is so erotic to me, the way it almost carries the sound of his voice.

And then he says the words: "I need you to take my virginity, Cody. I need it to be you."

Need.

He said need.

With my hands on him, I coax his body to turn around. The second he's facing me, I plant a kiss right on his cheek, then his chin, then his perfect, plump lips. I'm so fucking drunk on him, I could live with my face in his adorable one for centuries.

"Need?" I put a finger under his chin and lift his face to mine. His eyes sparkle in the dim light coming from the lamp in the corner of the room. "Why did you use that word? Why do you *need* it to be me?"

"It can't be anyone else," he answers like it's obvious.

"And why not?"

Trey swallows hard, then brings his hand to my chest all over again. He seems to be listening to my heartbeat for a while. "Cody, I think you've made me realize somethin' about myself. Somethin' no one's seen before."

I put a kiss on his forehead, then his cheek. I can't stop kissing him, even while he talks. I'm addicted to the touch of my lips against his soft skin. "What's that?"

"You made me realize I'm not some precious piece of glass." His eyes close as I kiss him. He leaves his lips parted between his words, breathing deeply. "You made me realize I'm ... I'm just like anyone else. I have desires, which you showed me. I'm flawed, which I proved to myself the day I lied to my father to protect those desires. And I realized that I deserve to experience all this world has to offer. Don't I? I'm sick of protectin' myself from it, as if feeling so much pleasure could destroy me."

"*I won't destroy you, babe,*" I whisper in his ear.

Trey grabs my face and pulls me in for a kiss.

Our bodies crash together.

Then I lose all control.

With our lips locked, I drag Trey down the hall to my room. My leg screams at me, but I ignore its every throbbing protest in favor of another throbbing part of me—a part that swells with my every furious heartbeat.

I push him over the edge of my bed face-first, his beautiful backside exposed to my every desire, and then slowly draw kisses down its length. Trey's body stiffens under the touch of my lips.

I could devour him whole right now. I still might.

"You're gonna feel everything," I growl as my face reaches his ass. I give one of his cheeks a bite. *I've been wanting to do that.*

"Everything ..." he moans back.

"Trust me, you will *never* forget how this feels." One of my hands is buried in the nightstand, fishing for the lube. "You will remember it every time you're sprawled out on a bed." I flick open the bottle, one-handed. "You will remember it every time you close your eyes and have a dirty dream." I squirt some into my palm. "You will remember it every time you slip on a pair of sexy underwear, or lick your lips after a tasty meal, or touch yourself."

"Oh, Cody ..."

I lather up my dick with the slippery lube, slicking it up from base to tip. There's no telling how far we're actually going to take this tonight, but if the squirming in his body and the throbbing firmness of mine is any indication, we might not be tiring out any time soon.

"What about a condom?"

I lift my eyes to his. "I don't have any."

Concern clouds his face. "But ... But shouldn't we—?"

"If you want to. But after all my time in that damned hospital, tests and blood tests and more tests, I can assure you by my word that I'm clean. And your virgin ass ain't done nothin' with nobody, so I doubt I've got anythin' to worry about with you."

He considers it for a moment. "Alright," he decides, relaxing. "I'm ... I'm fine without one. No condom."

I nod, then bring two slick fingers right to his pink hole. Trey sucks in air, then relaxes at once, as if he's so fucking pleased to feel my fingers down there at long last.

I grin. "Ever since I teased your hole that one time before," I moan at his back, "you've craved this feeling again, haven't you?"

"Yes," he groans, clawing the bed.

My two fingers slide in to the second knuckle with barely any resistance. I twist them around gently, stretching him as I watch and take pleasure in how much this is causing him to squirm.

Just wait until you get the real thing, boy.

"I want to look at you."

Trey twists his head around. "What?"

I slide my fingers out, then grip him by the waist and flip him over. He seems startled as I hook my arms underneath both his legs and pull his ass up against my waist. It causes a burst of pain in my left bicep, but I ignore that motherfucker. *No room for pain tonight.* My slicked-up dick flexes against his slicked-up hole, ready to slide right inside.

"I said I want to look at you," I tell him, my voice firm. "I don't want to miss a moment of this."

"Neither do I."

Trey, in all his strength, fierce morals, and convictions, looks so fucking vulnerable right now. It moves me, to be honest here. I want to cherish this moment as deeply and as significantly as I know Trey is right now. This isn't just sex for him; this is opening his soul to me and letting me inside him in a way I doubt either of us could have predicted a few weeks ago when we were practically at each other's throats.

I guess all of that passion was destined to lead us somewhere.

My grip under his legs tightens, despite the incessant ache in my arm. I can't wait to slide into him so deeply that I feel his body squeeze around my dick. I'm so fucking impatient for that first thrust of my hips as I cross the threshold and claim what's mine.

"You ready?"

Trey swallows once, then licks his lips. After a moment of his eyes searching mine, he finally gives me one slow, resolved nod.

The corner of my mouth curls up. "Strap in, baby."

I gently push my hips forward. With my dick right at his lubed hole, the tip slides in with ease. Trey's lips part, as if in surprise. I don't go in any farther, waiting for visual confirmation from his face that he isn't in any pain.

His eyes rock back drunkenly. His eyebrows lift, wrinkling up his forehead.

Nah, he ain't in any fuckin' pain.

I push some more, sliding even farther in. Now Trey groans and sucks in air. *God, I love when he makes that sound.* He's so fucking tight, too. I caress his body as I gently rock, slipping in a bit, then out a bit, over and over as I work him up. The feel of my bare dick in his slick hole is enough to get me to the edge in no time.

But I'm in no hurry. I can make this last for hours if I wanted. I want Trey's first time to be incredible.

He's going to be on the edge of ecstasy until I say so.

You won't forget a second of how this feels, Trey Arnold.

I never tire of watching the way he squirms on that bed. Time slips on by as Trey bites his lip, sucks in air, glances up at me with dreams in his eyes, then gets lost in a flood of ecstasy. He doesn't even notice how much deeper I've slid into his body. *If I actually manage to get deep enough to hit his prostate, he'll definitely feel it then.*

"Touch yourself," I murmur into the breaths and grunts.

Trey's lips part and his eyes reel onto mine. "I'm afraid to."

I quirk an eyebrow. "Why?"

"I'm so hard. I'm so hard I'm afraid I'll come."

"Somethin' about havin' a big, hard dick up your ass that just bones you right up, huh?"

Trey winces a bit—whether at my crude language or at my last powerful thrust which my thigh screams at, I don't know—but then he slowly draws a hand down to his dick, obeying. He only wraps his fingers around it, hesitating a second before doing so, and doesn't jerk.

Maybe he really is *already that close to the edge.* I slow down ever slightly, pumping him gently. He's relaxed so much down there, I'm pretty sure I could thrust my dick in all the way. I don't want to startle him or hurt him, though. The last thing I want him to remember from his first time is pain.

The last thing I ever want to cause Trey Arnold is pain.

"Focus on me."

Trey's eyes flap open. He meets my intense gaze as I lean over him, bringing my face as close to his as I can.

"Focus," I tell him as I thrust. Just the act of leaning over him pushed my dick in farther. Trey's mouth is agape, his face twisted into a mix of pleasure, ache, and disbelief. "Do you still feel safe?"

"I feel so good right now," he breathes.

"Do you feel safe in my arms?"

"I want you to make me come."

I quirk an eyebrow. *He's an eager boy.* "Already?"

"I can't hold it in much longer." Trey's breathing has turned erratic. He keeps switching from biting his lip to parting them, sucking in air, then hissing it out as he squirms under me. "I have to come. I feel so good, Cody, I want it so bad. *Oh ... this is torture.* Please make me come."

"You really want it that badly, huh?"

"Yes, but ... but I just have one thing ..."

"One thing?"

"One thing I want you to do."

I smirk, still gently pumping him. *He feels so fucking good and tight on my dick, hell, I'm almost willing to comply no matter what his request is.* "I'm all ears."

He reaches up with his free hand and touches the side of my face. "I want you to kiss me when I come."

Fuck. I am so turned on right now, those words alone almost made me lose my load. "Are you sure?"

"And I want you to come inside me."

He wants everything. He wants all of it all at once. He doesn't want me to hold back for a second.

"I'll do everything you want and more," I promise him. "I'm gonna kiss you as we come together, Trey. And I'm going to come inside you, too. You'll *feel* me empty myself inside you."

"I want to feel it so badly."

"There's no turning back."

"I liked it when you called me 'babe'."

I grin, amused and aroused by this sexy piece of meat beneath me. I don't want this moment to ever end. A part of me always knew this was going to happen between us.

Another part still doesn't believe it's happening at all.

"We're gonna come together," I tell him, "... *babe.*"

Trey groans, then starts to stroke himself.

I pump him deeper. The harder I go, the more my leg and arm hurt, but I have enough heat and blood chasing through me that I ignore it. No amount of pain can outmatch my pleasure.

I'm already on the edge, so it won't take much more to crash over the brink of orgasm. I feel it as certainly, as imminently, as unstoppably as a dam about to rip apart right down its center.

"Kiss me," he blurts suddenly, his eyes turning urgent.

I bend down to oblige.

He comes between our bodies so hard that halfway through our kiss, his mouth opens and he hollers out, groaning in pleasure. My dick, determined to enhance his state of unrivaled rapture, releases all my pent-up excitement into him right then like a flood. I part my lips, too, hollering out and thrusting against his ass harder and harder as I empty my whole load into him.

That was, by far, my most powerful orgasm I have ever had.

It's an orgasm that lasts so long, I can't tell when it began or when it ends.

That was a first time that *I* am going to remember forever.

I don't slip out of him after we finish. I've let go of his legs and find my arms cradling his body against me somehow. I'm not sure when that happened, but we're holding one another, all our mess and stickiness trapped between us, and our lips are glued to one another's, kissing each other tenderly.

Over and over in my head I hear the word—*babe, babe, babe*—and it makes me smile into our kiss, which seems to last forever. *He likes it when I call him "babe".*

24

TREY

I wake up a whole new person.

It's no joke, the way you feel after you lose your virginity.

Of course, gay virginity might be a little different. There's not a "cherry popping" involved. It's in the ass. It isn't procreative, as it doesn't have the chance of bearing a newborn in nine months.

But it changes you nonetheless.

After a particularly sensual shower—in which Cody caressed me under the water, then afterwards swatted my ass with his wet, rolled-up towel like some jock in the locker room—we shared a snack in his kitchen, brushed our teeth, then cuddled together on his bed. My phone was ditched somewhere in the living room with my clothes, and I didn't bother to check it.

Is that something else that changed in me, too? Did I become stronger magically? Did I break away a little bit more from my father and his heavy demands of me?

Did I veer off the Lord's path?

Am I free to do anything now? Am I free to try anything at all that's available to me on this planet full of infinite possibilities?

Have I been granted some kind of unspoken permission to do everything I ever dreamed of now?

Can I cuss?

I can fuckin' cuss if I fuckin' want to. Fuck.

I laugh suddenly at my own thoughts.

Cody stirs in my arms, then twists around to get a look at my face. His tired eyes squint, then he puts on a little smile when he sees the laughter in my eyes. "What's funny?"

I bite my lip, then shrug and answer, "I don't *fuckin'* know. You tell me."

His forehead screws up. "The hell's gotten into you?"

I giggle again, obviously and completely having lost my mind, then wriggle out of his sheets and get to my feet. I'm totally naked, by the way. "I'm gonna go make us some breakfast. How you want your eggs?"

He sits up and stares at me, appraising my odd behavior for a second, no doubt. "Scramble them fuckers up," he finally answers.

"Scrambled eggs comin' right up!" I announce, then make my way to the kitchen, leaving Cody there in a confused stupor.

The stupor doesn't last for long. He comes up behind me in the kitchen while I'm over a pan of sizzling eggs and grabs my ass. I ditch the pan and tackle him to the counter where we engage in a brief session of fierce, mouth-aching kisses.

When we part, he looks down at me like he doesn't recognize me, his eyes curious, yet deep in thought.

It's somewhere in his eyes that I find my courage. "I'm gonna tell my dad," I announce. "He's gonna find out anyway, right? So he might as well hear it from me."

"What exactly are you tellin' him?" Cody asks, wrinkling up his face. "That you got porked by his worst nightmare?"

"Or that I've been goin' behind my father's back for weeks to see you, even on my days off?"

"Or that I sucked you off more times than we got fingers for?"

"Oh, Cody. I *like* that wording."

"Well, yeah. Your ass needs to get the wordin' right, especially if you're going for givin' him a full-blown heart attack."

I shake my head. "Nah, not a heart attack. Just bad indigestion and a disapproving look that might last a day or two."

Cody smirks. "Better just go for the simple 'I'm seein' Cody' approach, then. 'We're a thing. Deal with it.' That'll do the trick."

"And then the *next* time we do it," I go on, feeling frisky, "we can do it in my bed. In my house. While my dad's asleep." I giggle at that, then turn back to tend to the eggs, shoving the spatula at them to keep the uncooked bits cooking.

Cody snorts at me. I turn to find him shaking his head, his eyes full of bewilderedness. "The fuck happened to you overnight? Shit, you've done lost your mind."

"That's not a bad thing," I point out. "My old mind was a bit boring. Time for a new one."

Cody only stares at me for a response, frozen in place.

I shoot him a wink as I turn back to the eggs. Suddenly, I find myself whistling a tune that was playing softly from the car radio on the way to the Strong ranch yesterday. It was a catchy tune, and for whatever reason, I absolutely must whistle it right now. I start to dance a bit too, shaking my butt and bobbing my head.

This is the energy that carries me for the next hour or so before I finally decide to make my way home.

"I have a shift at the clinic in a couple hours," I tell Cody when I'm dressed and at the front door, "but I can swing by afterwards if you want to hang out. Hey, maybe we could even do something fun, like catch a movie, or hit up the park, or—"

"Bell Lake," he throws out.

I quirk an eyebrow. "Really? You wanna go back?"

"Sure. Maybe you got some new 'exercise' you can show me." He smirks suggestively, a glint of desire in his eyes. "Don't act like your ass doesn't want to put your hands all over my thigh again."

"Alright. Skinny-dipping at Bell Lake it is." I chuckle, then lift my gaze upward, imagining it. "Y'know, I've never gone skinny-dipping. I really would like to try it."

"At Bell Lake?" Cody pushes air past his lips. "Fuck that. We're gonna have fish swimmin' up our asses."

Those words strike just the right note in me to tickle me silly. I laugh so hard, I'm certain all the neighbors are stirring in their beds wondering where that peculiar noise is coming from.

To be honest, I never knew I had such a loud laugh until now.

"Shit, you *sure* you didn't drink anything last night?" he asks, a hint of concern in his voice.

I cut off my own laughter abruptly and shoot him a look. "Cody Brian Davis, you know I ain't gonna put myself behind the wheel of a vehicle if I've had even a *drop* of alcohol. Don't you know me better?"

He eyes me. "Shit, boy, I ain't so sure I know this version of you much at all."

The more nervous I make him, the more Texan twang nestles itself in his words. I sort of like unsettling Cody. It gives me the same sort of pleasure that outing our relationship to my father is about to give me, I'm sure of it.

I bring my mouth to Cody's for one last kiss before I hit the road, then push through the door. "See your sexy ass later."

Cody watches me go for a bit, silent, then finally calls out, "I'd *better* see your ass later," at my back.

Oh, he will.

The second I get into my car, the cloying smell of spice and something *off* wafts over me overwhelmingly. I scrunch up my nose, confused, repulsed, then glance over my seat in pursuit of the saccharine stench.

Oh, crap. I'd forgotten about the carrot cake.

A carrot cake I was supposed to take home to my dad yesterday.

"Too late now," I decide out loud, then roll down my windows to let the car air out as I turn the key, back out of the driveway, and tear down the roads. It isn't long before the smell has thinned out enough to be bearable.

Don't worry, I console myself. *It's just a carrot cake. There are worse mistakes to be made.*

The whole drive home, I'm not thinking of mistakes at all. I'm humming to the nonsense on the radio. Actually, this nonsense is making me feel really good. Some top-of-the-charts pop song I can literally picture a slumber party full of twelve-year-old girls singing loudly to, decked out in PJs with all their hair twisted up in braids and ponytails and glitter. I grab hold of my phone and turn it into my microphone, singing my heart out with made-up lyrics as I drive, one-handed, across the whole town of Spruce.

I am the gayest son of a bitch right now.

Shame can't touch me this morning.

Invincible is my middle name.

When I pull into my driveway and cut off the engine, that's when the first sting of reality jabs into my mood. Maybe it's the eerie silence that follows after turning off the radio, sitting in my car and staring at the front of my house.

My father's in there.

"Who cares?" I ask out loud, defying my own fears, which are trying so desperately to bubble to the surface. Fear is paralyzing. Fear freezes the brain like a spell of ice. Fear causes the spine to curl and wither. "I'm not afraid," I announce to the dashboard. "I am proud of what I've done. I am proud of who I am. I am proud of whose house I just came from."

I'm so proud, I didn't even check my phone for missed calls or messages. I'm so "unafraid", I couldn't bear to see whether there were sixteen missed calls from my father, or a ton of urgent texts asking me to call, or six hundred voicemails demanding to know where I am.

I swallow hard. I'm totally not afraid at all.

The car door opens before I mean it to. Fumbling out of the vehicle, I grab the carrot cake from the back seat, then shut the car door at my back with a clumsy kick. I stumble on my way to the front door, nearly dropping the cake halfway there. I don't know why, but my legs don't seem to work properly. I swear I'm not drunk or high, unless you count the sex from last night.

Which was certainly a high.

The highest I've ever, ever, *ever* been. *It was that good.*

How am I even standing right now? Shouldn't I be walking bowlegged or something? I'm not. Shouldn't the inside of my butt hurt? It doesn't. Shouldn't I be aching everywhere? Other than the undersides of my legs, I don't feel a bit of ache at all. I might as well have returned from the gym after working out my quads for all the effect losing my virginity has had on me physically.

Mentally, though, is a completely different story.

Emotionally: a third completely different story as well.

I open the front door one-handed.

There's no disapproving dad in the front entryway awaiting me like I imagined. I move farther into the house, nearly tiptoeing. There's no one in the living room, either. *Odd.* I glance up at the banister of the second floor. Nothing, not even a sound.

Coming around into the kitchen, I find evidence of coffee having been made, but the machine is turned off and the half-full pot sits there, an empty mug by its side.

I set down the carrot cake, all its beautiful cream cheese frosting having melted and drooped down the sides like sad, old drapery. I experience a moment of grief for the cake. Was it one of Billy's? Was it ordered from Nadine's, Mrs. Strong's restaurant in Fairview? It doesn't matter now.

I continue on to the back glass windows, but don't find my father sitting in his usual chair, either. I stare at it, mystified. He should be home, unless he went to the church this morning for some reason. Was there an appointment I had forgotten about? Didn't he have an errand to run in Fairview today or something?

"The Parable of the Prodigal Son."

I spin around at the sound of the voice.

My father stands under the archway to the living room, his arms hanging at his sides. He wears pants and a loose shirt. His eyes look weary, his hair disheveled, and his jaw tensed up.

"What?" I respond, more a squeak than a word.

"A father's young son. Foolish. Impulsive. Acts on his own. He asks for his inheritance early. Then squanders it on a life of sin, on prostitutes, on extravagance and selfishness. Then, ashamed, he returns home." My father doesn't move, standing still as a statue as he talks. Somehow, it chills me to the bone. "And he stands before his father ... and knows he's disgraced him."

"Dad ..."

"You know what he asks of his father?" He grinds his teeth between his sentences. "He asks him to become his lowly servant, because he's no longer worthy of being called his son."

The coldness in his words pins my feet to the floor and urges my stomach to drop down there, too. I had so much courage just before opening that front door.

Where has all that courage gone?

"Where've you been, son?"

I try to stoke the flame of my indignance. All I find is a cough, an awkward shuffling of my feet, and no sparks at all. "I was with a f-friend." *Dang it, Trey, don't stutter.* "I was with a—"

"You were with the Davis boy."

I swallow hard. I try to lift my chin, but my stomach—filled with a breakfast of eggs and toast that I'm trying to keep down suddenly—is quickly converting into a black hole of despair, and it sucks all my confidence into its greedy, bottomless depths.

"That's fine," he states. "Of course it's fine. Why should I be upset with my son for that?" His tone is calm, which makes him all the more unsettling. "You are helping a boy in need."

"He's a man."

Why did I feel the arrogant need to correct him?

My father doesn't react at all—not on his face, at least. A small lilt in his voice is the only reveal of his inner hurt. "You are right. The Davis boy ... is a man. That must mean that *you* are the boy."

"I'm a man, too," I state, my voice quivering for some reason. I hate when my voice shakes. *I'm not afraid. It shouldn't be shaking.*

His words fall on my ears as hard as iron hammers. "Boys lie to their fathers."

My lips press together. The worst part is, I don't know which lie he's referring to. Is it simply my whereabouts, or did he learn something already that I haven't had a chance to divulge to him?

"I called your coworker Marybeth," he goes on. "You'd stayed there before. I thought something had happened to you, and I was panicked as any concerned parent would be. She was ... squirrely, to say the least. Of course I pressed her. It took all of ten seconds for her to crack, break down in tears, and confess that she couldn't lie to me any longer. She has a daughter of her own, and the thought of someone concealing where *her* daughter was running off to? Unspeakable. After Marybeth begged my forgiveness, she then told me where you likely were." His eyes darken. "*And why.*"

My insides turn cold as ice.

I don't blame Marybeth. This is all my fault. I did this.

"You and Cody? A '*thing*' ...?" My father shakes his head. "What is the matter with you, Trey? Are you *that* determined to disrespect me? To play out this ... *childish* rebelliousness of yours? Oh, son. I raised you better. Your mother raised you better."

The moment he brings up Mom, a surge of confidence rushes into me. "If a *boy* lies to his father, then maybe that *boy* has a reason." My nervous legs meander to the closer end of the couch, as if I'm putting it between us like a long defensive wall of fabric and wood and pocket change. "Maybe that *boy* lost trust in his father when he decided—"

"Trust?" My father bows his head slightly, but keeps his eyes firmly affixed to my face, burning. "How have you lost trust in me? What have I *possibly* done to break your trust, son?"

"You changed," I answer him. "And you know you have. Since the day I came out to you, you've treated me differently."

He flinches. "How could you say that? What do you mean? You think … You think I love you less because you're gay? Is that it? Goodness gracious, Trey, you know me better."

"Do I?" I challenge him, lifting my chin.

"Yes!" he cries out suddenly, spreading his hands. "What do you think Spruce Fellowship stands for? This has *absolutely nothing* to do with your sexual preference. This—"

"It's not a *preference*, Dad."

He huffs impatiently. "Your sexual orientation. Sexuality. You know exactly what I meant."

"Sure, of course, yes, you always mean well. Reverend Arnold *always* means well," I exclaim, my tone rising without my meaning it to, "but *Mr.* Arnold—my father—he is an oftentimes confusing man of many mixed signals. He officiates Billy and Tanner's big gay wedding, but then balks like a spooked horse when his own son tells him he's gay."

"I told you I'd need time. Darn it, Trey, isn't that a normal enough reaction?" He takes a breath. "Lord help me, is *that* what this whole thing is? You're acting out because I'm not trying to … fix you up with every gay guy from here to Little Water? Because I'm not taking you shopping every weekend for new shoes?"

"Jesus, Lord. Thank you, Dad, let's pull out *every* stereotype we can while we're at it. We'll go get mani-pedis, too. And if we can swing some tickets to the local *Cher* concert, then fucking *perfect*."

It's incredible, the power of one word.

One little, silly, insignificant, manmade word.

Seven letters.

Fucking.

In front of my *father*.

He doesn't respond at all. He doesn't even react. As if that seven-letter word itself was an exotic head full of snakes, my dear father has turned to stone at the sound of it.

I swallow, then stammer out my next words. "I-I'm sorry. I ... I didn't mean to say that."

"I told you." My father's words are so tiny and cold, they're almost gone, like bits of ice left on the edge of a cooler, biting your fingers when you touch them, yet melted in seconds.

I swallow again. For some odd reason, I can't seem to swallow right. "Told me what?"

"He would be a bad influence on you. He's bad news. Look at yourself, Trey. Look at what you've become. You and Cody? Why him? He's put ... *darkness* in you, son."

I suck in a breath. I want to cry suddenly, but I don't. *I won't.*

"Dad," I start, choosing my words carefully. "I don't think he's as bad an influence as you think. I ... I think he's helped me to—"

"Helped you?"

"Yes. *Helped* me ... to find myself. Dad, I've been lost. For years. I've been lost and—"

"Lost? No. You've been happy, son. I see the happiness in your eyes when you're one with God. Every Sunday. Every morning. My son, you don't know what you're talking about. You are confused."

"I'm not *confused.*"

"You are coming home late all the time," he presses on. "You are staying out all night, *lying* to my face about where you have been. Using foul language under our roof. You're—"

"I don't need the laundry list, *Dad*," I blurt before I can stop myself. "What I need is for my father to be a father to his *gay* son. I need him to *love* his gay son the way he *pretends* to in public."

"I never pretended! Where are you getting this from??" He is starting to lose his cool. I haven't seen him this undone in years, not since Mom died. "I'm learning, Trey. But you have to *teach* me. You have to *educate* me. I mean, what else do you want? I'm trying my best, and apparently, my best isn't enough. I'm trying to give you a good home, and you're running around behind my back with Cody Davis, doing God-knows-what. Do you know I pray for you every night?" he adds suddenly, nearly out of breath. "*Do you know that I prayed for you all last night while you were gone?*"

My father on his knees praying for my soul is not exactly the image I want to connect to what I was *really* doing last night.

"Ever since your mother left us, I've been doing this all on my own. And when I hear what you're doing ... oh, how it *breaks* my heart. I don't pray because I think you're too far gone to save," he tells me, his words strained. "I pray because I know you have the strength in you to stand up for what's right."

I face my father, my fingers curling into fists. "You know, I had to grow up real, *real* fast after Mom died. I took on a lot of responsibilities myself, running this house with you and trying to be your perfect son."

"Trey ..."

"I work *six* days a week," I go on, ignoring him. "Seven if you count my helpin' you at the church. I deserve a life of my own. I deserve friends of my own—friends that I choose. *Boyfriends that I choose.* And that's all without havin' to account for every *damned* minute I'm not here."

My father's face is so red, he looks sunburnt.

But I'm not finished. "And I think you're forgetting how the Parable of the Prodigal Son ends." I close the distance between us at last, bringing myself right up to him. "The father doesn't make his son a servant. The father welcomes his son home with open arms. He feeds him the best calf they own. He loves him. 'For what was lost is now found.' I've been found, Dad. I found myself, with *Cody Davis* to thank for it. And meanwhile, what have you done? You've wasted all your time with your eyes and ears closed to me, all these years—*not listening.*"

His lips quiver with unspoken words. His eyes turn to water.

"The one you ought to be praying for," I finish, "is yourself. Maybe you ought to be praying each night to have the strength ... to have just a *slice* of the strength and compassion that *Mom* had, because at least I know without a doubt how *she* would have loved me had I told her what I was before she—"

I choke on my words, the tears in my eyes stealing them away.

Far more annoyed with my uncontrollable, bubbling-over emotion than anything, I throw away the rest of my words and storm towards the stairs. I guess I've said it all anyway. My father calls out for me twice, his voice stern and cold.

The slam of my bedroom door is the only response he gets.

I drop onto my bed, everything before my eyes becoming a blur. It's the strangest sensation, to not be actively crying, yet to have tears escaping my eyes without my permission. I wipe one of them away, annoyed.

No crying. I won't give him any of my tears.

"Trey ..." he softly calls from the other side of the door. A soft tap of his knuckles follows, twice.

I bring my mother's seashell to my ear and drown him out with the rush and retreat of imaginary ocean waves. *In, out, in, out.*

25

CODY

This wasn't the text I was expecting to receive.

"He wants to '*wait 'til things cool off* ...?" I exclaim, staring at the text on my big, bright screen with my face all wrinkled up. "'*Big fight with my dad?*' The fuck is this shit ...?"

I call Trey back, unable to accept his wimpy-ass text.

He doesn't answer.

The next two hours of my life are filled with countless more calls and texts that Trey doesn't respond to.

They're also filled with too much groaning, thanks to my leg, which can barely carry my weight since last night. The throb in my arm is worse than it's ever been, too.

But both of those things are secondary to knowing where the fuck Trey is and what's going on with him.

"He's fallen down from his high," I mutter to myself as I stand over the sink by the can of beer I just downed and crushed on the counter. "He has second thoughts. He thinks he's gonna burn in eternal damnation now. He regrets ever knowin' me."

The thoughts keep torturing me. I go for another can, then find myself staring at it in my palm, my eyes stinging with anger. *Just like your old man,* a voice taunts me from the deep recesses of my head. *Go for another beer. Go right on ahead. Drink when life's tough. Take a sip. No pretty face is here to stop you.*

Have another drink, Cody.

I throw the beer back into the fridge, unopened, and slam the door shut with a huff, my body twisting in the effort. Just that simple action makes my leg scream out in protest, which causes me to stop at once and lean against the counter for support, all my weight shifted to my good side.

"You're such a fuckin' winner," I cheer myself on bitterly.

I've also become someone who talks to himself now, apparently.

But this isn't like my usual pain. Something warm and sharp lances down my whole left side. It's a fiery bolt of pain that, for a second, causes me worry.

Of all the days that Trey was here and I didn't need his help, of *course* today would be the one when I actually do.

And he's nowhere to be found.

Because I fucked all the courage out of him last night.

"Way to fuckin' go," I exclaim to my empty kitchen, my words tensed with pain.

I sit at my table with my phone in front of me, staring at it like it's about to vibrate to life with Trey's response at long last. I take apart and put back together my Remington again. Seven damned times I do that. Then I switch to my shotgun. If my hands aren't moving, then I'm dying a slow and agonizing death.

My phone stays still and silent as a stone.

I glare at it resentfully as I disassemble both my shotgun and my Remington again, and that's just how I leave everything: pulled apart, in a hundred pieces, and utterly abandoned.

Stubbornly pushing myself onto my feet, I go out back into the yard. Halfway across it, that same horrible pain from my leg wracks my whole body, and I'm on the ground the next instant.

Staring up at the sky, I wait as the pain subsides—or I become better at ignoring it with every passing second—and let my phone lie on my chest, waiting for Trey to return a damned call or text.

Storm clouds are rolling in. Practically in the space of ten tiny minutes, the sky has gone from a bright, noonish joy to a dark gray blanket of growling clouds. I stare up at those clouds and wonder if Trey's seeing them, too.

Why do I hurt so much? I'm not talking about my leg, either. Have I really invested so much of myself into Trey Arnold already? Is my heart completely committed to him? When the hell did I let him seep so fucking far down beneath my skin that I'm lying here on my back like a schoolgirl desperately waiting for her crush to return her call?

I close my eyes and wait. It's all I can do. I'm sure as hell not going to be able to drive around town on this leg looking for him.

Hell, he's a big boy, ain't he? He doesn't need me looking for him like a lost puppy on the streets.

When he's ready to talk, he'll pick up that phone and call.

A raindrop touches my nose.

I open my eyes.

That's when I hear the distant chime of a phone. It's not the one on my chest, however. I lift my head off the grass and turn my eyes quizzically toward the back door, perking an ear.

I hear it again.

It's my house phone.

Fighting through the pain, I clamber to my feet, shove my cell into a pocket, and limp to the back door as fast as I can. I'm hopping one-footed by the time I plunge into the house, which is damned dark inside from the clouds stealing away all the sunlight.

I rip the phone off the kitchen wall on the last ring. "Hello??"

The last voice on Earth I expected answers: "Cody."

My heart drops straight through the floor like a piece of lead. *Why is he calling me? What's happened?* "Reverend Arnold ...?"

"Is my son with you?" he asks me calmly.

I frown. "No, sir, he isn't." *Sir?* I pinch the bridge of my nose. "I've been callin' him all day. He hasn't answered once."

Reverend Arnold doesn't reply. A rumble of thunder shakes my back windows, bringing my attention to them.

I blink. "Sir?" I prompt him. "Reverend Arnold?"

"I just got a call from Dr. Emory, followed by another from his coworker Marybeth." He sighs. "Trey didn't show up for his shift today at the clinic."

My gaze casts to the floor in worry. "That's not like him."

"No," he agrees. "Do you know where he might've gone? He and I ..." He sighs again, deeper. "We had words. Last thing he told me was he needed some time alone. He packed a bag, including his mother's seashell, and took off. But I don't know where."

Mother's seashell? "When was this?"

"Two hours ago. I figured he'd gone to ... well, to *you*."

That was after he texted me. "What's this seashell you're talkin' about?" I ask over the rumble of more thunder. Raindrops start kissing my kitchen windows. I left the back door wide open, all the wind sweeping its way inside.

"His mother gave it to him. He listens to it when he's upset. It calms him. He likes being near water. I think to him, it's like being closer to his ... to his mother."

The words aren't easy for him to say, I can tell that much. But it still doesn't tell me where Trey is. I can't think of a valid reason why he wouldn't be answering his phone or making it to work on time. Sure, he's changed an awful lot in the past week or so, but he hasn't totally lost his mind. He would have shown up for work. He would have at least answered *someone's* texts or calls.

A bomb of thunder shakes my whole house. The rain starts to fall more evenly, tapping the windows hard.

"With the coming weather," Reverend Arnold goes on, "I don't want my son caught out in it. If there is *anything* you know about where he is, Cody ..."

"You think I'm holdin' out on you?" I limp across the kitchen and slam shut my back door. With Mother Nature trying to shove her way inside, it's an effort. I grimace and suck in a breath when I feel a stab from inside my thigh.

"What's wrong?"

He must've heard my grunt. "Nothin'. My bad leg. Listen, I don't know where he is. Like I said, he ain't callin' me. And if—"

Water.

He wanted some time alone. He took that seashell with him.

I freeze in the middle of my kitchen, a hand on the counter next to me. "I know where he is," I say and realize at once.

"Where?"

"Bell Lake." Another boom of thunder shakes the world. I lift two anxious, stony eyes to the dining room window. "It's west of here, out by—"

"I know where it is," he answers tersely. "But that's over an hour from here."

"Half an hour for me." I swipe my keys off the counter. There isn't a question in my mind that I have to do this, in pain or not. "I'll call you when I've found him."

"You can't possibly consider going after him in this weather."

"With all due respect, I'd go after your son in any weather."

He lifts his voice. "It's rainin' cats and dogs!"

I glance out the window. The rain is so dense, I can't even see the trees in my backyard. "Looks like just a light drizzle," I grunt.

"This storm is heading east towards us. I'm watching it on TV right now. Cody, you don't even know if he's *at* Bell Lake, or if—"

"He *has* to be there," I assure him. "And if the storm's headin' our way, that means he's already gettin' the worst of it right now. No time to waste. I'll call you."

Click.

After hanging up the house phone, I make a quick move for the front door. Every time my leg shouts at me, I grunt and push on faster, harder, more determined.

The adrenaline is pumping now. Nothing can stop me. Not a leg. Not a throbbing arm.

Not this tumultuous Noah's Ark fuckin' flood of a rainstorm.

I swing into my truck with a grunt and crank the gas. I'm out of the driveway before I even think whether I locked up my front door. *If someone's stupid enough to go out in this weather and ransack my library, more power to them. I hope they like Charles Dickens.*

I'm apparently stupid enough to go out in this storm.

I'd be stupid enough to do just about anything for Trey Arnold.

The houses whiz past me. So do the stop signs, which I ignore like a careless idiot. There ain't a damned soul anywhere on the roads of Spruce except reckless ol' life-endangering me.

I drive fast, even on these slick-as-sin roads. I don't know how I know it, but every cell in my body is certain that Trey Arnold is at Bell Lake right now, and that boy needs my help.

MOVE!

I'm not gonna let another damned warning go unheard. No more surprise bombs on my watch.

Not this time, Pete.

Thunder growls and laughs over my head tauntingly as I go. The rain tries to blind me, charging me in all directions. It's a war out here between wind and water, and the only armor I have is this truck and my sheer heedless stupidity.

And Trey is out there, caught right in the middle of nature's crossfire.

I'm on my way, babe.

I barely recognize the turn off the road I need to take, what with the sheets of rain pummeling my windshield. I turn too sharp for the slick roads, and my whole truck slides, scaring the shit out of me for exactly two seconds before my wheels right themselves and I'm back on track.

You'd think a scare like that would make my reckless ass drive more carefully.

Not when Trey Arnold is the destination.

The road is thinner than I remember. The trees, harder to see through the torrent of rainwater. When I get the feeling that I'm near where we stopped last time we were here, I slow down my truck and peel my eyes off the road, squinting in search of any sign of him.

I pull to a stop near the trees. My truck rumbles patiently as it awaits whether I plan to keep driving onward—or go on foot in crazy, aimless pursuit of him.

Considering the state of my leg, that's a risk I may not want to take; compromising my legs ain't gonna do Trey any good.

Is he even out here? I wonder, frustrated.

Doubt starts to punch into me the moment my adrenaline lets off. Did I just let my own panic and paranoia pull me all the way the fuck out here for nothing? What if Trey is fine and he simply made it to work late? What if he's at Billy and Tanner's, talking to them over mugs of coffee about his troubles? They might be sitting at a table right the fuck now, staring out the windows and saying to each other, "Goodness, it's storming hard out there. I hope no one's stupid enough to be out in this weather."

My jaw tightens.

Fuck. *What if he's not out here?*

I press my foot onto the gas pedal, ignoring the swelling, hot ache in my thigh that has not receded one bit in the past hour. *Talk about testing my resolve, this fuckin' leg of mine.*

It's five more long, slow, crawling minutes down the road that my eyes spot it.

Trey's car.

"Oh, fuck me," I cry out, putting pedal to the metal as I drive right up to his vehicle.

I suddenly find myself wishing I *had* overreacted—that my gut instinct was dead wrong and Trey *was* sitting in a warm house by the lake with Billy and Tanner.

I shove out of the truck the moment I park it, then race over the muddy street to Trey's vehicle. I press my head to the glass and find it empty inside. Trey's phone sits there on the passenger seat, abandoned. A backpack sits in the back seat, partly unzipped.

Fuck, fuck, fuck.

Rainwater pouring over my head in buckets, I lift my gaze and search around in circles. Nothing but field and grass to the west, a road behind me, a road ahead of me, and then the thicket of trees to the east, beyond which lies Bell Lake. No doubt that wimpy lake is flooded to near twice its size by now.

On just my first step toward the forest, my leg screams out so badly that I literally have to stop and cry out. *Something's wrong.* But I have no fucking time to figure out what; Trey is out there, and I'm that much farther from him with every passing second.

Gritting my teeth through the anguish, I push myself into the trees, stumbling over roots that try to trip me and pools of mud that suck greedily at my boots, making every step that much more laborious. I brace myself against a tree for two seconds for relief, then push onward toward the lake.

It's hard enough recognizing this landscape after having been here only once recently. Add to that the curtains of rain blasting at my face and disguising every once-familiar bunch of trees with a vague, watery blurriness, I don't know where the fuck I'm going.

"This what you come to show me?" comes the memory, my own voice as the pair of us walked this same path to the water only last week. *"Bell fuckin' Lake?"*

Trey's voice echoes in my memory, guiding me through the storm. *"And the least you could do is not spit out your curses now that we're here,"* he had shouted back over his shoulder, his face so fucking adorable I could've kissed it right then. *"You'll scare away the fish and all the beauty about it this time of day."*

There's no beauty here today. *It's a fucking nightmare.*

By the time the lake comes into view, I'm in full-blown soldier mode. My eyes are scoping every brush, every ripple of water, every tree. I'm fighting through the pain that might as well be a bullet wound from an enemy.

"TREY!" I call out. The one useless word is stolen away by the raging storm. "TREY!!" I shout again anyway.

I'm knee-deep in lake water, my boots sinking into the mud, before I come to another stop. Movement catches my attention to my left, but I realize it's just a branch floating in the raging water ahead where the worst of the rain pounds down from the sky.

Lightning flashes, blinding me. I hold up a hand to shield my eyes. The boom of thunder rolls over my back and seems to shake the very ground beneath my feet.

I move forward as fast as I can—which is frustratingly slow. Every single step is agony. *He isn't a fool,* I tell myself. *If he was out here when the rain rushed in, he would have sought higher ground or tried to make his way back to his car.*

For a moment, I catch myself looking out at the lake beyond the trees. It's flooded so much, you can't see the dock on the other side. And in its center, a whirl of twisting water and rain creates a breathtaking vision. The sky and the lake become long-lost lovers, reaching toward each other in this fleeting moment of the storm.

Amidst all the chaos thrashing around me, I find myself oddly taken by the terrifying beauty. This worldly appreciation shit isn't me at all, and here I am, momentarily impassioned by nature.

Damn, that boy has changed me in a seriously fundamental way.

I wonder if Trey is seeing this, too. *You'll never know unless you find him,* a dark voice tells me, inspiring fear to choke my heart all over again and yanking me back to reality.

The water is up to my waist now. *Time to backtrack.* I scope for any sign of movement that isn't jostling branches, airborne leaves, or twisting sheets of rain. In a matter of minutes, I'm out of the water and back on solid land, but with as thick as the mud on the ground is, it's still an agonizing effort to take even a single step, pain following me with every lift of my leg. I keep my feet moving, as quick as I can, and for a while, I'm doing fine.

Until my foot kicks into something hard on the ground.

I glance down at my feet. I see a peculiarly shaped mud-caked object. Seconds later, a wash of dirty water sweeps over my feet, and then its shape is revealed to my eyes.

A giant seashell that has no business being here.

I pick it up at once, then lift my eyes, surveying the area all around me with mounting urgency. "TREY!" I cry out once again, searching for him. "TREY! I'M HERE! TREY!"

It's right then, at long last, that I see him.

All of the pain in my body is forgotten in an instant. It's not even adrenaline carrying me, now. It's pure, unfiltered terror at what awaits me as I charge through the trees in pursuit of him.

Trey is on the ground, his back clumsily propped up against the side of a tree stump. For a second, it looks like the damned fool is just sitting there enjoying the view. He might as well have a picnic basket at his side.

Closer up tells a different story. "Trey!" I shout the moment I'm finally next to him. His eyes are closed. His lips are slightly parted, his jaw slack. "Trey! Wake up." I tap the side of his face gently at first, then more roughly. "Trey!" I feel for a pulse at his neck. He's got one. I tap his other cheek with such force, I might as well have just slapped him. "Wake up!"

In the midst of the stormy turmoil we're engulfed in, his face scrunches up and his eyes twist onto mine, confused for a second. Then the bastard says: "I'm ... I'm *fine*, ugh. I'm just ... I was just ..." And then his eyes go wide, looking all around him. "The heck ...?"

"It's flooding. A bad storm came in. Trey, what happened?" I hold him by the shoulders, my face inches from his. It's so fucking loud, the noise of the storm raging in our ears like charging trains.

"I'm *wet*," he complains groggily, then glances down at his leg. His eyes go wide again. "Uh-oh."

I look down. His pants are torn. The color of the mud beneath him is reddened by blood. There's a gash running down the length of his arm, too.

"Shit. You're bleeding bad." I go to tear a piece of his pants off, but the material is too thick and my left arm explodes with pain. I decide to go for the second best option: my shirt. I pull it up over my head—ice cold rainwater slapping my exposed skin—and bring it to Trey's leg. I have no idea how long he's been bleeding like this. "You must've fallen. Were you up in a tree or some shit? What the hell were you doin' out here?" I ask as I tie the shirt.

"My favorite tree," he confesses sleepily. "I just ... just wanted to see her again. I could've ... I could've sworn I saw her." He lifts his eyes toward the lake, squinting. "She was right there. She—"

"Trey, I have your shell," I tell him, lifting it to his eyes. Trey's eyes focus in on it like a cat to a red laser. "We need to get out of here. It's flooding and you're hurt."

"I fell out of a tree," he announces, confused. Then his eyes draw down my body, surprised. "You're shirtless."

Jesus, this guy. "You clearly hit your head, too, 'cause your ass sounds as drunk as I did last night," I tell him. "C'mon. We gotta get you to a hospital. My truck is through the trees by the road."

"I'm *fine*," he says again, then reaches to shove me off of him. He isn't successful. "Stop being such a drama—a drama ... *drama* ..."

His head droops to the side and his eyes rock back.

Fuck me. "Trey! Goddammit."

Without wasting a minute, I set down the seashell, then scoop him up into my arms. No, it isn't easy. This ain't a thirty pound dumbbell in my dining room we're talking about; this is a human body, and seeing as he's knocked out, he is all deadweight.

I holler out in agony as I lift him off the ground and start to move. I make it three steps before I collapse.

The raindrops slam like hammers against my exposed back as I assess whether I just broke my left arm. Despite it throbbing like a motherfucker, I can still move it. *That's a good sign, right?*

I go to pick him up again. This time, I can't even manage to get him off the ground without my arm or my leg giving out.

"Fuck this," I exclaim in exasperation, my voice cracking, and I come around to hook my hands under his armpits. Then I resort to dragging him like a sack of potatoes through the mud and rain.

It feels like my arm is being ripped from its socket.

It feels like someone is setting fire to my leg with every step.

An eternity later, we break through the trees. Our vehicles are within view by the road. Perhaps encouraged by the sight of them, a jolt of energy rejuvenates me, and I reach down and attempt to pick up Trey again the proper way.

Before I lift him, he stirs in my arms, then starts grunting and wrinkling his face.

"Trey!" I shout into it, giving his cheek another tap. "C'mon, babe. My truck is right there. Can you stand up for me?"

"*Babe ...*" he murmurs dreamily, half-smiling.

I yank him to his feet. He plants them, wobbly on his legs, and I guide him over to my truck, fighting the ice cold wind that threatens—out here in the open—to knock us on our asses.

"What the fuck is up with this storm?" I cry out as I pull open the door to my truck. "It ain't fuckin' hurricane season!"

"My mom ... was always fierce ... when she needed to be," Trey gets out as he settles into the passenger seat, his eyes half-open. He winces suddenly and brings a hand to his leg. "Oh, shoot. Babe, I'm bleedin' all over your truck."

"Hold my shirt tightly against the wound," I order him, then shut the door and limp quickly around the truck to my side. I pull open my door, swing into my seat, and slam it shut.

The half-silence from the angry noise of the storm is a reward I wasn't expecting.

"Hang tight, babe," I tell him as I turn the key in the ignition. My truck purrs to life, ready.

Trey seems to become alert in an instant, his eyes flapping wide open. "Oh my God. What have I done?" he blurts suddenly.

I swing the truck around carefully, then drive back the way I came, heading for the main road. "You just worry about keepin' that shirt wrapped tight around your leg. I don't care 'bout why your crazy ass was out here in this storm. Nearest hospital is down the road some ways, right off—"

"I-10. I know. I sort of volunteer there. Oh, jeez, it hurts."

"Hang on, babe." *If I keep saying the word "babe", maybe he'll stay with me and not pass out again.* "Damn, boy, you sure are one tough motherfucker."

"I'm so dizzy. Oh, I saw my mom. Did I tell you that? Did I tell you I saw my mom?"

Keep him talking. "Yeah, you did. What'd she say?"

"Oh, she didn't speak. But ..." Trey sighs, his head going slack.

"Babe, stay with me."

He doesn't respond, so I reach over to his lap and, after a second of fumbling, take hold of his hand.

He stiffens up, squeezing my hand back, and then he lifts his head. "Cody?"

"Yeah? Talk to me, babe. What is it?"

"Do you believe in God?"

I keep my eyes on the road. Despite all that's gone on in the last chaotic ten minutes, his question hits me right in the gut, and I find I have no clue how to respond. Is this a test? Are we okay? Is everything we've built in danger of collapsing depending on my answer to this one question?

"Why are you askin' me that? Why now?"

"How ... How can you not ... not believe in Him when He is the one who brought us ... together? When He is the one who ..."

Then Trey goes and passes out again.

"Babe." I squeeze his hand. No response. "Babe. Don't go out on me again, babe. Wake up. C'mon. TREY."

Nothing. *Goddammit.*

Trying not to swerve our asses off the road—as I'm steering with my bad arm—I turn over his wrist and feel for a pulse for the fucking second time since finding him. *Still there. Still beating. Still with me.*

I can't drive this fucking truck fast enough.

Sooner than I expect, we're already turning off the road with the hospital sitting on its corner. Just a shit load of rain and a few seconds of driving separates us.

"Trey, we're here," I call out as I pull up to the doors of the ER.

I swing out of the truck at once, then limp around the vehicle shouting like a hyena for help. Without even paying attention to who might be within earshot, I yank open the passenger side door and pull Trey out. He groans, to my surprise, then throws his arms over my shoulders.

"He saved both our lives," Trey murmurs in my ear as I walk him toward the door. "He saved both of 'em."

Two nurses appear out of thin air—two curly-haired miracles in tennis shoes—rushing up to meet us at the sliding glass doors. I blink, and then I'm watching Trey get taken away. The room spins, I blink again, and then my ears start to fill with cotton candy.

I stumble and fall against the wall, my cheek pressed against the cold surface. My fingers wrap around the nearest thing to catch my balance—the fabric leaves of a fake plant by the door.

A nurse's giant eyes are in front of my face. "Sir? ... Sir?"

I blink twice more. "Trey Arnold's his name," I mumble as the white walls close in around me. Why are the lights so fucking bright in here? "He fell from a tree. His leg ... take care of his ..."

My leg.

My leg is a well of molten fire.

MOVE!

I let go of the fake leaves, collapse the rest of the way to the ground, then kiss the tile. The silence takes me away.

26

TREY

Ocean waves lap playfully at my feet.

The smell of salt invades my nostrils and consumes my senses.

I feel so relaxed, I could just melt away into the sand at my back if I dared.

The sun beams overhead, but it isn't hot. It's cool somehow. Maybe it's something to do with the breeze, which brushes off the ocean lazily and dances over my nipples and bare toes like a cool, silken bed sheet.

I could just lie here forever.

"You really could," my mother languidly drawls in agreeance, sunbathing on the blanket next to me. "I mean, Trey, my darlin', goodness gracious, just *look* at this view."

I turn my face to her. Somehow, I'm not even shocked she's there. It's as if we do this every day. "I met a boy."

"That Cody fellow?" She snorts and shakes her head. A giant, floppy sunhat shades half her face. Somehow, on this beautiful beach, in this alternate reality, my mother knows I'm gay, and I never missed the chance to tell her. "He is messed up about you, that's for sure. God sent you a little angel, He sure did."

There's a fancy glass of rum punch in my hand suddenly, complete with a tiny lime green umbrella in it. I take a sip from it as if I've been holding it this whole time. "Yes, He did."

"You like him, don't you?" She wiggles her eyebrows.

"It's really, really early, but ..." I fight back a titter of glee. "I think I'm falling for him. He means the world to me."

"Early? Psh." She turns to me. "I married your daddy after knowin' him for just two weeks. You know that."

I blink at her. "I know, but ... I'm not *marrying* him. It's *way* too early for that. And besides, he's ... he doesn't really seem like the *marrying* type. Or the confess-your-feelings type. Or—"

"Oh, I'm not tellin' you to go off and get married, sweetie. You can wait with the Cody boy. You can wait a whole dang year, three months, and nineteen days if you want."

That was oddly specific. "Dad thinks he's a bad influence on me. He thinks Cody's pulling me off the Lord's path."

She lets out a long sigh, then yanks off her floppy hat and lets go of it. The thing floats away, carried into the sky by the wind. My mom's tangles of strawberry-blonde hair dance in the breeze, freed at last. "Your daddy's got the heart of a lion. Sadly, he's got the thick skin and thicker skull of one, too." She softly touches my shoulder. "Cut him some slack, sweetie. I know it's hard, but just try, alright? That dear, sweet man is really tryin' his hardest, and sometimes, he's just plain lost without me."

"I know." I exhale deeply, then nod again, more assuredly. "I know, Mom."

"He'll come around." She pats me on the cheek. "Besides, how are we supposed to know what the Lord's path is? Did you know that when your father met me, I was a waitress at Lucille's, a very skeezy bar in a very skeezy part of town, and I had ten different men's numbers tucked away in my apron? Didn't call a single one, but I had 'em. Your father—down on his luck, lost his faith, totally a mess—came into that bar and asked for a glass of milk." She lets out a bubble of laughter so infectious, I have to smile. "Milk! *Milk!* Dear me, the look on his face." She slaps a hand to her cheek, her eyes twinkling, overcome. "I fell in love with him right there."

I feel like I already know the story, yet hearing it now, it's like she's telling it for the first time. "Wow. I don't believe it."

"Oh, you'd better believe it! And I know, I know ... it all sounds so ... *unlikely.* Your daddy goin' to a skeezy bar like Lucille's. Me workin' there. This was many decades ago, before your father got his spiritual calling, mind you. And ain't neither of us was in a nice place, I'm tellin' you." Her eyes turn dreamy as she glances up at the sky. "But I don't look back at that day and think on how we saved each other. See, I don't look at it that way." She brings her gaze back to me importantly. "I see it as us *needin'* to fall off the Lord's path in order to find our happiness. If he had not come in and ordered that glass of milk ... If I had not taken the job at that filthy, sticky place ... neither of us would have found love. And you, my precious angel, wouldn't exist."

The rum punch is gone from my hand. My mom's no longer on a blanket. We're just, the two of us, sitting here in the warm, endless sand. I don't even hear the ocean waves anymore.

Suddenly, I become painfully aware of the fact that this little world I'm in is disappearing. "Mom, I miss you so much, it hurts."

Her face wrinkles up. "Well, that's an awful waste of time. I'm right in here, silly," she says, slapping a hand to my chest. "There ain't no need to miss me. I ain't gone."

"Mom ..."

"Oh, and before you do what you gotta do, please tell Cody I don't mind he left my shell where he found you. It's washed away, deep in Bell Lake by now. No one's gonna miss the heavy thing."

I throw my arms around her. The sand beneath us is slipping away. The ocean breeze is gone as fast as the waves fled, too.

"I love you, Mom." Tears are in my eyes—unless even those are a cruel illusion, disappearing as fast as everything else in this world. "I will honor you with all my days left God grants me."

"Sweetheart." She squeezes me back. I feel it. *I feel it.* "You just go and honor yourself."

Trey?

"Go and honor yourself."

Trey ...?

I open my eyes.

My father's face hovers in front of mine. His hands are on my shoulders, squeezing. "Trey." He collapses onto my chest—and the hospital bed I'm apparently lying on—with a hug. "My son. Oh, thank you, Lord. *Thank you.*"

I blink several times, confused, then bring a hand over his back in some lazy, groggy effort to hug him back. "Dad ..." I croak.

He brings his face back to mine, tears in his eyes. His lips are quivering like he's being electrocuted by all the emotion flooding through him. "Are you alright, son? Are you really alright? Oh, I thought I'd lost you last night. I would never have forgiven myself. I prayed by your side. Oh, how I've *prayed* ..."

"Calm down." I try to pat him on the back, but he's stood up already, too far away. My whole body feels like a heavy slab of stone sank to the bottom of a lake. "Everything's alright now." Then I try to sit up.

That was a mistake. Instantly, pain cripples me to the point that I holler out and flop back down onto the bed, groaning.

"Don't try to get up," my father tells me too late. "You injured your arm and leg. Some stitches were needed—twenty, I believe—and they gave you some meds to help with any possible infection."

My father knows how my mind works; he just answered the medical questions that were on my mind.

Well, some of them. "What exactly happened ...?"

"Just lie still, son," he urges me soothingly. "You fell from a tree, or so Cody told the nurse when he brought you in. You must have fallen pretty hard."

I blink at him in disbelief. "Cody? When Cody brought me—?"

The memory rushes back to my eyes like a splash of water in my face. I remember the cold rain. I remember noise—lots and lots of noise. I remember shouting. I remember the view from that tree overlooking the lake. I remember holding my mother's seashell close. I remember the snap of the branch. I remember ...

Cody in his truck. Me, bleeding. Lots of wind. Lots of pain.

"What were you doin' up in a tree?" asks my dad.

I try to let out a laugh of disbelief, but apparently my body doesn't have the strength to, because all that comes out is a small tuft of breath. "Actin' a fool," I answer, still grasping at all that I can remember from the accident.

Cody saved me. He got in his truck, came out into the heart of Hell's worst storm, and he rescued my sorry butt from Bell Lake.

I lift my eyes to my father's worried ones. Then another flood of memories rushes forth—darker ones, accompanied by a number of angry words, and an ill-timed decision of mine.

"I'm sorry for runnin' out," I tell my father. "And ... and for what I said. I'm sorry for so much of what I said and did. I put everyone's lives in danger."

His expression changes at once. He shuts his eyes, as if pained, then flicks them right back open. "No, this isn't right. *I'm* the one who ought to be apologizing."

"Dad ..."

"No, hear me out." He puts a hand on my head, stroking my hair like he used to when I was a sleepless kid at night suffering from nightmares. "You are a grown man, now. I forget that. I can't see past those eyes of yours sometimes because ... well, because they're your mother's eyes. I see them and ..." A flicker of pain passes over his face. "I just want to protect you, Trey. With all my strength. I fear every day that God might take you from me, too. I look in your eyes, I see *her*. I couldn't protect her when it counted. But ... I can protect *you* with every mortal ounce of my being." He kisses my forehead, then stays right there, speaking the rest of his words over my head, as if he can't look me in the eyes while saying them. "And I realize now that part of protecting you ... is letting you go. How can you find God's light if I'm snuffing it out by holding you so darned close to me that you suffocate?"

"Hold me as close as you want, Dad," I reply, touched. "Don't let me go completely."

"That Cody Davis is a good young man."

Those words, I was not expecting.

"He is a good young man. I judged him far too soon. Oh, how incredibly stubborn I've become since your mother left us." He pulls away and brings his eyes back to mine, tears in them. *Shoot, if I see him cry, I'm gonna cry.* "I told you a long time ago that I needed time to adjust. I realize now that that was just a poor excuse for not wantin' to face the truth. My son is gay. And he's the same son I've known his whole life. The same one your mother gave birth to and loved with all her dear heart." He puts a hand to my cheek, giving it a squeeze. "Son, if I ever let you down again ..."

"Dad ..."

"Then you just slap me right in the face. You slap the foolery right out of me and remind me what in tarnation our whole legacy stands for. Spruce Fellowship. I love you, son." He collapses onto me once again, all the air leaving my lungs when he does so. I feel him squeeze me as tight as he can. "I love you so much."

I hug him back, despite not being able to breathe easily with him on top of me like this. "I love you too, Dad."

We stay like this for a good while, embracing one another. I haven't felt this much outpouring of love from my dad since I can remember. The thought is enough to fill me with more love than any reasonable person might need in a lifetime. I've craved this closeness with my father for so long, I didn't even realize how much I missed it until now. I could hug him like this forever.

Until I realize I need another breath, that is. "Um, Dad," I get out. "About that whole suffocating thing ..."

"Sorry." He lets go of me. I breathe again. "I'll go get a nurse."

"Where's Cody?" I ask as he turns away, stopping him. "Can you send him in? I ... I really need to thank him."

My father turns back to me, somber. "He can't come just yet."

I quirk an eyebrow. "Why?"

"He's in surgery, son."

My heart races up my throat. I sit up, despite the pain. "What happened to him??"

"He's okay. He's going to be fine. He just, well ..." My father returns to the side of my bed. "Something ruptured inside his leg. His arm's bad, too, from what I gathered. It has to do with the—"

"The shrapnel," I blurt, catching on at once. "All that physical exertion ..."

"He's having some sort of nerve surgery, and they're going to remove the shrapnel, too. All of it. Leg and arm." My father sighs. "He's going to be bedridden for quite some time."

Cody ain't gonna like that one bit. "What exactly are they doing? There was a reason some of the doctors didn't want to take out the shrapnel in the first place. Are they sure they're—?"

"Don't worry about that. Bottom line is, he's going to be fine."

I swallow a sudden wave of tears, blink my eyes, then ask, "Is Cody's mother here? She should be here. Bethie—" I catch myself, having called her by her first name. "*Ms. Davis* will want to be here for her son."

"Oh, she's here. Just down the hall in the waiting room." My father sighs and shakes his head. "Cody is going to depend on you a lot while he recovers. It's going to be a long road for him, the physical therapy and everything. Well, if he sticks to it."

I let out a short, joyless chuckle, then roll my eyes. "*If he sticks to it*," I grunt. "He's gonna fight them every step of the way, just like he fought me."

Even my father chuckles at that. Then he lifts his eyebrows. "The good side of all of this that I heard is, since the shrapnel will be removed, he's looking at a potential of regaining full function of his arm, at the very least. Maybe his leg, too. Depending on how the nerve surgery goes, it may be very good news in the end."

I grab hold of my dad's hand right then, grateful for him being here. "Thank you for doing your best," I say, echoing my mother's words from our special moment on the beach—whether they were imagined or not. "Thank you for tryin' your hardest, even if at times you feel like you're doing it all alone. Thank you for havin' the heart of a lion and—" *Well, let's skip mentioning the thick skull of a lion, too.* "And ... for instilling it in me."

He smiles warmly, squeezing my hand tight. "I love you, son. Don't you ever forget it."

I avert my eyes, unsure how he'll take this next part. "Also, I think maybe that this June ... on the anniversary of ... of Mom ..." I swallow hard. "Maybe we could stop by ... by Lucille's, and ... oh, I don't know ... maybe order a couple glasses of milk. In her honor."

My dad's face turns to glass. Stunned doesn't cover it. He parts his lips to say something, then changes his mind and studies me with a look of utter bewilderment. Finally, after he's gathered his jaw off the floor, he tilts his head. "I ... told you about that? ... Or did your mother ...?"

I shrug. "It could've been either one of you. I don't remember. So does it sound like a plan? Would you like to do that?"

When my father smiles at me next, he looks more at peace than I've seen him in years. His answer is a soft, simple, thankful, resolute nod.

You're welcome, Mom.

* * *

I try to approach his room quietly, despite my crutch stabbing the ground every other step. It's the next morning, and my heart's pounding. I don't know what to expect.

"Well, don't go lurkin' out there like some shy puppy."

A smile breaks over my face. *Someone's clearly back to his old self.* I come around the door and step inside. Cody lies on the bed with his left arm and leg suspended in slings. His hair is a mess, there's a bruise on his cheek, but his eyes are bright and glowing.

I come halfway across the room. "I ain't no *shy puppy*," I sass back at him.

"Well, well, look who's limpin' around now," he notes with a smirk, nodding my way.

"I ain't limpin'. I have a crutch. There's a notable difference, if you use your dang eyes."

"Alright, whatever you say." He gives me a lopsided smile.

I'm by his bed. After a moment of hesitation, I reach for his right hand. To my surprise, he clasps my hand firmly, then starts to rub it with his thumb softly back and forth. His eyes are on mine, thick and full of emotion.

I tilt my head, watching him. "If it weren't for you—"

"There wasn't a question in my mind," he cuts me off. "You were in danger. Didn't matter how you got there. I wasn't gonna let no bossy-ass storm sweep away my man."

My man. Whether intended or not, my posture straightens a bit at those words. "You sure didn't. You carried me from the lake all the way to your truck."

"Carried you. Or dragged you halfway like a sack of potatoes." He shrugs. "I guess we'll remember that moment differently."

I laugh and shake my head. "Cody, Cody, Cody. You're gonna have to get used to me being around a lot, 'cause from what I hear, you're gonna need a *lot* of help bathing, eating ... pretty much everything I was doing before, and then some."

Cody purses his lips, likely preparing some snarky remark. Instead, he relents and simply nods. "Eighteen months or so, from what they said. You know what them fuckers did? They did nerve transfer surgery on me. Did you learn about that at your fancy nursing school? They went and harvested a nerve from my good leg and plugged a piece of it right into my arm. No idea what they did to my bad leg. Probably the same damned thing. Didn't realize we're all a bunch a' Frankensteins, able to do that to our bodies."

"The human anatomy is a wonder."

"Sure as hell is," he agrees.

"And they took out all the shrapnel, I heard?"

"Every bit of it." Cody shakes his head. "It'll basically be like startin' from square one all over again. Fuck. Just like how I was at Prairieland Medical. Fuckin' nightmare."

I lean into him. "Except *this* nightmare has an end, and its end might be you regainin' full function of your arm and leg."

"If I'm lucky."

"And it isn't gonna be a nightmare." I rub his hand. "I'll make sure of it."

Cody looks up at me. When the attitude drops away, there's an urgent need in his eyes, something hungry and exposed and beautiful. It pulls me right in and doesn't let me go.

"*I really want to kiss you right now,*" I confess in a whisper.

Cody smirks. "Maybe we can do it when my mom walks in," he reasons. "Get rid a' two birds with one stone. How's that sound? You ready to show her that her son's *gettin' his money's worth?*"

I snort. "No one's ever made me feel so cheap *and* so valuable in the same sentence as you just did." I get closer to his face, as close as I can while maintaining my cockeyed balance. "I don't think I can wait 'til she's here."

Cody reaches up, takes hold of the side of my face, and pulls my lips against his. I breathe him in, melting into the kiss.

It's one of those kisses where our foreheads seem to glue to one another, our faces never separating, and when each kiss ends, our lips hover, awaiting the next one. *And there's always a next one.*

"*You taste so fucking good,*" he whispers to me. "*I've missed these lips. Best damned lips in the world.*"

My insides are all aflutter, every particle of my body awake. I can't stand still. "*Yours aren't so bad, either.*"

"*Bet it gives you secret gratification. Big ol' told-you-so moment, me lyin' in this bed like this, havin' pushed my body too far ...*"

"*Not as much as I thought it would.*" I pull back and look him in his sharp, knowing eyes. "But I'll be here every step of the way."

He studies me long and hard. I swear, his beauty increases by the second. "Don't you ever go runnin' off again like that," he says, his voice firm. "Don't you ever do that to me or your father again."

I lift an eyebrow. "Or my father?" I snort. "When did the pair of you become so dang chummy?"

"You can say we came to an understandin'." He touches my hand with his fingers, running them up and down my palm, which I lift up for him. "Your dad cares a whole lot about you."

"So does your mom," I point out. His fingers freeze and he looks up at me. "Bethie ... came and visited me while you were recovering from your surgery. I told her that her son was a hero. *My* hero. That about made her explode with pride."

I expected that to make his face light up. Instead, he just tilts his head and smirks his Cody Davis smirk.

I never took him to be the kind who takes compliments well. "That also earned me an earful," I go on, "about how *lovely* and *brave* and *strong* you were as a kid growin' up. I didn't know you built a house when you were fourteen."

Cody's stoic demeanor breaks as he lets out a derisive laugh. "That is a gross fuckin' exaggeration of my mother's. I *helped* build my neighbor's *shed*," he clarifies. "And the only reason I got roped into that was because I was a rebellious little brat and my dad wouldn't do jack shit with me." He eyes me. "So you and my mom have become besties now, huh?"

"Well, mostly, she was just afraid that you were the reason I ran off into the woods." I shrug. "I mean, you *are* pretty scary. And there were—what, five?—nurses who were run off before me. You think you're gonna scare me off, Cody?"

"Just give it time." He grabs hold of the neck of my shirt and pulls me in for another kiss. I lose my balance, clumsy as I am on one leg, and drop onto the side of his bed. Impressively, our kiss is uninterrupted by the fall.

It sure don't look like I'm gettin' scared off anytime soon.

27

TREY

It's Sunday.

"Good evenin', ma'am!" I say, greeting Bethie at the door and welcoming her inside.

To clarify, it's a bunch of Sundays later.

"It's so good to see you!" she chirps happily. "Is my son here yet? That boy better not be late like he was last Sunday!"

Like, a whole lot *of Sundays later.*

"Cody's in the kitchen with my dad," I assure her. "We're just waitin' on some friends from the church. Oh, and Billy, who's gone to get some fancy new baked thing from his Shoppe. We're having it for dessert later." I wiggle my eyebrows.

"Oh my *God* you are too much with these potlucks! Sorry," she quickly adds. "*Gotta get outta that habit of sayin' His name in vain.*"

I chuckle and shake my head. "I really never minded and still don't."

She doesn't quite hear me over the roar of hellos that come from the living room, which is filled with the company of Tanner, his mother Nadine and father Paul, his younger brother Jimmy, Marybeth, and her daughter Jeanie. Carla, Mindy, Joel, and Billy's parents William and Laura Tucker are also there, along with some pretty girl Jimmy is apparently "seeing but they're totally not girlfriend-boyfriend so don't ask", according to Tanner.

It isn't long before the house is bustling with chatter, bubbly laughter, and smiling faces. With every Sunday potluck we host, the crowd seems to grow. I don't mind it in the least, except for having to bring out a second table to fit everyone. Maybe in a few weeks, we'll need a third. Completely recovered as I am (except for a tiny scar on my leg, which I doubt will ever go away), I'm happy to mingle with everyone and join in on some funny story William Tucker is sharing about a group of obnoxious teenagers he served at Biggie's Bites just last week. Apparently the super cocky captain of the wrestling team couldn't handle the heat of his hottest item: the Tackle Burger. Tanner finds that anecdote way too hilarious, apparently having some sort of personal relationship with that very item. "No, I ain't talkin' about it 'til Billy gets his butt here," he tells Marybeth, who sighs demonstratively with impatience after having prodded him for the story.

"Dinner's almost ready!" announces my dad from the kitchen.

That's the cue everyone's been waiting for. The teens—Jimmy and the girl he's "totally not seeing" and Marybeth's daughter—are the first to claim their spot at the end of the table. Since it's summer and we don't have all the magic amenities that the Strong ranch boasts of, we don't eat at the big table outside where the evil bugs feast on us more than we feast on the food. We populate the two tables pushed together in the actual dining room, which is as warmly lit as a family holiday every Sunday. Mindy and Joel, the newlyweds as of a month ago, sit with Tanner at the opposite end of the table from the teens, and they leave a spot for Billy, as well as for me and Cody's mom, who is still in the kitchen helping my dad finish things up. Everyone else piles into their seats, a dozen different conversations still lively and abuzz, filling the room.

Moments later—and right on time—Billy and Robby pour through the door with about five of the choirboys trailing behind, including Robinson, who is in a mood over some missed sharp note in today's service, which Robby has apologized to no end for—and to no avail. Billy's dessert is brought to the counter—two exquisitely arranged white chocolate cakes with strawberry sauce and swirly chocolate dollops decorating their tops. I have no idea what this particular Sunday did to deserve his masterful cake artistry, but I'm thankful for it (and make a private mental note to leave extra stomach room for it after dinner).

Some of the women brought side dishes to serve with tonight's meal, including deviled eggs with paprika, a spicy potato salad, green bean casserole, and the softest sweet bread I've ever tasted in my life, courtesy of Mr. Tucker. I'm so excited to dig in, every bone in my body is shaking with anticipation.

Before dinner is served, I move to the kitchen to check on Spruce's newest BFFs: Cody Davis and my father. The pair of them are laughing about something as my father cuts slices of honeyed ham onto a serving dish. Cody's mother Bethie is there, too, and whenever my father looks her way, something soft and friendly happens between their eyes, and it warms my heart. She takes a dish of broccoli and cheese casserole to the table, smiling over her shoulder at us (namely at my father) before disappearing into the dining room.

After his mother goes, Cody turns and catches my gaze, then shoots me a smile and flags me over with his good arm. He still has many months of physical therapy left before he's one hundred percent, but his improvement from that first day we were in the hospital together is substantial.

"Everyone here, babe?" he asks me.

I give him a quick nod. "Everyone and their stomachs." I put a kiss right on his lips, my insides fluttering, and then I give his ass a swat. "Go sit down. I'm carryin' these."

"Nah, I got it."

I eye Cody severely. "Stop bein' a stubborn butt. You *know* you aren't supposed to be doin' anything but sitting in a chair and not pushing yourself."

He eyes me. "Do I *look* like a sit-in-a-chair-and-do-nothin' kind of guy?"

"Go and *sit*," I order him, "before I go and spank you like a bad boy in front of all our friends."

My dad, having overheard my sass, makes a silly snort at that, then carries the plate of honeyed ham to the table. William Tucker appears out of thin air with his son Billy to help carry four of the other dishes to the table. Billy shoots me a smile on his way out.

Alone now in the kitchen for all of five seconds, Cody grabs my ass and pulls me against him. A deep, ferocious growl emits from somewhere deep in his chest as he brings his face right up to mine.

"You better be glad I love you, babe," he warns me, "or I'd spank that little smirk right off your face."

I didn't realize I was wearing a smirk. "Oh, is that so? Doesn't sound an awful lot like a punishment yet."

He delves into my face, his lips locked to mine in one very passionate, very aggressive show of affection. I set down whatever thing I was about to bring to the table and throw my arms around him wholeheartedly, pressing Cody to my body.

I love this man.

It was one day in the hospital, many, many weeks ago, that I had gone with him to one of his physical therapy sessions. He was in a particularly frustrated mood, despite how well the therapy had been going lately. At my arrival, all his frustration seemed to fall away like a heavy woolen robe shrugged off his back. We did the exercise together, and then after the therapist left, we broke all the rules by making love right there in that room. It was a bit careful. *And it was reckless. And it was very, very messy.* Heck, we didn't even bother to lock the door. Anyone in the world could have walked right in.

And afterwards, he kissed me so tenderly, I was lost in a sea of dreams, far, far away. He brought me back with the words: "I think I'm falling for you, Trey Arnold."

I looked into his eyes. My heart was thrumming so hard that it was troublesome to produce any words at first. "I'm falling for you too, Cody Davis. And I'm falling hard."

We kissed again.

And that night, I told Cody Brian Davis that I loved him for the first time. I haven't been able to stop saying it since. It's sort of like a bad twitch in my eye, now, actually. The dang words keep exploding from my mouth every time I see him, because I need him to hear it, to know it with all his heart, and to feel it in his bones as much as I do. *I love him. I love him. I love him.*

Cody kisses me once more. "Well, babe, we'd better go and join the others before they wonder if we're havin' sex in here."

"Let them wonder." Recklessly, I go in for another kiss.

I can't get enough of this beautiful man.

Later, after we've joined the rest of the guests, joined in a prayer led by my father, and we're all well into our second or third helpings of the array of delicious food, it occurs to me how very lucky I am to be among such friends. Every person at the table has a beautiful heart. Even ever-moody Robinson. Even Marybeth and her gossip-queen-in-training daughter. Even Robby, who eyes me suspiciously now and then, as if I'm hiding that Cody is actually a praying mantis in disguise, ready to eat me alive one of these days. His worries come from a place of love—*and that's what matters*.

"Trey?"

I turn to Cody at my side, who is visibly stuffed, leaning back slightly in his chair. "Yeah, babe?"

"Have you ... noticed our parents?" he asks, his voice low.

I glance over the table, curious. Bethie and my father, side by side, are sitting particularly close to one another. They are lost in some private conversation, Cody's mother giggling and my father smiling handsomely as he shares some story with her.

I blink. Why hadn't I noticed this before?

"You think they're gonna hook up?" Cody asks.

I purse my lips in thought. "Um ... should we be worried?"

"What's there to worry about, babe? If they hook up, that'll just make us stepbrothers who make out and fuck each other."

I eye Cody. "I swear, I'm gonna spank your hot ass so damned hard, you'll have to repeat your physical therapy a *third* time."

At that, Cody laughs so boisterously and hard that half the table's conversations cease as they look our way, thinking they're missing something. That half includes my father and Bethie, who glance at us with such a look of bewilderment that I'm inspired, quite suddenly and quite unexpectedly, to laugh just as hard.

If this is how we are stone sober, imagine this same sort of party with alcohol involved.

Lord help us all.

After dinner, some of the guests take their leave due to work in the morning. Jimmy and his not-girlfriend mention plans with some friends, who are trying to get in all the time together they can before everyone splits up and goes off to college in the fall. Tanner seems especially touched by that, since he's not looking forward at all to saying goodbye to his little brother, who has his eyes set on a school halfway across the country.

The rest stay, hanging in the living room with the TV on, or chatting outside by the bug repellant lights (which, in my opinion, don't do a damned thing to the persistent, immortal Texas bugs). Cody and I find ourselves situated at the end of the couch—nearly sitting in one another's laps—along with Mindy and Joel, who share stories about their exotic honeymoon in Jamaica.

Their sweet stories linger long after most of the rest of the guests start saying their goodbyes. Soon, it's just the two of us plus our parents on the couch watching the TV and enjoying plates of whatever's left of Billy's extravagant dessert. When our parents excuse themselves to the kitchen—Bethie insisting that she wants to help clean up—Cody and I remain cuddled in each other's arms on the couch. I doubt either of us are even paying attention to what's on the TV.

"Really gets you thinkin'," murmurs Cody, his voice vibrating through my ear, which is pressed to his chest as I hold on to him.

"What does?" I ask, my fingers gently stroking up and down his abdomen, which has gotten considerably softer over the long months. *It just makes him all that much more cuddly.*

"Their honeymoon."

"Mindy and Joel's?" I shrug. "Sounded really fun. All of those beaches. The sand ... the ocean ... Heck, I wouldn't need a big fancy hotel. Just give me the beach and a beautiful sunset."

"Noted."

I flinch, then lift my head off his chest to get a look at his face. "Noted?"

He smirks. "Babe, you're sure-as-spit crazy if you think my ass ain't marryin' yours someday."

The words strike a most harmonic chord in me. I'm dazed.

"Don't go all paralyzed on me," he teases, giving my face a gentle poke of his finger. "I gotta play it smart, here. If I don't snatch you up—"

"Cody ..."

"If I don't snatch you up while I've got you in my hold, then you could go runnin' off into the woods again. Or, worse, run off to Fairview where the guys are all richer. Or you might get snagged by that Bobby Parker fellow Jimmy took to prom, who's eighteen now and eyes you every damned Sunday from the back row of the church. I notice this shit, by the way."

"Shoot, the wicked things that cross your mind ..." I murmur, shaking my head.

"I'm gonna stake my claim on you. And I'm gonna do it right. Before I get on a knee, I'm gonna ask your father for his blessing."

"Good luck with that."

"He loves me. We're best buddies now. Just like our parents, apparently."

I chuckle at that, tickled. "What the heck are we gonna do about the naughty pair of 'em?"

"Absolutely nothin' at all." He holds me close, then brings his face right up to mine. "Babe, I'm gonna do this right. I'm gonna make you mine the proper way. Church bells, fancy tuxes, and rice flyin' over our heads. We'll run off to some pretty beach for our honeymoon where you can get all the big-ass seashells in the world that you want."

"Just keep callin' me 'babe', and you can't ever go wrong."

He grins. *"Babe, babe, babe ..."* He goes for my laughing face, shutting me right up with a tender kiss.

I'd be a fool to doubt how deeply Cody's love for me runs: *as deep as the ocean, its waves still singing in my ears with my mother's best wishes from Heaven.* With Cody Davis at my side, I know I will never be alone.

Epilogue
CODY

Exactly one whole dang year, three months,
and nineteen days later.

The bells are ringing atop Spruce Fellowship today.

My man is at the other end of the church getting spruced up in his sexy tux with the help of his friends, including Billy.

And I'm here with his better half, Tanner, and my emotional-ass mother who can't stop the waterworks.

"I just never thought I'd see the day!" she sings between her sniffles, straightening my bowtie. "Oh, I really wish you'd picked a better color. Green is just—"

"Green is what Trey wanted. It's a sentimental color, means a lot to him." I smirk at myself in the tall mirror as I straighten my posture and inspect my suit. *It's so fucking nice to be standing on two feet for once, comfortably, and having the use of both my arms, pain-free.*

Tanner stands a few feet away with his arms crossed, studying me. "Y'know, when Billy and I had *our* weddin', we had the whole high school football team here, and—"

"Nah, Trey didn't want to go all out."

"I'm just sayin'. It's never too late. One call, and all of 'em will be here to send you two off."

I snort at that, then nod his way. "You're a good man, Tanner. I sorta regret not knowin' you and Billy better back in school. Your little bro's grown into quite a fine man, too."

"Oh, don't get me started on that troublemakin' little punk." Tanner shakes his head. "First year of college down, he's already broken eight different girls' hearts. I can't even keep up with who he's seein' lately."

"That one girl he was 'not seeing' the summer before he left for college. She's still around, ain't she?"

"You bet she is. Though they're still pretending that they ain't all into each other. You know, sometimes, it's those first loves that stick." He shakes his head. "You better get Reverend Arnold to say a prayer for her before Jimmy goes and devours her whole."

It's those first loves that stick.

The words make me smile as I think about how far Trey and I have come over the last year. We're living together in my house, which Trey and I have gone all out in renovating. There is a full back patio now, complete with a hot tub and a garden. Who the hell knew I had a green thumb? I sure as fuck didn't. But with all the help and generous donations from various members of Spruce Fellowship and the friends we've made, we were able to afford fixing up my grandma's old place into something of a dream home for the pair of us to live in. Trey started taking some classes last fall, determined to become a full registered nurse in a few more years. There's nothing under the sun that boy can't do when he puts his mind to it.

My heart swells whenever I think about Trey Arnold, the man who's about to become my husband. I can't wait to walk down that aisle with him by my side.

The thought makes me wonder. "Is this what you and Billy did when y'all got married?" I ask Tanner, lifting an eyebrow. "Did you two walk down the aisle together?"

Tanner shook his head. "Nah. I stood at the front. Billy, mister fancy pants, walked the aisle with his pa, who gave him away."

"Wish I could a' been here to see it," I admit. "Was too busy dodgin' bombs overseas, I guess."

"Honey, please," complains my mom.

"Hey, just keepin' it real." I check a strand of hair that's out of place by my forehead. "Damned stubborn hair."

"You know I hate it when you make jokes about all of that."

I smirk as the thoughts make me think of Pete. He's contacted me a few times over the past year or so. We caught up one night (at two in the morning, thanks to the damned time zones) over a very bad Skype video chat. He was so happy for me, I swore I saw a tear in his eye when I broke the news that I was getting married. At first, of course, he gave me shit for it, calling me a softie and asking if "this Trey guy" was gonna bite and yank down a garter from between my legs. I laughed so hard and swore I'd throw a fist into his shoulder for that one.

For one fleeting, pained second, I missed the hard, toughened camaraderie of my fellow soldiers. I missed Pete and the strength he gave me when we looked out for one another. *MOVE!*

And boy, did I ever move. The very next second, I realized how far I've moved on from those days. The truth is, so much has changed inside of me since then. For one, I actually enjoy silence now. Trey planted some sort of tranquility spell inside me, I swear it. Somehow, in embracing my fears, I feel stronger than I've ever been. *That's all thanks to Trey.*

Pete wasn't able to take a leave in time for my wedding, but I know I'll be catching up with that fool someday. Maybe by then, Trey and I will have a kid running around our legs and shouting at us for attention. Who knows what's in my future? *Whatever it is, I'm ready for it.*

I stop my mom from fussing with my bowtie any longer, then bring my arms around her, hugging her tightly. "You're the best damned mother a stubborn fool like me could ask for. Thanks for bein' strong when I needed you to be strong. And thanks for ..." I let out a light chuckle. "Thanks for perseverin' enough to go and hire yet another nurse you thought I'd scare away."

She plants a teary-eyed, wet kiss right on my cheek. "Thanks for *not* scarin' this one away."

Indeed. *Thank the Lord for that.*

TREY

I have wrung my poor hands so much in the past hour, you'd think I'd have drawn a gallon of water out of them by now. I'll be lucky to have fingers left by the time I walk the aisle.

"Breathe," coaxes Billy with a hand on my back and another on my chest. "Just breathe. You'll be fine."

"I'm gonna barf all over my dad," I announce, the nightmare playing before my eyes. "In front of God and my friends and the whole population of Spruce. My dad's gonna ask me if I take that man to be my lawfully wedded husband, and I'm gonna answer with, 'I barf'. Hey, you got any more Tums?" I ask Robby, who's sipping from a glass of water in the corner of the room. He sets his glass down at once and quickly starts fishing through his pockets for the roll he stashed in them.

The door cracks open behind us. "It's time!" calls Marybeth with a headset on—my self-assigned wedding coordinator.

"No time for Tums," I call out at Robby, who looks up from his task, startled. "Do I look okay, y'all? Do I look pale? I can do this, right?" I blow air out my lips, then hop in place. "I can do this."

"Just picture the nice, sandy beach you and Cody are gonna banish yourselves to when this is all over with," Billy tells me, his voice soothing and calm. "Think about all the people out there who love you. They are just so damned excited to see you two get together finally after all this time! And they're gonna cheer you on when you both jump in that car and burn rubber on your way to your honeymoon." He grabs me by the shoulders and gives me a look. "And when you're in that car drivin' off, you'll miss all these pretty faces. You'll wish you enjoyed the moment more instead of bein' so dang scared of it."

Enjoy the moment more. Miss the pretty faces. I give him a nod to indicate that I heard him loud and clear. I'm not sure I can speak, considering what's trying to come up from my turning stomach.

"You ready?" Billy asks kindly.

Nope. "Yes," I force myself to answer. "I'm ... I'm ready."

"Then let's go meet that husband of yours!"

I nod at him, forcing myself to smile despite my nerves.

I'm still nodding as I walk down the hallway toward the doors to the chapel. My eyes are darting everywhere, drinking every tiny thing in, worried every step of the way that I'm forgetting something, or that my hair somehow got messed up in the last five minutes, or that my zipper is down and I'll be exposed to the world as I make my way down the aisle.

Then my eyes find Cody Brian Davis, my fiancé, waiting for me by the doors to the chapel.

That beautiful man is about to become my husband.

He is a sight to behold, that handsome, gorgeous hunk of a man. His tux is fitted perfectly to his beefy form, showing off each curve and bulge of muscle he's worked on regaining over the past year. His face is simply dashing, his beard shaved down to nearly nothing, which shows off his secret dimple. His eyes sparkle as they fall on mine.

At once, I'm put at ease. This man will be my husband in just a matter of minutes. This beautiful man is going to be my tether in life. This man will be my rock, my heart, and my love, from this day until the end of my days.

"You look stunning, babe," he tells me.

And then he goes and says somethin' like that. I melt, charmed all over again by his deep, inviting voice. "Right back at you."

Ms. Davis—the adorably attired Bethie in a cute pink gown—comes between us and extends her elbows. "Come now, boys. It's time to make our walk, ain't it?"

Cody shakes his head. "My mom's enjoyin' this attention way too much," he mumbles to me, which earns him a playful smack on his shoulder from his mother before he hooks arms with her right side.

I hook arms with her left, then lean towards her. "Thank you, Bethie, for giving me your son. I'll be sure to do something about that attitude of his."

"Oh, I have no doubt you will," she leans my way to reply.

Billy squeezes on by into the chapel with Tanner and Robby, taking their seats. Soon, a hush falls over the chapel, and then the music swells, filling the whole of Spruce Fellowship.

I glance over at Cody, as if to ask if he's ready.

His eyes, assured and happy, are my answer.

The three of us walk the aisle between countless packed rows of every single person in Spruce. I see faces from high school. I see faces from every Sunday's service. I see faces from around town. Happy faces. Adoring faces. Grinning faces. Wistfully smiling faces. Teary-eyed faces.

Straight on ahead, I see the most proud face of all: my own father, who stands at the front, ready to join us together, forever, in holy matrimony.

Boy, how far we've come.

Having reached the front, Cody breaks away to walk his sweet mother to her seat, then returns to his spot where we now face one another at the conclusion of the music, played by a thankfully good-mooded (and, daresay I, misty-eyed) Robinson.

As I stare into the eyes of Cody, my father faces us and the world and delivers his speech on forever, on love that spans more than just our short, mortal lifetimes, on God's eternal love for all His children, on the specialness of two people finding one another in this noisy world, and on the specialness of giving away his own son to such a fine man as Cody.

"Do you, Trey, my son, take this man to be your husband, now and for the rest of your days?"

"I do," I state into Cody's beautiful eyes with due pomp and carefulness. My man smiles warmly in return.

"Do you, Cody, take my son, Trey, to be your husband, now and for the rest of your days?"

"Oh, you bet I do," he sings with due cockiness, inspiring a wave of teary-eyed, warm tittering in the room.

"My men, bear witness to the love of God in this world, so that those—to whom love is a stranger—will find in you good and generous friends. By the power vested in me by God and by man, I now pronounce you husband and husband. You may now—"

Cody, entirely unable to restrain his boorish, eager self for a second longer, cuts my patiently-speaking father off by plunging his sexy lips right into my face, kissing me with enough fervor to rival the fireworks of a hundred New Years.

The room may be erupting in applause and cheers right now. There may be crying. There may be shouts of joy. There may be fists pumped in the air, or waving hands, or laughter.

I don't know a bit of it. The only thing I know is Cody and the sweet taste of his lips on mine. The only thing I feel is our heartbeats raging together as one. The only thing I hear is the peaceful bliss that swells between us like an ocean wave in my ear—a seashell that has no form or body, not anymore.

Somewhere in that peace, my mother is watching over us, and I know she's cheering us on with pride. Maybe she's even wearing that giant, floppy sunhat she had on in my dream of her on a beach so long ago, sipping from a garnished glass of rum punch.

When our kiss ends, I peer into his eyes longingly. "You ready to start our life together, Cody Brian Davis-Arnold?"

To my question, a broad and handsome grin spreads across his face. "Oh, I like the sound of that very much, babe."

"How 'bout we see how much more kissin' we can get away with before they gotta kick us outta the church?"

"Best idea I've heard all day," he answers with a grin.

To that, our smiling lips find one another's again. I wonder if there will ever come a day that'll outmatch the joy swelling in my heart right now. *Somehow, I doubt that very much.*

The End.

Made in the USA
Middletown, DE
15 April 2019